ELINOR

Books by Vicky Adin

The Cornish Knot
Portrait of a Man

Brigid The Girl from County Clare
Gwenna The Welsh Confectioner
The Costumier's Gift

The Disenchanted Soldier

The Art of Secrets
Elinor

THE ART OF SECRETS BOOK 2

ℰLINOR

VICKY ADIN

A catalogue record for this book is available from the National Library of New Zealand.

Produced for Vicky Adin by AM Publishing New Zealand
www.ampublishingnz.com

Cover Background Image: Bev Robitai

To order copies of Vicky Adin's print books:
www.vickyadin.co.nz, www.amazon.com

Ebooks available from www.amazon.com

Dedication

To my daughter and her daughter
With love

1

Warning Signs

The haunted look on Jessica's face propelled Emma to her feet. "What on earth's the matter? You look like you've seen a ghost." The hated cliché was out of her mouth in an instant but summed up her friend's distressed appearance. She had not seen Jess in weeks, and the person standing before her was a different woman – she'd lost weight, was pale and dispirited, her long, dark locks escaped limply from a large hair claw.

"Maybe I have." Jess handed her the creased newspaper cutting she'd been clutching.

"What's this?"

"Read it," whispered Jess. She perched on the wingback chair Emma guided her to and folded her arms, her knees bouncing up and down.

Emma placed a hand on Jess's shoulder, hoping to calm her while she read. "I don't understand. What's this all about?"

"I don't know exactly, but it's not right. It can't be right." Jess trembled. Unable to sit still, she suddenly stood, to stare beyond the window and the scene outside to a world far away. "My dad always said knowing your family and where you came from gave you roots. A realisation that we are all connected somehow."

"Yes, I understand that feeling, but what's upset you so much?"

Jess turned towards Emma, a frown marring her brow, but some colour had returned. "I found that funeral notice when I was cleaning out the house. The cuttings were in an old envelope under a whole bunch of other stuff." Jess's father had died last November, and his death had thrown her into turmoil. "Dad was so adamant about his family tree. He was always telling tales when I was growing up, about this aunt and that, or what one grandmother or another got up to. I used to get terribly confused with all the names and relationships, then after I left home, I forgot most of what he told me. Once I had a family, we were too busy with the immediate things to listen to his stories."

Emma knew how easily stories from the past got lost. In part, that was why she had become a ghostwriter – to help people find their roots. "That's normal, but I don't see why you're quite so distraught."

"I feel my whole life is falling apart and everything I knew and understood about myself has gone."

"I'm sure it's not that bad. So tell me, who is this 'Evelyn Somers, daughter of the indomitable Elinor Somers'?" asked Emma reading from the clipping.

"That's my problem. I don't remember. Dad could count back several generations and knew all about his various grandparents and their siblings." Jess sat again and rested her face in her hands as if she was trying to block something out or make sense of something behind closed eyes.

"Sorry, Jess, I don't understand the problem here."

At that moment, Emma's ever-patient husband Luke stuck his head around the door. "Anyone want coffee or anything?" he asked. "Hi, Jess. You okay? You rushed past me so fast I didn't get to say hello." Looking at Emma, he rolled his eyes towards Jess. "Everything all right?"

"Oh, hi, Luke. Sorry, I … um, well … it's just … Hi. Coffee would be great, thanks. White with two."

Emma looked at Jess in surprise at the unusual request for two sugars but let it slide. She glanced up at the clock. "Thanks, honey. I'll have tea, please. Can you do the school pickup?"

"Yep. One tea, one coffee, coming up."

Emma smiled her thanks, knowing he was aware how long this conversation could take. She and Jess had been friends since antenatal classes nine years ago. Their daughters had been born a couple of months apart and had more or less grown up in each other's houses. Until lately.

"Can you tell me why this has upset you so much?" asked Emma.

"The date. Look at the date she died."

"1999. I still don't …"

"Exactly. She was alive all those years when I should have had a grand-something-or-other, whatever she was, like other kids. Only I didn't. Dad said …" She broke off, struggling to make sense of her memories. "But now I come to think about it, I don't remember what he said. I just knew I didn't have grandparents. I suppose

I thought they were dead, like Mum's. But that funeral notice shows they weren't. Or this Evelyn wasn't."

"Listen, Jess, I do know what you're going through," soothed Emma, remembering how fragmented she felt when she discovered her own mother, alienated from her adopted parents, had kept those grandparents a secret until it was too late. "But let's not jump to conclusions. There must have been a reason your dad never told you."

"What possible reason could there be?"

"I don't know. But if your mother also kept quiet about this Evelyn, she must have supported him."

Jess fell silent, contemplating Emma's words. Her usually warm, dark eyes were now red and swollen, her face splotchy. She appeared completely at a loss.

"Here you go," said Luke, returning with a tray. "If you don't need anything else, I've got stuff to do. I'll pick the girls up on the way back." He winked at Emma. "Am I on cooking tonight?"

She squeezed his hand. "Thank you."

Emma passed the coffee mug to Jess and placed the biscuit plate on the side table. She moved the carver chair from the corner to sit within touching distance of her friend. "Let's start at the beginning, shall we? I know it's been a tough couple of months since your dad died, but what were you doing to find these cuttings?"

Clutching the coffee mug in both hands, Jess stared intently into the milky liquid and began to explain. "The lawyer said I had to clean the family house out because my sister wants it sold. ASAP. I know I've been putting it off, what with everything … Last week, I decided I'd better get started. Olivia wanted to come with me, so the two of us went over to the old house."

Jess talked about packing up all her dad's possessions ready to take to the hospice shop; how her eight-year-old daughter chose to keep a couple of things, and she'd collected a few items for herself, but all the furniture and other stuff had to go. "None of it would suit our place, and Martin wouldn't have it in the house anyway." Jess appeared to shudder as she said her husband's name. She placed the mug on the side table and ate two biscuits.

Emma waited until Jess was ready to continue.

"By Sunday, all that was left to sort was the paperwork. Dad had stuffed papers into every drawer, and the cupboards were full of boxes. Livvy got excited by the old photo albums and lay down on the floor to look at them while I tried to sort out what might be important and what was rubbish."

Jess sipped at her coffee, pulled a face and put the cup down. "It wasn't easy. Some of it I had no idea about. I think Mum and Dad kept every card and letter they'd ever received. After looking at twenty or so cards that said little beyond the obvious, and from people I didn't know, I chucked them. The letters I put into a box for later. Olivia kept asking if I knew who this or that person was in a photo. Sometimes I did, but not many. One drawer was full of loose photos. I glanced at a few on the top. One or two had names on them, most didn't and …" She paused, took another breath and continued. "… And I realised I didn't have a clue. I didn't have that connection with family that Dad had considered so important. And at that moment, I realised I'd lost touch with Dad. And it broke my heart."

Jess burst into tears. Emma found a box of tissues and put it on Jess's knee. Pulling several tissues out, Jess blew her nose and wiped her eyes. Her sobs subsided. "Sorry. I'm so topsy-turvy right now, I can't think straight."

"Don't be sorry. It's natural. You've lost your dad. Grief often comes at odd times, sparked by little things. Give it time. How's your mum?"

Emma knew better than to ask about the estranged sister, the one who'd stormed off, vowing never to speak to Jess or her father again after they'd gone against her wishes and put her mother into dementia care. That was over a year ago.

In return, Jess blamed her sister for putting added stress on their dad's heart and causing his death. There seemed no way to be reconciled, and with the lawyer breathing down Jess's neck to get the house ready for sale, Emma sympathised with her situation.

Jess attempted a smile. "I knew you'd understand. Mum's deteriorating, and she doesn't remember Dad's gone. She keeps talking about him as though they were young again."

"What do the doctors say?"

"Not much. There's not much to say. She's cared for, she's safe, she doesn't wander, she eats most of what is put in front of her. I can't ask for more. It was hard not being able to visit her through all the lockdowns last year. But in some ways, it was easier. It's impossible to talk to her about anything."

Jess stared out the window again as the sun lit up the roses swaying in the breeze. Her voice was almost a whisper. "Some days she doesn't know who I am. And I don't take Olivia now. She's too young to remember Mum as she was."

"Oh, Jess. That's a huge load to bear. No wonder

you're stressed. Let me help – what can I do? Meals or housework or something."

"No!" The instant retort was sharp and took Emma by surprise. "Sorry. I mean, no thanks. It's okay," stammered Jess. "Honestly. I'm managing. And Olivia is so good. She helps me a lot."

The ups and downs of life over the previous twelve months, as the pandemic sweeping the world reared its ugly head, had taken a toll on even the most placid people. Learning to live within the bounds of the various lockdown levels – anywhere from 'stay at home and only go out for essential supplies' through to 'free to go out anytime and mix with people' and back to isolation again – was often a challenge. Especially so for those with health, emotional or family problems. There was no telling if or when there'd be a new outbreak, which might necessitate another lockdown.

Over that time, mostly thanks to Luke's even-tempered nature, Emma's family bubble had managed well, but she was beginning to think Jess's household hadn't been as good. Their friendship had changed in that year. They didn't talk the way they used to. Emma put it down to spending more time at home with their own families; they'd communicated less and no longer reached out to each other as much.

Even so, Emma considered Jess's reaction to the old funeral notice a bit over the top. Why did it matter so much? Was it a culmination of her dad, her mum and her sister all rolled into one? Or was something else going on she didn't know about?

Uncertain how to introduce her concerns, she changed the subject. "Do you know who Elinor Somers was?"

"Not exactly. There were two Eleanors, I remember that, but I never knew their surnames. Dad used to rattle off on his fingers the five Es and he was number six, Edward. He was proud of his heritage, especially the female side, extending back to the 1860s or something. I forget now." Jess pulled out some more tissues and blew her nose again in what seemed to Emma a delaying tactic. "Oh, Emma, why did he lie to me? Why tell me they were all dead when they weren't? Why pretend?"

"Maybe he didn't. Maybe he was protecting you." Emma's experience with family histories often revealed stories people wanted to keep secret. The reasons were as varied as the people involved. "What do you know about your dad's mother?"

Jess looked confused. "Nothing. I don't remember who his mother was."

"Where did you find this?" Emma asked, returning to the cutting.

"I'd hardly dented the piles of papers before it was time to go home. You know, family stuff, and get Martin his dinner."

Another pause. Another vacant stare.

Emma frowned. Her instinct said something was wrong.

"I'd left everything pretty much as it was, and I've been back every day since trying to sort it all out. It was strange being there on my own – without Olivia, without Dad. I could almost hear …" Jess drifted off again, staring at the floor.

"Hear what, exactly?" Emma often felt a sensation of old houses 'talking' and wondered what Jess had experienced.

"Oh, never mind. Nothing much. Just old houses creaking in the wind. Anyway …" She rubbed her eyes.

"Jeepers, we collect a lot of paperwork in our lives. Screeds and screeds of it. I ended up with a box of what I thought were the most important and threw the rest away. Not that I care much. If that rotten sister of mine wants any, she can come and get them herself."

Jess pulled angrily at another tissue. "Then I started on the drawer of photos. I went back this morning to finish sorting them and check I hadn't missed anything. At the bottom of the drawer, I found an envelope with several clippings inside. I peeked at the first one and saw the name … I don't know quite what came over me, but I panicked. It was as if …"

Jess raised her tormented eyes and looked straight at Emma, begging her to understand, to help. And something else Emma couldn't put her finger on. "I had to get out of there."

"And that's why you came here?"

Jess nodded.

"Shall I come to the house with you and help finish the sorting?"

"Would you?"

"Of course. Anything to help." Emma looked at the clock again. "Luke should be back any minute with the girls. He can look after them for a couple of hours or so if you want to go today, or would tomorrow morning suit better?"

Jess jumped up. "Oh, damn, it's late. I'd better go. If you're sure you don't mind, I'd be grateful if you would help me sort out my dad's stuff and …" Jess gabbled. "Would you please find out if I really did have a grandmother until 1999? You're so clever at that. I'll give you a call. Is Luke back yet?"

"No, not yet. Oh wait, yes, I hear the car. Jess? What's going on?"

"Nothing." She shook her head. "Nothing. I have to go."

Emma followed as Jess raced towards the front door. She watched Jess wave goodbye to Luke, hustle Olivia into the car and take off in a hurry.

"Hi, Mum," said Rosie coming through the door and giving her mother a hug around the waist. "Anything to eat?"

"Course. Ask Dad."

"What was that all about?" said Luke, closing the front door behind him.

"Tell you in a minute." She put her finger to her lips. "Come into the library where ears can't listen," she whispered.

"That sounds like an invitation I can't refuse. Let me fix a snack for Rosie. I'll be there in a jiff."

The library was Emma's domain. Painted a pale aqua, lined with bookshelves and family treasures, the room was a haven of history and serenity. She had placed her desk and two computer screens directly in front of one set of shelves, facing the garden. A comfy armchair piled with cushions sat in one corner, an antique padded carver in the other, and her grandmother's precious leadlight cabinet filled with all her mementos was against the far wall. French doors opened onto the patio and led to the path her clients used.

"Rosie," Luke called, "remember, no TV until you've done your homework."

"Aw, Dad. Just while I eat my afternoon tea, please? Then I'll do my homework."

"Okay," Luke conceded. "Half an hour, while I talk to Mum."

Luke took Emma in his arms and kissed her. She stretched her arms around his neck. The colour of the walls brought her aquamarine eyes, shining with expectation, to life.

"You've got that look on your face again," said Luke, tucking one side of her blonde bob behind an ear. "I can feel a new case coming on. What's up?"

"Sit down and I'll tell you."

Resting one long leg across the other knee, Luke relaxed into the armchair while Emma began to tell him about Jess's discovery at her father's house.

"I know I shouldn't ask, but what's your involvement in all this?"

"I offered to help her sort some photos and whatever else she finds. If she's found one set of cuttings about a funeral twenty-plus years ago, I'm positive there'll be more. And possibly papers that will reveal other family secrets. Her dad was a hoarder. She'll need someone to explain the complexities."

Luke grinned at her growing enthusiasm. "Is that all you're going to do, my little sleuth? I know you too well. You're going to want to dig a bit deeper to see what you can find."

* * * * *

When Emma arrived at Jess's family home the next morning, she was captivated by its old-world charm.

The house was a typical Californian bungalow of the 1920s, set on a large section, with a white picket fence and a central pathway leading to the front door. The garden was a riot of colour, out-of-control roses and cottage garden plants.

"Are you ready to do this?" asked Emma, thinking how pale and drawn Jess looked as she answered the door, as if she hadn't slept well.

"I have to get it finished. That impossible sister of mine is wanting rid of everything, even though it's half mine. Come on, let's get on with it."

They spent the next few hours loading Emma's car with bags that she had offered to drop off at the hospice; those destined for the rubbish dump went into Jess's.

"I'd better call the auctioneers and see if they want any of this other stuff," said Jess, sounding unenthusiastic.

Looking around the rooms of furniture, lamps and ornaments, Emma was saddened that so many mementos would go to the second-hand shops to be disposed of, and any link with their previous owners would be gone. But she had to remember that not everyone was as nostalgic as her. Sometimes she felt more attuned to the past and people she'd never known than to many of the people she met in her current life.

Except for Luke. He understood. She'd had so little growing up, and lost so much in such a short space of time, long before they'd met, that it wasn't a surprise she hung on to sentimental objects.

"Let's clear the table and spread everything out until we can make sense of it," said Emma, putting a pile of photos on the table and roughly sorting them into recognisable groups.

They pulled out the remaining drawers in the drop-front writing desk and put the more-important-looking papers on the table.

"What do you want to do about all these receipts?" asked Emma.

"Dump them. They're old."

"Are you sure? There could be clues to your dad's life amongst them."

"Nah. Get rid of them. It's what she wants."

Emma wondered why Jess was being so compliant with her sister's wishes. "Do you?"

Jess shrugged as she added a few more handwritten letters to the box she'd started to fill. "Dunno what I'll do with this lot. I doubt they'll say anything interesting."

"How do you know? They could be a gold mine of dates and names."

"Maybe. But will they help me find my grandmothers – or whoever they were?"

"They might. I'd suggest you sort those letters into date order, and glance through *them* first. See what's there."

Jess took a handful from the box and began to place the letters into piles in decade order. "There's a couple here from way back, a few in the '30s and '40s, but most are later."

"What's this?" asked Emma. The desk appeared empty, but she spotted a small drawer in the top section that had been missed, and pulled the knob. "It's locked. Have you seen a key anywhere?"

Jess came to peer over her shoulder. "Is it? There's no obvious keyhole."

"Maybe it's stuck." Emma ran her hand along the front and sides, pushing and prodding. "Got it," she said, pressing on a tiny lever at the back. The drawer popped open. Inside lay a fat envelope full of bits of paper and family notices. She handed it to Jess. "I think we may have found something."

Emma noticed the front panel of the shallow drawer in the middle had extensions on either side. She pulled the drawer from its surrounds and, as she did, the entire front section slid out to reveal another set of letter slots and drawers behind. "Oh, wow! This is amazing. I didn't expect that. I've read about these secret cubbyholes but never seen one. What a treat."

Emma was eager to investigate further. Her love of antiques was almost as deep as her love of tracing family histories. "See how the drawer and the front set of racks are half the depth of the side? I hadn't noticed. This could be where your dad hid all his secrets."

The two women stared at the back section of tall narrow slots, which held several envelopes, and a centre section with three small drawers.

"Oh, Jess, this is beautiful. You can't sell this. It's so special."

A strangled gasp escaped Jess, and Emma turned to see what was wrong. Jess held her hands over her mouth, her eyes goggling. Not for the first time, Emma wondered what else was bothering Jess. It couldn't just be a bunch of old papers.

"Dad built that desk. A long time ago. I remember …"

"That's wonderful. Are you positive you don't want to keep it? If it was precious to your dad, maybe it's tied to your past and might reveal the 'indomitable Elinor Somers'."

2

On the Move

Near Levin, Horowhenua
26 January 1919

Elinor Somers closed her eyes and took a deep breath, hoping to reset her rising temper. Her children filled the space with noise as they squabbled, laughed and chased each other around the house. Every sound swirled, magnified and rang inside her head – the knife against the bowl as she chopped the butter, the pot lid she lifted to stir the soup. The dog barking outside was more than her nerves could stand. She rubbed her flour-coated wrist across her forehead to ease the tension. "Stop it!" she snapped. Stillness followed while the children waited. "Get outside. I can't stand your clatter any longer."

The heavy clumping of feet on wooden boards echoed in Elinor's head as her eldest daughter Ella ushered the three younger ones out. All except thirteen-month-old Dot, who looked up at her mother from the rug. The child's large, round eyes pooled with tears at her mother's sharp tone and dribble ran down her chin, wetting her bodice. Elinor quickly swept Dot into her arms before the girl could let out the wail building in the tiny body. Her head couldn't stand another din.

She had given her daughter a spoon dipped in honey to suck, moments before she heard the door opening. She turned, ready to scold the children again, only to see Joe. She glanced at the clock – mid-morning, with so much of the hot summer's day yet to come. Joe never came in at this time. Her body thrummed with fear.

"What's wrong?" She watched her husband of ten years as he pulled his boots off on the home-made wooden jack and came inside.

"Nothing. The youngsters came down to the shed and said you were upset."

Elinor stood straighter and glared at Joe. Her most striking feature was her height, closely followed by her piercing green eyes, which she now used to full advantage. She might be exhausted, she might want to fly off the handle at the slightest incident and run to the seclusion of her bedroom, but no one, not even Joe, was going to accuse her of weakness. "There's nothing wrong here, either. They were making such a racket I told them to get outside, that's all. They shouldn't have gone running to you. Now, scoot. Get about your work and leave me to get on."

"You don't have to pretend with me, Nellie."

"Get away with you. I've got work to do, even if you haven't."

Joe took Dot from her arms. "Now I'm here, how about you make me a cup of tea and I'll have this one awhile."

Elinor hurried to the coal range, moving the big kettle across to the heat while she threw tea leaves into the pot. She reached for the freshly baked bread, sliced off a couple of pieces, buttered them and handed them to Joe.

"How's the packing going?" he asked, jiggling the now-smiling infant on his knee.

Elinor frowned. "As well as I can with four youngsters underfoot and a baby to feed. Our Ella is doing her best to keep the little ones quiet, I know. And I shouldn't have lost my temper, but I'm nowhere near ready. How will we manage, what with all the furniture and the animals?"

"Your brothers will bring your father's truck. They'll help load the dray and take the animals."

"Are you sure we're doing the right thing, Joe?" She handed him a mug of hot tea, took Dot from him and put her on the floor to play.

With his mouth full, Joe didn't answer immediately. She could see the doubt in his eyes but wasn't surprised when he said, "Of course. Why wouldn't I be?"

They would walk off this place as they had walked off the last one, and the one before that, owning nothing. They never seemed able to get ahead, never got a break, despite their best efforts. All she wanted from life was security. A home she could call her own, a place overflowing with love and laughter and certainty for her family. She suspected it would be many years before her dream came true, but she lived in hope. "I'm not letting anyone defeat us, Joe. I'm not." She'd find a way.

The goal of owning a farm of their own had been her father's driving ambition, and now it drove her husband.

Moving had been a part of her life from an early age. Shifting from house to house, from town to town, as one place failed, the season ended or they'd heard of a better job, a better way of living. The nomadic lifestyle took its toll, and what for, she asked herself … what for?

She knew, of course. Land. The need to own a piece of dirt. A source of pride and a mark of success. But, like chasing rainbows, the pot was always a little out of reach. They'd moved so often, she began to plan for it as much as she planned for her next pregnancy.

She straightened her shoulders again.

"Take it easy, Nellie. We won't be beat, not in the long run, but right now we have no option. This land is no good."

She had tried to convince herself they could stay. That this time they'd find a way, but deep down, she'd known they wouldn't be able to make the farm pay. Joe was so easy-going and accepting, it often frustrated her. Sometimes she wished he would fight against their misfortunes, but that wasn't the nature of the man she loved.

Joe's old labouring job at the flax mill had been intermittent and low paid; farming seemed a good option and they'd leased a property. They'd tried milking cows, but the land wasn't right, according to her father, her brothers, his brothers. Everyone said they were crazy to try, but at least they had tried.

Another shiver of determination ran down her spine. She would not give up.

Seeing Elinor's distress, Joe rose from the table and took her into his arms, patting her back as she leant her head against his.

"I'm sorry you have to go through this again, Nellie. We'll do better one day, I promise."

"I know we will. And I'm sorry for moaning. It's just … well, because …" She glanced down at her belly.

He grinned. "We've another coming, don't we?"

Elinor nodded. "I didn't want to tell you till I knew for certain. It's early days."

"Well then, all the more reason for us to do this now. For the children. For you." He ran a finger down her cheek. "Thank you," he whispered in her ear, taking the opportunity to nibble it in anticipation of the night to come.

Pulling himself away, he kissed her forehead. "I'll be away back to work now. See you later. Chin up." He sounded so happy.

Elinor stared at the back of the door after Joe left, listening to him whistling a tune, too weary to carry on where she'd left off. She should be grateful. She was grateful, especially that the children had escaped the deadly sickness that had swept the land a matter of months before. As if the war hadn't brought enough misery, but to face a pandemic as well seemed cruel beyond words.

Nobody had given it much thought earlier in the year. It appeared to be a flu, like any other. Then the second wave struck between October and December last. People rapidly fell ill in their droves, contaminating everyone around them. And so many dead.

She quivered.

Eighteen thousand soldiers killed in four years of war was bad enough. But to lose another nine thousand people to something called the Spanish flu in a matter of weeks, many of them young, and many returning soldiers, was too much to comprehend.

1918 had been an unforgiving year, but she was thankful her loved ones were safe.

"Mam, Mam!" yelled Millie, rushing in the door, closely followed by the boys. "Ella's bein' ever so mean. She won't let us do anyfing. And she's not our boss. Tell her, Mam, tell her."

Elinor looked over the heads of the younger children to see her eldest girl struggling with a heavy basket of pine cones for the fire.

"I asked them to pick up the cones, not to carry 'em," said Ella, dumping the basket on the floor. "Sorry, Mam. The boys are too little, but this one," – she glared at her sister who, at seven, was only two years younger – "she refused and threw them everywhere. The boys thought it was a lovely game and took as many out of the basket as they put in."

"Millie, did you do that?" asked her mother, putting her hands on either side of the child's face so she could look into her eyes.

The girl looked chastened but undaunted, a trait inherited from her mother. "She was being bossy."

"Still, that wasn't a nice thing to do. I use those pine cones for the fire, and you are supposed to help. You're not a baby any more." Briefly closing her eyes, Elinor was thankful the girls would be off to school in the morning. "Now be a good girl and help me clean the boys up. Ella, keep an eye on Dot and stack the pine cones in the box, there's a love. And Ella …" The girl paused and turned to look at her mother. "Thank you." Her mother's compliment raised a small smile.

Elinor hustled Millie and the boys towards the bathroom. Filling the tub with steaming water, she stripped them of their clothes and left Millie to wash them. Watching the children play brought back memories of her childhood in Rangiora, not far from Christchurch. And how cold it had been in winter with little to make life comfortable. No running water in those days, a lukewarm washtub in front of the stove and only the coal range to cook on, with a rather useless fireplace in the living room. Not that they used that room often. She must have been about Ella's age when her father heard about a better job and they moved. Not that it worked out.

* * * * *

Elinor and Joe rose before dawn, ready to make their move to Pahīatua and a new life. Her brothers had arrived with her father's precious Model TT truck the night before, to help load the dray with their furniture and trunks, and whatever else they owned.

In the silence of the early morning, sounds carried. She could hear the men talking in the yard, the dogs yapping and snuffling as they were fed, and the birds starting their chorus.

"Come along, Sal," murmured Joe to the sturdy draught horse as he backed her into the traces and began to buckle the harness. He rubbed the mare's ears and clipped a feedbag under her nose. "You've a long day ahead of you today, my girl. Eat up." He was good with horses, knew how to handle them.

Elinor handed the three men a slab of bread and home-made jam to keep them going until she could disturb the children and serve a proper breakfast before they headed off.

"How long do you think it will take us?" Elinor asked, stacking boxes outside the door in readiness.

"No more than a couple of hours to load," said Joe. "Once we get going, as long as there's no slips or breakdowns along the way, we'll be there well before dark."

"I'll drive the horse and dray," offered her brother, Dick, as they discussed the route through the gorge alongside the Manawatū River between Ashhurst and Woodville. "With a full load, we'll have to walk Sal the whole way. It'll be after dark before we make it through." He turned to Elinor. "You look after them kiddies, Nell. Me and Johnny'll do the rest. Joe can drive the truck, and you can take the wagonette."

Elinor swallowed her concerns, but she was unsettled about driving alone, with a growing belly and all the children. What if anything went wrong? The gorge was notorious for slips.

Elinor put on her best smile when she saw Joe watching her.

"I'm not happy about Nell being on her own," he said. "I'll keep pace with her."

"Don't be stupid!" said Dick. "You can't travel that slow in the truck. She'll overheat." Dick kept walking to and fro, picking up another article to load on the dray. "You'll be there in two, two and a half hours. I'd say get going. And if you want to ride back, you two can always meet up somewhere along the way. You'll be great, sis. Don't fret."

That's easy for him to say, mused Elinor. He doesn't have five restless kids to contend with. "I'll be all right," she assured Joe.

She packed lunches for everyone, handed them out, put the hamper and their bags in the wagonette and organised blankets for the little ones. It would take her a good five or six hours without stops, even pushing their young gelding to a trot most of the way.

Elinor turned her head at the sound of another horse. "Oh, look, here's William. He's home." She waved out. "Will! How wonderful. I didn't know they'd let you out."

"It's good to be back, Nell. They couldn't keep me locked up forever, not with this arm as it is."

Elinor hadn't seen him since he'd returned from the work camp. She peered at him in the half-light. Always the quietest of the four brothers, he smiled at them, but behind it she saw his pain. Lines that hadn't been there before, a sallowness that belied the manual labour he'd been doing, and thin. So very thin.

"I'm so pleased to see you." She reached out to hug him.

"You, too, Nell." Briefly, he returned her embrace.

Tears rose in Elinor's eyes as she thought about William, and Joe's other two brothers. All dissidents to the crazy war fought in places she'd never heard of, year after relentless year. A war that tore families apart, broke hearts and minds, and destroyed communities. But now the slaughter was over. Peace was being negotiated, and the oft-postponed celebrations were being talked about again, but with so many loved ones lost and soldiers yet to return, the mood was sombre.

"Any news about Frank?" Poor Frank, the youngest, and not yet twenty-one when he was carted off.

William shook his head. "Still in England, so Pa says. Waiting for a ship to bring them home."

Joe's parents had taken it badly when Frank had been forcibly transported to England, some three years earlier, alongside that other objector, Archibald Baxter, and his mates. They'd had a terrible time. Too terrible to think about. Torture it was, sheer torture what they had to endure.

"And Harry?" Their other brother, who had already served almost three years hard labour in the South Island, considered himself lucky. Elinor wasn't so certain.

Will grimly shook his head for the second time. "Another eighteen months."

They wouldn't see him home again until nearly two years after the ceasefire. Elinor internally raged at the futility.

Given the treatment the authorities meted out to his brothers after they decided not to obey the call-up, she was glad Joe had listened to sense. He'd registered with the Reserves and received an exemption as a farmer with a wife and more than two children, but none of it sat well with him.

"I heard you're off again," said William as he rubbed his hands together. "I figured you might want some help?"

"Thank you, Will. That's kind of you. Going to a better place this time," said Elinor with her fingers crossed. "A chance to start again."

The sun hovered high in the clear sky by the time the men had finished the loading. All that remained was to get the stock onto the truck. Elinor had caged the half-dozen or so chickens she wanted, and Joe had previously herded their three sheep and two sows into the stock pens in readiness. He'd been forced to sell off the few cattle he had, which made the shift easier. They weren't doing well anyway, but he'd need to get a fresh herd to suit the Pahīatua farm. Another expense that weighed heavily on his mind.

"Let me drive the dray," said William when they'd finished. "If I get held up, I've got nothing to lose. And I might have to rest Sal along the way." He shrugged and smiled at Elinor. "Joe can ride my horse while you drive the kids. Dick and Johnny can take the truck."

The tension drained from Elinor's shoulders. "Thank you," she whispered with a smile, and set about organising extra food for him.

Will checked his dented old fob watch. "If we get going, you should all be tucking into dinner before the day is done."

"Ma will be waiting," said Dick, agreeing to William's plan. "She's got beds ready 'n all until you can get settled."

On that Sunday morning at the end of March, the little group set off without a backward glance. Elinor and Ella, nursing Dot, sat abreast on the front seat, while the younger children perched on the side-facing seats or sat on the floor of the wagonette. Joe rode Will's horse alongside as Elinor drove down the back road. Dick took the main route with the truckload of animals, and Will followed slowly behind with all their household goods.

Embarrassed by his failure, Joe didn't want the neighbours to see them leave. He watched the passing traffic – the new cars vying with the traditional horse vehicles – hoping he wouldn't see anyone he knew. With luck, respectable people would be at home or church, and not out poking their noses into other

25

people's business. Even so, Elinor watched him rub a hand over his face as if wiping away his shame.

"We've done nothing wrong, Joe," she said gently as they made their way north before they could turn east through the gorge. "We haven't taken anything that wasn't ours, and we don't owe anybody anything. We've just left."

Looking down as he rode alongside, Joe smiled, but Elinor wasn't convinced he believed her.

"I know," he mumbled, "but it's the fact we had to leave what's getting to me."

"But at least we're going to our own place, not a leasehold."

"Except, it's not ours, is it? The bank owns it." Joe slumped into silence.

They stopped once to let the children stretch their legs, and Elinor handed out sandwiches and cake to keep them going. Watching the children run around, laughing and having fun, they began to relax. The worst was over. They'd easily be at her mother's before nightfall.

Joe soon became anxious for them to continue. "I'll drive through the gorge. It's a bit narrow in places," he said.

"Do you not think me capable?" she challenged.

"You, my dear Nell, are capable of anything you set your mind to. I have no doubts about that. But it's my job to protect you and the children from harm. So let me do my job. I'll drive."

Elinor knew better than to dent Joe's ego any further. "Then that would be nice," she acquiesced.

Joe hitched his horse to the back while Elinor lay the

26

two younger ones down on the floor. She hoped they might sleep, watched over by Ella and Millie. Once seated, Joe handed Dot up to her before climbing in himself, and with a flick of the reins they were on their way again.

The sun glistened on the river, and Elinor admired the passing scenery. Picturesque views appeared with each bend of the narrow, winding road, but the track had its share of risks. She kept looking up at the cliff towering above them. The steep greywacke rock face was known to crumble and slip, sometimes blocking the way.

No sooner had the thought entered her head than she heard rumbling. She couldn't work out whether it was behind or in front. The sound swirled in the confined space. Will's horse reared up, squealing, pulling free of the rein holding him, and galloped ahead. Between the shafts, the gelding began to fight against the restraining bit. Elinor could see the muscles flexing in Joe's arms as he fought to keep the horse from bolting. The wagonette rocked and skewed as the young animal pranced and twisted, desperate to escape. The children clung to the sides, their frightened cries turning to fits of coughing as dust and rubble choked the air. Dot screamed incessantly, adding to the deafening noise.

Somehow, Joe scrambled onto the horse's back and managed to throw his jacket over its head. Dropping to the ground, he began to calm the trembling animal, urging him away from the danger moments before a section of the cliff slid down the face.

Elinor couldn't see for the grit in her eyes as debris crashed over the road and on down the bank to swash into the river below. Large chunks of sandstone bounced down the cliff face, shattering into smaller sizes with each jolt. Elinor let out a yell as one slice hit her on the shoulder. She lost her grasp and Dot slid from her hold and wedged in the footwell. The baby's cries grew louder as lumps of rock continued to rain down on them.

"Mam!" squealed Ella from behind. "Ricky's not moving, and there's blood."

Thrusting the rescued Dot at Ella, Elinor struggled to scrabble over the backboard, hampered by her skirts.

Joe reached him first. "Looks like he banged his head in the commotion. He's breathing fine."

Elinor released the breath she'd been holding, easing her burning lungs, and slowed her racing heart. She whipped off her apron to staunch the blood oozing from the child's temple and soothed his forehead. Licking her hanky, she wiped away the dust from his eyes and was rewarded as his eyelids fluttered.

"How is he?" shouted Joe above the ongoing noise. "The others are okay. A few bumps and cuts but no real harm."

They smiled to comfort one another, relieved no one else was injured.

"I think he'll be fine," said Elinor, lifting the boy onto her lap to nurse him in her arms. "The bleeding has stopped. But let's go. I'll feel happier when we're there. Hurry, please, Joe."

The frightened boy clung to his mother. The thunderous sounds faded away leaving a few scuttling fragments to break the ensuing silence. Joe tossed the larger bits of rock off the carriage floor while Elinor wiped the worst of the dust from the children with her hanky and apron, soothing them as best she could. After Joe inspected the horse and wagonette for damage, they continued their journey, ill at ease. They found Will's horse, still trembling, further along the track and retied him to the back.

Throughout the remainder of the nightmare journey, Elinor's eyes constantly scanned the road, the gorge and the cliff above. She jumped at every sound, and her voice held a shrill edge when she spoke to the children. Ricky had fallen asleep – she hoped he was asleep. He looked so pale, she struggled to stem her dread.

3

The Clouded Truth

Auckland
3 February 2021

Taking a break from her research to stretch, Emma looked out of the French doors to the garden and her roses; Charli's roses to be exact. Her grandmother had loved them. To her, they were a symbol of life repeating itself through the generations. They embodied people and personalities. It had taken Emma a long time to work out what Charli had meant, but in their short time together she'd learnt a lot, and without her, Emma would never have met Luke.

She and Luke had developed into quite a team over the years. He had taken over his late father's more-than-successful publishing house and grown it by adapting to modern technology. Now, thanks to many of the lockdown restrictions caused by the pandemic, they relished working from home.

She loved her special room, surrounded by her books and heirlooms, where she wrote contemporary novels using the pseudonym Amanda Grove, and as a researcher and ghostwriter of other people's family histories, biographies and memoirs using the pen name Emma Rose. Luke worked in his purpose-built, tiny-home-style super den, a matter of steps away, editing, designing, formatting and publishing for any number of clients, her included.

The recent snap lockdown had highlighted the benefits. But one of the surprise advantages was that if either became too preoccupied, the other would pick up the slack in the household. Emma took Luke at his word that he'd do dinner, and returned to her research.

She opened the genealogy website to continue work on the tree for a client who wanted a family history put together, but her mind wasn't on the task at hand. She kept thinking about Jess.

Clicking away from the page, Emma began to search the newspaper archives for some of the names Jess had mentioned, with little success. Maternal lines were inherently difficult to trace. She switched the timeline search and smiled as the name Elinor Somers came up for winning a prize at the local Women's Institute.

She had a starting point – a date and where she had lived. Satisfied she'd found something and determined not to get side-tracked, she returned to her client's tree and added a few more names. For an hour or more, she happily collated and searched and added extra details but couldn't resist checking on Elinor Somers again.

She'd persuaded Jess to take home the letters and cuttings they'd found in her father's desk and read them for herself, in case there was anything personal Jess didn't want Emma to know.

Emma wouldn't intrude further until she heard from Jess again, but she felt certain something was wrong. Something more than grief, but she had no idea what. For the time being, Emma put aside her suspicions and assumptions. She had far too much work on at present to get distracted anyway.

Instead, she began to check the history of New Zealand between the two world wars and improve her understanding of what life was like for the average woman of that era. Small-scale farming and large families were common, which meant not only did the women look after the children, the cooking and the household chores, they also helped on the farm.

Through her biographical writing, Emma had gained a vast knowledge of life in previous eras. For people who knew their genealogy, their story was easy to write, but to her, the best clients were the ones who knew little. She loved unearthing the facts for those who had a sketchy outline at best and needed help to flesh out their story. She'd developed an instinct to detect what was the truth and what was a false lead.

She reached for several of the research books from her collection and spread them out on the desk. One thing she had learnt – if she was going to write biographies, she had to check the facts. Taking a descendant's word that something had happened at one time or another was risky. Their version was often a variation on the truth. Myths and legends were carried through the generations, and secrets lay ready to be revealed – when you knew how.

* * * * *

"You said you had something to tell me," said Jess that Saturday when she arrived at Emma's house for coffee and a catch-up. She put her father's box of paperwork on Emma's desk. "I've brought you this lot. None of it makes sense to me. I'll leave it for you to sort. What have you found?"

The summer sun shone through the French doors, warming the room as Emma settled herself behind her desk, ignoring both Jess's tone and the unease fluttering in her stomach. She'd look at the box later, once she'd talked to Jess about the extent of the research required. But it didn't appear as if her friend had touched it. Emma picked up one of the paper-clipped sets of papers she'd prepared and handed it to Jess.

"If what you told me about the five Es is correct, then I may have tracked down your Elinor Somers."

"That's good."

Jess looked different today. Not as pale as last time, but tired and edgy. She watched Jess glance over the top page but not bother to look at the following ones. Emma's disquiet edged up another notch, but she retained her usual cheery tone. "To be honest, it's easier to trace people further back than it is in more recent years. Crazy, I know, what with today's social media and all the personal stuff that's posted online, but official information is covered by the Privacy Act."

Jess shrugged. "I wouldn't have a clue. How did you find her?"

Given Jess's curt and distant attitude of late, Emma couldn't decide whether she was genuinely interested in the process or simply making conversation. Either way, Emma wanted to explain.

"Practice. I use the archives and newspapers mostly, and I can go online and search the registers. Births more than a hundred years ago, marriages eighty years ago, deaths fifty years, depending on the age at death, and so on. I took that funeral notice for Evelyn dated 1999, guessed when she was born, trying to trace her mother Elinor, and worked backwards from there."

"I don't need to know all that detail. What did you find?"

Taken aback once more by Jess's sharpness and her lack of interest in the discoveries, Emma unclipped another set of pages and handed Jess a page at a time.

"I think your Elinor Somers was born in a small rural town near Christchurch in 1889. In those days, everyone would have known everyone else, so I should be able to discover a lot more if I keep digging."

Emma passed across another list of names and dates. "Her father was Robert – born in 1865. He married an Emily the same year Elinor was born. It could be fun adding all the in-laws and siblings to the list if you want to go that far. See, it's not hard when you know how. But it does take a lot of time."

Jess shuffled the papers she was holding into a neat pile, replaced the paper clip and laid them on the desk. "I don't want to know about all the others. I just want to know who Evelyn Somers was and why I didn't know her when she was alive."

Emma searched Jess's face, wondering why she wasn't more excited and asking any number of questions. Her gut instinct that all was not well resurfaced. "I know it's not much. Not yet. We don't know anything about their lives – where they lived and worked, or what happened during their lifetime – but it's a start."

Jess shrugged. "Where will you look next?"

"That depends on you. More coffee? Or will I start getting lunch ready?"

Emma got up from her desk and stacked the empty mugs onto the tray ready to take to the kitchen. She was looking forward to talking to Jess about how things were going with her sister and the house sale, and if she'd found anything of interest in the letters, worried something important may already have been thrown out. She had some ideas on where the family had lived that she wanted to talk to Jess about, hoping she might remember something her dad had said. But if Emma was reading the electoral rolls correctly, then Elinor and her household moved often.

"No thanks," said Jess, breaking into Emma's thoughts. "I'll have to go soon."

Emma glanced at the clock. Less than an hour and Jess was leaving already? In the past, they would spend half a day or more together without ever running out of things to say. The old Jess would have stayed for lunch. They'd have had a glass of wine and talked the afternoon away. Emma inwardly shrugged off the feeling of being pushed aside. She couldn't put her finger on what had changed, but suddenly she felt apprehensive.

"Oh, I see. Well, okay then …"

"What depends on me?" prompted Jess.

"Oh, I wondered if you could help me find more information. I can show you how to look things up."

Jess bit her lip. "I can't, sorry. You'll have to do it, but I need to know soon."

Emma had anticipated Jess would recognise the amount of work involved and understand the difference between helping a friend and working for a client. Jess knew what she did for a living.

"It's just that …"

Emma decided she couldn't express her feelings. If Jess wanted her to write the story Emma knew, deep down, was there, she would have to wait. "I'm sorry, Jess, but I don't have the time right now. I'm rather busy with clients. I've found your Elinor. I suspect she had a stack of children – they did in those days. But which one was your direct line leading to Evelyn I won't know without a lot more research."

Jess picked up the papers, glanced through them again and put them back on the desk. "Don't let me stop you. You must have time. You work from home."

Emma felt something sink in her stomach. What an odd thing to say. "I don't think I do. I've, um, got commitments, and … er … deadlines to meet."

Which wasn't strictly true. Her schedule was her own. She didn't have to meet any external deadlines other than the promises she'd made to her clients. But she didn't earn a cent if she didn't write the next book – hers or someone else's. She was too embarrassed to put it into words.

"I'm sure you'll find a way," said Jess. "I must be off now. Let me know what else you find. It's important."

Emma was left standing in the middle of the room wondering what had happened. Jess hadn't even looked at her, let alone apologised or explained, or said thank you. Whatever was troubling her friend was now affecting their friendship.

Stewing over Jess's behaviour, Emma made her way out to Luke's den. Noticing he was on a call, she wandered off into the garden. In her past life, before she met Luke, her anger and resentment would have left her with no doubts about what she should do: tell Jess to get lost. But she wasn't that person any longer – or she hoped not – so why was she feeling put upon by someone who was her friend? Aiming to distract herself, she was about to get her gloves and secateurs to do some deadheading when Luke called out.

"Did you want to see me?" He stood at the door, hands on the frame, half leaning out. The sun glinted off his dark hair and his eyes danced playfully.

"I wondered if you had time to stop for lunch."

He glanced behind him for a second, seeing what was still active. "Yes. I think I could. Give me fifteen minutes. Good idea."

Smiling, Emma went to the kitchen and had made fresh wraps by the time Luke appeared. They took their lunch out on the deck to sit in the sunshine, briefly admired the garden and chatted. Luke's client numbers and demands were steadily increasing, and he was happy in his work-from-home den.

"Best thing we ever did. But you didn't suggest lunch to talk about my work. What's up?"

"Jess," replied Emma. "Right now, she's not my favourite person."

"What's happened? You two used to be close."

"I know, and in some ways, that's the problem. I don't know how to handle the situation. I'm torn. One part of me says that, as a friend, I should do all I can to help her. I know she's struggling. I understand the stress she's under, but I feel she's taking advantage."

"That sounds out of character. Why would you think that?"

"She's pushing me to trace her family tree but refuses to help. Then today, she was abrupt and wouldn't talk about what I had discovered, little as it was. And then wanted me to spend more time searching."

"So why is that a problem? You're brilliant at all that stuff. I don't know how you do it. Does she want you to write their family history?"

"I don't know. She hasn't said exactly. It's tricky. As her friend, I feel I should keep digging, although I can't understand the rush. But if I do as she asks, I'm going to have to shelve my paid work. I have other people wanting their family trees done and their stories written. I've already got two on the go and it seems unfair to push them aside to do freebie work instead."

"Are you thinking she's asking too much of you because she hasn't offered to pay you? Is that it?"

"No!" Emma snapped, but Luke was partially right, and her guilt at having such thoughts rose to the surface. "Not really. Although if she had, I wouldn't have accepted. But, yes. In some ways. It's the principle. It's the way she expects me to do the work. If she was prepared to wait, I could do it outside of work hours. Or if she offered to do some things to share the load, or even showed she valued what I was doing, I might feel differently. But she's not. In fact, she's just dumped a whole load more on me."

"Have you said anything?"

"I don't know how to, exactly. It sounds so mercenary, and I don't mean it that way. It's simply a matter of priorities. And she's shutting me out of whatever's bothering her."

"Why don't you ask what's wrong?"

Emma shook her head. "I did try, but she shrugged it off. There's never been the right moment since. She's put up a barrier. She never stays long enough to talk about anything."

"I'm not sure how I can advise you. You're going to have to make your own decision about business versus friendship and which way those loyalties lie. But it sounds to me like your friend is in trouble and needs you."

Emma rested her hand over Luke's. "I can always rely on you to see through the fog. And I'm beginning to wonder if there's more to it somehow. She's on edge and seems frightened all the time. Maybe she thinks there's an inherited illness, or a lost inheritance."

"Well then. Take that approach. Give her some coincidences that could open up the conversation?"

Emma looked at him sharply, wondering if he knew something he wasn't telling her.

"Have you heard anything?"

"Me? Why would I hear anything? About what exactly?"

"Oh, I don't know. Something. Anything."

Emma poured herself another glass of water, fingering the condensation running down the jug, trying to order her thinking. "Has Martin lost his IT job? I know he worked from home throughout that big lockdown last year, but I haven't heard since."

"No idea. Didn't Jess say?"

"No."

"I must admit, that day she came roaring in here, she looked like the devil was chasing her."

"Maybe he was," Emma muttered.

"What are you talking about?"

"I don't know yet, but I have a suspicion."

4

A Mother's Doubts

Pahīatua
10 February 1919 – 23 May 1919

Her mother, Emily Harwood, and her brothers, Dick and Johnny, who had made much better time in the truck, came rushing out to meet them as soon as they heard the horse and wagon on the gravel driveway.

"Oh, Ma, we've had such a fright," said Elinor, handing a limp, grey-looking Ricky to her mother. "He was hit by a falling rock." She explained the whole experience as she clambered down.

"So were you, by the look of you," said her mother, which Elinor dismissed with a wave.

"Dick, Johnny, there's been a large rockfall in the gorge. It's blocked," said Joe, going on to describe exactly where the slip had happened.

"We'll set off now and see if we can head Will off before he gets to the gorge road. With luck we'll be able to send him over the track. And we'll tell the council bloke." They jumped in the truck and roared off down the driveway, scattering stones along the way.

Poor William, brooded Elinor briefly. A long night lay ahead of him. He might have to camp out overnight to rest old Sal, but right now her main concern was Ricky.

"He's awake," said her mother. "How are you feeling, Ricky lad?"

Ricky looked from her to his mother with big round eyes and reached out for Elinor to take him again. "There, there, lad," she whispered, still shaking as she tried to reassure both herself and the boy. "It's all over now. You're okay."

Ella carried a now-smiling Dot, while Millie and Ted ran around chasing away the nervous tension of the journey, plainly unaffected by the incident. But fear haunted Elinor throughout the night as she listened for the slightest change in Ricky's breathing, and for days after, she searched for signs of something being wrong with her precious youngest son.

"Oh, Sprout," she whispered, using her special name for her husband. "I couldn't bear to lose a child." Not like all those other mothers in the world who'd lost so many.

Lying side by side in the big bed her mother had made up for them, he comforted her. "He's fine, Nell, my love. Don't fret, my girl. I'll take care of you."

She nestled closer into him and let him take her worries away. But the fear remained.

Time passed, and her fears lessened. Ricky returned to the same romping boy he'd always been, and she slowly accepted no harm was done, but she would never forget that terrifying trip through the gorge.

* * * * *

Elinor settled into life over the hills, a short distance as the crow flies from where they'd come. The rundown farm her father had found for them, while an improvement on anything else they'd had, meant a lot more work. Harder in some ways. Better in others.

The daily chore of milking cows morning and night set the rhythm of the day. In between, fences needed mending, the boggy track to the ramshackle cowshed desperately required new gravel, the fire begged for dry wood to be chopped, and it fell to Elinor and the children to feed the hens and the pigs in makeshift pens. Joe settled to working the land as he'd always wanted.

A matter of weeks passed before dissent raised its head.

The door slammed behind Joe when he came in for his lunch and sat at the table. "I don't want to be rude to your father," he said, pointing his fork at Elinor, "but I'm sick of him telling me everything I do is wrong."

"Maybe not wrong," suggested Elinor, knowing her father's bluntness and his opinion that his way was the right way would test Joe's patience. "Maybe he's discovered a better way."

"Better, be damned. Always telling me I need to feed the land, feed the cattle, repair the fencing, fix the shed, keep a paddock for hay. How the hell can we afford that?"

She suspected her father was right on some things. Joe had a strong belief in everything would work out, even when it didn't. Worried over the additional bank loan they'd taken to buy the extra stock, he had held back on farm maintenance.

"I'm sure you know best, dear. As long as the cows are healthy and you're getting the milk yield you need, that's what matters." Elinor wished he'd listen to some advice in that direction.

"Where does he think the money is coming from, I ask you?" he mumbled, ignoring her hint.

Nevertheless, as the months slipped by, Elinor had begun to hope they'd found their home at last. That this place, near her folks and siblings, back where she'd spent her teen years before becoming a wife and mother, would see them settle and thrive. She looked forward to re-establishing the closeness they'd once had with her family, now they were living nearby.

The house certainly had potential. While newer than their last place, with running water and a wetback to heat the water, the place was run-down and uncared for. She could give it care, but what it needed most was time and money, neither of which they had. Joe worked from dawn till dusk. She couldn't ask more of him, yet she had a troubled feeling things weren't quite what they should be.

She'd spent the last couple of months making new curtains from cast-off linen her mother gave her. She'd spruced up every room until she was satisfied, even if her ever-growing belly frequently got in the way. Her sixth pregnancy was far more tiring than any of the others. The baby wasn't due for another three months, and she already felt like a balloon ready to pop .

This morning, she ached in every joint and muscle, and could barely climb out of bed. But she had breakfast to make when Joe came in after milking, and the girls to see on their way to school. She left the youngest three to entertain themselves as best they could, but she couldn't avoid the chores.

An hour later, she'd never been so happy to see her mother and little sister walk through the door.

"Good morning," called Lily. Putting her basket on the table, and wrapping her apron around her, she bustled around the kitchen, stoked the fire and put the kettle on to boil. "Take a load off your feet, love, while I make us a nice cup of tea." The considered cure-all for everything in life.

"Don't fuss, Ma. I'm okay, truly I am."

"Nonsense. Look at the size of those ankles. All swollen up like that. We'll have to do something about it, but right now you need to sit down and put those feet up." She pushed the pouffe under Elinor's legs and plumped up the cushion behind her back. "Patty, you go find the boys and keep them amused while I see to Nell here."

"How did you do it, Ma?" asked Elinor once her sister and the boys had gone outside.

"Do what?"

"Follow Pop from place to place with young ones underfoot?"

Elinor remembered her father always looking for new opportunities. They moved to the Hawke's Bay, where her baby brother died hardly having taken a breath. Two long decades ago, but never forgotten. Sorrow sent the family to the Manawatū, where they made new friends. Friends who became relations when Elinor married their son, Joe. Another move after that, and then another, until her father had finally beaten the odds.

He'd been nothing more than a labourer, like Joe, before he'd bought his first dairy farm a few miles north of Pahīatua and their life changed. Elinor dreamt she and Joe could beat the odds one day.

"I didn't have it like you do. For a start, we didn't move for nearly ten years after you were born. And mine weren't so close together. I only had the three of you at the time. Your sisters were born here, remember. And you were a big help. Your brother, too, from a young age; Dick was his da's shadow. Still is. Don't know where we'd be without Dick."

Her brother was, without doubt, the apple of her parents' eye, more so since the scare last year. Dick had caused a mighty ruckus and their da had been incensed. As defiant and stubborn as his father, Dick had taken it into his head not to do service, even though he'd signed up. He absconded and got himself arrested and thrown in the military prison. A severe bout of bronchitis ended any military career before it began, and weakened him for life. Even now, you could hear him wheezing sometimes.

"And now you're going to a new place," said Elinor. "I've mixed feelings about you leaving the farm I knew before I was wed. I have fond memories of the old place, but the one you're going to is closer to town and us, so that'll be nice."

"It will, dear. It was all because of that bush fire earlier in the year, not long before you came over. Really put the wind up your father. I don't think I've ever been so scared; or him. We came very close to losing the house and shed. And the heat. Dreadful it was; so intense. I've never heard such a noise either. Roaring and crackling. We were luckier than our neighbours who lost buildings. After that, your father was determined to find another, better property. And he did. The house is so much nicer and has all the modern appliances. The garden needs taming, but I don't mind doing that. The farm is what matters. Your father is as proud as punch at the gains he's made. It'll soon feel like home again."

Elinor closed her eyes while her mother talked. She could hear her moving around the room, folding washing, tidying things away and making the tea. She'd put Dot down for a sleep, hoping for a bit of peace, leaving the boys to be boys, watched over by Patty. For the first time in months – no, years – Elinor felt at home.

Home, that magical, mystical word that meant something different to all who used it. As she slipped into a restful drowse, Elinor's mind drifted through all the homes she'd known.

Granny Reta's kitchen smelt of freshly baked bread as she snuggled against her grandmother's shoulder, but a sadness permeated the house that she didn't understand and her father never explained.

She hadn't liked the smell of Grandma Nora's kitchen – a stale meat odour hung in the air and clung to the clothes drying on the rack and the furniture. She shuddered. She'd been named after her, but … something was wrong. Something didn't fit right in her dreams.

Now at her mother's hearth, and feeling so grown-up as the eldest with her baby brother to care for, then another brother, and another. She was an adult by the time her two sisters came along.

And then came her turn, and five children to go with five kitchens, none to call her own, none that gave her satisfaction or security, always moving, moving, moving …

"Elinor, wake up, girl. What's the matter with you, all that moaning? Come on, I've got that poultice ready."

"Poultice?" said Elinor, trying to shake the eerie sense of loss. "What?"

She looked blearily at her mother until the present came back into sharp focus as the baby stretched and turned, poking her this way and that. She made to stand up, but her mother pushed her back against the cushions.

"You should run a bath later and put Epsom salts in it and have a good long soak – the magnesium will help – then when you go to bed, sleep on your left side. That always helps the circulation. Keeps baby from pressing down, but right now I've chilled the cabbage leaves for those poor feet. You sit there, my girl, and let them do their work."

"Ooh … That feels nice," said Elinor while her mother pressed the cabbage leaves into place and massaged her feet. "But I can't sit here all day. I've work to do."

"Now you're 'back home', you don't have to do it all at once. I'll bring your sisters over later to help with bathing the children, and I've already got a stew in the oven and the potatoes are sitting in the pot waiting to be boiled."

Elinor kept her tongue still. She was in no mood to be bossed around or made to feel incapable. She well remembered times when she'd needed her mother, and her sisters. They'd not been so forthcoming then, but that was her father's doing, and all in the past. She must let sleeping dogs lie. Leave it for the menfolk to sort.

"How's Joe getting on? Is he happy with the stock and things?" continued her mother, her tone guarded, as if she knew something she wasn't saying.

"Why do you ask?" said Elinor.

"No reason in particular." Lily busied herself, changing the cabbage leaves over and getting rid of the used ones in the bucket for the pigs, and avoided making eye contact. "You've been here a couple of months now and I wondered how he was settling to the work."

"Why wouldn't he settle?" challenged Elinor. "All he's ever wanted was to work on the land. Just like Pop."

"I know, dear. Don't get cross with me. I'm only thinking of you."

"Who's said something?" Elinor was suspicious now.

"I don't know anything, Nell. But maybe you should ask Joe yourself. I'd better be off. Do those feet feel better now? Remember what I said about the bath." Before Elinor could think to say anything further, Lily was gone, calling Patty as she went.

Later that night, after supper, after the children were in bed, after she'd had her bath and was sitting up in bed, Elinor asked, "How's your day been? Is everything going well?"

Joe shrugged, his reply muffled as he pulled his shirt over his head, throwing it across the back of the chair for tomorrow, his trousers following. He pulled the bedclothes back and climbed in next to Nell. He pecked her on her cheek and rolled on his side away from her.

"Well?" she prompted, not expecting anything more loving, given the size she was, but he'd been quiet all evening. Quieter than normal.

"I'm tired, Nell. There's a lot of work to do and lots to know, that's all. Now turn out the lamp and let me get some sleep."

And if that wasn't a duck-shove, she didn't know what was. She'd get to the bottom of it before another night passed.

Whatever was going on, Joe was in no mood to answer her questions. For once, all her wiles were wasted and he wouldn't be drawn. Frustrated by his sidestepping, she turned her attention to sorting out five hungry children noisily demanding their breakfast.

She'd put the oats to soak the night before, and the thick, smooth porridge now bubbled gently on the range. Despite her irritation with Joe, she was grateful for the billy of milk he brought her every morning. The creamy liquid cooled the porridge, encouraging the children to attack the bowls with gusto.

"Ella, will you help Ricky, please, and Millie, leave Ted alone. He can eat his porridge by himself."

"Now, my lovely girl, how about you?" She plonked Dot in the high chair. "Are you going to eat nicely this morning?"

Dot had started to grab the spoon, attempting to copy her siblings, to feed herself, but Elinor was having none of that this morning. She held the little hands down and popped the spoon in her mouth. "Good girl," she said, kissing the child on the forehead. Dot opened her mouth for more and soon her bowl was scraped clean.

"Now then, off you go and do your chores before school," said Elinor, as she wiped hands and faces with a facecloth. "Ella, take Ted and bring in some more pine cones, and run down to the shed and tell your father I could do with extra firewood. Millie, you can help me with the dishes." Ignoring Millie's groans, she released Dot from the high chair and put her on the floor to play with Ricky, who, at four, was a good distraction.

Moments after Elinor had put the kettle on the range, the sound of the horse and gig alerted her to the arrival of her mother and two younger sisters, Patty and Stella. Even though her father had bought a car, Ma refused to learn to drive, considering it dangerous.

"I swear you can smell the teapot being warmed," she said, greeting her mother.

"Nothing like a good cup of tea to start the day. How are your feet?"

Elinor looked down and waggled one towards her mother. "Not as bad as yesterday but it's early in the day." She eased her back as the baby kicked.

Lily frowned at Elinor's discomfort. "I won't be able to come every day, but Patty can walk to school with Ella and Millie; that'll save you the worry. They'll need their coats, it's getting chilly out there. Stella will come as often as I can spare her, to take care of the boys. You are to *sit*," she said, pushing her daughter to the armchair.

"I can't sit doing nothing all day, I'll go mad."

"Then knit, or darn. Baby will need new clothes. Later, you can peel the vegetables, and there's buckets of apples that need doing. But you are to keep off those feet if you're going to stay fit for this next one."

Elinor accepted defeat – and the cup of tea her mother passed her. "All right, then. Stella, can you go into my room, please, and bring me the box from under the bed with Dot's old baby clothes? I can sort them out, I suppose, and make something new from them."

Soothed by the sounds of harmony after the older ones had gone to school and Stella had taken the boys outside, Elinor relaxed to her role, repairing the odd tear and hemming a set of towelling nappies.

"Are you happy, Ma?"

"What are you talking about, girl? What's happiness got to do with anything? Life is what it is, and you just get on with it," Lily said, as she continued with her baking and filling the tins with biscuits and cake to last the week.

"I know that, but there must be times when you're happy, or pleased with something. Like when all the fruit is bottled, or the kids are laughing, or you make a new dress."

Lily shrugged. "It's nice to see food in the pantry and not have to worry about where the next meal is coming from any longer. That makes me happy."

"Tell me about when you were first married. You were nineteen, same as me, when you had your first baby. Do you love Pop as I love Joe?"

"What's brought on this nonsense? Why does it matter? You marry, you make a life together, you have kids and you watch them grow up, hoping you can teach them not to make the same mistakes you made."

"That doesn't answer my question." Elinor put her sewing to one side and wriggled in the chair. "I'm getting a numb backside with all this sitting." She resettled and put a cushion under her knees. "Isn't there more to it than that?"

"What's all this blather about? Are you feeling sorry for yourself?" said Lily, as she handed Dot a biscuit. "Because I don't see any reason why you should."

"No, I'm not." Elinor tried thinking of a way she could explain how she felt. "Not at all."

"So what is it? What's irking you?"

Unsure what to say that her mother would understand, Elinor asked about something else that had bothered her. "Tell me about Grandma Nora."

"What about her?"

"She must be getting on now, but I haven't seen her in years. When was the last time you went south? You must miss her, and she you. I know I would."

"Hard to miss someone who tells you not to come home. Grandma Nora is a law unto herself," said Lily. "When your father decided to leave the town to look for better work, she told me not to come running back when things went wrong. She was a hard taskmaster, but then I suppose she'd had a difficult life. Eight kids, lost two, and Grandpa Jim was a hard man, violent, and a drinker."

"I remember the place had a peculiar smell about it."

"That'd be the stale blood. He was a slaughterman, remember? He reeked of it. His clothes were impossible to get clean and get the smell out. He ran the local butcher shop until he went bankrupt. More than once. After that he dragged Ma north to some town or other, and then wrecked that. She'll be happier back where she came from, now he's gone."

"Who is she closest to?" asked Elinor, wondering why women suffered so much at the hands of their menfolk. Why they couldn't stand up to them more. But she knew the answer – to have a home. A roof over their head, and food on the table. Security of sorts, in exchange for freedom.

"My eldest brother. The boys mattered to her; the girls not so much. Ma might be a tiny thing, but she's as tough as nails and doesn't let anyone close. She told me once, never get attached to anything or anyone as tomorrow it could be gone."

That was Elinor's greatest fear.

Elinor pushed herself to her feet, wincing at the pain. "I need to visit the dunny. Then you can tell me more." If she could articulate what troubled her. That feeling of instability, of fragility, that she might lose everything. Was she too attached to the idea of a home? It wasn't the physical challenges of moving that bothered her; Elinor struggled with an emptiness of spirit.

When she came back, the opportunity had been lost.

"Dick will be along in a minute," said Joe, dropping an armload of firewood beside the coal range. "He's been helping me in the shed so I said he could eat with us."

"And Stella is here somewhere; she's been looking after the boys. And Ma's been helping me with the chores," said Elinor with a glance at her mother. "There'll be plenty enough soup and bread for us all."

Lily was already untying her apron and folding it into her basket. "I'd better be getting back. Grandpop and the others will be hungry. I hadn't realised the time." Gathering her coat, she kissed her daughter, whispering, "We'll talk later."

Elinor watched her go, knowing she'd missed her chance.

In the momentary silence, a song she'd heard drifted through her mind. "I'm always chasing rainbows …" she hummed as she put the lunch on the table, wondering where she'd heard it, but it had stuck in her head. For such a slow, dreamy tune, the words were incredibly sad. "… I never even make a gain."

There had to be more to life. She didn't want a life like her grandmother, who shunned softness, or her mother's complaisance; she wanted a wholehearted family life.

She loved Joe. She loved the way he cared about her and the children, and he rarely lost his temper, but she knew deep down – even without her mother's hints, or her father's condescension – that Joe's farming skills were limited. In time, they would move again. Try someplace else. Only she didn't know when.

5

When the Past Makes More Sense

Auckland
8 February 2021

"What's going on, Jess?" Emma muttered to herself as she put the box of papers out of sight under the desk until she could decide what best to do, or say.

They'd entered another snap lockdown, and Emma decided to use the time to finish writing a client's history she considered more urgent. She'd done all the research, put together a family tree dating back five generations to when the foundation mother first arrived in New Zealand; now she needed to bring it to life.

Beneath her fingertips, her interpretation of New Zealand as a raw, unbroken land, when European settlers started arriving in the 1840s and 1850s, started to come together. She saw the beautiful but difficult landscape, from coastal flats to mountain ranges within a matter of miles, bush-clad at every step and criss-crossed with sparkling rivers and lush but treacherous ravines.

She imagined wagons loaded with all their household possessions, struggling along roads often no more than muddy tracks. The women driving the horses on, over rocks that jutted above the surface or through mud, while the man pushed from behind. Frightened children huddling close to their mother as the older boys, trying to be men, pushed alongside their fathers.

She could hear their voices calling out in frustration and disappointment mingled with a little fear, the huffing horses and the jangling and creaking of harness, the crunch of gravel under the wheels.

The mother trying to provide a hot meal for her tired and forlorn family over an open fire, if dry wood could be found in the damp native bushland. If not, a cold meal of bread and cheese might be the only offering before an enervating sleep.

The cities took shape more quickly with the arrival of skilled immigrants, but those who sought to work the land or seek their fortune during the gold rushes of the 1860s frequently found the climate disheartening, the native forests impassable and the isolation oppressive. Their rough-hewn huts, set amidst stunning scenery, were often surrounded by bush in need of clearing to create farmland before they could feed themselves or earn a penny.

Their ultimate reward was an abundance of water, clean fresh air, plenty of wood for building, and their independence – the right to be their own master, to create a better life. The reason they came.

What shone through was the determined spirit of the women, who got on with what needed to be done, helped their neighbours, raised their children and sang and laughed and succeeded. But this new life they'd come for was as far away and different to anything they had ever known.

The torrential rain beat against the tin roof, the din so loud her ears rang. Darkness suffused the room and she lit a few of her precious candles. She'd had no time to make new ones. For days, she'd focused all her energy on John, her little son who lay so ill in his cot. Whispering soothing sounds, she bathed his head with cold water hoping to break the relentless fever.

Day turned to night, and John's father had not returned with the doctor. She knew in her heart they would not make it in time. The mud would be too deep, the horse would toss its rider into the scrub, there'd be a slip blocking the track, the doctor couldn't be found. Any number of obstacles paraded through her mind.

The sound of the door opening alerted her to their arrival, but it wasn't them. A kuia, a Māori elder, entered, put her finger to her lips for silence and went to the boy. Overawed, daunted, Mary watched the old woman test his temperature and listen to his breathing. Removing some bits of plant material from a pouch hanging from her waist, she soaked the concoction in a bowl of hot water taken from the kettle hanging over the fire. When she was satisfied, she tipped some of the water off, leaving it to cool in a mug. She reheated the strained water in a pot found hanging above the hearth and added more leaves to the water. The aroma of the heating vegetation, while not unpleasant, was sharp. Mary took a deep breath, realising that her lungs felt refreshed. Chanting quietly, the kuia poured the liquid into another bowl and held it under the boy's nose, wafting the steam towards him. His breathing was shallow, but Mary could see his chest lift. The woman placed a piece of muslin over the boy's head, trapping the steam and allowing it to seep into his lungs.

Before long, he began to cough. The old one lifted him to a sitting position, leaning him over her arm and rubbing his back. After several coughs, he brought up phlegm she wiped away with a piece of towelling Mary gave her. The old woman held him semi-lying in her arms as she dribbled the cooled, clear liquid she'd saved into his mouth. Reheating the leaf concoction once more, the kuia repeated the process. Wafted the steam for him to breathe, rubbed his back again, gave him more of the liquid, and after another bout of coughing, rechecked his temperature and listened to his lungs.

Several hours passed until the kuia smiled, nodded and walked off into the rain from whence she'd come. No words had been spoken, they'd not been necessary; an innate sense of well-being had imbued the room. 'Thank you,' Mary called into the darkness. She rushed to Johnnie's side. His breathing was easier, he was cooler, he slept. Mary's tears spilled as relief flooded her body. She would not lose her son tonight.

Emma stopped writing, happy to have got through that section. The family took the story of the kuia to heart. Who she was, where she'd come from and what she'd used nobody knew – or the information had been lost with the passage of time – but the myth was passed on from generation to generation. Stories such as those became Emma's mainstay.

Too often, she was required to write about the loss of a child, in a scene that broke her heart as she recalled the loss of her first baby. Long before she'd met Luke; before Rosie had come into their lives. A secret she'd kept buried for so long it nearly destroyed her. Now she used the experience of that trauma when she wrote of such tragedies. A mother's heartbreak would have been no less in 1890 as in 1990, or any other time, but it left her drained.

Satisfied she'd done enough writing for the time being, Emma turned her focus to another client whose family tree was taking shape. She had no idea where her love of genealogy had come from, but putting together a story about the past, linking people together by blood and marriage, through love and loss, brought the past to life for her. She spent hours wandering off down rabbit holes looking for the right people and how they lived their lives.

"Are you ready to take a break?" asked Luke, popping his nose around the door.

Emma glanced at the clock. Near enough to the end of her working day. She was strict about working hours and family time. Nothing was more important than her family. "I am," she smiled. "Be there in a tick."

She saved the last file and closed it, bookmarked a web page, did one final check for emails then shut the computer down for the night. She loved the hour before dinner, preparing whatever they were eating that evening and chatting over the day's events. Rosie watched TV or sat nearby doing her colouring-in with her earbuds in, listening to music.

Luke had poured Emma a glass of wine by the time she arrived in the kitchen. "Take a seat, I've got this tonight."

She pulled out the bar stool and watched as Luke chopped red onion, garlic, capsicums and zucchini ready for the ratatouille he was making. Then he sliced and diced the chicken, seasoning it with basil and oregano and a healthy dollop of olive oil and red wine vinegar, and left it to marinate.

"You look happy with yourself, Mr Grainger. How's your day been?"

"I had a great day." He grinned and proceeded to tell her about a client who wanted a coffee table book with short stories, road trips and screeds of photos. "It's going to be a challenge laying it out, but fun. It's a great concept. I'd like to see if some of those vineyards she visited would sponsor the book, and we could showcase their wines and restaurant recipes."

Emma listened as he told her some of his ideas for putting the sections together, in what order, and how he wanted each double-page spread to look.

"Sounds great. This one's got you really motivated, hasn't it?"

"It has. It's not every day you get a job like this. I think it'll be a limited edition. But enough about me, how's your day been, Mrs Grainger ... or am I talking to one of your proxy personalities?"

Emma laughed, spluttering over her wine.

"You remind me so much of Charli sometimes with her pen names," Luke continued. "Loved her to bits – you, too, by the way – but she did get engrossed in her writing."

Her grandmother had indeed been a chameleon, writing under her own name, Charlotte Day, and as Georgina Strong and Amanda Grove. 'Georgina' had died with her, but Charlotte had gifted Amanda's pseudonym to Emma.

"She most certainly did. I'm glad I'm not that complicated. Amanda's next romantic adventure is on schedule. You'll get it in a week or two. They're easy to write since I'm able to adapt a beautiful love story from a family tree and recreate it in a contemporary setting. But right now, Emma Rose the wordsmith, is full up."

"Do you ever regret taking on other people's stories?"

"Not in the slightest. I love it. It fills my thirst for history. I managed to write a fascinating piece today, about rongoā – traditional Māori medicine – back in the late 1800s before the 1907 Tohunga Suppression Act came in. The family legend is that a kuia saved a boy's life and he went on to become a doctor. Did you know you could use the bark of the mamaku, the black tree fern, as a poultice for swollen feet and ankles and suchlike instead of cabbage leaves?"

"Now how would I know that?" laughed Luke, who openly admired her ability to research the tiniest of details.

"As for the other one I'm putting together, it's early days. I'm doing the research on a simpler family life full of all the successes and failures of large families. It's much less challenging. For me, anyway. Might not be for you."

"That sounds ominous." Luke wiped his hands clean and took a sip of his wine as he gently stirred the sauce.

"It's one of those where there are snippets of letters, newspaper cuttings, photographs and other such memorabilia to be included, so the layout will be tricky. Aren't I lucky that's your job!" She grinned happily as they clinked glasses acknowledging their teamwork and each other's skills.

"Have you spoken with Jess?" Luke asked as he turned his back to check the rice and stir-fry the chicken.

Emma frowned at the pile of used pots, pans and utensils already filling the sink. Since they took it in turns to cook and clean up, there was one problem with Luke cooking – he was messy.

"No. Not so far. I'm trying to work out which angle to come from and I've not had the time to do enough research yet. Now, what can I do to help?" said Emma, getting down from the stool to set the table.

"Nothing. And you're avoiding the issue."

"I'm not. I'm busy right now. I have to finish Amanda's latest – there's a memoir that isn't half finished and the family history book still needs a lot of work. I don't need Jess's family mess in the mix when she doesn't know what she wants so I'm not avoiding anything."

"Yes you are," said Luke firmly. "And if your latest book will be finished soon, you have another problem to face. Doesn't Jess beta read for you?"

Emma stopped mid-setting and stood upright holding a fork in her hand, staring at the tines as if they held the answer.

"The state she's in at the moment, I wouldn't ask her. It'd be an imposition. I'll figure it out." Irritated that their pleasant hour together had turned sour, Emma resumed setting the table and let the conversation drop.

"If dinner's ready, I'll get Rosie."

Except, Emma couldn't let it drop. The image of Jess's troubled face kept bothering her; her distress at discovering that an ancestor, if that's who she was, had been alive well into Jess's late teens seemed unreasonable on the surface, yet Emma could empathise. She'd missed out on so much with her own grandmother, she knew the gap it left. And she couldn't get the idea out of her head that her friend was in some way in need of help.

"Goodnight, darling. Time to go to sleep now," said Emma putting away the book she'd been reading to Rosie. She kissed her, turned off the lamp and returned to the lounge, where she snuggled up to Luke on the sofa.

"What are you watching?" she asked, even though she could see a game of cricket being played. Her one-sided argument with herself – that she was too busy – pitted against her impulse to support her friend.

"One of the World Test Championship games I recorded, why?" Luke barely took his eyes off the screen.

"Will it take long?" She knew her question was silly. The players were wearing white, which meant a test game and those took hours, if not days, unless it was a highlights package.

"Could do. Depends on why you're asking."

"If you're busy watching, do you mind if I go and do some research?" Even as she asked, she knew she was breaching their agreement of work during work hours, but there were times when the rule could be broken. Couldn't it?

"Hmmm? If you want to. Why? Oh, good shot. Did you see that stroke play down the offside?"

Emma ignored the cricket. "Rosie said Olivia doesn't want to be her friend any longer."

"Out! Did you see that. Good piece of bowling. That's four down now," said Luke, momentarily dragging his eyes away from the television. "That's girls being precious, isn't it? I wouldn't worry about it."

"Maybe. But it got me thinking. A passage about friendship in the story I read Rosie tonight made me feel guilty. I should try to do a little more research to ease Jess's mind."

Luke kissed the top of her head. "I knew you'd come around. Go. I'll call when it's time for a cup of tea."

As was usual when she was dealing with other people's histories, Emma wished her long-lost grandmother Charli was still around. They'd had such a short time to get to know one another, but Charli was never one for sentimentality. Get on with it, was her motto.

"Right. I'll get on with it then."

Emma retrieved the box of papers from under her desk and picked out a couple of funeral notices from the newspaper clippings. Settled in her chair, she clicked open the genealogy website and began to fill in more information starting with Jess, moving back to her father Edward, and struck a gap. She searched for more information on Edward's parents or siblings without success. Whoever Elinor Somers was, Emma felt sure she was the anchor to the story. She had no practical reason to think that, but her instinct didn't usually let her down. If she could find the link.

As she clicked through hints and studied the information, a list of questions formed in her head. What was she looking for exactly?

She was almost certain Elinor was born in 1889, so at the turn of the century, what did an eleven-year-old do in a small town? Was she still living there or had they moved by then? How did the household make a living? How old was she when she married, and where was she when war was declared?

More questions came to mind, and Emma started a list of things to search for so she wouldn't forget anything. While she spent most of her time researching online and wrote directly on the computer, she preferred to handwrite her lists. She could mind map and doodle around the edges as she pondered each question and where she might find the answers.

She had few answers so far, beyond what she knew in general about 1920s New Zealand. While electricity, cars and home appliances were starting to make life easier for some by the middle of the decade, other households still struggled with poverty and hardship – rural areas in particular. Families harboured the hope of better things to come.

But they didn't. If anything, the depression of the 1930s was worse.

Emma usually found women's stories began in the home. Her first task was to find out where Elinor had lived between the start of a new century and the First

World War. Clicking through to the New Zealand History website, Emma was starkly reminded about life after the fighting. Had they all survived? What about the Spanish flu epidemic? Were they involved in the Peace Celebrations? What had life been like for them?

Emma selected the archives website and entered the name Somers. A list appeared with links to a series of World War One records. A few more clicks and she was reading the military records for a family of dissenters. Emma's brain – and pulse – started racing. There was so much more to this story than she expected. About to pick one of the links and chase a lead, she stopped. These accounts, she reminded herself, were about the Somers men. Her task was to find the women, the maternal line. Not an easy task until she could pinpoint which of the Es had married which man?

Emma sighed and closed the computer. She needed to do a lot more mind mapping.

6
Peace at Home

Pahīatua
July 1919

The rains arrived in full force and the temperature dropped. While the winter provided some respite from the workload, they still had an endless number of chores. With the cows dried off until calving began later next month, Joe had time to do a few repairs and work around the house that Elinor wanted before the next baby arrived.

"Did you decide if we need to get any fertiliser?" asked Elinor. "We must send more milk to the factory next season to make ends meet."

"Don't you start! Your father's bad enough," Joe grumbled and grumped. "What with? The animals will have to cope. I can't afford to miss a bank payment because he thinks we need to add stuff to the grass. I'll let them graze the long acre if they need more feed."

Elinor held her tongue. Grazing the land along either side of the roadway was frowned upon. He'd get another fine if he wasn't careful.

"Anyway, there'll be a new litter of piglets soon. They'll bring in a fair bit."

The pigs had certainly helped, and Joe bred from them as often as he could. While young Ella happily looked after the hens and collected the eggs, the pigs overwhelmed her. Since Elinor was in no shape to handle them, it was as well that Joe was fond of them.

"Come along, girls. Wash the boys' hands and get up to the table."

Elinor liked winter, despite the cold and wet. The evenings closed in early and she could pull the curtains and create a cosy nest away from the troubles of the world. And to Elinor, the world seemed greatly troubled still, even though the war was officially over. She'd read about the signing of a treaty at some unpronounceable place in France last month. Five years to the day since someone killed that Archduke Ferdinand and started years of bloodshed and violence that left the earth grieving. Grieving for a life that was, the lives that were taken, the disintegration of trust and optimism, of neighbourliness and respect.

With little understanding of why they had to go to war in the first place, Elinor simply wanted a peaceful life for everyone.

And a home to call their own.

"Tell Pa what you've been up to today," she said, as she piled the plates with a mutton stew from the sheep Joe had killed. "Ricky, you start."

The four-year-old sat up straight, wiped his nose with the back of his hand and promptly wiped it on his shorts, receiving a smart tap from his mother. "Ow." He studied his hand, staring up at her in surprise. "I picked fruit."

"So did I," piped up Ted; fifteen months older, he considered himself grown-up. "And we helped in the garden digging and picking."

"We all helped, Pa. Mam said," added Millie.

"I peeled the apples while Mam bottled them, and we made pie," explained Ella. "The younger ones weren't much help with that."

"I was, too," squeaked Millie. "I'm as good as you."

"No you're not."

"I am so."

"Stop it, girls," snapped Joe. "That is no way to behave at the table."

"I want pie," said Ricky.

"Eat your vegetables first," said Elinor, watching him pick them out from the meat. She smoothed the boy's hair and pointed to his plate. "Those beans and that carrot are the ones you collected."

Ricky eyed his mother cautiously as he picked up a bean and nibbled one end.

"Use your fork," said his mother.

He wiped greasy fingers on his shorts, received another smack on his fingers and took hold of his fork to stab the carrot.

"Sounds like it's been all go," said Joe, smiling at the faces around the table. "I'm glad to hear you were helping your mother. I can see how busy you've all been. Hasn't Mam done a good job?" He nodded towards the line-up of bottled fruit and the remaining clutter of jars and cooking utensils ready for the next batch. He'd already taken several bucketloads of peelings out to the pigs, and another one awaited.

Elinor eased her back and guided Ricky to eat

another piece of carrot. "No more than any other time. When the fruit and vegetables are ready, we have to harvest them. It's a team effort and Ma helped. And aren't we always thankful for the bottled fruit come winter?"

"We are. Especially after all the hard work. Will you be up to going to Saturday's Peace Celebrations?" asked Joe, a worried look crossing his face. "You're looking tired."

"Our class is part of the parade and I've done a painting …" began Ella.

"So's my class," butted in Millie. "We've got to be at school …"

Ella punched her in the arm and hissed. "Be quiet. I haven't finished."

"Enough, you two," growled Joe. "I won't speak to you again or you'll get to feel the weight of my hand. You're behaving like two squalling babies."

"I'm not a baby," howled Millie, who immediately hung her head at the glaring look she received from her father.

Elinor intervened. "Clear the plates please, girls, and start washing up." She turned to Joe. "I'm okay. A little tired, but I plan to go on Saturday. There's a good programme over the whole weekend, and I'll bake a cake for the Bring and Buy."

"I'd 'ave preferred to take the train to Dannevirke, but the coal situation put a stop to that. How can the government not have enough coal, for God's sake? Ridiculous situation."

"No use getting het up about it," replied Elinor, smoothing over the matter. "And it's not a coal shortage as such, it's because there's not enough men to do the work. That's the real problem. Anyway, I'm happy to stay local." She rubbed her overlarge belly. "I can come home when it gets too much."

* * * * *

Saturday morning dawned grey and overcast, but the weather was promised to hold. After hitching their gelding to the wagonette, Joe helped Elinor clamber up on the seat, while the children piled in the back.

"There's a picnic lunch for all the schoolchildren before the parade," said an excited Ella. "And we can have another feed at afternoon tea. *And* there's a dance, Mam."

Elinor laughed. "I don't think I'll be going to any dance, sweetheart. There's no way this baby will let me do that."

The town buzzed with voices and the clatter of horses' hooves, cars chugged by and the train whistle sounded as Joe pulled the wagon to a stop in the school field. Neighbours and friends stood gossiping in the street while the children ran around letting off steam, calling out to one another. Elinor saw her mother talking to some other women and waved, but her father and brothers weren't anywhere to be seen. At 11.30, the crowd was called together by Mr Harding, chair of the Patriotic Society.

"Welcome, one and all, to this day of celebration that peace has settled on our nation and across the world. We are here to give thanks to those who came home and tomorrow afternoon we will remember those who gave their lives in our name, at a service in the Drill Hall. But for the moment, children you are invited to feast in the hall before the parade begins. And parents, do avail yourselves of the tea-making facilities. The parade will begin at 12.30 sharp."

He climbed down from the box he stood on and ushered everyone inside.

"What's all this about a service?" Joe frowned. He wasn't much of a churchgoer at the best of times.

"It's a thanksgiving service, tomorrow. I thought we should go and say our thanks."

"What have we to be thankful about?"

"A lot. And …"

"After what those bastards did to my brothers?"

"You can't change what's gone, Joe. I am thankful the war is over, that no more have to die, that our family survived and that none of mine fell sick with the flu. That your brothers are alive. That we have hope for the future. Aren't you? It's not about us, Joe, it's about what we, as a country, do next that matters."

She left him standing there looking stunned as she took her cake to the stall and joined the children inside.

The sound of the bands warming up and getting into position alerted people to the time. Everyone hurried to get a place to watch the parade starting at the Post Office. With handkerchiefs and flags in hand, people lined the route around the town all the way to the Drill Hall where the mayor and others would address everyone before the service.

The drum major tossed his baton and the bands began to march, each with a group of schoolchildren positioned between them, some waving and calling to people they knew, others taking their task more seriously, marching in time as best they could. Elinor strapped Dot to her with her shawl and held tightly to the boys' coat collars. She was frightened she'd lose them in the crowd.

Standing on tiptoes, she watched until she could see the girls. "Look, boys," she pointed. "There they are. Wave now. Wave your flags. Wave them high." She had no idea where Joe was. She hoped he wasn't in the pub, where many of the men had threatened to go, drowning his sorrows. He wasn't much of a drinker, and she never denied him the occasional one or two. Not like those temperance women. She didn't have any truck with them. Going too far, in her opinion. But he'd be irritated with her for challenging him earlier.

Joe appeared next to her, flashing a grin of apology. He lifted Ricky onto his shoulders. Elinor smiled, happy to have him beside her. Shaking away the threatening memories of past failures, she put her hand on Joe's shoulder, letting the love she felt for him shine in her eyes. With him by her side, they would succeed. She had much to be grateful for.

"Come on," he said, covering her hand with his before putting Ricky down again. "Let's follow the parade."

The boys laughed and skipped as they ran along the road barely keeping out of the way of the marching bands.

Soon they arrived at the hall where all the dignitaries and guests were already assembled. Elinor found a spot to stand out of the cold wind in the shelter of one of the buildings. The girls were still with the school group, and Joe stood out in the open area to listen to the speeches, the boys beside him. With a few moments to herself, she relaxed. The voices droned on while she entertained Dot until she heard a raised voice.

"That's all very well for you, in your fancy clothes and fancy house, but what about us?" demanded the man. "No jobs, no money, what's the government doing to help us? That's what I want to know."

Shouts of agreement came as others joined in. Elinor couldn't quite make out what some of the gripes were about. She knew some of the returned soldiers were struggling on small farms on marginal land to make ends meet. Others were in poor-paying jobs. Foreclosures were threatened. Some unlucky ones lost everything. Elinor didn't agree that banks should be allowed to take homes away from families because they were struggling to earn enough to live on. It wasn't through lack of trying.

Mayor Horne raised his voice above the heckler. "Have some respect, sir. Now is not the time. We are here today to honour our war heroes, those who returned to us and those who were lost. Today is a day of ..."

The man's insulting taunts were soon drowned by those surrounding him. A scuffle broke out as a few tried to restrain the heckler and push him away. Elinor began to think peace had been restored until she heard Joe's voice.

"For heaven's sake, shut up. Didn't you hear the man? Now's not the time."

Elinor's stomach churned. Why had Joe spoken up? What on earth had possessed him?

"You! Keep yer gob shut. It's got nowt to do with you. You and your conchie brothers don't deserve to stand alongside decent men like me." He spat on the ground and wiped his mouth on his sleeve.

Elinor's heart skipped a beat as she silently begged Joe not to respond, but the mutterings grew louder. She'd hoped *that* knowledge would not follow them through the gorge, but she should have known better. Small towns knew everyone's business.

Officially, as a farmer and a man with several children, Joe was not an objector. Even so, she understood how grieving, angry people wouldn't appreciate the difference.

She could see a group of men surround Joe and worried what it might mean. A similar group congregated around the heckler who was forcing his way through the crowd, dragging cohorts with him. Elinor turned her head from side to side, searching for the boys, trying to pinpoint where they'd gone, hoping they were not amongst the fray. She couldn't see them anywhere and chided herself for not knowing when and how they'd escaped her notice. Undecided whether to look for the children or try and get Joe away, she hovered a few seconds longer on the edge of the proceedings.

Arguments, raised voices, grumbles and a general hubbub reached her ears, but nothing made sense until she saw the raised fist and heard the thud. The stranger had struck Joe full on the jaw. He staggered, but those behind kept him on his feet. Then Joe charged at the man, who waited for him. Wrapped in a wrestling hold, both men pushed and grunted, each trying to get their arms free of the other, as a circle formed around them.

"Fight! Fight!" came the chant from the ones behind the man, while those behind Joe tried to pull him back, but not before he'd landed a blow in return.

The blast of a police whistle alerted a relieved Elinor to the arrival of the local copper and his offsider, forcing through to the centre of the crowd, growling at anyone in their way.

"Calm down now, Fred," said the sergeant, putting his hand on the man's shoulder and pushing him backwards. "Now's not the time for all this. If you don't behave, I'll take you down to the station. Do you hear me?"

Fred glared at Joe over the policeman's shoulder. He wiped his mouth with the side of his hand where a split lip had started to bleed. Never taking his eyes off Joe, the man spat.

"And you, sir," said the sergeant, addressing Joe and preventing any further clash, "should know better. Least said, I say. Least said. Now I'd suggest you be on your way, and let proceedings continue."

Joe picked his hat up from the ground and strode away, patently angry but choosing the lesser trouble. Elinor hurried in his direction.

"Joe! Wait. Joe!"

He paused in his stride and looked around for her. "We're going," he barked. "Where are the children?"

"I don't know. We have to find them."

The look on his face changed as he picked up her panic. At that moment, the four of them appeared from behind the building.

"I kept the boys with us," said Ella as they rushed to cling to their mother's skirts. "I didn't want them to get lost in the crowd. They were frightened by the shouting."

"You did well, Ella. Thank you," said Elinor, hugging them in relief and smiling at her daughter.

"Didn't you say it was bad to fight, Pa?" asked Ted.

"I did, son. I did," replied Joe, ruffling the boy's hair. "And I still believe that. I didn't ask for him to hit me." Ted looked less than convinced as he bit the side of his lip. "Let's go," said Joe. "We're leaving."

"No, Pa, please. No," begged Ella. "I don't want to go home. Please can we stay. There's afternoon tea and then a movie. I'd like to go."

"Yes. Please, Pa," chipped in Millie. "I want to stay, too. It's for school and everyfing," she added wishfully, thinking something as important as that would persuade him.

The scowl had not left his face and deepened when Elinor backed her daughters. "Don't spoil their fun, Joe. Let them stay."

"Remember, there's the concert after, and the dance," said Ella, her face shining with expectation.

Elinor laughed. "Nice try, sweetheart, but I won't be going to any dance and neither are you. There'll be other times, you'll see. You can go to the movie and that's all."

The look she gave Joe said she'd made her mind up and she would brook no argument. "Now, let me look at that face of yours." She reached up to touch Joe's jaw.

"Stop fussing, woman. I'm fine."

He brushed her hand away and plonked his hat back on his head. Leaning down to speak to the children, he rubbed his hands together. "Come on then, boys, let's go play some games."

Deciding the damage to his face was minimal and she could put ointment on it later, Elinor let them go. "But remember, tomorrow afternoon, we are going to that Service of Thanks and …"

"I'm not going to any service," he growled.

"Yes. You. Are. Joe. We all are. We are not going to run away and hide our heads in shame. You and me are going to that service, and that's the end of it."

"Aw. Do we have to?" moaned Millie. "It smells in there, all stale and horrible, and it's sooo cold."

"You'll do what your mam says, and that's final," snapped Joe, automatically reprimanding his daughter for answering back, even though Elinor knew he wanted to argue the point.

Elinor patted Joe on the arm. "Off you go now. It's Children's Day. Today is for them. Soldiers' Day isn't until Monday, and you know I wouldn't ask you to have anything to do with soldiers."

He nodded and immediately ran off with the boys to the field where various games were being played.

"Thanks, Mam," said Ella and Millie simultaneously.

"All right, girls, we can wander back to the school now and see what's going on there, and when you are settled, I'll get Pa to take me and the boys home. He'll come back for you when it's finished."

Elinor was exhausted by the time she got back to the house. "Would you take the boys out on the farm somewhere and keep them occupied for a while, please ,Joe? I'll put Dot down for a sleep and take a moment to myself."

"Are you all right? There's nothing wrong with the baby, is there?"

"No. Don't fret none. I'm tired, that's all. I'll be right as rain by the time you get back with the girls."

Elinor thankfully retreated to her room, put Dot on one half of the bed and settled herself on the other. She lay there propped up on pillows, wriggling her swollen feet, admiring the room she had created. She loved this bedroom. It was her peaceful, happy place. She'd decorated it all in blues. On the dressing table that had belonged to Joe's mother, a wedding present a decade ago, sat the blue and white ewer and bowl she used every day. Only yesterday, she'd replenished the vase with bluebells and irises growing randomly around the house – courtesy of another woman who'd planted the bulbs – and placed them beside the wedding photo of her and Joe. Not that they were in wedding finery, Joe dressed in his best suit and she in her best dress with the brooch he'd given her fastened at her throat.

She'd filled a blue glass bowl she'd been given with beeswax and created a candle. Lying open on the hand-crocheted cloth was her diary. She liked to write down what happened in their life, even the smallest things mattered. Life was precious, and one never knew when it could be taken away.

She smiled at the toddler asleep next to her and closed her eyes. Within the month, they would welcome another child into the world and she needed to be strong by then. They relied on her. She'd made certain of that.

Joe's voice, soft and gentle nudged her senses. "Wake up, Nell. Wake up, there's my girl. There's been an accident."

"What?" She sat up abruptly, struggling to gather her wits and move her over-large body off the bed. "The girls? Are they all right?"

"Yes, they're fine. Your father's car went into the ditch on the way home from the concert."

Her eyes widened with foreboding. "How? Oh Sprout, how bad is it?" She scanned his face for signs of grim news. "Is he all right?"

Elinor ran her hands over her sleep-tousled hair, absently thinking about her hairbrush. "I need to go to him."

Joe held her by the shoulders, stopping her from getting up. "No, Nellie. You can't do that. They are okay."

"They?" Anxiety flared.

"Your mother was in the car with him, but no one is hurt. Bruised and a little shaken up, but unharmed. Truly, there's no need to panic. Dick says it was a gentle slide off the road in the wet. It started raining while you were asleep. The car's a bit banged up, but no harm done. I think he'd had a drop too much by all accounts. They're home now, he says."

She tried to work out what the time was. How long had she slept? "I don't care about the car. As long as Ma and Pop are all right."

Only then did she realise the child was no longer on the bed beside her. "Where's Dot?" Sitting on the side of the bed, she shook her head and gazed at Joe. "And who's looking after the boys?" She stood up and started to push past Joe to find out for herself, but he held her back.

"Don't fret, Nell, love. The kids are all right. I decided to let you sleep. You looked so peaceful lying there. I went and got the girls and they've seen to the boys. You don't have to worry about anything."

Momentarily, Elinor bristled at the idea she wasn't needed. She was their mother. She ran the household. She was the heart of the home. Of course she was needed.

"They'll want their dinner." Still disoriented, she wondered again about the time. Through the window, the sky was black, but that didn't help. In the middle of winter, the sky darkened early.

Joe reassured her. "They've had some bread and cheese, and Ella's put some veges on to boil to make soup. Get yourself tidied up and come out when you're ready."

Feeling the panic subside, she remembered something else. She put her hand up to his face, fixing her eyes on his. "I'm sorry about what happened today, Joe. But you don't need to carry any shame, or fight your brothers' battles. You are a good man, Joe. A good husband and father. Don't let that man cloud your judgement or upset you. Do you hear me?"

"But I don't believe in war and killing. I'd have done the same as my brothers, if it hadn't been for you and the children. And I'll stand up for my right to say so."

"I know that, Sprout. But getting into a brawl about it won't help and won't change anything. Neither will getting down in the dumps and morose help you, or us. We love you."

He kissed her then, loving her the way he always had.

That Joe had avoided being called up was thanks to her. She'd made the decision as soon as war was declared. No one was going to take her family away from her – ever. If the only way to keep her husband from the authorities was to have children, then she and Joe were going to have a houseful.

As she'd planned, by the time conscription came into force, Joe was considered essential to the economy to work the farm and support those at home.

She'd have more children. She knew that without a doubt. But for now, enough filled the house with noise and companionship and heart.

He smiled. "You are so good for me. I love you, Nellie. I love you so much." He crushed her to him before letting her go. "Take as long as you like. Everything's in hand out there."

After he'd gone, Elinor stared at herself in the mirror, dishevelled and huge. She brushed her hair into a bun at the base of her neck and changed into a clean house dress. She mustn't let things slide. What was she thinking, going to sleep in the afternoon! She pinched her cheeks to put some colour into them and gnawed her bottom lip. Satisfied she looked less like a ghost, she entered the kitchen.

"Mam," squealed several voices, rushing up to hug her leg, waist, arm, whatever part of her they could hold on to. A surge of joy infused her. She pulled Ella to her chest and whispered a thank you in her ear, while she tousled a son's hair. Balance was restored.

"What have we got here, then? What's this mess on the table? Where are we going to eat?"

The children quickly started putting away the things they'd been doing and reset the table with cutlery. Elinor stirred the pot of vegetables boiling on the range, added some salt and fresh-cut herbs, and chopped some of the pieces a bit smaller.

"You've done well, Ella. This soup is going to be just what we need."

She checked on Dot who was a contented child, happy to play with whatever was put in front of her, to find Ella had everything in hand. *She's going to make a good mother when her time comes*, concluded Elinor, well satisfied.

"Are you sure Ma and Pop aren't injured? Are you sure I shouldn't go down there?"

"Yes, I am. Johnny said Dick had taken them home and your mother was resting. Your father was angrier about the state of the road than anything else."

Elinor smiled to herself. "Yes. That sounds like Pop. I'll go up and see them tomorrow."

Joe never did go to the thanksgiving service.

7

Too Many Missing Links

Auckland
11 February 2021

"Hey, Jess," said Emma when she called a few days later. She'd received a couple of texts asking if she'd discovered anything yet, and a curious message saying 'you must help me', but Jess hadn't replied to any of her responses. "How are you? I haven't heard from you this week. Is everything okay? Do you want to come around?"

"No, I don't have a car right now, and Martin needs me to give him a hand. Maybe some other time."

Emma listened to the excuses. That strange emotion she got when something didn't feel right settled in her stomach yet again. "How about I pick you up then, after school? We could go for coffee. Or a walk, if you'd prefer? Luke will have the girls if that's what you're worried about."

They'd had another Covid scare and another three-day lockdown. Everyone was being warned to be cautious, but Emma decided Jess was more important.

"No."

Did Emma hear panic in Jess's voice?

"Um. No, I can't. Tomorrow doesn't suit either. Let me get back to you."

"Okay, then. I'd like to talk to you about what I've found. It's not as much as I'd expected. I've struck a few dead ends, but I'm hoping something might jog your memory from what your dad used to tell you."

"Oh, I see. Well, maybe next week. Gotta go."

Emma heard Jess hang up and again wondered what on earth was going on with her friend. But if she wouldn't meet up anywhere, or talk over the phone, then how was Emma supposed to help her?

Her last foray into the records had revealed some idiosyncrasies. Maybe she could use that as a lever. Instinct kicked in. She grabbed her bag and car keys and called to Luke she'd be out for a couple of hours. She saw his hand wave in answer and left.

The more she reflected, the more Emma realised she'd completely missed Jess's constant references of late about having to do something or be somewhere because of Martin. But Jess had a job – or used to. Working part-time as a florist. Part-time because Martin always insisted she had to be home for Olivia, but she'd loved her job. Her home was dotted with vases of every shape and size filled with everything from a single flower to twigs to huge branches of greenery.

The two friends had a mutual admiration society. Jess thought Emma extremely talented because of her way with words; Emma considered Jess to be hugely creative and artistic.

Then Emma recalled Jess saying last year that she

was receiving the lockdown payment the government offered to retail businesses when they couldn't open. Had she returned to work? Emma knew she'd taken some time off when her dad died but that was over two months ago. Was she still on leave?

Emma didn't know, and that knowledge heightened her misgivings.

Jess had loved being a stay-at-home mum when the girls were young, and Emma admitted it had helped her enormously when she needed someone to look after Rosie. When the girls started school, Jess had moved around a few part-time jobs that Emma considered she was too good for but had finally settled into the florist's role. The flexibility of part-time meant the two friends could meet up after school, go for walks, have coffee, a wine or two, a movie evening. But that was before the lockdowns, Emma realised and cursed herself for not noticing the distance opening up between them, or doing anything about it.

She pulled up two doors from Jess's house. There was one car in the driveway, but no way of telling who was home. Emma picked up the envelope she intended to give Jess with a list of questions and walked along the footpath, looking around for any signs that something was different. The house looked the same. The garden tidy, and filled with flowers for picking. She could hear the soothing sounds of doves cooing and tūi chortling in the background, but the doors and windows were all shut despite the summer heat. Not knowing what she was looking for or expecting, Emma knocked on the door.

A moment or two passed before Jess answered. The look of fear on her face shook Emma.

Jess had time for a quick shake of her head before being pushed aside.

"I thought I said we don't want anyone coming here," commanded Martin.

He smiled as he turned to Emma, but his grey eyes were steely. She could sense his animosity. "We're fine, if that's what you're wondering. We just don't want any visitors. You know," he shrugged one shoulder. "Covid safety and everything. Do you hear me? I'd appreciate it if you didn't come again. I'm sure you understand."

He shut the door in Emma's face.

She heard noises and Martin's raised voice but not what he was saying. She stood there in shock, staring at the door for several seconds, wondering what to do next.

"He sounded calm and reasonable, but he was so cold," Emma explained to Luke when she got home. "And Jess looked awful. I know people are scared of this virus. Last year was dreadful, but things are so much better now with all the precautions being taken. I don't understand why he is inflicting whatever's bothering him on Jess. I'm worried. She looked absolutely terrified. Put that with Olivia saying she doesn't want to be friends with Rosie and I think there's more to it."

"What are you thinking of doing?" asked Luke.

"I don't know. I have no solid evidence of abuse or anything, nothing to prove my instinct."

"Whoa. That's a leap out of the blue. What makes you think it's that serious?"

"I don't know exactly. It's the way Jess's been behaving. But I can't do anything without her say-so, so I'm stuck."

"Have you tried to contact her?"

Emma nodded. "Text and email. No reply. I suppose I'll have to wait until she contacts me. Meanwhile, I'd better get back to work."

Unduly distracted by what had happened, Emma couldn't settle to adding to the novel. She was so close and knew where it was going, but the words wouldn't come. She turned instead to the family history she was collating. Maybe she could push that onto Luke a bit sooner and free up some time to work on Jess's history.

A couple of hours later, after checking the order and adding a few more pages of explanation, she was done. She downloaded the marked-up file, the photographs and various photocopied documents onto a USB and took it across to Luke. "Here's the family history file I told you about. The photos are all numbered with a list of captions to match. I'll leave you to organise the layout."

"You finished that quicker than I expected."

"I had to. I can't ignore Jess's plea any longer."

Luke reached for her hand and rubbed his thumb along one side. "You are my favourite person, you know that? Love you, now scram and get digging."

Needing no second prompting, Emma returned to her computer, ideas already swimming in her head.

After she focused on building Jess's family tree, Emma found many of the links waiting for her to follow. As she told Jess, it was surprisingly easy to trace someone generations ago if you had an inkling about names and places. Fortunately, the slightly unusual spelling of Elinor helped. She certainly had moved around. Emma found her, or her family, listed in the electoral rolls in Canterbury, Hawke's Bay, Horowhenua, Pahīatua and three different addresses in Manawatū. But there were gaps, and electoral rolls didn't list anyone under voting age, so she was struggling to find how many children Elinor had or which of them was Jess's direct line. Neither had she discovered any reason why this Elinor was considered 'indomitable' and, most importantly, why Jess's father had kept his relation, whoever Evelyn was, hidden from his child.

An hour or so later, Emma pulled herself out of one of the rabbit holes she'd been following, realising she still didn't have answers. She'd found a few old newspaper notices covering the death of Elinor's paternal grandfather, in 1874, and from that managed to discover he'd arrived in New Zealand with a wife and young child in 1860 to work in the flax industry – a common occupation of the time. There were other notices several years later, signed by Elinor's father, distancing himself from debts belonging to his brother-in-law, who later went bankrupt. One article, about a court decision that four brothers, including Elinor's father, should pay a regular amount to another brother for the care of their mother intrigued her the most.

Family feuds occurred quite often within large families, usually sparked by money – or, as in many cases, lack of money. Emma wasn't surprised to see that money was the issue with this family in the 1890s. She discovered one branch had settled in Taranaki around the time Elinor was born, which didn't help her search at all. The more she followed the branches, the more twigs she found on both sides of the family – interesting twigs, showing a string of failures and a few successes – none of which hinted at any secret inheritance – but each one took her further away from solving Jess's dilemma.

The only information of any help was the discovery of Elinor's father, mother and siblings living in the Pahīatua district as dairy farmers. Emma guessed Elinor Somers and her husband were also dairy farmers. Running a family farm was typical of the day. Dozens of smallholdings, providing both a home and an income, dotted the countryside for decades after the war. Some succeeded better than others, depending on the quality of the land and the skill of the person. She wondered which of the pair was the stronger minded.

"I think I'd have liked a family farm lifestyle," she said to Luke when they caught up for their evening wine on the deck. Her head was too full of information to decide what to cook so she opted for Thai takeaway delivery. Even Rosie loved pad thai.

"Why's that?" asked Luke, a born-and-bred city boy.

"Fresh-grown vegetables, space to roam, chooks for eggs, a pet, or even a lamb. Do you remember school calf club day when you were little? I wasn't allowed a pet, but we did do baking and crafts. I remember creating faces and shapes from vegetables and fruit and things."

"I don't remember any calf club, but we did have our end-of-year school fair with cake stalls and games," said Luke. "I enjoyed the races the best."

"The three-legged race, or egg and spoon?"

"Yes. And remember the dunk-the-teacher stall?"

The two were soon laughing over old school activities, reminiscing about their childhood. Emma's rather unorthodox upbringing, with a transient mother who moved around, brought back different memories, but she'd had a good life and a good, if different, education.

Luke's had been far more regular and stable and, according to his older siblings, he got away with mischief. He was also the one to work in the business with his father whom he was close to. Especially after he lost his mother.

"So shall we move to the country?" asked Luke, grinning with enthusiasm. "Rosie could have a horse. It'll need grooming and the stall mucking out. And we'll have at least two dogs. You could train them, and then there's the house cow to milk. Sheep for the freezer, if you could bear to kill one, and pigs to clean up the scraps, and the mud. Don't forget the mud."

Emma pulled a face. "Maybe smelly farming isn't for me after all, but I think there were advantages. Large families were more common then. They worked together to do the heavy work, the actual farming, and harvest the home-grown fruit and vegetables for bottling and preserving. They were probably fitter, since they walked everywhere. Or had horses and wagons to get around, before cars became affordable and more commonplace. They learnt skills for home maintenance and there was always a companion in a sibling."

"And arguments. I remember the arguments," Luke reminded her.

Emma didn't know about those. Her view of past times was tinted with a love of antiques. "It can't have been all good, I know. Lots of hard physical work, but I think the slower pace of life that wasn't driven by social media and the pressure to earn more, buy more, own more, must have been better. But then having no money would have had its problems."

"Where are you with your research?"

"I'm not sure. Lots of general stuff about the '20s. And I've worked out Jess's three-times grandmother is probably Elinor, born in the Christchurch area, and those who I think are her parents and grandparents. That was relatively straightforward if I've followed the line correctly. There were a lot of children, many who stayed put and just as many who moved elsewhere, presumably for work. But I haven't managed to capture their 'reality'. Who they were as people. I'm missing a connection."

"That's not like you. You're very good at visualising who people were and how they lived."

Emma fidgeted and fiddled with her hair. "Usually, I know. But I can't get a grasp on this Elinor and her children. Someone should know them, should know how they looked or sounded. Photographs, the sound of a laugh, a story handed down, but Jess has nothing." She took a deep mouthful of her wine and let her eyes wander over the garden, the roses, the trees waving in the breeze, and the blue, blue sky above. She'd had nothing either, but then fate had intervened and she'd found Charli and Luke. "I'm trying to put dates together and they don't fit. Either they're too far apart or too close together. They don't make sense."

"Run them past me and let's see if we can pick up a pattern. What do you know?"

Emma glanced at the clock. Ten minutes before dinner was due to arrive. She might get her head sorted if she thought out loud. "Okay. Let's go. Elinor was born

1889, married in 1909. First child born 1910. Living in Pahīatua not long after World War One. I don't pick her up on the electoral rolls again for another decade. One or two more names on the list by then that I need to follow. Could be children old enough to appear on the rolls but I don't know which one is Jess's direct line, so I can't move forward."

She paused to check Luke was following, took a sip of wine and continued. "Moving back from Jess to her father. He was born not long after World War Two and died late last year. From what Jess said, he knew his maternal line – from the 1860s to this ancestor Jess is wishing she knew – who lived until the turn of the millennium – back through five generations of Es. Women whose name started with the letter E. His name was Edward and without any sisters that we know of, the direct maternal line is broken, so he was number six."

"Okay. So far so good."

"But. I think I've found Elinor's daughter, Ella, born in 1910. If she married about the age of 19 or 20 as was the norm, around 1929, I can't fit in two more generations between then and 1946 when Edward was born. If Elinor is the third generation, that makes her daughter number four in the line. Who is number five? I can't work out which of the five Es is Edward's mother and which is his grandmother. There's a link missing."

"I see your problem. There does seem to be something amiss."

"More importantly, what happened in the nearly forty years after Edward's birth, and before Jess, that split the family apart?"

8

Nothing She Could Do

Pahīatua
August 1922 – March 1923

Every August they celebrated three birthdays. This year she was thirty-three, Millie ten, and Connie four, but this year Elinor's spirits were low. She made a special effort to bake a cake and pretended all was well, but the last few years had been harder than she'd expected, and the future looked gloomy. She wondered if they'd ever get a break. The elation and growth immediately after the war had come to a grinding halt by the end of 1921.

"Don't be down in the glums, Nellie love," said Joe, trying to jolly her along. "It's not like we can do anything about it. We're all in the same boat, us farmers. Those Brits stopped taking our goods, and the price has dropped out of the market."

"I know what happened, Joe. Like I know there are men walking around looking for work, near starving to death, after being forced off their land. What if that happened to us? The government's already slashed spending to the bone. How is everyone going to survive?" She glared at him across the table. "You wouldn't lie to me, would you? We're okay, aren't we?"

"Of course we are. The kids have been great, and the girls are old enough now to be a real help."

"Don't try and shift the conversation to them. We've seven now with Dan, and another on the way. I need to be sure we can feed and house them properly."

"We'll be fine, Nell. I've talked to the bank. They understand it's not easy."

"As long as you are certain, Joe. About the bank … That makes me feel better."

Elinor feared the bank foreclosing and the loss of a haven for her family more than anything else in life.

The decade had begun with such hope. People shook off the shackles of the past and were embracing new ideas, such as electricity, home appliances and cars. Her father had been one of the first to install the new Lalley-Light electric power plant to run the milking shed and electric light to the house on the more prosperous farm they'd moved to. He was going from strength to strength while she and Joe missed out every step of the way, and yet her father never once offered them any opportunity. Never once offered a helping hand. It was as though he wanted Joe to fail so he could say, 'I told yer so.'

Her mother never expressed an opinion her father didn't have, but she was delighted to show off the new electric iron and electric kettle, neither of which Elinor would afford. Her folks even talked about getting a gramophone and a radio, to rub salt into the wound.

From then on, a great number of new and exciting innovations and events began happening. Aeroplanes criss-crossed the skies, the mail could now travel by air, war monuments were being erected and an official public holiday was declared for 25 April to commemorate the fallen soldiers. Not that Joe would attend, but she was quite taken with the new idea of raising the flag at school every day and singing the anthem.

With money tighter than ever, it was up to her to find ways to feed and entertain the youngsters that didn't cost anything. She expanded the vegetable garden and had meat if Joe could afford a piglet, or lamb, or shot a rabbit now and then. They'd even had to relinquish the wagonette and the young gelding. Poor Sally had died, and they'd needed a younger, stronger draught horse for the farm work. They couldn't afford to keep both.

Her biggest regret was not being able to go to Granny Nora's funeral earlier in the year. What a to-do that had been. Of them all, Elinor was the one who was the most distraught.

"I feel I've missed so much, Ma, by not having my grandma around. My kids see you all the time, and it's made me realise how important generations of Mas are to making sense of family."

Her mother snorted. "Not with my mother, you wouldn't. My father never wanted girls. He blamed Ma when we did anything to upset him. The sooner we left, the better. It saved her from the beatings."

Sadness spread through Elinor. Whenever she thought of family, she thought of 'home' as the heart, a place of love, not a place to escape. "Is that why you've hardly visited since?"

Lily frowned. "I've been a couple of times since my father died, but Ma never did change. If you want to go, we'll pay if you can't afford it," offered her mother, which meant her father had told her to.

"I can't do that," said Elinor, shaking her head. She wouldn't shame Joe by accepting her father's money.

Pop had tried to twist it so it was her fault. "You're too stubborn for your own good, my girl. You never listen. I'm glad your sisters will be there to support your poor mother."

But Elinor stuck to her principles. "I won't accept charity. And since it seems you're happy to see us fail rather than talk to Joe about working together and sharing resources, like you do with the Dick, you can keep your money."

How the argument turned to the farm rather than family she didn't know, but she refused to back down. For a time, she did wonder if she'd done the right thing.

Elinor didn't know anything about Granny Nora's past, her parents or where she'd come from. But it was she who had started the tradition of naming. It was her one gift to her girls. According to Granny, generations of kinswomen had named the eldest daughter starting with the letter E. Granny was Eleanor, next came Emily, but known as Lily, then came Elinor, Lily's daughter, named after Granny but spelt differently. Then she and Joe had named their daughter Ella. In that way, Granny Nora lived on.

The other thing she remembered about Granny Nora was that she always had a needle in her hand. Despite her work-worn fingers, Granny was a fine seamstress.

Which reminded her, she had repairs in need of doing. Time to stop daydreaming about the past. "Ella, bring me my sewing basket and come help me with some of this mending. And Millie, you can start preparing the vegetables. Is that meat in the oven yet?"

The girls no longer grumbled – they knew what was needed – but she was glad the two eldest were girls. Even at twelve and ten, they were a great help to her. Ella looked after the small animals and was very good with the youngest children. She was also the brightest at school and enjoyed her schoolwork. She'd even won the end-of-year prize. Millie was turning into a good cook, and nine-year-old Ted was the living image of his father. He followed his pa around all day, prepared to do as much as was needed and not one iota more, which was nothing like Joe.

With needle and thread in hand, Elinor repaired and patched the clothes as best she could, turning collars and cuffs, and adding braiding to hide hem marks where she'd had to let the girl's dresses down. She was grateful for the sewing machine she'd purchased for a pittance a couple of years ago. It was a boon, but she'd been torn at the time, wanting to buy it but knowing the woman who owned it was so down in circumstances that she only had a few personal items remaining to start a new life. Such was the reality of bankruptcy and bank foreclosures.

Surely, the worst was over. They'd be all right now. Joe had promised.

* * * * *

A matter of months later, Elinor ran from the house until she could breathe no longer. A burning rage erupted. She stood frozen to the spot, half bent over as a roar erupted from deep within. Nothing in her life before had exposed such raw emotion.

Something had to be done. But what? How could this happen? How would she regain what she'd lost, after this?

"I'm sorry, love," said Joe when Elinor returned to the house. "So, so sorry."

"You promised, Joe. You promised."

"I know I did, but I didn't have a choice."

She knew all about choices – or the lack of them. "How much time do I have?"

"For what?" asked Joe, failing to understand what she was talking about.

"You said the bank has threatened to foreclose if we don't make the next payment and pay the arrears. You said we have to rent this house to someone else to make ends meet."

"If we want to save the farm, then yes. I know the place I found isn't much but …" He trailed off at the hostile look Elinor threw his way.

"How could you fail to make a payment and not tell me? How could you!" She would lose the house she'd started to call home.

"I'm sorry, Nell …"

"Don't you 'I'm sorry' me. If we have to move again. I repeat, how much time do I have?"

"The next payment to the bank is due at the end of the month."

She did a quick calculation. If they were to get someone paying rent in time to meet that payment, she had a matter of days, if not hours, to make the move. She nodded. "I'd better get on with it then."

There was no time for sentimentality. The comparative hovel she was being forced to move to would only accommodate half of what they owned. The rest would be left for the new people.

She looked around the kitchen, imagining the other rooms. She would take the table and enough chairs for them all, her favourite armchair and some of the beds. They'd have to double up and share best they could.

In the face of her silence, Joe shuffled out the door while she began to toss what she needed from the kitchen into packing boxes, crates, flour sacks, trunks, whatever she could find. She moved to the other rooms and did the same. She didn't stop – not for the children, not for Joe, not for her mother – and worked through the night until she was finished. Damn the bank. Damn Joe for letting things get out of hand. Damn her father and her brothers for not saying something sooner. Damn them all. She'd show them what she was made of.

In her haste, she left a fallen candle, an oven mitt dropped beside the stove, a rolled-up newspaper on the hearth and an oil lamp on a windowsill.

By the time the family rose the following morning, Elinor was back to her normal self with a ready smile, the stove blazing, plentiful food on the table, the house cow milked and the eggs collected.

Joe put his arm around her waist and kissed her cheek. "Morning, love. You seem in good spirits this morning."

"Good enough," she said, not pulling away and letting him think all was well. The children squabbled over the last of the jam for their slice of fresh-made bread. "What must be done gets done. I just need to get on with it."

Ignoring the children still bickering at the table, she

left them – and Joe – to sort it out. Picking up the nearest cardboard box, she heaved it onto her hip, opened the back door and went and stacked it with others beside the driveway, then returned for another load.

"Joe, hitch the dray up so I can start to take a load."

"We don't have to do it all today, Nell. There's time."

"No," she said, shaking her head, her lips pressed in a tight line. "I don't think so. I need to get this done today. As soon as possible. Because if I stop and think about it, I won't be able to do it. Now, are you going to help me? Because if you're not, you need to get out of my way."

She strode into the house and collected more things to add to the pile outside. Back and forth, without stopping. Then, collecting a bucket and throwing various cleaning cloths and soap into it, she marched off down the road to the poor example of a farmhouse the neighbour was letting them use for a pittance. 'To help us out,' Joe had said. *To gloat, more like*, fumed Elinor.

She shivered as she pushed the front door open. The house was cold, even on a sunny day. They'd have to keep the coal range burning all day and night if it was going to be liveable. Slowly wandering from room to room, assessing what changes were needed, she saw a large tin bath hanging from the wall. She bit her lip. Back to the worst of basics. No bathroom, no running water. She fought back the tears, returned to the kitchen and let out a sigh. Her shoulders sagged, easing the tension, when she saw a wetback had been added. She might have to fill it by hand, but at least hot water was to be had. Through the window, she saw a water tank. Joe's first job would be to connect it to the house. Maybe it wouldn't be so bad after all.

She heard the dray pull up, and she and Joe silently began to set up the beds and put what furniture fitted in place. Beyond instructions as to where she wanted things, she refused to speak to him. Her youngest brother, Johnnie, turned up unexpectedly to give them a hand, but nothing she said would draw him on what their father said about him helping or the farm failing. After the men had gone, she turned her mind to cleaning.

Hours later, back aching, fingernails broken and her hair awry, she returned to the place she considered home. Why was home such a fleeting promise, always just out of reach, something everyone else had, except her?

She stood at the door staring at the peaceful scene before her. Ella was playing with Dot and keeping a careful eye on the baby asleep in his basket. Millie and the two boys were playing a game. She looked up at her mother who had moved from the coal range to greet her.

Lily's face looked drawn and the way she teased the towel in her hands gave away her agitation. "Let me take that," said Lily, reaching for the bucket. "Supper's ready. I'll serve it as soon as you say. Do you want to take a hot bath first?"

"What are you doing here?" Elinor's voice, barely above a whisper, came out thin and tight.

"I wanted to help, that's all. I ..."

Elinor cut in. "Help? It's a bit late for that. Pop should have said. You should have said. You should have warned me."

"I did try," faltered Lily, "but ..."

"But nothing!" Elinor put both hands to her face, rubbed vigorously, trying to dispel the anger.

"You've refused your father's offer, he tells me. Why?"

"Why? You have the nerve to ask why?" Elinor was so enraged she couldn't stop shaking. His offer to buy the farm from the bank for the pitiful amount they were asking and employ Joe as a labourer was more than she could stand. No talk of a partnership or equity; he was prepared to see them brought to their knees. "He knows why I won't take his offer. I will never be at his mercy. Not now. I won't be shamed by him. He could have done so much more when it had mattered. Get out of my way."

Elinor pushed past her mother and headed for the sanctity of her bedroom to meet Joe, skin glowing, coming from the bathroom.

"Nellie," he called, reaching out for her, but she evaded his grasp.

"I'm all dirty."

"I've been worried. Are you all right? Where have you been all this time?"

She stared at him, eyes wide, mouth open. What was he talking about? Did he honestly have no idea? She shuddered.

"At that hovel, the next roof over our heads, trying to make it clean enough to live in. Where else do you think I've been?" Her temper boiled over, and she pushed him out of the way.

"Nellie?" came his plaintive cry as she slammed the door shut.

"Children." Elinor cleared away the breakfast things and put the last of the dishes into a box to take with her.

"I want you to grab the bags I packed each of you and take them out to your father. Ella, can you carry Dan?"

"Yes, Mam."

"Well, get started over to the house and I'll be there soon. Millie, you can start to walk with Ted and Ricky. Don't get distracted on the way. I'll take care of the others. Now get going."

Last night had been an example of what to expect from now on. With few chairs remaining to sit on, the youngest ones had sat on the floor with their bowls to eat, and restless, grizzling children trying to sleep three to a bed had kept her up most of the night.

"I can take the younger ones if you want," said Joe, coming inside. "There's enough room on the dray for them. We've not got much else to take except the suitcases. Are you coming?"

"No, not yet, but you taking the kids would be a big help. Tell Ella she can give Archie some milk, and Millie can see if she can find any eggs. And get the fire going. I've got some things to finish off here."

"Okay. See you later."

Elinor wandered around the house checking she'd taken everything that mattered to her. She wouldn't leave anything personal for strangers to gawk at. She picked up a crocheted wool rug one of the children had dropped and held it to her nose, smelling the lingering scent of her handmade soap, but all that was left of the house were the bones. Basic furniture she would miss but didn't have room for. The new people could move in and start living in her house without a second thought.

She put the last of her things by the door and set to cleaning. She couldn't abide a dirty house, and she could vent her anger on the floors as she scrubbed. She lit the lamps and stoked the fire for the hot water, satisfied everything was as it should be. The evenings were drawing in and, as the afternoon light faded, Elinor slowly walked away from her home, towards the worst house she'd ever lived in.

Hours later, after the children had been fed, the babies asleep and the girls playing a game of snakes and ladders, Joe sat at the table studying the paper. Elinor slumped in the armchair by the fire. With her head rested against the back, her eyes closed, she let the exhaustion and anguish of the last few days wash away.

Joe moved the lamp closer and turned in his seat to read the paper better. A moment later, he let out a yell. "What's that?" He pointed out of the curtain-less window to a glow in the sky.

"What's what?" Elinor kept her eyes closed.

"That glow. Look, Nellie, look."

She opened her eyes and turned her head but didn't get out of the chair, too exhausted to move. Joe stood by the window, trying to get a better look. All Elinor could think was that she'd need to make some curtains soon.

"Fire," shouted Joe. "The house is on fire!" He raced out the door before she could say anything.

Where he was going or what he thought he could do, she had no idea. There was no fire brigade, not enough people, not enough water. There was nothing he could do.

Elinor closed her eyes. The house would be gone by morning. The fire would see to that. No one would take her home from her now. The fire had done that.

She smiled.

9

False Assumptions

Auckland
12 February 2021

Emma searched online for information about what a friend could do to help a woman she suspected was being emotionally and mentally threatened. It felt intrusive to phone any of the likely organisations in case they asked for details. She wasn't ready for that yet, but the websites aimed at physically abused women didn't help her much.

Eventually, she found one outlining a scenario that struck a chord. In hindsight, Emma had missed so many hints Jess had tried to give her, she felt guilty. She couldn't be certain, but she didn't believe Martin's behaviour pattern was long-lived but something that had changed since last year's lockdowns.

Jess's life had changed dramatically. She *had* lost her job and now spent all her time with Martin, who controlled her movements and whom she could talk to. Jess had no one who would notice that she wasn't around like she used to be – except Emma.

The website suggested how to handle the situation and refocus the conversation to a more equal partnership. But it all relied on the woman being prepared to have the discussion, and that was Emma's problem. If she couldn't talk with Jess, how could she help her?

As she read through the list of ways people could be controlled, which fitted what she knew of Jess's situation, Emma's thoughts drifted to her historical characters. In times past, women had less say about how they could live their lives, but while some managed to stand up for themselves, domestic violence was always an issue. More often, lack of financial independence caused the greatest problems. Men who gambled or drank their wages away, farmers and business people who couldn't juggle the workload and costs and fell foul of the banks and moneylenders, widows left destitute. No wonder the women grouped together to improve their lot.

With no idea how to help her friend, Emma once again turned to Jess's family tree. Maybe there was something there she could hang on to and use as a breakthrough, but she suspected the family hadn't had the easiest of lives.

"Oh, where is this story!" wailed Emma aloud to her computer. "Why can't I find the missing connections?"

Emma began to doodle.

Jess's dad had been adamant about his connection to his five Es maternal line. Yet Jess didn't know any of them. Emma flicked back pages of her notes looking for the list she wrote when Jess had rattled off their names: Elinor, Evie, Ella, Emily, Eleanor. She wasn't certain if that was the right order or even which way it went. Top down, or bottom up.

As she doodled, she wondered why she had spelt the two Elinors differently. She couldn't have known at the time, but intuition told her the Elinor Somers she was trying to trace was the anchor to it all reasserted itself. But she couldn't see how to fit in both an Evie and an Ella in Edward's life. Unless …

Her phone beeped. A message from Jess. With a surge of expectation, Emma opened the text. *Dads.* Maybe Jess would talk to her after all.

Some instinct told Emma not to text back to ask what she meant. Emma racked her brain. What about her dad? There were endless questions about her father. Nothing made sense. Why was he estranged from those he talked about all the time? Why was Jess's sister – she couldn't even remember her name – so offside with her father? When she'd visited yesterday, Emma hadn't left the envelope with the list of questions she wanted Jess to look at. Neither had she waded through the box of old letters Jess had left behind.

"I've got an idea Jess's asked me to meet her," said Emma when she wandered out to Luke's workshop to tell him. "Her father's house hasn't sold yet, and I think she wants to meet me there. There's nothing else I can think of."

"It's worth a shot. Go around and look anyway. You've nothing to lose."

Minutes later, Emma was driving towards the Shaws' place still trying to slot pieces of the complicated jigsaw together. She pulled up outside the old house. There was no sign of Jess's car or that the house was open. Emma got out and stood at the gate in the middle of the white picket fence, thinking the house looked forlorn. A driveway to the side led to the freestanding garage at the back. Emma wandered up the driveway wondering if Jess was there. Had she guessed wrongly? Sadly, Emma wondered if the house would be knocked down by its new owner. With the price of land the way it was, a developer would have a field day with a section this big.

"Jess? Are you here?"

"Ems," said a quiet voice. "Shh, I'm here. Behind the garage."

Emma looked around, feeling ridiculously like an intruder, but couldn't see any cars, or neighbours watching through a window. Satisfied no one was looking, she slipped behind the garage to find Jess huddled in the corner where the old apple tree stood. The dappled sunlight offered a secluded spot that felt strangely protected from the world.

"Jess, are you all right? You look awful." Thinking her words weren't terribly reassuring, she reached out to hug her friend. "You gave me quite a scare when I saw you yesterday."

"I don't know how to start, or even where, but Martin is sick."

"Has he caught Covid?" Emma gasped, her fear of catching it unfolding.

"No, no nothing like that. I mean mentally."

Emma's face crumpled. "Tell me what's happening. We need to get help."

"He won't listen. I've tried. He tells me there's nothing wrong with him. It's all my fault. I fuss too much or I want to trick him into taking medication. He thinks I've gone to visit Mum, so I haven't got long but I wanted you to know. He times me when I'm out, saying he worries that something has happened to me if I don't get back in time. He denies it, but I know he checks my phone messages, and he's forbidden me to see you. He says he's frightened you'll infect Olivia, which is nonsense."

"Oh Jess, I'm so sorry. If there's anything I can do, let me know. We can set up a code." Emma almost laughed but restrained herself in time. She was hardly spy material. She was far better at uncovering things than hiding them.

"I'll try using 'Dads' again sometime when I can. Martin told Olivia not to be friends with Rosie. So tell Rosie it's not her fault."

"How long has he been like this?"

"It started during lockdown last year. He was nervous about catching the virus and became super vigilant about washing his hands and wearing a mask. But he's got worse. We have set routines when Olivia and I can go for walks or play outside. I order everything online, and click and collect. It's a wonder Livvy is still allowed to go to school. He's quite out of control. And so angry all the time."

Emma's gut had warned her something serious was going on and now Jess had confirmed it. "Oh, that's awful."

Jess hugged Emma, wiping away a tear. "Sorry. I'm so stressed I don't know what to do. But I'd better go. I'll have to lie about going to Mum's."

"Now I understand why you've been acting so strange. Are you okay? Truly?"

"I am. It's frustrating, but there's nothing physical, so

I'm safe. And it's easier for me to do what he wants for now. I just need to get Dad's stuff sorted."

Emma couldn't begin to think how she would fare, carrying such a high emotional load as Jess had. "Do you want me to continue with your family tree? What else can I do?"

"Nothing. But please keep digging. My sister is stirring the pot now. There's something there somewhere."

"Will do. Where's your car?"

"In the other street. I snuck in through the fence. There's been a gap since I was a teenager. My sister and I used to use it when Dad didn't know we were out late."

"Remind me, what's your sister's name?"

"Lily."

"I've got a confession to make," said Emma when she returned home. "I've misjudged the situation. Jess says Martin's ill. Stressed beyond reason about Covid, and he's become utterly obsessed with being clean and tidy. He always was a bit that way inclined. Hated clutter and junk lying around, but she steered around most of it. Now he's worse, rearranging everything until it's perfect, and he's become domineering. To the point, he won't let Jess out of the house except to collect the groceries and see her mother – but he times her."

"Not an easy situation, but it does make more sense," agreed Luke. "You must feel better knowing that."

"I do in some ways, but it's still abuse in my opinion. Emotional abuse. She says she's coping, but I think she gives in and chooses the path of least resistance. It's probably easier that way, but not safe, or healthy. She asked me to keep looking into her family tree."

"No excuses then? And one less thing for her to worry about."

Emma grinned at him. "No. No excuses. But I'm worried about her."

"Sometimes your writer's instinct for drama is a little too well attuned." Luke chuckled and grinned at her, taking away any unintended sting.

"Well, it's not like I'm wrong exactly. But yes, I did think something more serious had happened to Jess."

Emma poured herself a glass of water and offered one to Luke, who shook his head. "It troubles me how commonplace mental health issues are. But it isn't a new phenomenon. Most of us today understand what soldiers suffered during and after the war. Now they would be treated for post-traumatic stress disorder, but no one knew such a thing existed then and treated troubled souls as lost causes who were making it up. Such a shame."

"You have such a soft heart, my darling, you'd give anyone the benefit of the doubt." Luke wrapped his arms around her and kissed the top of her head.

"Now, maybe. I've learnt a lot since my days of wanting to be the hard-nosed journalist everyone hated but respected, because I nailed the big stories. Except, of course, I didn't. I was small-time, at best, and angry. And had no idea who I was or should be."

"Ah. An identity crisis. Off to the psychologist with you," laughed Luke, trying to distract her from her self-analysis, as he usually did. "Charli soon fixed that, didn't she?"

Emma could laugh about it these days. "She certainly did. I wonder how my life would have turned out without her. I wouldn't have you, that's for certain."

"Well you do, so stop worrying about might-have-beens. You are who you are simply because she showed you the way, not because she inherently changed you. When people find their purpose in life, there's no holding them back. So off you go and fulfil your purpose."

Back at her desk, Emma began to put words on the screen. Random words about family, but as she wrote, she remembered a class at university where they'd debated 'Who Am I?' Not what one did in terms of a job or hobby, or who you were in relation to someone else, but who you were inside. Were you a conformist or a rebel? Were you shy or outspoken? Did you rely on other people to shape you or were you someone who shaped your own life? Were you determined, frightened, reliant, or a leader? There were no right or wrong answers, but it made each student think about how to answer the question.

Now Emma wondered about the characters she was writing about. Who were they? Gender roles were more defined in the past. Societal expectations made sure people conformed to those beliefs or suffered the consequences if they didn't. Precepts that passed the test of time, or did they?

One thing she did know, she had enormous empathy for Elinor Somers, someone who was constantly moving house, from the South Island to the North, from one region to another, having to make new friends, discover new locations, new ways of doing things … and for what purpose?

The more she wrote about the original settlers in Jess's line coming to New Zealand, the more she understood the difficulties. Mid-nineteenth-century life in a small South Island town wouldn't have been easy. A place where everyone knew your business. Reassuring, on one hand; daunting on the other.

Elinor's paternal grandfather Thomas Harwood would have been hard at work all day cutting flax. His wife Margaret at home with the children making do as best she could. The couple had left England during winter with one son, and months later arrived in a New Zealand summer with two. The thought of giving birth on a sailing ship gave Emma the shivers. They wouldn't have had any comforts, crammed together in steerage. While Margaret probably had the help of the other women on board, she'd take a bet Thomas wasn't around.

When they arrived, they'd have found the housing situation completely different from what they were used to. Simple houses built of wood, often draughty, cold, with no running water or facilities. Before long another son, followed by young Robert, Elinor's father, arrived in quick succession, but the baby girl lived less than a day. Then one more son, and the news from England that her mother and two sisters had been taken by the smallpox epidemic sweeping the country. Who would comfort the woman? Who would help her grieve, share her chores, manage her sons, the eldest of whom was barely ten? Another son a year later, before a daughter. A precious daughter. A mother's helpmeet.

But worse was to come. At the age of thirty-six, with six sons and a baby daughter, Thomas was taken from her. A healthy thirty-eight-year-old man died of a heart attack, leaving his widow destitute. The family was never the same again. Soon the boys were in trouble with the law, one disowned another, the years passed and they separated to live elsewhere. Some would never rejoin the family, as the newspaper articles testified.

After putting the bare facts in place ready for her to expand later, Emma was both sad and exhausted. She often lived the emotional trauma of those she wrote about.

On cue, Luke appeared with some tea. "I figured you might need this. You've been in here for hours, tapping away."

Emma cleared a space for the cup and saucer, and Luke sank comfortably into the armchair. Emma took a welcome sip of her steaming drink.

"What's the scoop?" Luke asked.

"Elinor's paternal grandparents' life paints a terribly sad picture. But I'm now certain that none of the E women I'm after came from Elinor's father's side."

"Well, that's a step forward, isn't it?"

"It is, and it'll save me following unnecessary branches."

"What about the maternal side?"

Emma grinned. "That's where the mystery begins."

10

Reactions and Interactions

Glen Oroua, Manawatū
1925-1926

March 1925

The move back across the hills to the Manawatū had been an upheaval. She shuddered when she remembered the hovel they'd been forced to move into when the bank had threatened to foreclose. Even though the insurance for the fire had paid the mortgage arrears and replaced the furniture they'd lost, life was still uncertain.

The rental house they'd moved into was adequate but, without spending money on fertilisers and updated equipment, Joe had struggled to make the farm efficient enough to pay its way. Being forced to sell the Pahīatua farmland hurt immensely, but Elinor would never let on to anyone how she felt. She would never betray Joe. Stoic had become her middle name. For all that, she decided the move was for the best, but she'd never let herself be put in that position ever again, and started to squirrel away every penny she could.

She would always believe they were better off not labouring for her father, whatever he said. She was confident they could make something of this place back on the Manawatū side of the gorge. It offered more opportunities, or at least that's what Joe had said.

"Granny Reta's died," said Elinor clutching the telegram her mother had sent. "Pop's mother. I don't know what to do."

Joe put his cup back on the saucer and took her hand across the table. "You should go see your father. When's the funeral?"

"It doesn't say. But I doubt Pop will go. You know him. Too stubborn for his own good. He's never forgiven his brother George for taking the other brothers to court all those years ago."

Joe looked at the clock and settled back into his seat. "Did you ever find out why?" he encouraged, refilling the teacups.

"No. Not exactly. Pop said his brother was mean-spirited and it wasn't fair. I must have been five or six at the time, but he's not let it go since. I can't remember the last time I saw Granny Reta. I have vague memories of her from when I was little. Sitting in a small, dark room with the coal range burning, and the smell of bread. It's funny how the smell of fresh-baked bread still reminds me of her, but she seemed a sad old lady to me, even then. We moved after Dick was born and I don't think I ever saw her again."

"Do you want to go to the funeral?"

Elinor shook her head wearily, thinking back to Grandma Nora and now Granny Reta and how she hadn't known either of them. "I don't think so. We don't

117

have the money, for starters, and I don't know any of those relations over that way anyway."

She wondered what had gone wrong within the family that a grandparent didn't know their grandchild. She hoped that would never happen to her. Although her father's attitude was making it harder to stay in touch.

Joe got up from his chair. "If you're sure. We could find the money if we had to." He collected his hat from behind the door and paused in the entranceway. "If you asked me, I would say you should go back to the farm and see your folks. I could manage with the older kids for a couple of days. If you take Archie and Dan, Ella and Millie can help with the girls, and the boys are old enough to be of use."

"I'll think about it."

"I'll drive you to the train, and Dick will pick you up at the other end. It'll be easy enough for you," he persisted.

Elinor nodded. "Thanks. Maybe I should."

She hadn't told him yet she was pregnant again.

* * * * *

Elinor had barely stepped inside her parents' home before the arguments began.

"I am not going and that is final!"

"But she's your mother. You should show some respect. What will the others think?"

"I don't give a damn about the others. They never considered me. *She* never considered me. And she's not likely to notice I'm not there, is she?"

Elinor wandered around the garden with the two boys, trying not to eavesdrop, but her father's voice carried. How could a son not want to weep at his mother's graveside for what he'd lost? But it sounded as though he'd lost his mother a long time ago. She'd have to work harder to guarantee that never happened with her boys.

"Look, you two. Look at the bee."

The lush garden, with its abundant display of flowers, shone in the autumn sunshine. Her mother had done a great job of the grounds in the six years they'd lived at the farm.

"Careful now," said Elinor, pulling enquiring little fingers away from the creature collecting nectar from the flowers, their heads bobbing in the breeze. "Don't disturb her or she might sting you."

Elinor loved all her children and tried not to favour one above another, but she loved them most when they were babies and toddlers, while the world was a place of wonder to explore. Dan, who was nearly four, was his mother's boy. He hadn't yet gravitated to his brothers and father and the outdoors. Archie, at eighteen months, was at the cheeky, chatty, huggable age she adored. She must find a way to ensure her children always wanted to be together as a family.

Looking around the homestead, her parents were undoubtedly prosperous, employing her brothers on the farm and supporting her unmarried sisters. Elinor held out hope such comfort and security would be hers one day in the future.

He'd done well, she'd give him that. At her age, her father had been a labourer. The farm she'd loved on the north side of Pahīatua, that they'd moved to nearly twenty years ago, had been their stepping stone, a place where they learnt the ropes. In time, her father and brothers had become well known for their stock breeding programme. Partners – on a farm she knew would pass to her brothers. She wished he and Joe could have worked together, become partners. If she'd recognised sooner it was never going to happen, she might have saved them a lot of misery. She never understood why he wanted Joe to fail, but he'd never offered them anything other than miserable charity.

"And I'm not paying for any funeral or ridiculous headstone either. George can go jump," yelled her father.

Elinor heard a door slam and assumed her father had gone out onto the farm. She returned inside to find her mother in the kitchen preparing vegetables. Without being asked, Elinor donned an apron and worked beside her mother while the boys sat on the floor playing with a few pea pods. In the background, the new radiogram was on, playing the occasional song amongst the patter. She recognised the one epitomising her life. Was she chasing rainbows?

Mother and daughter chatted easily about the local gossip, how things were growing in the garden, what meetings her mother had attended, a new recipe Lily liked. They avoided discussing Joe or last season's move back to the Manawatū after the fire. Something Elinor knew her parents objected to.

"I'm enjoying my National Women's Institute meetings," said Elinor. "It's early days yet, but they have big plans for more groups and to expand how they can support women. It takes me out of the house once a month, and I'm meeting new people."

"That's good, dear. I haven't bothered. I've enough to do."

As if I haven't. But Elinor kept that to herself.

"Have you read about the New Zealand and South Seas Exhibition?" asked Lily. "It's to be held later this year in Dunedin. I wish we could go. Not that your father would consider it, but the displays sound marvellous with so many new things on offer. I can't quite believe some of it myself."

"Can't say I have much," replied Elinor. "We won't be able to go or afford anything new. But I have been looking at the new fashions and hairstyles. I think I could make myself a couple of those new-style dresses. That straight-through look would suit my height. And I might get my hair cut into one of those bob styles they're talking about."

"Oh, your father would not approve of me doing anything like that."

"I doubt Joe would either, but it's not his hair and he doesn't have to wash it. One thing we all know, it'll grow back."

For a house in mourning, the occupants carried on with life as though nothing had changed. There were no tears, no reminiscing, no expressions of loss. If anything, anger rose to the surface more often. Elinor felt removed, wondering if she should be there, if she was adding a burden to their lives. Her sisters were glad to see her and wanted to chat about the latest fashions and hairstyles. And they happily played with the boys, providing her with time to ponder.

"How long are you staying?" asked her father over supper.

"I'll go back tomorrow. I can't leave Joe on his own for long with the other children."

"I don't know why you bothered to come at all, if you think he can't manage without you for a few days." *There he goes again*, brooded Elinor, *always complaining.*

"I came to see you. I thought you might want the whole family together at a time like this." Her eyes glistened. Not with sadness, but with regret, and anger. Why did he always put Joe down? He would never have permitted her mother to go anywhere without taking all the children with her, regardless. At least Joe was managing the other six, more than her father had ever done.

"I'm glad you came," said her mother, patting her hand. "It's lovely to see the two little ones, and hear all about the older ones. How are they doing at school? What's Ella up to?"

"I'm pleased with their school reports, and Ella is growing up so fast. Didn't I tell you all this in my last letter?"

Her father folded his newspaper with a huff and pushed his chair back from the table. Her eyes followed him as he wordlessly left the room, wondering which of life's dilemmas had changed him so much. Growing up, she didn't remember him being so disapproving.

She turned her head towards her mother and the look on her face took Elinor aback. Emily had also watched her husband leave, and her look of sadness, resignation and regret spoke volumes. Elinor was transported back to a conversation she'd had with her mother earlier, not long after arriving in Pahīatua, about being in love and being happy. Her mother had not given her a satisfactory reply. Elinor wondered if she'd finally got the answer she sought. Was her mother happy living in a lovely home, on a prosperous farm, surrounded by her children? Elinor didn't think so.

She glanced at her sisters, so much younger than her. Nearly twenty years between her and Stella, who was only two years older than her own Ella. Had her mother wanted more children at that late stage? Had she been happy then? Elinor probably would never know, but suddenly she wanted to get home to Joe. With baby number nine growing in her belly, the realisation of how happy she felt and how much she loved Joe was almost overpowering. She had so much to be grateful for, so much to value.

"Penny for them?" she asked, startling her mother.

"What? Oh, they're not worth anything. Now, what was I saying? Oh yes. Did Patty show you her scrapbook from being May Queen last year?"

Accepting her mother would never talk about her innermost feelings, Elinor smiled. "No. I didn't know she kept a scrapbook."

Patty immediately leapt to her feet and returned a few breathless minutes later carrying her gown and a book of memorabilia. "Look, there's me with the tiara, and here, I'm being presented with the sash."

Elinor oohed and aahed over every photograph, newspaper article and other miscellaneous items, from a ticket stub and programme to the pressed bouquet. "I'm sorry I couldn't see you in person. It's never a good time of year on the farm." Even as Elinor explained, she knew her words sounded hollow. Everyone knew what farming was like at any time of the year. "But I have missed you, so much," she added, wanting to be close to them again. If she was being honest she would tell them her father's attitude to Joe kept her away, but the moment passed and she held her tongue. She didn't want to spoil Patty's moment.

Neither would she tell them about the new baby. Her mother hadn't noticed. Her father would disapprove, and Joe deserved to know first.

* * * * *

October 1925
"You are impossible to reason with!" growled Elinor's mother, as she bustled around ordering the girls to do this and that.

"We know what to do, Grandma Lily," said Ella as calmly as she could, resentment showing in every scowl and shrug she and Millie sneaked behind her back.

"And so you should. I don't know what you are thinking, Nell, but this place is a shambles."

Elinor bristled. What did she expect? Ten people lived in a house with four bedrooms – eleven if she counted the new baby coming – one of which had been vacated for Lily's visit, leaving the girls to double up. Archie still slept in their room, until the latest one arrived. There was never enough room for everyone's clothes and schoolbooks. While she admitted clean washing waited to be folded, she put schoolwork ahead of such chores. The newspaper pile could be tidier, and the last lot of wood the boys had brought in had left a trail of debris, but she was not letting her mother get the upper hand.

"Ma, if you are going to come here and complain, you can pack your bags and go back to Pop." Elinor was in no mood to put up with her mother's pontificating. "Either you are here to visit, or you are not. Now what's it to be?"

Mother and daughter stared each other down, but this was Elinor's house – she couldn't call it home yet, only somewhere she lived. A ramshackle house on a leased farm.

"Very well," said Lily, patting her hair into place. "But I hope you have aired the bed properly," she added caustically.

Elinor gritted her teeth but withheld the sharp retort. "Naturally. I do know how to run a house."

"Of course, dear, but when you wrote, you said you were at your wits end with the farm work, and what with the baby due any time … I came straight away, without another thought, to help you." Lily responded to Elinor's chastising by once again playing on the sacrifices she'd made.

"Being busy and stretched to find time does not mean I don't know what to do. And that was weeks ago. Now Ma. Behave. None of us are in this situation by choice," Elinor reminded her mother, "but that's life, and I will face up to it beside Joe."

"As you always have, my dear. As you always have." No one could miss the note of reprimand in Lily's voice. Not even the girls.

"I'll put your bag in the room on the left, Grandma Lily," said Ella. "It's as comfortable as we can make it." Behind her, Millie tried not to laugh, covering her mouth with her hand.

Elinor raised an eyebrow wondering what trick the girls might be playing. "It better be. Or you'll answer to me." She could fight with her mother, but her children would not be disrespectful.

"I'll check," Ella conceded, "and take through a ewer and jug for you. We've only the one bathroom," she finished, stating the obvious. There was only ever one bathroom, but this one was inside – sort of, more of a lean-to attachment accessed from the porch – and had running water, even if the gaps in the walls made it a chilly place in the mornings.

Elinor was fairly certain this baby would come any day now. It was already sitting low, but in comparison to her others, this one was small. She hoped it would stay awhile longer and grow a bit bigger.

Secretly, she wished for a daughter. If the pattern of two girls, two boys, repeated itself again, then number nine might be another girl. Joe, of course, wanted more boys. Boys to carry on the name, men to help him run the farm. He had plans, did Joe. Big plans. Pop's cousin Thomas, a well-respected horse breeder and trainer who'd died a couple of years ago, had given Joe ideas. But ideas cost money. And if she could put her dreams on hold, then so could he.

The aroma of roast meat lingered in the warmth of the kitchen as Lily and Elinor sat around the table chatting after supper, having a cup of tea.

"I belong to the local Women's Institute," said Elinor. "I think I told you before. There's a meeting on Tuesday. Would you like to come with me?"

"You can't go out in your condition!" cried her mother. "It's not seemly."

"Oh, for heaven's sake, Ma. It's 1925, not the dark ages. Who cares? I don't, that's for certain. And I'm sure they won't either."

Elinor rose, gathered the cups, saucers and plates, and carried them to the sink. Her mother's voice followed. "Don't bang them around so much, dear. You'll chip them."

She forced herself not to snap back, but her mother had irritated her enough already. "Why don't you see what Joe and the kids are doing while I finish these. I'll join you when I'm done."

She heard her mother's chair scrape back and relaxed, relieved to have a few moments to herself before she chivvied the younger boys to bed and made sure the older ones had done their homework. She knew Joe would be reading the paper and studying the race form. He enjoyed the odd bet or two, more for the fun of it and to extend his knowledge of breeding. She wouldn't let him waste money. *He should be looking at the milk yield,* fretted Elinor, but that had become her job.

She plastered a smile on her face and joined them in the living room, which for once was surprisingly quiet but cool. No one had shut the curtains against the October sky. She'd be glad when the evenings got longer and this room would be warmer.

"It's a bit chilly in here," said Lily, hugging her cardigan tighter around her. "Doesn't the fire draw well?"

Elinor gritted her teeth. "Connie, go get your grandmother the crocheted rug off my bed, please, there's a dear." She turned to her mother. "I'm sorry you're cold. The rug will help you feel warmer, but please stop criticising. I can't do anything about any of it."

"I'll fetch more wood," said Joe, folding his paper and getting to his feet. He put the paper down and patted Elinor's arm as he passed. "It's okay," he whispered. They had agreed to save the wood and only light the fire when necessary. Tonight, it seemed, was one of those occasions.

"Where's Ella?"

Millie, with her nose in a book, shrugged; Ted and Ricky continued with their game as if she hadn't spoken, until Dot answered. "Hiding."

"Hiding where?"

"Anywhere we aren't. She says we're too noisy and she can't think straight."

Elinor sympathised. She understood completely. She wouldn't say anything now, not with Grandma Lily here to add her weight to the situation, but she'd find out where the girl had gone. She'd be sixteen in January, and Elinor had her suspicions Ella was growing up a little fast for her liking.

* * * * *

Elinor decided digging into Ella's indiscretions could wait as the next labour pain bit deep.

"Joe, ask Ella to come and see me. There's no time to lose." She paused for breath as she felt the baby move and her muscles tense in preparation. "And you'd better tell Ma."

Before long, the house was ablaze with light, the coal range stoked into life and water boiled in as many pots and kettles as could fit. Her mother placed rubber matting over the bed and set towelling and sheeting rags at the ready. For a moment, Elinor wished they'd leave her alone. She'd done this before and would do it again, and didn't need this level of fuss and bother, but she kept her thoughts to herself. Including the one that this baby was not like the others.

Someone dabbed a cold, damp cloth on her forehead, and the door opened and closed letting cooling air waft across the room. Time passed in a blur. Voices drifted in and out of her consciousness but nothing she could interpret as warning signs. She let the pains ebb and flow. Dawn approached. It wouldn't be long now.

She was vaguely aware of grunts and bellows she assumed were her own, and voices encouraging her. She didn't need to be told when to push or pant. Her body knew the routine and she let instinct take over.

"It's a boy," said her mother, followed by a quiet mew rather than the lusty yell she'd hoped for.

Elinor tensed. She'd been wrong. She felt certain this one was a girl.

"He's a fine wee fella, with all his fingers and toes and bits and pieces."

She knew how tiny he would be, and fretted her boy might not be as robust as the first four.

Lily and Ella helped clean Elinor up and put a clean nightgown on while the midwife saw to the baby. A few minutes later, Elinor was sitting up in bed nursing her newest son.

"He's breathing fine," said the midwife. "But I'd get the doctor to look him over next time you see him, just to be sure."

"I will," agreed Elinor, not knowing when that might be.

Over the next few weeks, baby Matthew blossomed and Elinor's concerns faded as the rush up to Christmas occupied the house. The news that Joe's father was not his usual self, added to the collective eagerness to have a family gathering with as many generations as possible. At eighty-three, Pa still drew his sons to him like a magnet, and they were unshakeably loyal to their mother. Home was where the brothers could share their common beliefs without having to defend themselves every time.

* * * * *

January 1926
"What a life he had, Joe. Worthy of a book," said Elinor as they returned from the funeral. "I'm glad I knew him. Don't let his story go with him. You boys must tell your own boys."

They all knew his death had been imminent, but knowledge and acceptance were different emotions and Joe was coming to terms with his. The whole family was now grateful for the Christmas Day celebrations at their parents' home. It had been a wonderful day, full of laughter and storytelling, with plentiful food and harmony. A day they would treasure in years to come. Grandpa Somers had welcomed baby Matthew into the fold, blessing him with home and hearth.

A tear rose in Elinor's eye. Joe's parents had a hard life with few comforts. Only in recent years, no more than five, did they have somewhere to call their own, a shelter from all that had gone before. Now Granny Somers would live there alone.

11

Threats and Promises

Auckland
18 February 2021

"Luke," called Emma, appearing at the door to his workshop late one afternoon. "Have you got a minute?"

"What's up?" Luke pushed his chair back.

"I've received a letter and wondered what you thought?"

"Who from?" He reached out and took the letter Emma offered him.

"Lily Shaw. Jess's older sister."

He glanced up from the letter threatening to report Emma to the Privacy Commissioner. "That's a bit odd."

"I don't think I've ever met her. Only the other day I had to ask Jess her name. I'd forgotten."

"Well, it seems she's taken a dislike to you."

"But I don't understand why."

Luke glanced at the clock. "Shall we grab a drink and sit for a minute?"

They wandered back to the kitchen where Luke made

them each a G&T and took them outside to the sofa. He patted the seat beside him and Emma sat down.

"This is a nice treat," she said, taking a sip of her drink.

"What time did you say Rosie was due back?"

"Not until seven. One of the other dance mums is taking them tonight."

"Then we should take advantage of the opportunity. Dinner?" he said.

"Sounds good to me," said Emma. "I'm glad Rosie decided to take up dance this year. Now Olivia is no longer her bestie, it's nice she has some other friends."

"Any news on that front?"

Emma shook her head. "No. And I don't expect much. Jess said she'd contact me when she could. It's only been a few days."

"So, what about this?" Luke nudged the letter on the table.

"I don't know what to make of it. Can she really charge me with breach of privacy?"

"Charge is a rather loaded word. I don't think there's a charge per se, and no one can sue for money. They can make a complaint to the Privacy Commissioner but I'm guessing nothing much happens after that, beyond a wet bus ticket and a 'cease and desist' order. Possibly a fine if the police get involved. But on what grounds?"

"You tell me? In short, her letter says I'm to stop digging into her family's past or she's going to charge me. So, okay, charge is the wrong word, but shouldn't her complaint be with Jess, not me? I'm simply following a client's instructions. But, more importantly, how does she know what I'm doing?"

Luke replaced his glass on the table. "I don't have the answer to that one. But one thing I'm fairly certain about is the dead can't complain."

"But Lily's not dead!"

"No, but the people you're researching are. What secrets do they hold that could upset Lily so much she's threatening you?"

Emma's eyes gleamed. "Now that's an interesting notion. I could possibly do something with that."

"Don't get carried away, but there must be something that sparked the woman's interest."

"True. Question is, what do I do now?"

"Ask Jess first, I suppose. Since you don't know this woman, you haven't done anything wrong. You've not stolen her identity or anything like that. But it would help to know what the fallout is between them."

Emma nodded. She loved the evenings in their west-facing garden, and this part of the house was the last to lose the sun. Watching the movement of grasses and flowers in the evening breeze and listening to the rustle of the trees was her favourite distraction. It had become a haven during the lockdowns of 2020.

"I don't want to disturb Jess unless I have to. She was so uptight when we spoke, I said I'd wait until she got in touch with me."

"I understand that, but be careful. Until you know what it is and can counter it, this Lily is likely to be persistent."

Emma was alarmed. "Why would you think that?"

He shrugged. "A hunch, I guess. Now, seeing as they lifted the latest lockdown rules, let's go get that bite before our little missy returns?"

They scanned in at the local Italian restaurant and once seated were quick to remove their masks. Emma happily let Luke distract her by chatting about his work as they ate.

They got back, clutching Rosie's favourite pasta takeaway, moments before she arrived home from dancing. The busyness of catching up with her day and getting her ready for bed pushed all thoughts of what to do about Jess's family research out of Emma's head.

During the night, with Luke snoring softly beside her, Emma's brain began to whirl. Not awake enough to think straight, but in a semi-doze that let her mind roam free, Emma tried to recall what Jess had said over time about her sister.

Emma knew Lily was unreasonably angry with their father for putting their mother in dementia care, and she blamed Jess for being 'Daddy's little angel'. Where had that phrase come from? Emma turned over, trying to get comfortable and empty her mind, desperately wanting to get back to sleep.

Jess's voice came to her: *She always said things like that. I shouldn't be so smug; that she knew something I would never know – Your daddy is not the person he pretends to be – Don't think you're special.*

Emma woke feeling decidedly groggy. She hated nights where her thoughts overtook her sleep, but unfortunately, it happened too often for comfort.

Luckily for her, Luke was an early bird. Cheerfully chatting in the kitchen with Rosie, he handed Emma a cup of tea the minute she appeared.

"We're all done. I'll drop Rosie at school and be back soon." He kissed Emma's forehead, gathered Rosie's bags, put her lunch box and drink bottle inside and guided her out the door.

Emma sat on the bar stool, leaning on the bench holding her cup in both hands trying to recall the phrases she'd 'heard' during the night. What did they all mean?

Both Jess's parents had been teachers if she remembered correctly. They'd settled in the city around the time Lily started school as far as she could tell. Nothing out of the ordinary in their life that Emma could find.

Jess had put up with Lily's superiority. Five years was a lot when you're a child trying to work out what adults mean. And what big sisters think they know. How much do you trust your instinct and eyes, and how much whispered tattle?

But that was years ago. What about since? When had Lily and Jess become disconnected?

Dates.

It had something to do with dates.

Emma finished her tea and jumped in the shower. She was eating a slice of Vogel's toast with avocado when Luke returned.

"No walk this morning?" he asked, seeing her dressed in casual pants and a soft blouse. "You've got that look about you again. Had a brainwave, have you?"

Emma nodded and mumbled through a mouthful of toast. "I'll go for a walk later when I need to reset the brain, but yes, I think I'm on to something."

"Sounds like I'd better leave you to it. I've got a busy day. Lots of little bits and pieces to clear for clients before I'm ready to work on the final layout for your family tree book. You did warn me it was huge, and you were right."

"And I think you got the easy part. But it'll be a real heirloom for them when it's done. I'm going to double-check Jess's information and sort a few dates first. See you later."

In her library, Emma opened up her computers, turned her scribble pad to a clean page and started her search. She began by writing down birth and death dates for each family member and matched marriage dates against birth dates. Even in the days of strict moral codes, it wasn't surprising to find couples getting married 'just in time' before the baby arrived. She remembered one case she'd worked on where the mother was considerably younger than the father – well before the Legitimation Act, 1894. Emma had discovered six of their seven children born before they married. When she went in search of the original birth certificates, the officials barred Emma from seeing them, stating the newer registration of their birth after the parents' marriage under the Act superseded the original versions.

The fact that records with the same birth date for all six children – or registration date, in that case – had alerted her to the truth in the first place, had made no difference. She shook her head at the strange rules relating to privacy.

After an hour of checking and double-checking, Emma had found little to go on. A couple of coincidences interested her but she couldn't quite see what difference they made. The Elinor Somers she was investigating had died the same year as Jess's sister Lily was born, and she'd found an Ella Shaw who'd died the year Jess was born, but Emma couldn't make any connection between them. With no digitised newspapers much beyond World War Two to look up, she was at a stalemate.

Nothing alerted her to anything out of the ordinary until another more intriguing coincidence, in 1928. Something about it caused a prickly sense of possibility she couldn't ignore.

The phrases that had flitted through her dreams returned. What did Lily know that Jess didn't?

Her phone pinged. Thinking it could be Jess, Emma opened the text: *Mind your own business.*

The message came from a generic 'no reply' link. With her heart rate up a notch and her mind racing, she grabbed her laptop bag and car keys.

"I'm off to the library," she called to Luke.

"In the city?"

"Hopefully not, but I might have to go to the archives. I'll text you." She'd tell him about the message later. No need to worry him for the moment.

Barely two Ks down the road, Emma realised the car behind her was the same one she'd spotted parked in her street. She shrugged it off, telling herself not to imagine something that wasn't there. Cars went about their own business all the time, like her.

Emma waved to the librarian and found a study desk she could lay claim to and opened her laptop. She'd found it easier to search the library catalogue that way and pinpoint exactly what would help her. A few minutes later and she'd collected a stack of books. Flipping through the index and several paragraphs about the late 1920s, Emma began to get a better picture. Maybe some inspiration at last.

Not after exact wording or even specific applications, Emma began to mind map, linking names and dates. Arrows criss-crossed her page and scribbles filled the gaps. She looked up the New Zealand Archives website but could find nothing interesting enough to draw her into their office for the moment.

"Hi, Emma," said the librarian as Emma checked out a few reference books, slipping in a couple of novels that had caught her eye. "It's wonderful to see you again. Keeping busy?"

"I am. Researching a family tree for a friend at the moment."

Without taking her eyes off her task, the librarian casually added, "There's a woman over there who followed you in. She's been watching you ever since."

Resisting the urge to turn around, Emma moved slightly and caught the woman's reflection in the glass panel on the desk. "Thanks for letting me know. I don't think I know her."

Dressed in designer sports gear, the tall, thin woman wore her dark ponytail pulled through the matching baseball cap, partially hiding her face. By the way she fidgeted, Emma could tell the woman was nervous. She had no idea who she was but had the instinctive feeling it might be Lily. If so, then she looked nothing like Jess, except for the dark hair.

"Maybe she's read about what you do and is too shy to approach you," suggested the librarian.

"Maybe. But if that's the case, I don't want the commission anyway. Clients like that can be difficult. I want to help people with their research, not battle them about what I find."

Thanking the librarian, Emma considered whether to do a couple of errands first or go straight home. The notion of being followed didn't sit well. Sitting in her car, trying to decide if she should phone Luke and tell him, or leave it until something happened to prove her theory, Emma nervously kept watch on the library door.

As far as she could tell, the woman was still inside, but maybe she was playing the watching–waiting game as well. With her nerves getting the better of her, Emma started the car and turned the opposite way to home. If she took the long way around, she'd know for certain.

By the time she pulled up in her garage, Emma had convinced herself she'd panicked over nothing. No one had followed her.

She pushed the button to lower the garage door and saw the car she imagined had trailed her into town pull up on the opposite side of the road. She gasped in fright, and her pulse skyrocketed again. She couldn't see the driver because of the window reflection, but intuition said it was the same woman. The roller door clanged shut bringing Emma back to the present.

What was going on?

And, more significantly, how could she find out about the woman and if she had anything to do with the letter?

Emma sat before her computer and started typing. Words flowed from her as they often did when an idea took hold. As she wrote, anchored to a past that felt very real, she decided the two events were random coincidences. To think anything else was too bizarre. Pushing aside the worrying letter, Emma became lost in Elinor's childhood.

Elinor could not have been more excited at finally being on a farm, with a proper house and a bedroom she shared with her baby sister. She'd found the years of moving from house to house searching for work, unsettling, but her father Robert had promised she would have a home, a place where she could be happy, as soon as he could save and borrow enough to buy his own place.

The years of hard labouring had taken their toll from his time collecting flax in the wet. Even though her mother Emily refused to accept reality, her father was past forty and not as strong as in his younger years when they shifted onto the first of the Pahīatua farms.

From an early age, Elinor understood that wherever they lived, life could be hard. While farming was the most common occupation for families of the time, not all farmers knew as much about good farming practices as they should have, and had to learn. Her father included. Get it wrong, and life would be a hand-to-mouth situation within a season.

From the beginning, Elinor loved farm life. She loved the animals: the pigs to take the excess skimmed milk and vegetable scraps, the chickens providing eggs and many a good soup, the sheep for wool and meat, and the dairy cows that provided the income. At the age of fifteen, while still helping to care for her young brother and baby sister, Elinor and her brother, Dick, two years younger, learnt what to do and what not to do from their father as he learnt best practices from other more-experienced farmers.

Elinor would rise early, happy to help chase the cows into the milking shed. She loved the smells and sounds of early morning as the mist rose from hot breath and the sun climbed over the hilltops. Her father and brother had a knack with animals, and before too many years had passed, their skill at breeding changed their lifestyle and prosperity.

Her mother loved her garden and grew whatever flowers and vegetables she could. A variety of fruit trees already existed on the property and in season, the kitchen would be a hive of industry as mother and daughter bottled everything in readiness for the winter, all of which proved kinder than the winters down south. Over the long dark months, they spun wool and knitted by the hearth. She'd learned many skills that she would take into her own home and teach her daughters in times to come. The family soon found themselves at the heart of the community, involved with the hall, the school, charity events and the entertainments that abounded.

But they never forgot their friends back over the ranges in the Manawatū and they visited as often as they could. The train trip through the gorge became a regular event, but sometimes they needed to take the horse and dray. Any journey through the gorge could vary from hair-raising to a pleasure, depending on the state of the rock face, but Elinor considered it worth making the trip, whichever way they travelled.

Yet she chose to walk away from that good fortune and marry the man of her dreams. A man she'd secretly loved for several years. The eldest son of their Manawatū friends. But first, her parents celebrated the birth of yet another daughter, welcoming Patty to the family, not six months before Elinor was due to wed. While she found it a wrench to leave her baby sister, the knowledge that Stella, now six years old, would step up and help their mother soothed her mind. One day soon, she would hold a baby of her own, in a home of her own.

In April 1909, at the age of nineteen, Elinor walked down the aisle of the Church of St John the Baptist to become Mrs Joseph Somers. Stella was her bridesmaid, with Johnny as page. Standing tall and straight, in a well-fitted but plain brown dress with a white stand-up ruffled collar and bronze chevron braiding, Elinor's plans for the future took flight.

She was ready to face whatever lay ahead, shoulder to shoulder with her husband.

She wanted what her mother had, what all women wanted – a family and a home.

12

New Beginnings

Glen Oroua, Manawatū
February 1928

In the four years they'd lived in the big draughty house, Elinor had grown used to its idiosyncrasies. She'd re-established her blue bedroom with all the trimmings, often picking the more readily available blue hydrangeas when she couldn't find irises. And she had treated herself to a few more 'blue' items now Joe had mastered the farm.

They weren't flush with money by any stretch of the word, but neither was money as tight as it used to be. The government's Family Allowance payment of two shillings a week for each child she'd started receiving a couple of years since had helped, especially with so many children. They now had an electricity generator that operated the milking shed and ran the house. Elinor's life was considerably easier after purchasing a refrigerator and an electric iron. Although she'd decided against an electric cleaner and other appliances in favour of Joe's pride and joy, a second-hand car.

"Look, Nell," he cried as he pulled to stop in front of the house.

Elinor and the children ran outside, rubbing their hands over the paintwork, opening the doors and squashing into the back seat. Elinor sat in the passenger seat.

"It's beautiful," she said, admiring the wood panelling, the red leather and matching carpet.

"It's a Studebaker tourer," he said, continuing to explain aspects of the motor that meant nothing to her. "We'll be able to go into town together and take picnics. Especially now, with the new trial of putting the clocks forward an hour over summer. We'll be able to go out after milking. Won't that be wonderful?"

Elinor agreed it would be wonderful, as long as they could afford to keep up the monthly payments and run it. And to do that, it would need to be useful, more than simply jaunting around.

But above everything, the item that brought her the most pleasure was the radiogram. She and Joe loved to listen in the evenings after dinner and talk about what they'd heard. They especially enjoyed hearing the news updates, about politics and current and local affairs, and the latest songs had her tapping her toes. Elinor was surprised at how much she was learning from the radio, which brought her around to her latest worry.

The younger girls, especially Connie, enjoyed school; the boys, not so much. They preferred being out on the farm with their father. "I shouldn't complain," she said to Joe that night. "They're good lads, but I don't want Ricky to drop out of school the way Ted did. They need to learn more than they have."

"Why? As long as they can read and do their sums, that's all they need."

Elinor couldn't find the words to explain why she wanted them to have more schooling, or what they should learn exactly. "What if the farm failed? What if they needed to find work? Other than labouring, what jobs could they get?" She didn't want her sons to have the same life as generations of their forefathers. "Surely, we can do better for them than that?

"Stop fretting. The farm is going well, and the boys do their bit, bringing in extra when they can, helping with the haymaking and fencing when the neighbours need it. A good day's hard work for a good day's pay never hurt anyone."

But she couldn't stop fretting. As in the past, Elinor was getting nowhere arguing with Joe about the boys' schooling beyond their compulsory years. The girls, she had more control over. Or did she? The younger ones, maybe, for a while, but not so much the older ones. These days, girls had so many distractions, and options to choose from. Thankfully, Dot and Connie were too young to get up to mischief, and Dan and Archie still clung to her skirts, despite coming up seven and five, but even she had to admit life in the 1920s was a lot more fun than the pre-war years.

Permissive was the phrase on the older generation's disapproving lips, but Elinor enjoyed the more easy-going lifestyle, with less pressure to conform and more freedom to be herself and do things for the pleasure of it. And speak her mind.

That concept had bypassed Millie. She preferred to work around the house and had become an excellent cook. She was equally at home in the garden but hated the animals and refused to return to school once she'd turned fourteen.

"I don't need all that," said Millie. "I want to keep the best house, and I can learn more from you than from any school."

Elinor could hardly object to that ideal, but she wished for more for her second daughter. A better life. A gentler life than she'd had.

* * * * *

Out of the blue, Ella announced, "I've got myself a job with a dressmaker. I'll be able to pay towards the food bill."

While she was learning a good skill, Elinor believed Ella could do better than being a machinist. Ella. Her firstborn. Her anchor. The one whom she'd relied on many a time when she'd needed help with the children, in the garden, in the kitchen and on the farm. But as a mother, she'd gone wrong somewhere. Ella had a rebel streak in her.

"And I'm going to get myself a car," she said. "I've seen a small English one, second-hand, and I'm learning how to drive." She grinned and laughed, full of the joys of life.

Now there was no holding her back. Always off to dances at the community hall, to race meets with her father and uncles, to fairs and theatre shows. The sooner she found a bloke and married, the better. Elinor had a suspicion that a fella was in the mix somewhere, but so far Ella hadn't confided in her, and she didn't dare mention her suspicions to Joe. He'd hit the roof.

As if to prove her point, a few nights later, while they busily cleaned up the kitchen and dinner dishes, Ella said, "Mam? Can I ask you something?"

The tone of voice immediately alerted Elinor that the 'something' was of importance. "Of course. What do you want to talk about?"

"How's your day been?"

"Ella, you don't want to know how my day's been or how the garden is growing. What is it you want to say?"

"I've met someone."

"I wondered when you might. You're the right age and a fine-looking girl. Who is he?"

"Just a boy … um … from the big farm down the way."

Elinor was about to ask which way exactly when the penny dropped. "You mean the one with the stables?"

Ella mumbled and nodded.

"They're a bit grand for the likes of us, sweetheart. I can't see his pa liking that at all. He'll have grander plans for his son."

Ella laughed as she dried another dish and put it away. "Not *his* son. I wouldn't want anything to do with that stuck-up egg. No, he's, um, the stable hand."

Elinor's heart slipped into her stomach. She was no snob by any means, but she wanted more for her girls than the lifetime of struggle she'd had. Love brought you contentment, but money bought the comforts. "What's his prospects, pet? That's the first thing your pa will want to know." She hoped she sounded interested rather than discouraging.

"Do you have to tell him?"

Hearing the panic in the girl's voice, Elinor wiped her hands dry, watching her daughter all the time. She pulled out a chair and sat down. "Not if you don't want me to. But why the secrets? Is this boy not keen? Or are you imagining more than there is?"

Ella spun around, pretending to do something at the sink, but not before Elinor saw the blush infuse her face. "It's not that," Ella muttered with her back still to her mother. "It's … well you see, I've not told him where I live. He thinks I live in town."

Elinor contemplated her daughter's words and wondered what she wasn't saying. "And why would he think that? Unless that's what you told him."

"I didn't exactly, but he's seen me leave work and visit a friend who lives nearby, and he put two and two together."

"And made more. I see. He thinks you're independent, and not living with your parents. Do I know this 'friend' you visit?"

Ella topped up the kettle and put it on to boil, knowing a cup of tea was always the order of the day whenever anything needed discussing. She set out the cups and saucers, collected the milk from the safe and refilled the sugar bowl, careful to replace the crocheted doily to keep the flies away. "No. She's a girl at work, but she lets me use her place sometimes to get changed if I'm going out."

"I see," repeated Elinor. "These, I presume, are the nights you are supposedly working late or going to the moving pictures?"

Ella continued to flit around the kitchen doing anything to avoid looking at her mother. "Don't sound so disapproving, Mam. I'm eighteen. I'm not a little girl any more. And I'm only having a bit of fun."

Alarm bells rang. "Be careful about what sort of fun you're having, my girl. It'll be you paying the price. Now tell me more about this boy."

In one movement, Ella had flung herself on the chair facing her mother, her face flushed and her words coming nineteen to the dozen. "He's twenty-one and saving for his own place. He wants to buy a mare and stallion soon and breed from them. He says he knows all about what the boss does and thinks he can do as well. He needs somewhere to graze the horses, and a barn, and I said …"

"Whoa. Slow down. One thing at a time. Are you suggesting he graze them here?"

"Well, he could, couldn't he?"

"Not without your father's permission, which I doubt would be forthcoming anytime soon, especially since you don't want me to tell him about this lad. Make up your mind, girl. Now let's start at the beginning. What's his name?"

"Jack. Johnny Redway to be exact. He says he met your cousin Tom and they talked about his future in the industry."

"Thomas? But he's been gone for several years. What's he trying to pull?"

Ella frowned and nibbled at her lips, suddenly doubting what she'd said. "I don't think he meant the old one. Another one. Oh, I lose track of all your cousins."

Elinor smiled at that comment. "So do I. I've not seen half of them in many a year, but he must mean one of Walt's boys, but I've not seen them for a long time either."

Briefly, Elinor wondered why that was. She knew all Joe's brothers and sisters and everyone in their families.

They often ran into one or more groups when they visited his mother on a Sunday, but her father – and her mother, for that matter – kept their family at arm's length. She had written it all down in her diaries so she wouldn't forget, but some people were nothing more than names. Maybe she should get to know them better one day. "Tell me more about this boy. What's he like?"

"He's got gorgeous red hair – not carroty, but darker, more bronze. And blue, blue eyes. He says his mother is Scottish and he talks with a lilt in his voice. I could listen to him for hours. He's clever, too. He knows so much about horses and the stables."

Elinor restrained herself from making any teasing remarks. Joe would put her through enough of a grilling before the boy would even set foot on the place. And as for horses, she'd like to think he'd say no – horses did nothing to improve the land – but the whole family had a love of horses, breeding and racing, Joe's poor deceased father included. She suspected the idea of owning a few hairs on the tail would thrill him. "What next with wonder boy, then?"

Ella picked at her nails and avoided her mother's eye. "We want to get married." If Ella heard the intake of breath, she didn't look up.

"This is all a bit sudden, isn't it?"

Ella's shoulders moved, dismissing her mother's comment. "Why wait? We like each other, he's got a good job. I've got a job. He's of age. I'm old enough. What more is there?"

Elinor desperately wanted to tell her what more there was. To put a wiser head on her young shoulders. But as with every generation before and, she suspected, every generation to come, that wasn't likely to happen.

"You've not mentioned love. Love is the glue that holds you together. How much time have you spent with this boy? How well do you know him?"

Ella's head popped up and the eager, pleading look she gave her mother softened Elinor's heart. "Of course I love him. And he loves me, but you've always said you have to *like* someone as well. You have to be friends. Don't you say 'I love you' before you tell us off? It's the same thing, isn't it?"

"All right, I'll accept that. But what else? How is he with money? Who are his family? Where will you live? I presume he lives on the farm."

Ella nodded. "In the dorm with the other single blokes. But we could find a place ... We won't need much. A cottage. Can you talk to Pa for me, please?"

"What good will that do? He's not going to be happy until he meets this boy and decides for himself. But I will talk to him *with* you."

Ella beamed and got up from the table and threw her arms around her mother's neck.

"What's all this, then?" asked Joe, entering the kitchen. "I came in to see where my cuppa is."

"Sorry, Pa," said Ella. "It's all ready. Sit there and I'll pour one for you. Do you want a piece of cake?"

"Well, since you're offering, I won't say no." Joe looked quizzically at Elinor wondering what was going on. "What have you two been chatting about for so long? I thought you'd never finish the dishes. You missed a good programme on the radio."

Ella stood behind her father, her eyes pleading with

her mother to start the conversation. She put the teapot on the table and poured.

"Some mother–daughter stuff, about growing up and becoming a woman. It's a complex business. Especially when you meet someone."

To give him his due, Joe calmly accepted the cup he'd been handed and said thank you for the cake presented to him on a plate. "I suppose you mean someone that's a bit more special than the usual people you meet?"

Joe's eyes bored into Ella. She twisted her apron in her hands, smoothed it out, sat down, and stood up again, all within a few seconds.

"Well? Who is this someone?"

Ella rattled off something similar to what she'd told her mother.

"I don't give a monkey's uncle about his eyes or his voice. I want to know how he earns his keep, and how he thinks he can look after you. Can you tell me that?"

To Elinor's ear, Joe sounded gruff, but she knew better. She hoped Ella had realised that.

"I'll go check on the children, make sure they don't disturb you." She rested her hand on his shoulder as she passed, looking into his eyes with a gentle smile and soft tone. "Please, Joe. Go easy, listen to what the girl has to say before you jump to conclusions."

He patted her hand and she left them to it.

By the time she returned, Ella was sobbing.

Joe glared at her. "You should have told me."

Taking a quick inward sigh, Elinor soothed her voice. "Calm down, Joe. She told me this evening. If you hadn't come in when you did, she'd have held back for longer."

"She's not to see him again. Do you hear me?" He thumped the table. "Both of you. Do you hear me, Ella? You are not to go near him."

Ella raced from the room, slamming the door.

"Well that didn't take long to fall apart, did it?" said Elinor, replenishing the teapot with boiling water. "What happened?"

"I'm not having any jumped-up, smart-arse horsey bloke telling me what to do."

"Goodness, why would he be telling you what to do? The girl wants to marry him, not employ him."

"She's got some crazy idea that he could set up a stable on the farm. I soon put a stop to that, I can tell you."

"One step at a time, Joe. He doesn't own any horses yet. It's a goal, that's all. It's what he wants to do with his life. I seem to remember you had goals at his age. Still do. You wanted a farm and a family – and now we have both. Sometimes things work out sooner, sometimes later, but we have to have hope. Ella's getting ahead of herself, that's all. What's the harm?"

Joe grunted rather than answer, but Elinor knew she'd broken through. "He's getting the right training where he's working, and they'd have to find somewhere else to live. I can't see him being any bother to you at all. I'd like to meet him, and if she's set her heart, who are we to stop her?"

* * * * *

A week later, Ella brought Jack to the house. He fiddled with his hat, wiped his hands on his trouser leg twice before shaking hands, cleared his throat and ummed and ahhed when spoken to, but Elinor liked him. The way he looked at Ella warmed her soul, and Ella clearly adored him. She clung to his arm to give him confidence. They had obviously been seeing each other for a while and had built that rapport that comes to two people of like mind. Not that she'd mention that to Joe. Some things were better left unsaid, but the boy was polite and spoke well with that lilt Ella had mentioned.

"Yes, Mr Somers. I aim to work there for some time to come," answered Jack with enthusiasm. "I love my job, but I've still a lot to learn."

"And he's good at it, Pa," said Ella.

Jack looked embarrassed. "The boss says so, anyway. Has me handle the more difficult colts."

Elinor shifted them into the kitchen, and over a pot of tea and a plate of scones, the awkwardness eased.

Joe fired more questions, barely giving the lad time to breathe.

"Yes, sir. My boss treats me well. He says he's willing to give me a hand up when the time comes."

"Do you ride, lad?" asked Elinor.

"Yes, Mrs Somers. I do the early-morning runs. I'll never be a jockey. Too tall. But I get to know what the horses like and don't like, and can tell 'em what I know."

Joe cleared his throat. "Why do you want to marry my daughter?" The question they had all been waiting for but dodging.

Jack got up from his chair and tucked it under the table to stand behind it. He cleared his throat, covering his mouth with his fist while he considered his answer. He stood upright with his hands on the chair back.

"Your daughter is very special. She is refreshing, not frightened by challenges, and loves her family very much. And that's all down to you," he began, obviously having practised his speech. "It's that love, that loyalty, that drew me to her. I want to share my life with her." He paused to look at Ella for encouragement and she smiled back, nodding. "I, um, I think we could make each other happy, and I promise to take good care of her. I earn a good wage. I'm a free man with no debts or liabilities. If you would allow it, I'm asking your permission to take Ella as my wife. It would be a great honour." His shoulders relaxed, relieved to have finished.

Elinor wanted to clap. Jack had convinced her. She waited to see if Joe had been won over. From behind the door, where the other children had been listening, came squeals of laughter, giggles, and goodness knows what else. But it seemed they were pleased with the idea.

"Say yes. Please, Pa?" Ella bobbed down beside her father sitting in his chair and took his hand. "Please say yes. I do love Jack, and I want to have what you and Mam share. I want to know a love like that, of my own."

Joe peered down at his eldest daughter, his love for her shining through his doubts and anxieties. "If that's what your heart is set on, then you have my permission."

Ella kissed him on the cheek and raced around to stand beside Jack, clutching his arm, almost bouncing on the spot.

Joe rose and offered his hand to Jack. "Congratulations, young man. You have a special prize there. She is fierce about what she believes in, loyal and determined, but she will be a handful. I will hold you to your promise to take good care of her."

"I will. And thank you."

Elinor stood looking at the happy young couple and let memories of when she and Joe first got together fill her with warmth and love. Back then, she was barely older than Ella was now when hope permeated the air and the future looked promising.

With all her being, Elinor wished them a peace-filled life of happiness, prosperity, love and family.

13

Voices from the Past

Auckland
19 February 2021

Emma hadn't yet told Luke about the strange car and the stranger woman from yesterday. She didn't quite know what to say. It sounded so cloak-and-daggerish, and ridiculous. Things like that didn't happen to ordinary people. And she had no way of telling if either situation had anything to do with the even stranger letter from Lily or the warning text.

Luke was still out on the school drop-off. She sent a text to say she was going for her run, noting the time as she set off. Her route usually took a little under an hour if she headed through the park, along the beachfront and back home, even allowing for her to walk back up the hill – especially if she didn't linger gazing at the scenery, taking in the smells and sounds of nature, as she was wont to do. This time of year it was so tempting to sit and listen to the birds chirping and watch the waves lap on the shore. The old Emma would never have been calm enough or happy enough to be bothered, but the new Emma was someone she liked much better.

Music played through her earbuds as she happily jogged along, thinking about what she'd uncovered and how she could tell Jess. She wondered if she could drop a letter in their box. Would that upset Martin? She didn't know. From what she understood, this virus was unlikely to be spread by contact with paper or something handled by someone else. It was worth a try.

Emma felt a touch, milliseconds before she tumbled on the gravel path and rolled onto the grassy bank. Wondering what on earth had happened, she raised her head in time to see a woman in black running out of sight over the rise, her ponytail flaring out the back of her cap.

Emma sat up, wincing at the unexpected pain, and inspected the damage. Holes in both knees of her running pants where she'd hit the ground, dirt and gravel clung to the grazes, and blood oozed from a cut. She brushed a couple of stones off and looked at her palms, similarly grazed and dirty, but she didn't think a lot of damage had been done.

Until she tried to stand up.

Her left knee folded as soon as she put weight on it and a pain shot up her leg into her lower back. Rolling onto her right side, she managed to get to her feet, but she wasn't walking far without help. She limped to a low retaining wall next to the path and gingerly sat down. Her breathing was shallow and her hands clammy as she reached for her phone in her belt bag.

"Luke?" Her voice cracked, as a wave of nausea swept through her. She cleared her throat. "I fell," she said, not ready to try and explain what had happened. *Did that woman push me? Surely not, I must have tripped. Why would someone knock me over and keep running?* "Can you come and get me?"

Emma heard the alarm in Luke's voice. "Stay put, I'm on my way."

She ran the incident over and over through her head while she waited. It was a coincidence. It had to be. A woman running past had distracted her and she'd stumbled. She couldn't believe someone had deliberately pushed her. But she couldn't shake that niggling thought.

Later that morning, long after she'd had a warm bath with Epsom salts and bandaged her wounds, and the trembling had stopped, Luke started to question her.

"One minute I'm running along in a world of my own, music playing, thinking about my research, and the next I'm on the ground, wondering how I got there." She was clutching a cup of hot tea, feeling her body settle down as the muscle ache set in.

"Are you certain about this woman?"

"I can't be certain about anything, Luke. If I hadn't seen her, I'd have said I'd been clumsy and fallen, not paying attention. I don't know if or why she might have had anything to do with it."

"Why would you think that?" His questioning became terser.

Emma realised her mistake too late. Why had she mentioned the woman at all? "Letting my imagination get away with me, I suppose," she said, guilt adding to her plight for not telling Luke everything. What she'd said was true, but maybe not the whole truth.

She wanted, really wanted to believe that everything was a series of unconnected incidents, even if her gut told her differently. She needed to work it out for herself first or Luke would want to do something about it.

"Do you think it's got anything to do with Jess's sister and that letter?"

"Surely not. It's all a bit far-fetched, isn't it? Like something out of a badly written crime series." Emma hoped she was right and she'd conjured it all up, but the woman must have seen her fall so why didn't she stop to see if Emma was okay? Wouldn't most people do that?

Luke wasn't letting go. "We need to challenge this Lily person about that letter. I won't let you be bullied."

Emma baulked. "There's no need for that, is there? Let's leave it, Luke. You told me it can't come to anything, so let's forget it. Please?" She reached across to put her hand on his knee, feeling justified in not telling him about how she'd been followed. It would make matters worse, and he'd go off the deep end if he thought she was at risk.

He took her hand and kissed it. "I don't know what I'd do if anything happened to you. You scared me today."

"Love you," she smiled. "But it was only a fall and I'm okay, honestly I am. Nothing broken. No real damage done. I'll be fine. Now," she added, pushing herself out of the armchair, wincing as she straightened, "back to work with you. I've got things to do."

"Are you sure?" He came to her side to steady her.

"I am. I'll probably stiffen up as the day goes on, but my brain is still functioning perfectly, thank you. Now off you go."

Except Emma discovered her brain wasn't working that well as she sat at her desk trying to concentrate. Her mind kept flitting between events but nothing made sense. She was certain Luke would be calling the police, or something equally silly, if she told him about all the coincidences coming so close on top of one another. And she couldn't let him do that.

But what scared Emma the most wasn't any one thing, but one thing *after another*. What was she missing? Why did Lily want her to stop researching?

Emma decided to take the offensive and contact Jess. One way or another, she needed to know what Jess knew – if anything. Martin couldn't keep her locked up forever – Covid or no Covid. There'd been no cases in months, and life had returned to near normal for most people. She felt Jess should be seeking treatment for Martin rather than kowtowing to his demands. But she was no psychologist to know what was best.

Can we talk? Emma hesitated for a few moments, wondering if she was doing the right thing, but finally pushed send. All she could do was wait. Still rather shaken, she decided to tidy her desk. When she became engrossed in work, she tended to have piles of interesting papers and loads of scribbled notes scattered around. She bent down to the rubbish bin and saw Jess's box of letters. She'd shoved it under her desk some time ago and forgotten about it.

Maybe now was a good time to get started. Clearing the last of her desk and putting away the papers she no longer needed, Emma began to make new piles. Handwritten letters by decades, business letters, accounts. She quickly put the accounts and documents relating to a farm to one side. Nothing personal or obvious jumped out so Emma dug a little deeper into the box. She found a few more newspaper cuttings, mostly weddings and funerals. She put them aside to spend time on later, as she'd need to match names against the family tree she was building.

At the bottom, she came across a small notebook. As soon as Emma opened it and read the first entry, she realised it was much more. This was a diary, a chronicle of life – or part of one. Unfortunately, Emma had no idea who had written it. With no dates to guide her, no idea when, other than it was old, with faded writing and splotchy paper, and as much about feelings as facts.

Emma settled into her armchair and began to read the dozen or so random jottings. She was soon drawn into another world: a time of hardship, of longing, and belief that the best was yet to be. Whoever this person was, her main regret was moving house all the time, but her biggest joy was her family, the love of her life, someone she called Sprout.

'What a terrible time we are having, I wish I could do or say more to help my beloved firstborn, but in a time of such tragedy, no words will heal her pain. Only time and whatever inner strength she possesses will help her to recover. I sincerely hope something of her father will exist within her. His staunch nature will help her through.'

Whatever the situation, to Emma, abiding affection, warmth and devotion poured from the pages, but the arbitrary writings came to an abrupt stop partway through.

Putting the notebook to one side, she began reading through the letters.

The earlier ones were generally between 'Nell' and 'Ma' and talked about the children and farm life. She assumed the Nell in the letters was the Elinor she was researching. Nell was a common enough variant. She wished all the nicknames were as easy. Sometimes pet names had little or no relevance to the person's name at all and often had more to do with their personality or behaviour. She suspected Sprout was one of those.

Emma ticked off the names she found against her list and carried on reading, but little in the letters touched her. In contrast to the diary, the letters were distant and factual. Emma decided the writer couldn't have been the same person.

* * * * *

Her phone buzzed. Emma opened it to find a reply from Jess. This time the text said, *Mums*.

Somewhere in the pile of papers, Emma had written the name of the care home. She scrabbled through and found it, checked the clock and went out to Luke. "I've got a text from Jess. She wants to meet me at her mother's care home. I don't know how long Jess has. I'll text you when I'm ready to leave. Okay?"

"Are you feeling up to it?"

"I am. I'm much better, and this will help distract me." She bent down and kissed his cheek, wondering why they didn't have special pet names for each other. It wasn't something that came up. They used endearments, yes, but not names. Was that a modern thing, or a personal preference, she wondered, thinking to add it to her list of dots to connect.

"Okay. Good luck. Will you mention Lily's letter?"

"Haven't decided yet. I'll see how she is first and catch up on the latest with Martin."

The garage door went up and Emma backed out but stopped in the driveway. Getting out of the car, she went onto the footpath and surveyed the street both ways for parked cars and anyone possibly watching the house. She couldn't see the one that had followed her, so with a breath of relief, hopped back in and drove to the care home without incident.

Jess was at the front door. "I waited for you so I could sign you in as my guest. They wouldn't have let you in otherwise."

They walked down a hospital-style corridor that unsettled Emma a little. She didn't like to think of people living out their lives in such an institutional environment when they should be surrounded by the cosy companionship of family.

"Thanks, Ems. Thanks for coming. I'm glad you understood the message. This is the one place Martin lets me come alone. He doesn't like it in here. Too clinical for him. I think the place scares him."

"No trouble. But I don't want to intrude on your time with your mother."

Emma noticed Jess's eyes tear up as they stopped by a door. "You won't. Believe me. You'll understand when you see her."

Anne Shaw's appearance came as a shock – frail, slightly dishevelled, sitting in her dressing gown in a large rocker-style chair staring out the window. She didn't turn her head when her daughter entered.

"Hello, Mum," said Jess brightly, pulling the upright chair next to her mother. "I came to see how you are today. It's such a lovely day with the sun shining on the flowers, and I can hear birds singing."

Jess chatted on without any noticeable response from her mother, whose almost translucent, vein-ridden hands sat listlessly on her lap. Emma had little experience with older generations, other than Charli, who was as witty and in control of her life on the day she died as she had always been. The woman who sat in the chair in front of her looked the exact opposite. Her almost immobile state filled Emma with sadness. If this was dementia, it was no wonder such a diagnosis frightened people. How awful it must be to lose your memory, and for Anne, any normality or degree of enthusiasm for life.

Jess signalled for Emma to pull up another chair. Her movement attracted Anne's attention and her eyes followed Emma as she sat down.

"Who is that? Who are you? I don't know you," Anne demanded, suddenly becoming agitated, flapping her hands and shaking her head from side to side as if trying to dislodge a thought or image. She tried to get out of her chair but didn't have the strength to lift herself. "What do you want? Are you come to make trouble? Yes. That's who you are. You want to make trouble. You're Lily. Get away from me. Get away ..."

As quickly as she had become agitated, tears began to fall. She sat in the chair again, still and seemingly calm.

"This is my friend Emma, Mum," explained Jess. "She won't hurt you. She won't cause trouble. It's not Lily. Lily isn't here. Let me rub your hands with cream."

Jess squeezed some hand cream from the tube on the side table and began to gently massage her mother's fingers and palm, pushing up the sleeve of her dressing gown and massaging her arms. Anne closed her eyes and sighed, peace restored.

"Mum gets easily upset these days," whispered Jess to Emma, as she continued the treatment. "Something about my sister is distressing her but I don't know what it is. I grew up thinking Mum preferred her to me, but now I'm not so sure."

Jess stopped what she was doing and pulled the sleeves of her mother's gown back into place.

"Do you remember the time Evie came to see us, Eddie?" The words came from Anne, but the voice sounded much different from her outburst of a few moments ago. "She changed our lives, didn't she, Eddie? She did. I remember."

Anne perked up and pushed herself out of the chair she'd failed to get up from earlier. Jess rushed to help, but Anne didn't need any help. She stood upright and steady, her eyes skimming the room as if trying to work out where she was. "I must get changed. She mustn't see me like this. She is always so beautifully dressed. I wonder who her dressmaker is."

Anne turned towards Emma and looked puzzled. She smiled warily. "Hello, Evie. Are you here already? I must brush my hair."

Anne walked like a far younger woman to her wardrobe, pulled out a floral day dress and began to strip off her dressing gown. Jess glanced between Emma and her mother as if Emma had the answer. Anne pulled the dress on over her nightie, found her hairbrush in the drawer and styled her hair into place, even going as far as to pat it, as if she'd removed a hat.

"Hello, Evie," said Anne sitting down. "It's so nice of you to visit. Eddie, come and say hello." She looked around the room again. Stared at Jess and then at Emma again. "Ed?" her voice faltered. "Where are you?" She wrung her hands in her lap and her eyes darted left and right with rising agitation. "Where is that man? Edward?"

Her voice drifted off. The Anne they'd seen disappeared.

With Emma's help, Jess eased Anne back into her recliner and wrapped a blanket over her knees.

"What just happened?" asked Emma.

"Her memory returned for a brief moment. It happens sometimes. We can talk now. Mum won't hear us, let alone understand."

Emma glanced at Anne and saw the vacant expression, confirming Jess's words.

"Oh, Jess, I'm so sorry you have to cope with this, especially after losing your dad and being at loggerheads with your sister. It's too much. I never understood how dementia affects people or how they respond and react. I never expected this. I've been a terrible friend, not understanding what it meant. Forgive me. And now there's Martin. Is there anything I can do?"

Emma felt naïve and insensitive but Jess dismissed her concerns.

"You've been a good friend, Ems. Better than you

realise, because you never treated me differently. You just expected me to be like you and have fun. And for that I'll always be grateful. But yes, things have changed. Mum is more withdrawn than before and rarely recognises me. Sometimes she rejects me completely, and the nurses have to calm her down."

Emma remained silent as Jess turned to look at her.

"What worries me most is what sets her off. Sometimes I have no idea. Relatives do get some training on how to respond, what to say and how to react to keep patients calm, but it's not easy. I never hear my name. Sometimes she speaks of Dad in the past, like then, but recently my sister's name crops up whenever someone new comes in – nurses, cleaners, physios, anyone really. Sorry. I should have thought, but this seemed the best place to meet."

Emma's heart did a tumble, both at the way Jess spoke, appearing detached from her mother, turning her into a patient, and the fact they needed to hide to talk. Emma mentally pulled herself together, deciding to be practical rather than sentimental. It wouldn't help Jess for her to get emotional. She needed to provide Jess with something to hang on to.

"I have got some things to tell you, but before I start, why would your Mum think I was your sister? Does she look like me?"

"No. Not at all. Her hair is dark and she's tall and skinny, the opposite to me, and highly strung. She often looks displeased. Why?"

Emma held back the gasp of recognition that made her stomach flip. "I wondered why I would be mistaken for her, that's all." She wiped her hands on her jeans.

"I wouldn't worry. Mum thought you were this Evie person after that. Do we know anything about her yet?"

"I've done some digging and have some ideas, but there's not much. Tell me about your situation with Martin first. How is he? And how's Olivia?"

"Livvy's fine. He's good with her. Distant, but he helps her with her schoolwork if she asks. She wouldn't have any idea there was anything wrong, and I'm grateful for that."

"And you?" asked Emma, hesitant about knowing.

"I've learnt how to manage him. As long as I keep to a routine, keep everything as he likes it, we're okay. I'm okay. He keeps his stares and threats to himself. I cook what he likes best and put everything away as I finish. But he's become obsessed about something – illness or cleanliness, or something. That's why he wants to know where I am all the time. In his way, he's protecting me."

"That's a heavy weight to carry. How do you manage to get away to see your mum?"

"I guilt-trip him. He lets me come straight here and back, but I have a feeling he checks the speedo and he's definitely time watching. If I say I'll be back by 'whenever', I need to be five minutes early or he goes crazy."

Emma couldn't imagine the stress that must cause and admired how Jess appeared to muddle along. From being worried about Jess and wanting to fix her situation, Emma now appreciated that Jess was stronger than she'd thought. "What do you need me to do?"

For the first time in ages, Jess smiled. "Be you. Be the generous spirit you are and appreciate what you have. For me, there's something about my sister – don't say her name, that will start Mum off – that isn't right. I don't know what exactly. I've had another letter ordering me to finalise the house sale and the disposal of everything in it, and close the file with the lawyer. But it bordered on irrational, even paranoiac, and I want to know what she's hiding. There has to be more to it."

Emma flinched, ill at ease with the whole concept. She wriggled in her chair, not wanting to let her friend down but still be honest. "I'm hardly the right person for that job, Jess. I research the past not the present. I'm not a sleuth, but since you mention it …"

"What?" Jess pounced on her reticence. "What's happened?"

"I got a letter from … um, you know, telling me to stop digging into the family tree. How did she know I was doing that?"

Jess looked guilty for a moment. "I told her."

14

A Three-pronged Onslaught

Glen Oroua, Manawatū
19 February 1928

"Can we have the wedding soon?" pleaded Ella, in her element choosing fabrics and designs and stitching her gown. "I don't want to wait until next summer and winter is such a horrible time to get married. So wet and gloomy."

Elinor began to wonder why the haste, but Ella seemed completely unfazed by her concerns. She simply wanted to be Jack's wife as soon as possible. Jack said he was keen and after a lot of debate, they chose a late April date.

"While the garden still has flowers and greenery for the bouquets and decorations," said Elinor, thinking out loud.

The women made a fruit cake, soaked it in brandy and put it away to mature. "And we'll have to stock up on butter to make pies and pastries."

Elinor added something new to her list every day, including reminding Joe to organise tables and chairs from the hall. She didn't quite know what they'd do if it rained. Would they be able to borrow or hire a marquee? She'd book the hall as well, just in case.

In amongst Ella's endless questions and the purchases of ribbons and baubles came the arguments. "I want my friend Mary to be my chief bridesmaid," she stated defiantly.

"That's not fair," bawled Millie, who'd expected to be chosen.

"You can follow along with Dot and Connie in their flower girls' outfits, and make sure the page boys behave themselves."

"That's a very large bridal party you're talking about. I think we should reconsider," said Elinor quickly, before Millie got more upset, and gently steered Ella to be reasonable. "For every girl there must be a boy. Apart from the time involved, there's the cost of all the dresses and suits. And who is Jack's best man? Will he want anyone else to make up the party as groomsmen or pages?"

"I thought Ted would be best man and Ricky would be groomsman and partner Millie."

"I don't want my younger brother as my partner," bemoaned Millie. "That's silly."

"Shut up, Millie. It's not your wedding."

Elinor was sometimes overly lenient with her eldest, but there were times when she pushed too far. "That's enough, Ella. There's no need for that behaviour. Now say sorry to your sister and we'll start again."

Ella and Millie glared at each other, but Ella gave enough of an apology to satisfy Elinor. "Now, back to

Jack. What you're suggesting isn't fair to him. You can't expect that. The man chooses his own supporters."

"Oh, fiddlesticks. I had it all planned. Each of the girls would be in different shades of floral organza ..."

"I can promise you that is not happening," interrupted Elinor. "The cost alone is one thing, but we won't be able to make that many outfits in the time, and do all the cooking. If you want an early wedding, you'll have to make do with one bridesmaid and Jack with his best man. Or you put it off until next summer. Your choice."

Ella huffed and puffed and flounced, complaining about how mean everyone was being, trying to spoil her big day. Elinor ignored her until Ella settled and grudgingly conceded. "But I'm going to get a gramophone and play music. You can't stop me doing that."

Elinor watched her daughter head out the door, wondering when her reliable, steadfast girl had disappeared, and where this rebellious, determined woman had come from. She smiled inside. Maybe she hadn't let her down after all. Maybe Ella would be the strong and resilient one. Elinor certainly hoped so. You never knew what life could throw at you, or when.

The weeks flew by as the busyness intensified. In addition to Ella's wedding turmoil, there was a household of eleven to organise and cook and clean for – from two-year-old Matthew up to Joe, now in his mid-forties. Joe was busy on the farm – or that was his excuse whenever Elinor wanted to talk to him about wedding plans – and Matt was becoming excessively grizzly. Elinor was exhausted. She retired earlier than usual simply for some peace. But listening to Matt breathing in the cot beside her increased her anxiety rather than gave her rest.

Since he'd been a newborn, Matt had struggled to thrive. His lungs were small, they said, and the doctors believed he would never work outdoors. He suffered from asthma, coughs and sniffles, and needed to be wrapped up warmer than any of her other children. No one explained to her why, but Matt lacked the robustness of the others.

She rose from her bed, lowered the window slightly to restrict the draught, even on such a warm night, tucked the blanket further up his chest and watched him sleeping. At times like this, she felt helpless, unable to transfer her health and mettle onto him so he would grow stronger. She dreaded the thought of winter and the cold winds and damp walls. Those dark months always set him off. She'd have to speak to Joe about making the house warmer, if that were possible, or lining the bathroom.

The weather held well into autumn, the sun shone and, while the air had chilled off night and morning, the days were beautiful, except for the wind. Strong, gusty winds were a guarantee of change. Ella fretted about what would happen if it rained, if the wind blew her veil away, if she got dust in her eye. Elinor let her fuss, there was nothing anyone could do. The wind always had been, and always would be, a factor of life in the Manawatū. The only difference was the strength of it on any one day.

When the rain fell ten days before the wedding, Elinor relaxed. The timing was perfect. The lawn, flowers and greenery would freshen up, and there was time for the ground to dry out and the wind to clear the air before the following Friday.

Joe appeared after the morning milking, shaking the moisture off his hat and raincoat and hanging them on the peg on the porch, before pulling off his gumboots. "This rain is very welcome, the ground needs it, it's parched, but it's a bit heavy for my liking. It's not soaking in, and the tracks are slippery as blazes. There's runnels everywhere and the dirt's turned to mud."

"How did you get on with the milking?" asked Elinor.

"Okay. A few muddy tails in my face, and the shed was a mess, but the cows'll find the driest parts. They know their way. I'll give them a bit more time. But I could do with a cuppa and something to eat before I head out again. Could be a long day if this keeps up."

The rain persisted for hours and lowering clouds immersed the house in gloom. Elinor turned on the lights and made a fresh pot of soup for lunch, the appetising aroma spreading throughout the house. She pulled out the apple slice she'd been saving, hoping to lift a few spirits. Food was usually a good antidote, but no amount of jollying was going to boost Ella's mood. She'd already magnified the weather out of all proportion, but everyone else was pleased to be sitting around the table filling their bellies with warm food.

The sound of a car arriving interrupted their happy chatter, plunging the family into silence. Elinor quickly looked out the window. The fact someone was out in such conditions and that she didn't recognise the car set off alarm bells.

Joe opened the door to welcome the stranger. "Come under the shelter," he called from the porch, raising his voice above the rain pounding on the iron roof. "What can I do for you?"

"Is this the home of Miss Ella Somers?" asked the man of about thirty, dripping wet and covered in mud.

Joe frowned. "It is. Why?"

Elinor went to stand beside him, hoping to block the children's view until they knew what was happening.

"I didn't know if anybody's told you or not, but Jack and me were friends. He told me all about Miss Somers and the wedding and everything, and I didn't want her to find out from anyone else." He gasped for breath after he'd finished his non-stop speech.

"Tell us what, man? What is it?" Joe placed his hand over Elinor's resting in his arm. The anxious look he cast her way did little to allay her fears.

"Did I hear Jack's name? Is he here?" asked Ella, coming out onto the porch and pulling her cardigan around her in the cooler air. "Oh, hello. Haven't I seen you at the stables?"

The man pulled his hat off, allowing the rain to drip off a lock of his hair now falling across his forehead. "That's right, Miss Somers, I work with Jack. He …"

"Has he sent me a message?"

"Not rightly, miss. It's just … I'm so sorry. What with the wedding and everything. He was that excited."

"Never mind that. What about Jack?" Joe demanded.

"Jack said he needed to take the colt for a run this morning, as usual, despite the heavy rain. I watched him head off into the mist, warning him to be careful as the training track had likely turned to mush. He'd take it slow, he said, but summat must have happened, 'cos next thing I know the colt comes galloping back, all skittish like, without him."

"Is Jack hurt?" squeaked Ella. "Where is he? I must go see him?"

"No," snapped the stranger. "You can't. You mustn't. It's worse than you think, miss. Um, well, you see … Jack must 'ave broke his neck when he fell. I found him when I walked the track. He'd gone by then. I'm sorry I couldn't get here sooner, but I had to get the others, and someone needed to tell the boss. I'm sorry for your loss, but I gotta go now. I'll leave you to your grief. Jack was a good bloke. He'll be sorely missed."

Elinor held her daughter upright even as her own energy drained away. All her hopes for Ella were dashed, knowing the life she'd planned had ended as surely as Jack's life had been taken.

Before her eyes, Ella turned into a wraith as the blood left her face. Her hands turned to ice and she stared, unblinking, into the distance trying to take in the shocking news. Her silence frightened them more than if she'd broken down. Had she heard what the man said? Did she understand?

Joe took her arm. "Come on, love, come inside and sit down."

When they returned to the kitchen, the other children stared back. Not a peep could be heard, not even from Matt. The food lay untouched on the table, the soup coagulating, while five-year-old Archie chewed on a crust.

Joe stood behind the chair they'd coaxed Ella into, with his hand on her shoulder; Elinor crouched in front saying soothing words of encouragement. Blank eyes turned towards her but they held no awareness.

Ella's eyes began to water and tears rolled down her face, but she sat erect, not moving to stop them or the shaking that had taken hold.

Elinor mopped the teardrops and tried to force a mouthful of the sugared tea Millie had made between her pale lips.

The keen, when it came, choked the room with pain. The shuddering gasps of air intensified her agony as Ella rocked back and forth clutching her stomach.

Jack was gone, and the Ella everyone knew went with him.

* * * * *

The King's birthday celebrations
5 June 1928

As if losing Jack wasn't enough, Ella had more to bear.

Elinor restrained herself from admonishing the girl for being a fool, since no amount of remonstrating would change the reality. They talked for hours, days, when Ella discovered she was pregnant a month after losing Jack. If the wedding had gone ahead as planned, no one would have been the wiser, but the situation had changed completely and now she would be an unmarried mother. Any chance of a future would be wiped away.

Elinor kept the news to herself, not wanting to tell Joe until she'd made a plan. She wanted to protect her daughter, shield her from more pain, give her something to look forward to.

Ella had become so quiet and withdrawn, almost morose, and had lost weight. She moped around the house, matching the unusually wet weather, not taking any interest in any of the things that had once excited her. Her only joy, if you could call it that, was caring for her baby brother.

As Elinor had feared, Matt's stamina had diminished as the weather worsened. Since the rains began in April, they'd not let up. The damper and colder it got, the more Matt coughed, the less spark he had. Ella nursed him, sang to him, played when he could, fed him and made him the focus of her day.

Elinor sat beside her children on the sofa. "I've an idea," she said, seeing how attached Ella was to Matt. "We'd both have to agree, and I will have to tell your pa."

"Don't tell Pa!" Ella panicked. "He'll be so disappointed in me."

"If we do nothing, I won't have to tell him. He'll be able to see for himself. Trust me in this." The despondency in Ella's eyes distressed Elinor so much she was determined to put her plan into action. "Have you noticed I'm pregnant again?"

Ella's mouth dropped open. "No. I hadn't. Truly?" She paused, studying her mother. "Are you happy about it? I wasn't sure you'd have another after Matt. But that's exciting in some ways. We'll both be having babies at the same time. They can grow up together and be friends, and I can learn from you."

Elinor smiled. A spark at last. "You don't have much to learn, my love. You've been by my side with all the babies for a long time. But no, there will only be one new baby in the house."

"I don't understand," said Ella, now frowning, alarm etched on her face. "Are you sending me away?"

"On the contrary, my sweet girl." Elinor put her arm across Ella's shoulder. "I'm suggesting the opposite. I'm suggesting you continue your life here as if nothing has happened. If you're willing, I will pretend your baby is mine. I'm not pregnant, but you believed me. So will others. I can tell everyone I'm expecting again. No one will think twice of it."

"How will that work? And the delivery and everything?"

Elinor could see the fear in her child's eyes. "I will teach you. Prepare you for the worst. But you will need to be brave and do exactly as I tell you. It'll just be you and me. It won't be easy, but you've seen me give birth many a time. You know what to expect and we will do it together. You'll be fine, I promise."

Ella looked unconvinced.

"I will appear increasingly pregnant while you simply put on a little weight. You can raise the baby here in this house and no one, except your father, will be any the wiser. To the world, the child will be mine."

Ella stared dumbfounded at her mother, a hint of hope in her eyes. "Are you serious?"

Elinor kissed her daughter's cheek. "I am. You're wonderful with the children. Look how you are with Matt. That's what gave me the idea. You can be the child's big sister, but do all the mothering things you need to do to satisfy your yearning – and you will yearn. The younger children won't notice or think anything is out of the ordinary. They're used to me being pregnant and you helping. Your father would be suspicious so we'd have to include him in our secret."

"Would he do that?"

"For you, yes. I think he'd do anything to see you smile again." Elinor could see the churning emotions in the girl's face. "Think about it. There's time – a little, at least. But we'll need to put plans in place so don't think too hard or too long."

"Thank you, Sprout," said Elinor. "I'm grateful." She pressed her body against his and kissed him. "You are such a lovely man."

"If we can save Ella shame, then so be it," he said, between nibbling her neck and ear and working his way down her body. "She was silly to let Jack have his way before the wedding, but she isn't the first by a long way. Now, enough talking, turn out the lamp, there's a good woman."

As long as she didn't fall pregnant herself. That would ruin everything.

Elinor cleverly made undergarments that hid Ella's tummy under the loose-fitting house apron with large side pockets she constantly wore. She'd lost weight since losing Jack so they had plenty of leeway. She then made a front arrangement for herself where she could add filling as time passed. Millie might possibly twig, but she doubted it, and she would never say anything.

Elinor's prediction that the winter would bring drier weather didn't materialise, but the temperature fell.

"We'll have snow on the hills by August," said Joe, coming in for his lunch and rubbing his hands together over the cooking range to warm them. "It'll cause no end of trouble for the calves and lambs if it's bad enough." Not that they had many sheep, but they couldn't afford to lose any either.

This year, more than most, Elinor was glad they'd had so many sons and daughters. Joe couldn't have managed the farm without the older boys. Fence posts collapsed in the mud, races became quagmires and the dray often got stuck on the driveway taking the cream cans to the gate for the dairy factory lorry to collect. Repairs were constant.

Matthew's health worsened. Elinor was back and forth to the doctor seeking more medicines, more suggestions, but in her heart, she knew she was about to lose one of her children.

"Mrs Somers, I strongly urge you to keep your own strength up. You are far too pale. You must eat. Drink soup and take a hot cocoa before you go to bed; it will help you sleep."

She nodded at the doctor, but she could hardly get anything past her lips. Joe and Ella weren't much better. Only the younger ones were eating properly and Joe enough to keep working.

A lump settled in her stomach, her eyes ached with unshed tears and her lungs could barely get enough air. Fear tormented her every moment. His breathing caused her physical pain. She was his mother. It was her job to protect him, to save him, but knowing she couldn't made the pain worse.

All she could do was take his photograph. She swaddled the little boy in a knitted blanket designed for a much younger child, but Matt was so tiny, it didn't matter. She pulled the top up to frame his head and protect him from draughts and laid him in Joe's arms.

"You hold him, Joe, keep him warm. And Millie, turn on all the lights; we need more light in this room."

Her hands shook as she held the box camera in front of her. She knew little about photography and had no idea how it would turn out, but she could see the sadness in Joe's expression. She took several snaps, for once not worried about the cost of developing. She wanted the best, the nicest photograph for the wall.

A few days later, Elinor hung the photo of Joe and Matt, mounted in a large oval frame with bevelled glass, on the wall above the corner chair where they could all see it. Matt's big dark eyes stood out against the white of the blanket surrounding him.

"It's pneumonia," said the doctor. "I'm so sorry. Keep him warm, and give him this elixir; it'll help his breathing but I don't expect him to last the night."

Each of them took turns holding him. The younger ones were eventually put to bed, while Elinor, Joe and the older ones sat around in the living room, listening to the radio. They avoided talking about the one thing they wanted to talk about most. What was the point? There was nothing to say, and so much to say. So many memories, and so few memories.

Joe nursed him, propping him against the arm of the chair. The boy's lips were blue and his skin pale, but while his lungs rattled with air, there was hope.

Until there wasn't.

The room stilled, everyone holding their breath to be certain no sound came from Matthew. Slowly, quiet sobs replaced the silence. On a midwinter night at the end of July, Elinor's youngest child left them.

Four months after they buried Matthew, Elinor and Joe welcomed a new baby. A child of light, not a replacement for Matthew, but a child who restored harmony after months of heartbreaking turmoil.

15

Tribulations

Auckland
19 February 2021

Emma was still coming to terms with Jess's revelation that she'd told Lily about wanting to trace the family tree. The fuss had nothing to do with Emma, Jess told her, but was more, according to Lily, to do with Jess not having the right to do such a thing without asking.

Emma hadn't known until that moment that Jess and Lily had been in touch with one another. The last she knew, the two sisters were still not talking and were arguing through the lawyer. Emma was now torn between carrying on her task as Jess wanted, or waiting until the two sisters had sorted it out between them. Whatever the 'it' was.

She also felt guilty.

From Jess's description, it was highly probable that Lily was the woman who had followed her to the library, and to the park. Whether she'd been pushed or had simply tripped, Emma still couldn't say with certainty.

The letter she'd received had definitely come from Lily but she had no way to prove the text had. And now she'd received another text: *Back off.* But she couldn't bring herself to tell Luke about the parts he didn't know.

That fact alone was eating at her. She and Luke had always been honest with each other, and here she was keeping secrets, but she didn't want him worrying if there was nothing to worry about.

She soothed her conscience by telling herself she never talked about her clients in detail. She only talked about her discoveries if one of the ancestors had been an important person or achieved something of significance.

She knew Luke wouldn't be happy with that excuse since she'd become the target, but for the moment she wanted to know more before revealing the truth. Emma thought there was more to Anne's seemingly random ramblings.

The distressed woman had talked about Edward as if he was in the room, or nearby, but adding the name of Evie to the conversation changed the timeline. Evie – if it was the same Evelyn as in the newspaper clipping – had died late in 1999. Edward had been gone a few months, but with Anne suffering the way she did, she probably had little, if any, cognisance of time. Emma believed Anne had remembered something from much earlier.

As usual, when she wanted to think, she let her fingers do the talking. Even after reading some of the letters, she still didn't have any sense of who she was writing about. She decided to start on the overview, a chapter she included in all her reports about significant events of the time and how the ancestral family may have fitted.

In 1920s New Zealand, the rural–urban split increased as towns and cities grew faster. Urban residents quickly adopted the latest in fashion, technology and lifestyle, becoming less conservative in their values. They enjoyed new-found freedoms, leaving rural dwellers behind.

New farming methods, including electrified milking sheds and tractors, boosted production; the application of superphosphates improved the land for those with the means. Exports of meat, dairy and wool were up, providing a reasonable standard of living for many, but the gap between rich and poor was still wide. Small rural farmers relied on the whims of overseas markets.

At the same time, travel during the first half of the decade became less of a luxury, as the railways throughout New Zealand became a popular and affordable means of getting around. During the second half of the decade, one in nine people owned a car.

Emma stopped typing, read through what she'd written and groaned. None of the words captured the individuals, the family, or the emotions. She wasn't writing a history book, she was writing about people. Her problem was she didn't know these people well enough yet – a glimmer about one person but no idea who that person was. All she knew was they were rural people.

Emma flicked through the major events within each year, desperately searching for something meaningful as an anchor to Elinor's life. What might have captured her interest and how much to include?

When Emma read about the first recession in 1921, when a glut of primary products forced prices for wool and meat to slump, she realised how fragile farming life was for many. She wondered how Elinor's household fared during that time? There were insufficient records during the 1920s to show where they lived or their occupation, but the record before that had them living in Pahīatua as farmers, and the next outside Palmerston North, in the Manawatū. Maybe they'd weathered the storm sufficiently well after all.

The more Emma delved, the more she became captivated by past details and facts, but as she opened another page, she reminded herself that none of the historic events would have impacted Elinor's life. They might've been shocked, it could've been a topic of conversation for a time, if nothing more immediate took precedence, but it wasn't helping Emma reimagine their lives.

She sat staring at the computer, disheartened. She'd found nothing to connect her to this mysterious Elinor or to help discover the elusive Evie. The lack of stories, of memories, of some sort of familial enthusiasm, kept Emma going around in circles.

Her saviour popped his head around the corner. "Hey, you. Have you seen the time?"

Dressed in well-cut jeans and an open-neck shirt, Luke looked hip and smart and a sight for Emma's sore eyes.

"I have now." Emma stretched. It had been a long day.

"And since Rosie is at dancing …" Luke ventured further into the room, pulled Emma to her feet and wrapped his arms about her.

"Hmmm. What have I done to deserve such attention?" she murmured in his ear.

"Nothing special. Just you. Being you." He nibbled at her neck, kissing her temples, forehead and lips between each phrase. "The generous. Warm-hearted. Spirit. That. You. Are."

Jess's words echoed in Emma's mind. She'd said the same thing. Was she so deserving?

"Nice compliment, but what are you up to?"

Luke pretended to look shocked. "Do I need an excuse to compliment my wife?"

Emma giggled. "No, of course not."

"I've got something to show you."

Taking her hand, he led her into the kitchen where a bright bouquet of florist flowers sat on the bench.

Emma reached for the card stapled to the paper.

Thank you, my dearest friend, for your love and moral support. You're a special lady. I don't deserve someone as good as you, but I value your friendship. I'm sorry I told Lily.

Jess.

Tears pooled in Emma's eyes. "That's such a wonderful thing to say, but what have I done to deserve it?"

"Enough, I would say." Luke handed Emma a glass of wine and clinked his against hers. He winked at her and took a sip before putting his glass down. "Now, there's another matter I'd like to discuss." His tone alerted Emma to a move from playful to serious.

He took a folded piece of paper from his pocket and handed it to her. Putting her glass down, she flicked open the paper. Her stomach flipped as her hand automatically flew to her mouth: *I'm watching you.*

"Where did this come from?" Emma's voice shook as her eyes pleaded with Luke.

"I found it in the letterbox. It's from Lily, isn't it."

"I don't know. Possibly. Probably." Emma put the paper on the bench and retrieved her glass. Feeling the sudden need to sit down, she collapsed onto the sofa.

"She had something to do with your fall, didn't she?" asked Luke, following her.

Emma took a sip of her wine. Her fears, doubts and guilt threatened to overtake her.

"Ems, sweetheart, what are you keeping from me?" Perturbed, Luke perched on the sofa half-turned towards her.

"I'm sorry."

She watched the emotions flit across his face as she told him the whole story, including the texts and what Jess had said. "I should have told you sooner. I suppose I didn't take it seriously enough."

Luke glared at her. "You most certainly did not. For Pete's sake, Emma, you could've been seriously hurt!" He tried to sound cross but failed. He was more rattled than angry. This was something beyond his control. "So what now?"

"Jess wants me to keep researching. She's convinced there's a secret being kept from her, one that Lily knows, which is why the threats, I suppose. I'd like to keep looking. How will she know whether I've stopped or not?"

"Can Jess talk to her? Can she stop her hounding you?"

"Possibly, but the situation with Martin seems to have settled for the time being. I don't want to stir things up. I'm not happy with what's going on either, but I have to respect Jess's wishes. I can't do anything if she doesn't want me to. Jess will text me the next time we can meet at her mother's rest home. In the meantime …?" Emma left the question dangling, hoping Luke wouldn't argue against her carrying on. She turned on her brightest smile and sparkling eyes and batted her eyelids.

He burst out laughing.

They clinked glasses again and the tension faded.

"Any idea what this secret is?" asked Luke.

'No, and right now I'm floundering around in the history pages looking for inspiration – and failing."

"That's not like you. What's missing this time?"

"I've been through the major events, and little jumps out and tells me my – I mean Jess's – family would have been interested or involved. Take 1929, for example. Fascinating history, I could write a book about it, but would it matter to them?"

"Ha ha, very funny. I thought you were writing a book."

Emma nudged him playfully. "I am, but not that sort of book. Their family history, their stories, the things that made them tick are what I'm looking at. There's heaps of other details. Take the Murchison earthquake that killed seventeen, or the opening of Auckland's Civic Theatre and Chateau Tongariro not long before the next economic slump, but can you see how any of that fits their daily life?"

Luke pondered her question. His knowledge of New Zealand history was almost as good as hers, but he often came from a different perspective. "Put like that, no."

"I often think I'm glad we were born in the latter half of the twentieth century. The first fifty years were absolute hell. Two world wars, and the Spanish flu – it's a miracle any of them survived." Emma took a breath and continued while she was on a roll. "And that's apart from several economic upheavals before the Depression years, and an unsettled monarchy with four kings in five decades. At least the next fifty years were better."

"Except for the Korean and Vietnam wars, and the Cold War," Luke reminded her, "but for the most part, you're right, especially for people living in New Zealand. Life was pretty good."

Emma agreed. "It still is. And I wish people would stop the moaning and finger-pointing. Don't they realise how lucky we are? Even with this awful pandemic, and all the civil and religious strife decimating parts of the world, most of us are far more fortunate than our ancestors."

Luke cuddled in beside her. "I know I'm lucky." He kissed her arm. "And you're lucky." He kissed her neck. "And we're lucky." He kissed her throat. "But can we put all the history behind us," – he kissed her mouth – "and focus on the here and now?"

Enveloped in his arms, she responded to his deepening kiss, until someone banged on the door.

16

Before the Downfall

Glen Oroua, Manawatū
February 1930 – 1931

Lying in bed, unexpectedly exhausted after the birth of her newest son, Elinor felt old and guilty. They needed her; she couldn't let them down, not on washday. It was always a three-woman job.

"I'm sorry, Ella. Maybe the girls could do a few chores. Dot's almost big enough. Connie's too young …"

"Stop worrying, Mam. I can manage. The girls need to be in school anyway. You rest now. You've been through a rough time with this little fellow. But can you look after Evie for me? It won't be too much for you, will it?"

"Of course not. Put her here on the bed beside me. We'll entertain each other."

Elinor cooed at two-day-old Sam lying in her arms and Ella's fourteen-month-old daughter Evie beside her, wondering how they'd manage. They couldn't afford another baby, but that's the way things were and they'd

193

have to make the best of it. Not that they'd ever had much, but they had less now, thanks to the whims of the overseas markets.

The usual ups and downs of the economy had worsened considerably in the past few months. Prices fell almost overnight as demand for exports came to a halt. Men were out of work in their thousands, and businesses had come to a standstill. Not that she understood how or why it happened so quickly, but the collapse of the share market in America caused a worldwide depression that had stretched its fingers as far as New Zealand.

She put Sam down to sleep on the pillow and lifted Evie onto her lap, laughing and tickling her. "You are two lucky youngsters, do you know that? You're going to grow up surrounded by so many people who love you."

Elinor wasn't used to having so little to do and chattered ceaselessly to fill the space. "I don't know what life will be like in the future, but I hope you'll always be laughing, with never a worry. That's what I wish for you both. One day, Evie my girl, I'll give you all my diaries to read so you will know my story. They're nothing much, mostly jottings about moments that gave me happiness. Or moments of great sadness. And there's been a few of those. You'll be surprised at the life I've lived. From a young girl of eighteen, when I met Pa, to now. I just wish …" But she couldn't put her wish into words. Not today …

'I promise I'll work twice as hard if you let me stay home,' Ella had said the year before, after Evie's birth, knowing the loss of her wages would make a huge difference. But Elinor couldn't deny her.

True to her word, Ella had worked relentlessly.

Elinor, Ella and Millie shared the heavy load of domestic duties between them without most of the new gadgets available, many of which her ma had – although she was grateful for the refrigerator that kept the food fresher longer.

They worked as a well-oiled team, taking it in turns to look after the five younger children and get them to school, prepare the vast quantity of food needed for twelve people, do the cooking, bottling and baking, and the housework, beating rugs, washing floors, as well as the weekly wash. Thanks to the skills she'd learnt while working for the dressmaker, Ella sewed for everyone.

On top of that, Ella had tended the garden. She'd read the *Yates Annual* and learnt the modern ways of gardening, growing plants from seed, and feeding and spraying. At her request, Joe built a larger hen nesting house and various frames for the climbing beans, peas and tomatoes. After school, all the girls, and the younger boys, were expected to work in the expanded vegetable garden, weeding, watering, staking, picking and killing any white butterflies.

Another section of land had been turned over to potatoes, kūmara and pumpkins Ella had grown from seed. Anything to save on food bills. Ted and Ricky helped harvest the root crops and the fruit in season, but most of it was Ella's work. Now the garden met much of their fresh food needs.

She was a godsend. But such a different Ella to the one before Jack had been killed. All she did was work without any of the exuberance for life she once had. Only Evie made her smile, only Evie could make her laugh.

At the time, Ella had argued black was blue with them over the child's name.

'I want to call her Jackie, after Jack,' she'd told her parents.

'You can't do that,' her father had thundered. 'People will put two and two together in minutes. And after all we've done to protect you. No, I say. Your mother deserves better. We deserve better.'

Elinor had been more pragmatic and tried to soothe the way between Joe and Ella. 'You know that won't do, Ella, but you could use Jackie as a second name, and continue the maternal tradition of naming her with something starting with E. It's a good compromise, don't you think?'

Ella had tried every angle to make them change their minds, but Joe was adamant. Ella was as stubborn, and days went by before the child had a name.

'I've decided on Evelyn,' said Ella eventually. 'Evie. But her middle name will be Jackie. I won't change my mind on that.'

Joe had accepted the compromise, and duly registered the child, bestowing the girl with his surname. Now Joe would register yet another child with his name. Samuel Joseph Somers, the youngest of ten – not forgetting Matthew – with five sisters and four brothers, who all carried the middle name Joseph ...

"I'm whacked," said Ella later that afternoon as she dumped a basket of dry washing on the floor and dropped into the fireside armchair opposite her mother.

"Why are you out of bed? I hope you haven't been doing too much."

Sam lay asleep in the basket at Elinor's feet, while Evie played with her toys. "I'm fine, Ella, but I couldn't lie in bed all day. If nothing else, I had Sam and Evie to see to, as well as the others when they got home from school. You know what they're like if there's no one to organise them."

"Indeed I do," replied Ella. "But now, you sit there and let me and Millie do tea."

Thankfully, the evening meal was the usual leftover cold meat from the Sunday roast, with bread, cheese and pickles, and whatever else was on hand. No one had the energy to do anything more on washing day. The task of heating the water in the copper, lifting the heavy washing in and out, rinsing it twice with blue, and pegging it on the long line hoisted by poles to dry in the sun and wind was exhausting enough. Wintertime was worse because the rinse water was so cold. Their hands would turn purple and ache badly, but rainy days created endless difficulties. The inadequate porch line was constantly in use as they moved items around. Smaller things hung on racks in front of and above the coal range, and for days on end, the kitchen stank of damp washing in various stages of drying.

"You look done in, Ella. Let Millie and Dot get the meal on the table," said Elinor. "I'm still a bit wobbly on my feet myself, or I'd do it. The chooks have been fed, and the food scraps have gone to the pigs, and some extra wood brought in, so those jobs are done. But I can sort the washing." She dragged the basket closer to her and began to fold, thinking she might be able to do some of the ironing tomorrow. Or maybe churn some butter. And she needed to make more cheese.

Happy to sit for a few minutes longer, Ella called, "Dot, have you done those potatoes? Pa and the others will be hungry when they get in from milking. And Connie, Millie needs those peas shelled. What've you been doing?" She ignored the usual groans. "And then set the table, you two. You know the routine. Don't expect anything from Millie and me tonight. Or Mam. Get the boys to help. It's time they learnt."

Elinor watched her two eldest girls. What a blessing they were. One as different as the other. Ella, the organiser, outspoken and sometimes bossy in her good-natured manner, never stopped working or finding ways to save money. She'd got up to Evie every night when she was a baby and still did a full day's work. She never complained about being tired, even though Elinor knew she must have been exhausted at times.

Millie was the quiet one, withdrawn and sometimes stand-offish, who efficiently got on with whatever needed doing without having to be told, and never asked for help. Millie did the baking and made the bread, always had a batch of jams or pickles on the go, helped Elinor bottle the fruit and vegetables, preserved eggs for baking and cooked most of the meals. At night, she would sit in her favourite chair and knit or crochet, making jumpers, cardigans and rugs for the whole family as Elinor spun the wool.

They were regulars at the Women's Institute branch meetings. Nationally, the institute had plans to expand and have festivals showcasing choral singing, writings and domestic arts. Locally, Millie often collected the prize for her baking, Elinor was the best spinner by far, and Ella more often than not won the sewing prize.

Ella would unpick and remake the hand-me-downs, reusing buttons and precious zip-fasteners when they were to be had. Collars and cuffs would be turned, hems braided to hide the marks, sheets would be topped and turned or remade into aprons; old aprons turned into dishcloths and cleaning rags. She was a master at making do with any fabric she could get her hands on. Sometimes she'd pick clothing up from the second-hand shop to remake, or buy fabric when it was on sale. Elinor was always impressed, but she had a hunch they would need all their make-do-and-mend skills in the coming months, if not years. The future looked bleaker than ever.

Even with the farm providing milk and meat, as well as fresh garden supplies, Elinor worried about the account at the store. They still needed basics such as flour and sugar in vast quantities. She hoped none of that would become unavailable.

At forty-one, and feeling every one of those years, life was still a struggle. Joe would be forty-seven soon and he looked older. The house she lived in belonged to someone else, with the uncertainty of whether they could renew the lease hanging over their heads, and now they were living in the middle of a financial depression.

They would manage, somehow – as they always had – but Elinor felt less certain about their future than ever before.

3 February 1931

"Quake!" yelled Elinor.

The atmosphere had been strange all morning on that third day of February, steamy and eerily still for a normally windy district. Elinor had no idea where the quake had struck but instinctively knew it was a big one.

A few minutes later, she heard the clomp of Joe's boots on the porch, followed soon after by Ted and Ricky.

"Are you okay?" he asked. Relief etched his face and he visibly relaxed when he saw everyone.

Elinor had trained the children from an early age to find her when an earthquake threatened. The area was known for having the shakes – most of them barely rocked the curtains, others would throw items off the shelves – but Elinor wanted the little ones with her. That way she knew they were out of harm's way.

"Yes, we're fine. No damage and, I suspect, not close."

"Turn the radio on; no doubt a bulletin will tell us."

Through the crackle, they heard how bad it had been.

"At 10.47 am, an earthquake lasting two and a half minutes and measuring 7.8 on the Richter scale struck Napier and Hastings, devastating a great percentage of the two townships.

Thankfully, HMS Veronica was moored at the nearby wharf and all navy personnel have been deployed to rescue people trapped by debris, and help collect those killed. The ship immediately sent out radio messages around the country to report the damage and further

*ships were despatched from the Devonport Naval Base
in Auckland, bringing additional doctors and nurses.*

*We have no information as to the numbers injured or
killed so far, but reports say many buildings have been
levelled, electricity has been lost and fires have started,
with little water available to douse them. Local civil
defence organisers are on hand to co-ordinate rescue
efforts, but the damage is extensive."*

Joe turned the radio off and rubbed his hands through his hair. "That's awful news. I have a feeling it's not going to turn out well. There'll be many dead after this, for certain."

"I feel sorry for the children," said Elinor. "They must have been so frightened. It'll be something they'll remember for the rest of their lives."

Little could be said. They'd only visited Napier once and didn't know it well enough to remember the buildings.

"Well, I'd better get back to work," said Joe, collecting his hat from the back of the door. "Come on, you two, can't sit around here all day wondering."

"We're off to help with the clean-up in Napier," said Ted, as he and Ricky sat down at the table that evening.

"Already?" said Elinor. "Isn't it a disaster area?"

Ted shrugged. "Yeah. But when we went into town I heard some say workmen are needed, so we volunteered."

Ricky chipped in. "It's summat different to do. And they need manpower."

"Did you know about this, Joe?" His nod was enough.

She didn't like arguing with Joe in front of the children, but sometimes it was necessary. "And you let them, without telling me?"

When her temper got up, everyone knew to stay clear.

"Don't fuss, Nell. Let them go. Food in their mouths and a few extra pence in their pocket won't be a bad thing." Joe kept eating, reaching for another slice of bread and butter. She wondered how he managed to be so complaisant about life when she wanted to rail against it.

"I'm not fussing, but the place is such a mess. Where will you sleep, and eat?" She knew she was bothering over silly things the boys could sort for themselves, but she couldn't help herself.

"It's all right, Mam, we'll be fine. A bit of dust and dirt won't hurt us. And we're used to hard work, thanks to the slave driver here." Ted winked at his father as he teased him, to soften the blow of them going. "Anyway, it'll save you having to feed us. You need it for the little ones."

Elinor couldn't deny that truth, nor their intent. She was proud they wanted to help those in need, but she'd miss them.

"How long will you be gone?" She was anxious they might like the area and stay.

"Who knows," shrugged Ted. "Depends on what we end up doing. We might find farm work, or repair work if we can't get anything official."

"Don't matter much," agreed Ricky, cementing Elinor's fears. "But we'll miss all this." He grabbed the last slice of cake. "Hey, sis! Any more of this going? It's delish."

Later that night, Elinor lay in bed, wide awake, fretting over the small things, aware she was being unreasonable. Caring for her children was all she knew, and she couldn't do that from a distance – even if they didn't want or need her protection any longer.

The household would be quieter without them, but she'd welcome the extra food. Ella was already altering clothes as the three women lost weight, pretending they weren't hungry so the younger ones could have more. She didn't know what else she could do to tighten the belt.

But how would Joe manage the farm without the boys? If only for a short time. Dan was not yet ten, and Archie seven. Too young to do real work. Nothing like Ted and Ricky tackled. She'd have to talk to Ella or Millie. One of them would have to help their pa with the milking, and she'd have to pick up the extra load in the house. Dot and Connie were getting old enough to do more chores, but she didn't want to interrupt their schooling …

Her head spun at each new thought. The danger they were going into kept her from sleep.

She rose the next morning with a thumping headache and her nerves on edge, but she kept her counsel and tried to be agreeable, if not cheerful. "Are you sure you've got everything?" she asked, tucking a bag of fruit and some bread into their haversacks. "Have you got enough warm clothes with you?"

"It's summer, Mam," laughed Ricky.

"We'll be fine, Mam," said Ted. "Rest assured, I'll look after him."

At eighteen and sixteen, Ted and Ricky had become inseparable, working in tandem on chores around the farm. Ricky was the taller and thicker-set of the two and was often mistaken as the older. Together they were a force to be reckoned with.

Ricky punched him on the arm. "Who's going to look after who, shorty?"

Their easy-going banter broke the strain. The boys kissed their mother's cheek and patted her shoulder.

"We'll write when we can," said Ted, waving goodbye.

Joe would drive them to the station, but they had no idea how long it would take or how close the train could get to Napier.

Elinor stood on the porch, surrounded by all the other children returning their wave, determined to keep her emotions under control. They were doing the right thing, but she still felt bereft.

The news from Napier worsened as the aftershocks continued. The newspapers and radio reported on the increasing number of uninhabitable homes with no water, sewerage or chimneys. More buildings collapsed and others were being demolished for safety. With each report, Elinor's sympathy went out to the poor women and children left destitute, who'd lost their homes, but those who'd lost loved ones tore her heart to shreds. Refugee camps away from the disaster zone were being set up in numerous small towns outside the area for them, while the call for able-bodied men to help with the demolition and clean-up continued.

"Our boys will be there by now doing their bit," she said to Joe a few days later as they sat listening to the radio. She could no longer begrudge her sons going to do what they could. "But it must be an awful sight to see."

They listened to the story of the miraculous rescue of a ninety-one-year-old from the rubble days after, but a story that rescuers had been killed and injured when the building they were working in collapsed sent Elinor's heart racing.

"Don't get yourself worked up, Nell. They'll be all right."

"I hope so. I wish they'd write. Then I'd know they are safe."

"Give them time, Nell love. Give them time."

Ten days later, a 7.3 magnitude earthquake rocked what buildings remained standing, shattering an already devastated city. The injury toll reached the thousands, and two hundred and fifty-six people died.

17

Perturbations

Auckland
19 February 2021

The banging on the front door persisted as Luke disentangled himself from Emma's embrace, breaking the spell.

"Sounds urgent, whoever it is," she said, hoping it was nothing to do with Rosie at dance class.

"Okay, okay, I'm coming," shouted Luke, frustrated by the rude interruption. "You don't need to break it down."

The second Luke turned the latch, Martin pushed past him into the entranceway, dragging Jess behind him. He let go of her wrist and beckoned to Olivia.

Martin pointed at Emma, who had emerged from the living room. "You said you wanted to talk. So here she is. Talk. And she's not to come back until she's sorted out that deranged sister of hers."

For a few seconds, they stood awkwardly, unsure who should speak or act first. Martin held Olivia in front of him. Emma moved towards Jess, who seemed remarkably unruffled, and put her arm around her. Emma trembled inside at the sudden aggression Martin displayed.

"Would you like to come in and sit down?" asked Luke cooly, shutting the door. "So we can work through whatever the problem is."

"There's no problem," said Martin. "I'm just sick and tired of people meddling in our lives."

"Which people would that be, exactly?" asked Luke.

"Women! Always butting in where they're not wanted." He pointed at Emma. "Interfering bitch."

"Watch your language, mate," said Luke, taking a step towards Martin.

Martin glared at Emma. "I'm watching you." He ignored Luke and repeated, "I'm watching you."

"That's enough. Be very careful what you say," warned Luke, catching Emma's eye. "Now let's stay calm, shall we?"

Emma saw the slight shake of Jess's head. She had no idea how to interpret the movement but those words … weren't they the same as the note shoved in their letterbox? Was Martin threatening her?

"Would Olivia like to stay?" asked Emma, restraining herself until she could talk to Luke about it. "Rosie should be home from dancing soon. She'd love to see her. A sleepover would be fun for them both. It's been so long."

"No. Olivia stays with me."

Olivia looked up at her father. "Please, Dad, can I?" she whispered. "Please?"

"Hey, don't spoil their fun," said Luke, wanting to

lighten the conversation. "It's nothing to do with them, whatever this is about. I'll drop them both to school in the morning. How about it?"

Martin glared at Jess and Emma, then turned to Luke. "How do I know she and that mad sister of hers won't turn Livvy against me?"

"Why would she?" countered Luke, keeping his rising temper in check. "Have you done something to upset her or make her angry?"

For a few seconds Martin simply glared at Luke.

"Well, have you?"

Martin's shoulders suddenly sagged. He gently pushed Olivia forward and she ran to her mother. "I didn't mean it, Jess. I'm sorry. I didn't mean what I said."

Leaving Olivia with Emma, Jess moved towards Martin. She put both hands on his chest. "It's okay, Martin. You worked yourself into a knot over nothing and need to settle down."

His arms enveloped Jess in a bear hug, and he buried his head into her neck, his hostility fading away.

"It's over now. You can relax," said Jess.

Emma was amazed at how reasonably Jess defused the situation, but something about it niggled. Was he often this belligerent?

"Shall we go home now?" asked Jess.

Martin's head moved against her shoulder and she pulled herself out of his grip.

"Sorry to have barged in on you like this. Lily made him angry. I'll tell you more later. Are you sure it's okay for Olivia to stay?"

"Of course, any time," said Emma.

Returning to Olivia's side, Jess lifted the girl's chin.

"Love you, sweetheart. Daddy loves you, too. He's a bit upset. You know how he gets. Do you want to stay?" Olivia nodded. "That's a good girl. See you tomorrow."

They stood barely a metre apart in a tense ring as Jess turned first to one, then the other. "Thank you, Luke. If you could drop Olivia home after school as well, that would be a big help. And thank you, Ems. We'll talk, I promise."

"Oh, um, thanks for the flowers," replied Emma, her arm draped over Olivia's shoulder. "They're lovely."

"You're welcome. I'll explain later. Something good will come of this, you'll see."

Jess took Martin's hand as Luke opened the door for them to leave.

"Night, Mummy," said Olivia. Wriggling out of Emma's embrace, she ran to her father and hugged him. "Love you, Daddy."

Martin lifted his daughter and kissed her. "I love you, baby girl, and I'm sorry I got cross."

A moment later, they'd gone. Emma and Luke eyeballed each other, the one looking as nonplussed as the other, until Emma realised Olivia was in her school uniform.

"How about you go have a shower. Raid Rosie's drawers for some PJs, and I'll wash your clothes ready for tomorrow. Come down when you're ready. Anything particular you want in your sandwiches for lunch?"

"Vegemite and cheese, please?"

"Done."

Once the girl had gone, Luke and Emma returned to the kitchen, rustling up a quick meal of chicken pasta and making the lunches.

"That was a bit of an eye-opener," said Luke, wrapping the sandwiches. "I never expected that. Nor for it to resolve itself so fast."

"Me neither, but didn't Jess handle it well? I'd have been quite frightened, but she took it in her stride." Emma was now certain Jess hadn't told her the full story. She didn't trust Martin one bit.

"It's obviously happened before. Didn't you tell me he was on medication or something?"

"I thought so, but I can't be sure." Emma drained the pasta and stirred the sauce through. "I know Jess said accessing mental services was difficult at the best of times. I don't think he's always like that. Just bursts of it when he feels out of control. I wonder what happened."

"I suppose we'll have to wait until Jess comes around and tells you. We can't question Olivia."

"Oh, no. I wouldn't dream of it," agreed Emma. "And it's none of our business."

"It is when it's in our house," said Luke, displeased. "I'm not having that happen again." Luke heard the door open. "Ah, here's Rosie now."

The girl ran into the kitchen, dumped her bag on the floor. "I'm starving."

"Hello, sweetheart," said her mother. "How about you run and have a shower first, and see who's up there waiting for you?"

"Who?"

"Go see. And be quick. Dinner's ready," said her father.

"And we shouldn't say anything to Rosie, either," said Emma. "If Olivia wants to talk to her, that's up to her, but we shouldn't."

"Okay. Fair enough. But Martin and I are going to have a little talk."

The next morning, before Luke headed out the door on the school run, Emma persuaded him to wait until she'd heard from Jess again before charging around to see Martin.

"Their situation is terrible, but interfering at the wrong time when you're angry might make things worse."

In Emma's opinion, they needed expert help. Both of them. Something was seriously amiss.

While Luke was out, Emma turned her mind to work. She answered her emails, turned down a job someone asked her to look into – until later, after she'd sorted Jess's family tree out – and cleared everything she could from her 'To Do' list, including ideas for her next novel. She needed to take a much more concerted, chronological and coordinated approach to Jess's story. There were too many gaps.

Again, Emma cursed not knowing all the surnames. Maternal lines were hard enough to trace through the generations, even with some idea who they married. As she tried to explain to Jess, without the person or their next of kin giving express permission to the authorities, current information was covered by privacy laws.

Her morning became more frustrating as the hours ticked by. Any search for deaths through the Births, Deaths and Marriages register stopped in 1971. Evelyn died in 1999. Marriages couldn't be searched beyond 1941, and births were the hardest. They needed to be over a hundred years old.

The births she was looking for in the 1920s through

to the 1940s simply weren't there unless someone had put a notice in the newspapers. Those clippings Jess had brought to her in the first place might reveal something.

With a small sense of expectation, she pulled out the folders she'd created. Putting the business papers to one side, she began scanning the letters again, looking for names that could help her. She jotted a few down before spotting the name Lily. Checking the date to be certain it couldn't be Jess's sister, she did a BDM search and found an Emily Marshall had married a Robert Harwood in 1889. A further search revealed an Elinor born a few months later. Maybe she'd found something after all.

Emma double-checked: Elinor had married Joseph Somers in 1909 and, bingo, her maiden name was Harwood. That confirmed it. Emma now had two generations of the five Es.

Feeling a little more elated, she reviewed the next chart of the family tree and saw an Ella showing as Elinor's daughter, giving her three. Emma looked at the list of five she'd written down. Still missing was one Eleanor and the mysterious Evie.

She took a stab that Eleanor was probably the older generation. If she ordered the marriage certificate for Emily and Robert, she could likely prove it, but that wouldn't help her find Evie, the one her instinct said fitted in the gap between Ella and Jess's father Edward. Somehow.

Emma had been down this track earlier and had met a dead end, but she wasn't one to give up easily. She began to make notes.

1. ***Eleanor*** – the original. Could have been called Nora, common nickname in the 1800s.
   A search of the electoral rolls for an Eleanor – possible married name of Marshall – was inconclusive. Need husband's name to confirm.

2. ***Emily*** – known as Lily. Aged 19 when she married Robert Harwood. Probable daughter of Eleanor, the original, and mother of the next Elinor.

3. ***Elinor*** – born 1889, married 1909. Around 19 or 20 then, depending on dates. Possibly named after her grandmother Eleanor, the original. Also a common naming pattern of the day. Traced through the electoral rolls to several different addresses.
   D. 1978, the same year Jess's sister Lily was born. Is there a connection?
   Ask Jess if her sister's full name is Emily. Could she have been named after her 2 x great-grandmother if the direct line is proven?

4. ***Ella*** – daughter of Elinor, possibly born 1909–1910? If parents married in 1909.
   Did she marry? Who & when? Have children? Possible mother (at age 36??) of Edward born 1946. No known father.
   Find death date if possible.

5. ***Evie*** – still no clues how she fits in the direct line. One of Gen3 Elinor's daughters as per newspaper notice. Sister to Ella (and others)?
   Born ??? D. 1999. Check age at death.

No evidence of a marriage.

Not on any electoral roll under the name of Evelyn Somers.

6. **Edward** – born 1946. Surname Shaw.

   Who was his mother?

   Jess must have more information about her father. She – or the lawyers – could apply for a copy of his birth certificate. That might prove who his parents were …

   unless he was adopted.

Emma drew more mind-mapping lines and doodled as her mind raced. Why did the adoption idea pop into her head? There'd never been any suggestion of adoption before, except in Emma's experience it was often the one secret that families kept.

While not much further ahead in proving anything, Emma felt happier with it all written down. She now had a clearer basis to work from. She could probably find lots of information about Elinor Somers, her mother Emily and grandmother Eleanor if she went searching. Historic details were easier to find. But none of those searches would help her find Ella without more information, like a marriage or death, for which she needed a surname. Nor would she find Evelyn online.

Emma remembered she'd been intrigued by a death and a birth in 1928 attributed to Elinor. Opening up the newspaper archives, Emma did a diligent search throughout the year. Flicking through the personal announcements, she came across an engagement notice in the February for Ella, daughter of Mr and Mrs J Somers, and John, son of the late Mr John and Mrs J Redway. How had she missed that? Thrilled by the find, Emma trolled through every website and register she could think of, but no amount of searching showed the couple ever married.

Disappointed, she continued scrolling and soon found two more entries. In the July of that year, the death of a boy. Matthew Joseph Somers, aged two years eight months, followed a few months later by the birth of a baby girl, Evelyn Jackie Somers, in the November.

"Poor woman. Poor parents," whispered Emma, as memories of her loss resurfaced. "To be pregnant with the next child as you bury your previous one. I can't imagine anything more awful. Such grief and such joy so close together."

However, had she found the mysterious Evelyn, known as Evie, as the daughter of Elinor as she expected? Feeling a surge of excitement at the possibility, and mindlessly thinking Jackie was an unusual middle name for that time, she switched to scanning the general notices. She came across a news article about a local man, Jack Redway, known for his skill with horses, who was tragically killed in an early-morning riding accident in the April.

What a terrible year for Elinor's family, mused Emma as she noted the dates and the obvious reason Ella never married her fiancé. If she eventually recovered from her grief, she may well have married later in life but, regardless of which angle Emma took, she could find no evidence of Ella marrying before 1941, when the records stopped.

Feeling a strange sense of loss, she marked 'Evelyn Jackie' as the possible Evie and continued searching. The newspapers soon turned to stories of personal tragedies as the country dipped into the gloom and despair of the Great Depression, as it became known, and the years passed with little to differentiate between them. Not until after the bilateral and imperial trade agreements late in 1932 was there any relief. A change of government in 1935, with the election of Michael Joseph Savage, finally saw the start of a new way and a better life.

Emma had known, right from the first day Jess rushed into her room, that Elinor's story was one worthy of a full-scale biography. Not because of any significant achievements, but as a social history of families of the time. The more she discovered, the more she wanted to write Elinor's story. Anticipation rippled through Emma as she began to map out how to tackle the challenge of conveying the drama and emotions of life's day-to-day struggles, and do it justice.

If she could fill the gaps.

18

The Endlessness of It All

Glen Oroua, Manawatū
1932

Elinor ceased listening to the radio bulletins that brought more bad news with each day. "I can't take much more of this gloom and doom," she snapped as she got up from her chair and clicked the knob to off. "I don't want to hear about it any longer."

The coalition government, formed late the previous year to combat the effects of the downturn, had brought even more austerity to those already suffering hardship. Amongst many other cost-cutting initiatives, the government introduced a transport licence system.

"How is anyone supposed to make a living from nothing? If I have to pay for a permit to transport goods more than 30 mile, it'll not be worth it."

Joe had stormed and raged for days about the unfairness of the situation.

"I can barely make ends meet now. Extra costs will break us." He was thankful his cream didn't have to travel far, but he often traded the pigs and sheep further afield when he could.

Elinor's greater concern was that, in another effort to reduce government spending, the school starting age had been raised from five.

"I'm not happy with this, at all. It means the younger ones have to be six now to start school. That'll not be good for Evie."

Not that she or Joe had much schooling, nor some of her older children, if she was honest. They'd resisted school in favour of the farm and left the day they could, but the older she got, its importance increased in her mind.

"It's not fair. We need more well-educated people, not less. We need working people to argue against the rich who think they know best," she protested. "How will the future be any different if we don't learn from the past?"

Throughout the year, riots broke out in Auckland, Wellington and Dunedin, demanding better government assistance. Elinor and Joe had neither the money nor the energy to get involved, even if Joe wanted to.

"It's not right, Nell. It's bad government to get us into a mess like this. We need to stand up for ourselves." He thumped the table in frustration. "I should join them. Protest. Do something instead of letting it fall apart around my ears."

They read about the mass fights between the unemployed and desperate workers and the authorities, heard on the radio how windows were smashed and people arrested, and watched the mood of the nation plummet further.

"Don't get involved, Joe. There's nothing we can do, and what's the point of all the fighting just to end up in gaol? Tell me that. How are you going to work the farm from gaol, I ask you?" Distressing as times were, Elinor's objective was to keep her family safe and save every penny they could. "You can't leave me here alone with the children, Joe. We have to keep working."

Eventually, the government introduced worker relief camps for those desperate enough, but the work proved to be little more than slave labour, with men doing meaningless work on roads and ditches for little return, and in appalling conditions.

Elinor and Joe hung on, despite the decreasing payout. All they did was work. The cows needed milking, regardless, until calving time. Farm repairs couldn't be ignored even if making do and mending became the norm when no new fence posts or wire could be afforded. Joe and the younger boys spent days painstakingly taking apart the existing fences that had broken down and reusing the materials. Joe was waiting for the next litter of piglets he could sell to make a few bob.

"Times'll get better. They will, I'm sure," Elinor reassured them as she tended to rips in their hands from the barbs and rubbed her home-made liniments into aching muscles. She had no idea when that day would come, but she had to believe it would.

As she'd feared, the two older boys, Ted and Ricky, had stayed in Napier. A year on from the disaster, there was still a lot of clean-up required even as the rebuilding began. Not that they'd been granted official work, given the numbers of local men in need of employment, but there was enough farm labouring to be had, and private clean-up work if you asked in the right places, or so they said. It was better than those relief work camps she'd heard about, but Elinor dreaded them being so far away and the conditions they had to put up with.

"We've a letter from Ricky," said Elinor excitedly as she ripped open the envelope, glad to feel connected with her sons even through a piece of paper. She missed them terribly, but she was proud of her boys. Proud that they were willing to forego their comforts to help others.

"What's it say?" asked Joe.

"They're well, and fit. So that's good. The rebuilding is going well with over a hundred new buildings nearly finished. He says they are different to the usual and called art deco. What a funny name. They're built of concrete and boxy, with rounded corners and flat roofs. But the authorities say they will withstand future earthquakes better." She lowered the letter and turned to Joe. "I hope there's no big earthquakes like that again. It would have been so frightening. The little ones we have shake us around enough." She turned the page sideways and deciphered a few more sentences. "They are still doing fencing and rubble removal but enjoy the sunshine. He sends their love."

Their few-and-far between letters told her little and she suspected only half the truth. The cost of getting home would keep them away longer than she'd hoped.

She felt so isolated from them. Like half a mother. She carried their latest letter in her pocket, reading it and rereading it, trying to interpret something new until she knew every one by heart.

Ella tended the vegetable garden, coaxing more food

from each plant, enough to make soup if nothing else. Fruit trees needed harvesting and pruning to allow room for growth. She chivvied her siblings to do their part and more, so she could remake and mend their clothes. The younger ones were growing and needed larger, longer clothing. Underwear was created from any leftover scraps she could piece together. Nothing was wasted, not food, not materials, not time. Elinor and Millie did all the cooking now, although washday was still a three-person job.

"It itches," moaned Dot as she tried on the latest dress Ella had remade from an old coat of their mother's. "And it's ugly." At fifteen, Dot drooled over the newspaper advertisements for things well out of her reach. Elinor never begrudged anyone anything, but she resented that some people still appeared to have money when they had none.

"Be grateful you're not wearing remade flour sacks like some people," growled Ella, pinning the hem. "At least you have a dress, and a warm one. I'll make you a slip from the lining, that'll help. You'll be thankful in the winter."

The boys were more of a struggle to sew for. They were harder on their clothes as they tried to help their father with farm chores now their older brothers were away, and fabric was more difficult to source. Elinor was thankful for their few sheep for their wool. She spun new wool, while the girls knitted and crocheted, and they made felt from old jumpers and rugs to make into jackets and hats. She couldn't see how they could become more self-sufficient.

Their one joy was the radio.

"Come on, Mam," called Dot, pulling her mother to her feet. "Dance with me."

The women and girls loved listening to the latest songs from America, jigging to stars such as Bing Crosby and Fred Astaire, Jeanette MacDonald and Ethel Merman, Duke Ellington, and Rudy Vallée. Music from Jerome Kern, Irving Berlin, Oscar Hammerstein, Richard Rodgers, and Noel Coward and so many more, brought smiles to their lips and dreams to their hearts.

Little Evie bounced up and down and waved her arms in time to the music, copying her older sisters until she dropped. Then she'd lie down in front of the radiogram and fall asleep to the sound of singing.

* * * * *

Summer always brought hope. As the year progressed and the weather improved, so did their spirits, even if the situation had changed little.

Towards the end of November, Evie turned four. Small things, like celebrating birthdays with a special cake and singing their favourite songs, had made the year something better than it would otherwise have been. They'd each had their turn, but Evie's birthday was one everyone enjoyed, thanks to her effervescence and unbridled joy. Maybe she was a bit spoilt with so many older sisters, but she was the liveliest of them all, and no one begrudged her a thing.

Elinor made up a silly ditty that lit up Evie's face. She clapped and laughed as the others hugged her and passed her around like a little parcel.

When you were one, we loved you like the sun
When you were two, you were still near new
When you were three, you sat on our knee
And now you are four, we'll love you for ever more.

Sick of the general malaise and feeling weighed down with life, Elinor, Ella and Millie concocted a plan to make Christmas worth celebrating. Ella wrote to her brothers and made them promise to come home. Joe was instructed to kill a sheep, and Ella picked out an old hen she could spare. The summer vegetables were timed to perfection, and the plums gathered off the trees went into tarts. Elinor made fruit wine and cider, for once jolly enough to spend money on the extra sugar needed. As a final touch, they decorated the house with a branch off a pine tree, hung with papier mâché balls they'd made during winter. Colourful paper chains hung from the ceiling.

"You're home!" cried Elinor in delight, throwing her arms around Ted and Ricky before they were barely through the door where they were met with Christmas Eve hugs and kisses and squeals of happiness.

"It's good to be home," said Ted, his eyes aglow as he scanned the room looking at all the familiar faces and homeliness he'd missed.

"And have we got some adventures to tell you," said Ricky, laughing.

That evening, sitting around the table, they entertained the family with tales of their exploits, some of which Elinor decided were youthful hijinks and others were wishes. Once again laughter filled the house and Elinor felt whole.

The youngsters were up early Christmas morning, eager to see what gifts they might have. Elinor always tried to give them a treat of some sort. Oranges were something she spent her pennies on to put at the bottom of their stockings, along with one special gift. The adults shared home-made gifts of sweets or shortbread, a new pair of socks, an embroidered handkerchief.

"You shouldn't have," said Elinor, flicking through the pages of the recently released *New Zealand Woman's Weekly* magazine. Filled with recipes, knitting patterns, gossip and a romantic story, she and the girls would have many hours of enjoyment from it.

Her eyes gleamed as she looked at Joe. "Thank you." She took his hand in hers. "Isn't this wonderful. Having all the family around us again."

"It is," agreed Joe. "A reward at the end of a bad year. Let's hope for something better next year."

But the year hadn't ended, and the next day brought news that shattered Elinor's heart.

FATHER DIED THIS AM. HEART ATTACK.

Elinor stared at the telegram. One part of her wanted to crumble like a little girl and weep for the loss of the father she'd known as a child. Another part said she needed to be strong for her mother, her sisters and her children who'd lost their grandfather.

Joe put his arm around her and led her to a chair. "Ella, love, put the kettle on, there's a girl, and make us all a cup of tea. And can you pack us some things?" He turned his attention to Elinor. "We'll take the train up this afternoon."

"Can you spare the time?" asked Elinor. He'd do anything for her, she knew.

"I'll make time. Especially now the boys are home. They know what to do."

Elinor nodded. She didn't want to leave her family, not now they were all together again, but her place was with her mother and siblings. They would need her.

The train journey through the Manawatū Gorge back to Pahīatua felt incredibly long and slow even though she knew its speed was the same as always.

"We'll be there soon," Joe assured her every few minutes.

When they finally arrived, it was near teatime, but it looked as if nothing had been done all day. Her mother sat silently in her armchair. After briefly grabbing Elinor's hand in a vice-like grip, she returned to her solitary thoughts.

"Put the kettle on, one of you, and make us a cup of tea, there's a dear," said Elinor to her sisters. "What happened?" she asked of her brothers.

"Dunno," replied Dick who sat grim-faced at the dining table.

Elinor knew how close her brother and father were.

"He was fine yesterday. Ate a hearty lunch, enjoyed the games and fun and went to bed last night as usual." He stared out the window, across the garden to the farmland beyond. "He seemed okay first thing. Complained of having eaten too much yesterday and said he'd better walk it off today. Then at breakfast he keeled over."

Letting her young brother and her sisters chip in, Elinor learnt he'd sat down to a full plate of bacon, eggs, sausages, tomato and mushrooms with toast, which he'd lathered with butter. A pot of tea to wash it all down and he was a happy man.

"Until he stood up," said Johnny. "He went all red and blew out his cheeks, like, and fell flat on the floor. He were as white as a sheet by then."

Dick grimaced. "He was gone just like that. Wham bang!"

"Can you talk to Ma?" asked Stella. "Nothing Patty and I say is making any difference."

"I'll try. Has she been like this all day?"

Stella nodded. "Pretty much. Ever since the doctor came and they took Pop away. I've tried to make suggestions, but she won't lie down. She won't eat, and she won't talk to us. I don't know what to do."

Elinor assured her that their mother's reaction was normal and not to fret. "I'll talk to her, but leave her be for now. She'll come around in her own time."

The local vicar had called earlier to briefly discuss a date for the service. The undertaker had taken the body and asked them to decide whether to have the coffin brought home again for friends and family to have time to say goodbye or to do all of it at the church.

"What do you mean no decision has been made? Why not?"

Dick was quick to push responsibility onto her. "You decide. And do we bury him down south where he came from, or start a new family plot somewhere around here?"

"Why would we bury him down there?"

Dick shrugged. "He's got brothers there, hasn't he?"

"Yes, and his father is buried down that way somewhere. But what's that got to do with it? Don't make problems where there aren't any. Don't you remember the arguments over his mother's funeral in Taranaki and all the fuss that caused? That was awful. We don't want a repeat of anything like that."

Elinor also remembered how little they had grieved at the time. Would it be the same for her father? Looking at her mother, she thought not, but for herself, would she miss him? The man he was, rather than the man he'd become. She'd miss the certainty of having a father, but she wouldn't miss his obstinacy or his callousness towards Joe. Nevertheless, she had good memories of her childhood.

Someone had to decide what to do next but why did it have to be her? "He wouldn't want to be down there. This is his home now. Anyway, the one brother he's closest to is up this way. It's got to be nearby, and we bring him home until the service."

Everyone suddenly wanted to have an opinion on who should have an opinion and why it mattered. Voices rose and arguments ensued. Elinor was ready to scream. What should have been a simple decision almost turned into a feud. Elinor was often surprised at the way people reacted to death. As if only their grief counted, as if tearing the family to pieces, saying hurtful things to each other, could be justified because the deceased wasn't around to speak for themselves.

"He will come home and be buried at Pahīatua." Cutting through the babble of noise, her mother's voice confirmed Elinor's decision.

At last! breathed Elinor with a sigh of relief. "That's settled then," she said. "Now, girls. Let's get some food on the table."

She and Joe retreated to the room they would use for the night. "You should go home in the morning," Elinor said, unpacking the things Ella had put together for her. "I'll stay on and talk to the undertaker and the vicar, and help arrange the service. In this heat we'll have to have the funeral as soon as we can, but we need time to put notices in the paper and tell everyone so they have a chance to get here."

"Are you sure? There's plenty of work waiting for me at home. Dick and Johnny don't want any help on the farm here, not with a young labourer around. I don't think your father had done much for a while from what I could gather. Just appeared at inappropriate times and gave orders. Seems like your brothers have been running the farm."

"That's sounds like Pop. But yes, you go home. I'll send you a telegram when we know the date and time and you can come back then. Should you bring all the children, do you think? How well did they know him anyway? "

"Is that the point? What does Grandma Lily want? What do you want? That's what matters."

He's right, of course, mulled Elinor, but she suspected Grandma Lily wouldn't know or care who was there. She'd lost her husband, the man she'd shared her life with for more than forty years, despite their difficulties. No one would replace him, and nothing would ever fill her life as much again. Yet nothing much would change, either. Dick and Johnny would inherit and continue to work the farm, building additional homes when they found wives; their mother would stay in the house until she passed, and the girls would stay until they married.

Whatever they did, Elinor instinctively knew it would be up to her to keep the relationships alive. "Bring them all," she said, suddenly smiling, relishing her newfound role. "Family should be together at a time like this."

It had taken the loss of her father for reality to take over. It would fall on her to become the matriarch, the centre, and provide a place to visit, a place to stay, a place of welcome where people talked and laughed and remembered. A place everyone could call home, wherever she was.

19

When Life Takes a Turn

Auckland
19 February 2021

Emma looked up at the sound of tapping on the French doors. "Jess! Am I pleased to see you! Come in."

Jess hovered in the doorway. "I wasn't sure of my welcome after last night. That's why I came round this way."

"Don't be silly. Of course you're welcome. You're my friend."

Emma indicated Jess should sit in the wingback chair while she returned to her desk.

"Is Luke mad at us?"

"Not mad exactly, but surprised. He said he wanted 'a word' with Martin about it, but I persuaded him to wait until you'd talked to me – and here you are. And it's lovely to see you, but will you please tell me what's going on."

Jess perched on the edge of the chair looking at the floor and if not exactly wringing her hands then fiddling with them.

"Come on, Jess," said Emma trying not to show her irritation. "One minute you want me to research your family, but you won't talk to me about it, then Martin says I'm not allowed to visit or talk to you, but then he brings you to our house and makes a scene. And what about this sister of yours and her threats?"

"Sorry, Ems. I don't know quite how to explain. But Martin is sorry for his outburst. So am I."

Emma tried to reassure her friend and get to the point. "Apology accepted. But can we sort out what is going on? What happened with Lily that sent Martin off the deep end?"

"I'll get to that, but in a funny way, I think last night was Martin's way of reaching out and asking for help. His way of saying he'd reached crisis point and didn't know what to do."

"Well, I agree, it was certainly a funny way of showing it. I could think of better." Emma hoped she'd kept her tone light and free of sarcasm. None of this was Jess's fault although, in Emma's opinion, she was enabling it. "What went on after you'd gone?"

Jess sat back in the chair and stared at Emma's cabinet instead of looking at her. "We sat down and talked and talked, the first time in ages. I discovered he's been getting more and more anxious. He hoped being at home all the time, working from home, with only Olivia and me there, that he'd feel secure and safe, but it didn't work out that way."

"I didn't realise he was that anxious about life."

"He always has been, since childhood, insecure in himself, doubting his self-worth. He needs to be in charge of what happens around him. Then those lockdowns last year gave him a chance to be in total control of his environment because he couldn't go anywhere or do anything or be evaluated or judged by anyone. Thankfully his IT job could be done from home or I don't know what would have happened financially. I didn't notice any changes in his behaviour until Dad died."

"Why then particularly?"

Jess turned to look at her. "Outside intrusions. The need for me to be talking on the phone, seeing other people and not at home under his control."

"But Jess, you should never be under his control. No one should control another person," protested Emma.

"No, I don't mean control as such, but more within his view, safe, where he could see me. He only wants to protect Olivia and me. He's scared he'll lose us somehow."

Emma refrained from suggesting if he kept acting as he was, he deserved to lose them. Instead, she said, "So what are you going to do?"

Jess sat forward suddenly, an eagerness replacing her uncertainty. "I forced an appointment with his doctor this morning. We have a prescription that should help. He's already taken the first dose and felt calmer, he said. And we're arranging for some counselling for both of us. It could take a while to get an appointment but that's okay. We are on our way back. I can cope in the meantime, now I know what went wrong."

Emma relaxed a little hearing that news. "And this time, if you need help, call me. Don't keep it to yourself."

Jess smiled. "I'm sorry, I should have come to you in the first place. He'll be okay now. But I have to persuade him to let me go out and do things."

Emma knew there was a long way to go in sorting Martin's problems. At least it wasn't what she'd first suspected, but he … they … would need help to get his paranoia under control. "So why did your Dad's passing spark him off?"

"He hated the undertaker coming around, and the funeral stressed him completely. All the well-wishers and people calling at the house. Then all the phone calls and letters from lawyers, Lily turning strange and demanding I sort the house and sell it immediately. Until then, he was okay with Livvy going to school and dancing, or me going to the shops and talking to you and a few others, but it's like he freaked out completely. Ridiculous, I know, but yesterday brought everything to a head."

"What happened before you came here?"

Emma still believed Jess was too forgiving and underestimating the level Martin bullied her, but while she wanted to be his saviour, she wasn't going to listen to reason. But then, Emma had never had to deal with anyone behaving irrationally before so couldn't judge how she'd behave in response.

"Lily turned up," sighed Jess with an overwhelming sense of defeat.

"And …?"

"She threatened me. Said she'd rain down all manner of legal challenges on my head if I didn't sell the house, lock stock and barrel, right now, and stop digging into the past."

"Oh, wow. I can see why Martin would lose his cool at that. Luke would. And not much rattles him. But what's Lily so worked up about?"

"Something about leaving the secrets where they belong."

After Jess left, saying she wanted to be home for Olivia, Emma pondered ways to help her friend.

If Jess believed she could regulate Martin's delusions now he was on medication, then she didn't want to get involved. Emma recognised that out-of-control sensation when life hadn't worked out as planned. Her grandmother Charli had seen her desperation and steered her in the right direction, but she didn't think she was someone who could help Martin or Jess deal with theirs.

What she could do was try to discover what secrets Lily knew that Jess didn't, and why she didn't want them known. Martin had called Lily deranged. Given the irrational bullying she'd received at Lily's hands, something wasn't right. Jess said it all linked back to their father's death. What was hiding in that house that Lily didn't want found?

Emma returned to the box of letters, checking her notes, but she knew she was wasting time. Whatever was missing wasn't in that box. "Think!" she railed out loud.

She'd ignored the photos, mostly because Jess said she didn't have a clue who many of the people were, and Emma certainly would have no idea, but she decided to take a look, in case a note on the back of one might inspire something.

As Jess had said, most were old photos with no names and no indication of who or where. She could only guess at when from the age of the photo or the style of clothing. After a time, she began to recognise the odd face and put those in the same pile, hoping she might find a trail.

At the bottom were three framed photos. One was of a man, moustached, in a formal, three-piece suit and high-collared shirt, carrying a fob watch. He was standing beside a seated woman with beautifully coiffed hair, dressed in a dark, braided gown, white collar and brooch.

"Who are you?" whispered Emma, rubbing her fingers over the image trying to sense the answer.

The second photo was of a suited man, sadness written on his face, holding a swaddled infant. She'd swear it was an older version of the man in the first photo.

The third brought Emma up short. The formal studio photo, taken, Emma estimated, around the 1940s, showed a moustached man sitting in the centre next to a grey-haired woman, surrounded by four men, four women, one boy, and a girl around twelve. It was, without a doubt, the same man again.

Emma glanced between the two images comparing the woman's features. Although the woman was obviously much older and wearing her hair differently, Emma decided those two images were of the same person.

Emma set the three frames up side by side and studied each one in turn. A story lived in those photos, and if she could put a name to one of them, she might be able to find it.

Going by instinct alone, Emma decided that *if* the woman was Elinor Somers, the image of the couple could have been taken around the time of their wedding. The second photo almost made Emma weep. The man's eyes were filled with such pain. Was the child sick? Maybe the child died? And the third was a simple family portrait. She studied the faces again and noticed how much alike they all looked, and she could see a resemblance to the older man and woman. Again, assuming this was Elinor and her husband, and the others were their children, they'd had a larger family than Emma had considered. They also appeared to be arranged by age, with the two youngest in the centre.

Emma began to scribble down more questions, cursing the difficulties she faced with BDM timelines, and the unavailable, missing and inconsistent census records and electoral rolls. But she hadn't completely lost her journalistic know-how. "You can't hide ten children." She returned to the box of photos. "They must be here somewhere."

"What on earth are you doing?" asked Luke when he returned from the school run, finding Emma down on her hands and knees among photos spread all over the floor. Some were spaced singly, many were in small piles, more lay on various surfaces.

"I'm looking for the children of one of Jess's ancestors. Trouble is, I don't know their names so I'm trying to put a timeline together through photos."

"Don't ask me to help," he said.

Emma got to her feet and stretched. Reaching up, she kissed his cheek. "Don't worry. I know you don't have the eye for that. What are you doing this afternoon?"

"I've got work in the studio I'd like to catch up on."

"Okay. See you later." Emma eased her neck and shoulders.

"Hello, Mum," said Rosie, munching on the afternoon snack Emma had prepared earlier and left in the kitchen for her.

"Hello, my lovely girl," she said, hugging her daughter. "Did you have a good day at school?"

Rosie shrugged. "Suppose so. I'm glad Olivia is allowed to play with me again."

"So am I, sweetheart. Now, can you do me a favour?"

"What is it?"

"It's a game of spot the face. If you see two photos of the same person I want you to show me and we'll add them to their personal pile."

"Okay. Cool."

Rosie wiped her hands on her school skirt, plonked herself down on the floor and began looking at the photos, crawling around on her hands and knees, turning back to one or another.

"Here's two," she said, handing them to her mother.

"That was quick. Good girl. You're much quicker than me."

"That's because you look at too much other stuff."

Emma smothered a laugh. The girl was right. She did get involved with each photo trying to place it in context. Rosie didn't care. A face was a face.

An hour later, after several other photos had been added to piles, Emma decided they'd done enough for the day. "Let's go play a game before Dad comes in, shall we?"

"If you like. I don't mind. Here's some of a girl. She reminds me of Livvy."

Emma took the three photos Rosie held out to her and could see what she meant. The young girl did have some resemblance to Olivia. The latest one of a girl of maybe eighteen to twenty, smiling broadly, Emma knew was taken in Auckland. She recognised the Civic Theatre building behind her. Not that it helped Emma discover who she was, but maybe it was another clue.

For the first time, Rosie looked at the framed photos lined up on Emma's desk. "That girl there," – she pointed to the youngest one in the centre of the family group – "she's the one. And that man there, he looks like Livvy's grandad."

"Why do you say that?"

Rosie shrugged again. She was good at shrugging. "I've seen some photos of her grandad and that man looks like him."

Astonished, Emma stared at the man, wondering why she'd never asked Jess for a photo of her father. The man, if Emma wasn't mistaken, was one of Elinor's sons.

20

Changing of the Guard

Glen Oroua, Manawatū
1933-1934

Elinor wrapped her arms around her husband. "Oh, Joe, that's marvellous news."

After more than three long, harsh years of deprivation and stark, government cost-cutting policies, the economy lifted at a stroke. Farming exports were back in demand, and the markets rose almost immediately.

"A weight has been lifted off our shoulders, that's for sure. We're back in business. I'm so glad our boys are home again. I couldn't keep up with the workload without them."

He'd tried to explain, as best he understood it, what had led to the huge devaluation of the New Zealand pound against sterling in the January. It had restored activity, and New Zealand's trade position strengthened with Britain.

"It's over, Nell. The worst is over."

Much of the detail went over their heads. All Elinor

knew was they had slightly more money in their pockets each month. Within weeks, the local economy was more confident, incomes rose, spending increased and banks reinstated more favourable lending policies. Something Elinor tucked into the back of her mind. They weren't ready yet, but soon.

Elinor went about her work with renewed vigour. They didn't have the money to buy any modern appliances, but lengths of fabric for Ella to make new clothes were first on the shopping list. That, and a few treats.

"I still think home-made is best," said Joe, biting into a chocolate bar. "Shouldn't we save our money for more useful things?"

"You're right, Joe, but I couldn't resist this once – for the children's sake. They will hardly remember what it was like to eat something not home-made, and a few sweets won't break the bank. The atmosphere in town was so lively and optimistic. What do the blokes at the saleyards say?"

"Business is better, especially for meat and wool, if not yet booming; they can see a future now. Dairy is up, 'n all, but we mustn't rush it. There's still need for caution, but there's hope, Nell. There's hope."

After her father's death two years earlier, her mother settled into a simple domestic life at home, in her garden, as Elinor had expected. The boys worked the farm, and the girls – although, at nearly thirty and twenty-five Stella and Patty were hardly girls any longer – ran the house and appeared content to live at home.

As time passed, her mother became more withdrawn. She was happy enough to see Elinor when she visited but preferred it when she came alone without Joe or the children.

"Ma," asked Elinor. "Why don't you want family to visit? I love it when the house is full but you're the matriarch. Isn't that your responsibility? Where's the place the family can meet and catch up with all the gossip and news, and feel welcome?"

"I can't be bothered with all that nonsense any longer. I'm happy on my own in my garden and with the girls for company."

Elinor noticed she hadn't mentioned the boys. "But what happens if they marry?"

"There's no sign of that happening, dear. But don't let me stop you. If you want to play the matriarch, go ahead."

Elinor inwardly grinned. She'd intended to anyway but didn't want to offend her mother. Satisfied, she began planning for August. Birthday month for her, Millie and Connie. At forty-four, and after forty-four months of deprivation, surviving the depression years as best they could, Elinor knew how she wanted to celebrate.

"I want to throw a party, Sprout," she whispered when they were alone that night.

While the house they'd leased for the last nine years was deteriorating before her eyes and they didn't yet have the money to do it up, Elinor had long since decided that people mattered more than the walls surrounding them.

"Whatever for?" asked Joe, taking her in his arms.

"I think we need a treat. We've never fully celebrated my birthday. It's always been for the children, but this year, I think it's my turn. And ..."

"And what, my darling Nell?"

Between kisses, she tried to explain her wish. "I want to turn our home into a meeting place where everyone is welcome. I want your brothers and sisters and their families to visit us and share a cuppa, and food, and feel at home. I want my family to do the same and mix with your family. I want our children to never want to leave home – even though I know they will one day – because their hearts are here with us, knowing they will return to that heart time and time again."

"I love you, my Nellie. You are the most wonderful, generous, warm-hearted person, and I will never want to leave your side."

After that, words were unnecessary.

* * * * *

As the rain clattered on the roof, Elinor welcomed visitors through her door. They rushed from their cars with hats, newspapers and raincoats held over their heads and leapt onto the porch to be met by hugs. Chatter accompanied the hanging up of coats and hats on the hooks beside the door as plates of food were carried inside.

The fire burnt brightly in the coal range, comfortably warming the room on a chilly afternoon. The kettle bubbled. Every chair was occupied, the youngsters sat on the floor, wanting to be in the same room, all together. Elinor's spirit swelled as the volume increased, laughter tinkled and contentment settled.

The applause was spontaneous when Millie revealed the birthday cake she'd baked. Beer, cider and fruit wines were poured, ready to toast the birthday girls.

"For they are jolly good fellows … and so say all of us. Hip hip hooray!" came the shout after they'd sung the obligatory happy birthday song.

Elinor hugged her daughters, one on either side of her. Fourteen-year-old Connie blushed and shyly accepted the best wishes and gifts, so many gifts, overcome by so many people.

Millie similarly embraced the love of family. "Thank you, Mam. For everything."

Elinor's soul surged. She looked around the room at the happy faces. Maybe she had achieved her dream after all.

* * * * *

September 1933

"Look at this, Joe," said Elinor, holding up the newspaper. "Elizabeth McCombs has won the Lyttelton by-election for Labour by a landslide, after the sudden death of her husband." More thrilled than she expected, Elinor read on. " 'Mrs McCombs has had an astonishing career in a male-dominated sphere. She became the first woman elected to the Christchurch City Council in 1921 and has now become the first woman in Parliament.' Isn't that marvellous, Joe?"

Over the years, much of it due to her mother-in-law's influence, Elinor's interest in politics sharpened. On election days, they walked arm in arm to the booth to cast their vote, both recognising and respecting the efforts of previous generations who had won women the right to vote back in 1893.

"Things are looking up," continued Elinor. "Women in Parliament will be the way of the future from now on. I hope they'll be able to exert some influence when it comes to family issues."

"I wouldn't hold your breath," replied Joe. "But we do need some different ideas to what we've had in the past. Life is different now."

The year marched on through a gloomy winter, but as summer approached spirits lifted, and Elinor rethought what she'd planned for Evelyn's birthday. "Joe, I've made some enquiries and found a local woman who teaches dancing. Evie so loves music and dances to the radio all the time. I'd like her to have lessons and learn to dance properly. You never know, she might make something of it."

"How much is that going to cost? Can we afford it?"

"I've a bit put by," she answered. "From the housekeeping and the child allowance. It could be a birthday present."

The following Saturday morning, Elinor, Ella and Evie piled in Ella's car and drove into town. They went up the stairs to the large studio above the shops where Evie's eyes lit up. Mirrors lined the wall, and little tutus and other costumes hung on coat hangers on the racks along one wall. A piano sat in one corner, and a dozen girls stood in a group chatting until the teacher, Miss Gwen Gibbs, called attention.

"I want to welcome our newest recruit, Miss Evelyn Somers, to the group. You must show her the way and look after her since you've all been here longer. Now say hello."

A welcome hello chorused in unison until Miss Gibbs clapped her hands and the girls fell into place.

"Come along, Evelyn, join in and follow what the other girls do."

Elinor and Ella sat on the hard, upright chairs against the wall and watched with growing delight. Sharing a moment of pride, Elinor took Ella's hand and squeezed it.

Evie was a natural, they could tell. She quickly picked up the steps and arm movements and exuded a natural gracefulness they'd never noticed before.

All too soon the lesson was over. Evie raced over to them breathless with excitement. "I've had the bestest fun. Can I come again?"

Ella hugged her. "What a clever girl you are. I'm that glad for you."

Elinor stood as Miss Gibbs approached them. "Well done, young lady," she said, resting her hand on Evie's shoulder. "For your first lesson, you've done well. Would you like to come back again?"

Evie nodded her head so vigorously her hair fell about her face.

"Very well, if your mother is willing, I will accept you into the school of dance."

Miss Gibbs looked between Elinor and Ella as if determining which woman was the girl's mother.

"Thank you, Miss Gibbs," said Elinor quickly, settling the matter. "I would be delighted for my daughter to attend your school. She's danced and jigged to music since she could stand."

Evie ran back to the other girls while Elinor and Miss Gibbs finalised the details. Out of the corner of her eye, Elinor saw one girl hug Evie, and smiled. She must write this episode in her diary. A precious moment in a precious life.

"My eldest daughter, Ella, will bring her in future," said Elinor. "Come along, Evie, we must go now."

Evie took Ella's hand and they pranced down the stairs together, laughing and chatting. Elinor's heart stirred to see the two of them so close, knowing how much Ella had sacrificed for her daughter who would never call her Mam.

Evie was disappointed to learn that the dance school would close over Christmas and she couldn't go to lessons again until school restarted, but was delighted when Elinor said she could bring her new friend to the house for her birthday.

"Can I really? That would be so much fun," squealed Evie.

For Evie's birthday the following week, Ella made her a new dress, Millie baked a fancier cake than usual, her friend played all the girls' games Evie loved, and together they put on a mini dance show for the adults that was met with great applause.

"I had a lovely day," said Evie, worn out from the afternoon's activities. "Thank you, Mam."

Elinor tucked her into bed and kissed her forehead, aware of Ella standing by the door watching, waiting her turn to kiss Evie goodnight. As she left, Elinor rested her hand on Ella's shoulder. "You should be very proud."

5 March 1934

Elinor shot out of bed the moment the earthquake struck. A loud cracking sound followed by a bolt of lightning had her running to three-year-old Samuel, to find him, Archie and Dan still asleep and oblivious. "Those boys would sleep through anything," she muttered to Ella who had emerged from her room to see to Evie and the other girls.

"All's well there."

"What time is it?" asked Joe, tying his dressing gown around his waist.

"Nearly midnight."

"I'll look outside," he said, grabbing a torch.

The two women checked for damage, finding a few things on the floor and the larder a mess. The loss of their bottled fruit would mean more work, but otherwise the house was unscathed.

"Everything looks okay out there," said Joe, coming back inside as another jolt shook the house. He instinctively wrapped his arms around both women until the shaking stopped. Elinor nervously scanned the room. Crockery rattled and the fire flared briefly.

Living in the Manawatū, they were used to shakes, most of them barely worth mentioning, but now and then a bigger one struck. They always seemed worse in the middle of the night – and this one was big, reminding Elinor of the Hawke's Bay quake three years ago.

Two further aftershocks followed several hours apart. On edge, and her eyes burning from lack of sleep, Elinor got up before dawn when Joe rose to round up the animals.

Earthquake or not, the cows needed milking. He

shook Ted and Ricky awake, and Elinor watched them disappear into the darkness.

When they returned, they shared a quiet cup of tea discussing the raft of other quakes.

"Let's hope nothing bad strikes here," murmured Elinor.

One by one, the others appeared and were told about the events of the night.

"How did we sleep through all that?" wondered Dan.

"Who knows," answered his mother. "We've certainly been lucky this time."

She dished up bowls of the porridge she'd had simmering on the stove and put the bread and toppings on the table. "We should call on the neighbours. See how they fared."

With no telephone in the house yet, Joe would need to drive over to see how they were. "I'll go after breakfast," he said, turning on the radio.

"A violent and devasting earthquake of magnitude 7.6 struck shortly before midnight last night. The Sydney Observatory reported it recorded one of the most disastrous earthquakes to date some 1,500 miles offshore. The centre is believed to have been somewhere near Pahīatua. Tremors could be felt throughout the lower North Island and as far away as Auckland and Dunedin. Reports of major damage are coming in from nearly every township in the region ..."

"Pahīatua!" cried Elinor, her stomach fluttering and her thoughts flying to her mother. The family listened, with growing horror, to the litany: chimneys down, buildings fractured and teetering, sheets of plate glass shattered over roads, broken goods lying smashed on shop floors, blowholes on the river flats at Foxton throwing sand and debris far and wide chasing campers from their beds, the railway lines twisted and snapped, and tramway lines down.

"How on earth did we escape unscathed?" whispered Elinor, shaken.

"There is news of sightseers flocking into the centre of towns throughout the dark hours, unable to sleep and unwilling to go home. Authorities are asking people to stay away and let them get on with assessing the damage, while they start the clean-up. Water mains have cracked and some fissures have appeared, and the roads are unsafe. A few minor car accidents have been reported, but miraculously, no deaths or major injuries at this time."

"You'd better head to your mother and brothers in Foxton," said Elinor, switching to crisis mode. There was work to be done. "I'll go to the neighbours and see if they're all right and use their phone to call Dick. If it was centred over there ..." Elinor bit her lip and drew a couple of deep breaths. She was determined not to let her concern for her mother and siblings overwhelm her. In an emergency, there was no room for panic. She needed to put first things first and find out the rest later.

"Don't you want to see how things are in Pahīatua?" said Joe, hovering nervously. "Then I'll go to Ma."

She could tell Joe wanted to see his mother, but he would never leave Elinor alone when she needed him.

She pushed aside her worst imaginings. "Don't be silly. She's half an hour down the road. It'll take hours to get through to Pahīatua, if at all. Go. But send a message back as soon as you can. I'll see if I can phone through to the farm. We can go later if we need to – if the road is passable."

With practised hands, Elinor and the girls worked quickly to gather a basket of supplies, piling in bandages, water, food, thermos and blankets.

"Ted and Dot, you go with your father and see what you can do to help the Somerses. Take this with you, you might need it. Now go, your father's waiting. Hopefully you can get through, but go carefully." Only her terse tone and rapid movements gave any hint of her inner fears.

No sooner had Joe left than Elinor was giving orders to the rest of the family. Busy hands had no time to fret. "Ella, come with me to the neighbours. See how their faring, and use their phone. Millie, look after the youngsters, they'll need breakfast. And get baking. The Women's Institute might set up food relief. Ricky, go into town and get some newspapers. Find out how bad things are."

"What about the larder?" asked Ella.

"It can wait. What's lost is lost. We'll clean up afterwards when we know how people are faring."

Two hours later, everyone was home again.

"All's well at Ma's," said Joe as he entered the kitchen smiling. "No one's hurt and there's no damage to the house."

Elinor hugged him, relieved to see him home and unharmed. He held her tight for a few moments, letting the tension ease. It could have been so much worse.

"Some others I saw weren't so lucky. Poor sods," said Joe. "After my brothers tidy up a bit, they'll head into Foxton to help with the clean-up there."

"We ducked into the village to have a look," added Ted, hanging his cap on the peg. "The place is a mess – roads cracked, stuff everywhere and the town hall is badly smashed up. I've never seen anything like it."

There would be months of repair work ahead if things were that bad.

Her stomach still churning with what might have been, Elinor passed on her news. "The neighbours escaped unharmed and let me phone through to Pahīatua. It's good there, too. Stella assured me all was well. A few trees down and some fissures, but the house and sheds escaped unscathed."

"Connie and I did a pile of baking and made pies in case the WI need it," said Millie, wanting to share her role in the emergency. "And we helped cleaned up the larder with Mam."

"I walked over the farm, Pa," said Ricky. "Nothing much. There's a few branches down, and the big tree in the bottom field keeled over. The pig pen'll need a bit of repair, but the cows are all good."

They pored over the newspapers Ricky had brought home, commenting on the differing levels of destruction between one place and the next, their fears allayed, and empathising with those not so lucky.

Elinor's relief was immense as she listened to their chatter. They'd seen out another onslaught with no harm done, and every one of her family was safe.

21

Playing Cat and Mouse

Auckland
22 February 2021

After dropping Rosie at school the following day, Emma opted to go for a walk on the beach before going home. It would help sort out her thoughts. On the way there, she saw a car similar to the one that had followed her before, but after a distance decided she was imagining things. She parked, glanced at the vehicles around her and, seeing nothing untoward, headed off along the sand.

With the sounds of the waves sweeping in and ripping out, the wind rustling the trees and birds calling, Emma set her mind to plotting Elinor's story. She closed her eyes, tilted her head back and breathed in the sharp tang of seaweed, filling her lungs with fresh, salt-laden air before striding out, gathering pace and rhythm.

Elinor Somers, matriarch, countrywoman, wife and mother, lived to be nearly ninety. In her lifetime, she lived through two wars, the Spanish flu, the Great Depression, and many natural disasters of varying magnitude. She saw the transition from horse and carriage to motor cars, from kerosene lamps to electricity and modern living, the introduction of a welfare state and the post-war boom years. She knew the value of each day and, in Emma's eyes, was a remarkable woman.

From what Emma had discovered, Elinor's life story, while mundane on the surface, was truly fascinating set in its historical perspective. Still bound within a patriarchal society and throughout years of deprivation, she clothed and fed her family with little in the way of amenities and kept them close by her side. She had been involved in the Women's Institute from its inception, along with two daughters, often picking up prizes for their skills.

How well Elinor adapted to modern living was a moot point. She raised ten children that Emma knew of and, if her instincts were correct, lost at least one. How many grandchildren and great-grandchildren would that amount to?

Doing a quick calculation based on each person on average having two children, there would be something close to forty by the third generation. Add in the spouses, mix up the generations and a family gathering in the 1970s would be sizeable. Plus another two generations to bring it up to Jess and Lily's time. Getting lost down the twigs and branches of various lines was easy; sticking to the direct maternal line – and finding all the correct information – not so easy.

But none of that mattered in the slightest if she couldn't link the direct line.

Her stumbling block was Edward Shaw's mother.

None of the searches had answered her questions. She didn't have authorised access to his records, and they were a long way off appearing online. There was only one thing for it – Jess had to request her father's information, even if Lily objected.

Checking her time on her phone, Emma made one last turn along the beach and headed back. She'd walked long enough. Time for action.

She saw the long scratch running the length of her car before she reached it. The parking spaces beside her were empty and few people were around to ask if anyone had seen anything.

Cursing, she got in, barely paying attention to other vehicles. She started to back out before realising a black SUV with dark tinted windows had pulled up behind her. She stopped millimetres before hitting it.

"Idiot. Why'd you stop there? There's plenty of space to park properly," she muttered, her pulse racing at the near miss.

Seeing she had room to do a turn, Emma put the car into drive and moved forward enough to swing around and head to the other exit. She'd barely gone two car lengths before the car pulled in front of her. Emma began to shake. This was no random incident.

She backed up a little and steered around a parked car to get to the exit lane, only to have the SUV meet her head-on. Emma's heart pounded, and she began to puff. Several seconds passed before the vehicle suddenly backed up and drove off through the car park giving Emma space to make her escape. She'd almost reached the exit lane, when the other car sped across her path. Emma braked hard to avoid sideswiping it.

Frantic now, she glanced left and right and in her mirrors, trying to place where the car had gone. She spotted it heading to the end of a line of parked cars. Emma quickly accelerated along the exit lane to the stop sign joining the main road.

"Come on, come on," she said to the line of cars, thumping the steering wheel. The SUV appeared behind her, edging closer and closer until it nudged her. Emma gasped, and peered in the mirror but couldn't see the driver. She checked the traffic again. The SUV nudged her again, and again, inching her forward.

Emma saw a gap and accelerated, narrowly avoiding the car in front as she shot into the lane. Looking back, she could see the SUV still at the stop sign. She took the first turn, looking for a different route home. She swiftly turned this way and that, through various backstreets, hoping to lose whoever it was who'd threatened her. She had a good idea who it might be, but all she wanted to do was get home safely. She'd think about the rest later.

Emma pulled into her driveway and collapsed over the steering wheel. Resting her head on her sweaty hands, she took several deep breaths trying to calm down.

Once she had her breathing under control, she went inside to find Luke in the kitchen.

One look was enough. "My God, Emma, what's happened?"

Emma sank into the chair and shakily outlined the events. In hindsight, frightening as it had been, she realised she hadn't been in real danger. Dodging cars in a car park at walking pace was hardly life-threatening, but why was she being harassed?

Luke was hopping mad. "Are you sure you weren't followed?"

Emma nodded, nursing the sickly sweet tea he had given her, which she didn't want but he'd said she needed. "Yes. I'd have recognised it straight away if I had been."

"Did you get the licence plate?" By now, endeavouring to keep his temper, Luke had paced the floor so many times Emma began to think he'd wear a hole in it.

"Don't be silly! I was too busy trying not to hit the damn thing – or be hit by *it* – to think about that. I just wanted to get away." She sipped at the tea but couldn't swallow any more.

"How can you be certain it didn't follow you when you can't tell me the make or anything much about it other than it was black? Do you know how many black SUVs there are on the road?"

Emma didn't bother to answer. He was right. She didn't know anything about the car, except it hadn't been the one that followed her previously. So who was it?

"I need to talk to Jess."

Emma was still shaking on the inside, almost as uneasy about confronting Jess with her suspicions as she was about the whole incident.

"Jess, can I come around? We need to talk." She expected Jess would be as mad as Luke – or at least as shocked – when she found out.

"I was thinking of going to see Mum later. Maybe we could meet there. Sounds serious."

"It is, but I don't want to talk about it over the phone."

It had to be Lily, but there was nothing she could prove.

"I'm driving you," said Luke when Emma told him she was meeting Jess.

"No. Please don't. I'm quite capable. Anyway, you'll need to get the girls from school if I'm not back in time, and I don't think it'll happen twice in one day."

"I'm not happy about this," he argued.

"And you think I am?" Emma heard her voice rising an octave and took a deep breath. She didn't want to fight. She was upset enough and Luke was pushing all the wrong buttons. "I'll be fine. Let me do this my way." She hoped she was right because, if she was honest, Luke had hit the mark. Getting back into the car was a bit scary, but she wasn't prepared to let it take hold and stop her from driving.

"Promise me you'll be careful?"

"Yes," she answered a little forcefully, and softened her tone. "I need to do this by myself, for myself." She rested her hand on his upper arm. "Please, Luke."

"If that's what you want. Just take care."

Luke waved her out of the driveway and kept an eye open, ready to follow should a car pull out after her, but saw nothing.

Constantly watching her mirrors, Emma drove to the nursing home without any further incident, which helped restore her composure.

Once again, Jess was waiting at the door. "Ems," she said with a hug. "I'm sorry for the hassle. I hope you don't mind coming here?"

"No, of course not. It's fine."

Jess operated the keypad to open the door and signed them in.

"Mum's not good," she warned as they walked down the same corridor as last time. "I don't think she's got long. If I didn't know better, I'd swear she's given up since Dad's gone. But she doesn't understand or have any sense of time and place."

Jess opened the door to her mother's room and stood stock still, mouth open. "What the hell are you doing here?"

A dark-haired, thin woman stood by Anne's bed, holding her hand. "She's my mother. I'm entitled to be here." Emma heard the defiant tone slip into despair. "You can't stop me. She's my mother."

For the first time, Emma came face to face with Lily. The same woman she had seen in the library. She looked utterly forlorn, tired, wan. And frightened.

"We'll see about that," said Jess, swinging on her heel and marching down the corridor leaving Emma hovering.

"Um, I'm …"

"I know who you are." Lily's voice sounded flat, but Emma recognised pain and defeat in her eyes. "I'm sorry …" Lily paused, looked down at her mother, smoothing Anne's flaccid hand. "But Jess mustn't know. She mustn't. It's not fair."

"I don't understand. Know what?"

"I'm hardly going to tell you, am I? You're the one trying to dig up the past. It's got to stop." Lily paused again, dropped her head, and in an almost-whisper said, "Stop. Please. Just stop."

Emma could sense Lily's suffering. She didn't understand what was causing such torment, or how she was involved, but the woman was hurting. "That's up to

Jess. She's the one who asked me to trace her family tree. If that's what she wants, then I will."

Pain or no pain, this woman had a lot of explaining to do before Emma could forgive her behaviour – if it was all Lily's doing.

"Please don't say anything to Jess." Lily took a deep breath. "Because she won't understand unless I tell her what I don't want her to know."

"What don't you want me to know?" asked Jess, shutting the door behind her. "That you've been coming here all this time and didn't tell me? That you made the staff promise never to tell me, knowing that Mum couldn't, and I was likely to think she was talking about earlier times if she did mention your name? Is there anything else I should know? Like why you want Dad's house sold so desperately, why you've been so up yourself, why you couldn't be the sister I needed. Why any of this?" Fists clenched at her side, she fought back the anger, trying to calm down and not upset her mother who was plucking at her blanket, moving her head from side to side and muttering as Jess's voice rose.

"I think I should go," said Emma.

"No," said Jess and Lily in unison, taking Jess by surprise.

Jess glared at her sister. "What gives, *Em*ily?" she asked, emphasising the Em.

Emma's brain clicked when she heard the name. One of her questions was answered. Not that it would make any difference. She suspected her role was nearly over. No more family tree and no biography. "This sounds like family business to me. I think you'd both be more comfortable and able to talk more freely without me."

"Stay," came the response from Lily. "You need to hear this, too. Then you'll both understand."

Puzzled at Lily's request, Jess nodded. "Okay, but let's try not to upset Mum, shall we?"

Lily promptly sat in the chair beside her mother. Emma chose a chair by the window, while Jess went to the other side of Anne's bed and took her hand.

"Hello, Mum. It's Jess. I've come to see you. I've brought my friend Emma with me." Anne's eyes scanned the room and looked back at Jess but showed no signs of recognising anything she'd said. "Lily has come to see you. We're going to talk about old times. That's always nice. The three of us chatting like we used to."

A slight smile flickered around Anne's lips. Jess raised the back of the bed so Anne was in a more comfortable position. Emma saw how much frailer she'd become even in the short time since her last visit.

Jess sat in her mother's armchair. Keeping her voice smooth and even, she asked, "What *do* you want, Lily? I'm so confused I don't know what to think. All I know is my sister has turned into some she-devil, and that makes no sense."

Lily hung her head. "To go back to when Dad and Mum and us two were a family."

Jess scoffed. "Well that clearly can't happen, so let's try again. What's got into you? Are you the one who's been following Emma and sending her texts and stuff? Because if you have, you owe her a big apology and me a big explanation."

Immediately defensive, Lily snapped. "You're not the only one whose world has been tipped on its head, you know. I've lost as much as you, maybe more."

Emma assumed Jess would also hear the sadness in Lily's voice, but if she had, she ignored it. "You brought much of it on yourself when you fought with Dad about putting Mum in here. He couldn't have coped any longer."

Lily nodded. "I know, and I was wrong, but I was so …" She paused, looking for the right words. "In denial, I suppose. I couldn't accept I'd lost Mum like that. I wanted to hang on to her, to the memories I had." Lily reached for a tissue and blew her nose. "I'm sorry. I've been so very sorry for a long time."

Emma's intuition told her Lily was telling the truth and maybe Jess would give her some credit. But it seemed not. She was far too angry.

"You didn't show it much. Poor Dad was beside himself worrying if he'd done the right thing."

"I know. I know. But I did make it up to him. Last year, between lockdowns, I used to visit him and I'd bring him here sometimes."

Emma thought back to the previous year. If she remembered correctly, Anne had spent the previous Christmas at home until a bed had been found for her at the end of January. Two months later, they were in total lockdown, confined to their homes for a full month, followed by lesser degrees of restrictions for the months following. But rest homes were out of bounds.

Emma remembered how anxious Jess had been about when she was allowed to visit and she followed the rules about not mixing when she did. As far she knew, her Dad went every day when allowed, but then, in the last few weeks leading into summer, with Covid looking as if it was under control and people could return to a near-normal life, Jess's father died. That final Christmas in the house was the last Christmas they shared.

Jess's voice had lost the calmness she'd strived for. "You what? Why didn't Dad tell me?"

The two sisters were so intent on their tussle, with Jess becoming increasingly resentful, they failed to notice Anne becoming more and more agitated.

Lily attempted a smile, as if remembering something. Her voice was kinder when she answered. "I made him promise not to, or I would stop coming. I'm sorry, Jess, truly I am. I didn't want you to know the details. I wanted to safeguard you from the truth."

"The truth? What truth?" she asked cynically, with an edge to her voice.

The ghastly croaking sound from Anne prevented Lily from answering. She pushed the bell button three times, long and hard.

22

Race Day Adventure

Glen Oroua, Manawatū
1934–1935

June 1934

Elinor had had so much fun planning and hosting the birthday celebrations for herself and two daughters last August, she decided to throw a surprise fiftieth birthday party for Joe. "You've got to keep it a secret," she said to Ella and Millie. "But I need your help."

June weather was unreliable. Always cold, snow often coated the surrounding hills, and the constant wind turned icy. But if it should rain, it would make things much more difficult.

Attending the Foxton races had become a regular event. Over the years, Joe's love of horses had grown. Even with motorised vehicles to do the heavy work, Joe still kept one working draught horse on the farm. Being around them gave him a thrill that Elinor could not deny him. One day, he wanted to graze breeding mares.

"Come along," he said, "we'll be late. The first race starts soon."

Elinor pinned her hat in place and picked up her handbag. Ella and Millie stood at the door and waved them off.

Joe lined up at the racecourse gate, and as they were about to pay their entry fee, a course steward approached them.

"Would you come with me, please, sir. Madam."

Joe looked at her, questioningly. Elinor shrugged, hiding a smile while Joe strode along behind the man leading the way to the members' section. Elinor was almost running trying to keep up with him as her new court shoes echoed on the cobbles.

"What's going on?" asked Joe.

"All will come clear in due course, sir."

The president of the club, whom Joe didn't know, welcomed him at the door. "Good afternoon, Mr Somers. We, the club that is, would like to invite you to join us in the members' section for the day, and partake of members' privileges."

"Why thank you," replied Joe, with a wide grin. "I don't know what to say. Thank you," he repeated, turning to look at Elinor and back at the man, his face aglow.

They were led to the members' seating area, right on the finishing line, given one-day members' tags, offered drinks and sandwiches. Several members came up and congratulated Joe.

"What on earth is going on, Nell?"

"Why do you think I would know?" Elinor tried to look and sound innocent, but sooner or later the game would be up. It was the last meet of the season and a week earlier than his actual birthday; luckily, he hadn't connected the two.

A race book appeared in his hand. "I trust you'll have an excellent day," said the man. "I've marked a few tips you might find helpful."

Joe looked bewildered as the man disappeared. "Who was he?"

"How would I know?" Elinor didn't know the man but assumed he was part of the secret.

They looked at the race book together and commented on the horses they knew by name, a trainer or two Joe was aware of, and aligned their choices to the ones the stranger had recommended.

"I'll pop to the tote and put a few bets on. Don't go anywhere. I'll never find you again in this crowd."

As soon as Joe was out of sight, the trainer Elinor had contacted appeared by her side. He winked. "All going to plan?" He'd helped her enormously in putting her plan into action and added a couple of extras. She'd been taken aback at the time when she'd realised he was the same young man who had come to their house all those years before and told them about Jack.

"Yes, and I can't thank you enough. I don't know how you pulled so many strings, but Joe will be ever so grateful. As am I."

"I'm happy I could do you a favour. Jack was my friend and he'd have wanted me to do something if he'd been here."

Elinor thought of all they'd missed, and how different Ella's life would be today if Jack had lived. She'd liked Jack, the few times they'd met. But it hadn't happened.

Joe was back, tote tickets in hand. He took his seat beside her looking around, taking in the details and the atmosphere. "Go, you beauty. Go!" he yelled, waving his hand in the air and jumping on the spot as his first pick came home. "I'd not have picked that one without that chap's suggestion."

They didn't win every race, and two of Joe's picks came in second and third and paid a small dividend, but the man's tips brought in more return than Joe had ever had.

"It pays to be in the know, doesn't it?" he said.

"One day, you'll be able to afford a full membership, and then you'll be in the know," said Elinor, happy to see Joe enjoying himself. "Knowing the trainers and the horses better must help, but it's never a certainty, surely? Animals are fickle and jockeys change."

"Nothing is ever certain, Nell." But that wouldn't stop him from enjoying the day.

Dashing around between his seat, the bar, the tote and the refreshment room, Joe absorbed the sights, sounds and smells. From the bugle calls, the thunder of the horses' hooves and the course stewards in their colourful jackets, to being up close to the horses in the parade ring – another members' perk – Joe was in his element. He was having such a great day, Elinor was almost sorry it would end.

Time for the second-to-last race, and the big race of the day. Suddenly she was nervous.

"What's the matter?" asked Joe. "You're jumping around like a flea."

"Am I? Sorry. It's all the excitement. I can't sit still. It's so thrilling."

Joe was yelling for his picks before they'd rounded the bend, and continued to yell all the way to the finish line. He'd won. He was jumping up and down, hugging her, throwing his arms in the air, his grin larger than ever.

The loudspeaker broke into their celebrations. "Would Mr Joseph Somers please make his way to the Winner's Circle to present the Cup Ribbon to the winning horse? Mr Joe Somers, please."

"What's all this?" he asked.

Someone beckoned him. He grabbed her hand and pulled her after him as he made his way down the steps. More people pointed to where he should go.

Elinor pulled her hand free. "I'll wait here. Go. This is for you."

He made his way onto the podium, where a steward handed him a royal-blue ribbon emblazoned with the race details. The loudspeaker came to life and announced the owners, the trainer, the jockey and the strapper as Joe placed the ribbon over the horse's neck.

Elinor could see him patting the animal, in awe at being part of the proceedings. He would go home with a full heart and a full pocket. She couldn't have wished for better.

On their way back, Joe was still talking about the day, as excited as any five-year-old receiving a gift. He didn't notice how quiet everything was as he pulled the car to a stop in front of the house.

"Come in with me," said Elinor. "Come and tell the others about it. Ted can put the car in the shed later."

They walked up the steps. Joe opened the door to let her go in before him and the second he stepped through the door he was met with a chorus of "Surprise!"

Twenty people filled the room that Ella and Millie had decorated. They sang, they cheered, they blew whistles.

The boys had brought in an extra keg of beer, and the table was laden. A large birthday cake sat in the centre waiting to be cut.

"Thank you all for coming," said Joe once the room had quietened. "I've had such an amazing day, I can't believe my good fortune. And thank you to my beautiful wife, who must have been the one to organise all this."

She'd write about it in her diary.

Was life turning around at last? She certainly hoped so.

January 1935

Elinor sat under the shade of the trees and watched her family laughing and enjoying their day at the beach, running in and out of the water, playing a haphazard game of touch rugby and munching through a mountain of food.

Joe flopped down on the towel beside her and flicked the water from his hair.

"Oi, you, look out. You're getting me all wet."

He grinned and rubbed his wet hands up and down her arms and quickly kissed her, right there in public.

"Joe Somers, don't embarrass me."

"Relax, Nell. There's no shame in a man kissing his wife."

"Stop teasing," she said, giving him a gentle push. "Enjoying yourself, are you?"

"I am. And so are the others."

They gazed along the long expanse of beach where other families were picnicking, and watched Ella strolling along the water's edge, picking up random shells.

"Will she ever marry?" asked Joe. "She'll be twenty-five this year. She should have a home of her own."

"Maybe one day, but a broken heart takes a long time to heal, and there's Evie to consider. Anyway, I like having them all at home. I'm in no hurry to see them leave. And neither are you. How would you run the farm without Ted and Ricky?"

"That's true. I'd need a farm labourer instead, and I'm not keen on that idea. It's better our boys than someone else's lads. And Dan and Archie are coming along."

Like bees to a honeypot, a few minutes later each of their children returned from whatever they'd been doing, looking for more food or something to drink. Dan and Archie had been on a treasure hunt and wanted everyone to inspect their finds. Dot and Connie laid out their towels ready to sunbathe. Millie, the most serious-minded and quietest of them all, had been building sandcastles with young Sam and Evie. Ted and Ricky, covered in sand from a wrestling game, landed where they fell, spraying sand over everyone else, provoking squeals of protest.

The sense of freedom that came with the lift in the economy over the last couple of years brought with it a chance to get out and enjoy life more. While unemployment remained high and failing government work schemes were often challenged, farmers such as them were marginally better off. No longer counting every ha'penny, the Somers family were going out more, joining in with others at sports events and local groups, going to local dances and meeting new people.

Life was looking up, and the fun day at the beach cost nothing, but reaped numerous rewards. Elinor was happiest when her children were happy. She couldn't prevent the fights and arguments that came from so many personalities living in close quarters, but mostly they enjoyed each other's company and no one held a grudge. That she would not tolerate.

As with all good things, the day came to an end.

"Come along, everyone," said Joe. "There's work to be done."

"Can we stay a bit longer, Pa?" asked Connie, backed up by her younger siblings.

"No, we can't," answered Elinor. "You know the rules. Now help pack everything up and let's go."

Despite the occasional grizzle, she wouldn't change her life; she had a good life. A husband she loved and a family who made her feel complete.

Slowly, over time, Elinor had encouraged extended family to visit. Sunday afternoons, birthday lunches, special celebrations, any excuse she could make to invite people, she used, until it all culminated at Christmas. Everybody – or nearly everybody – their parents and single siblings, and those not needed to stay on the farm or be with another family group – had congregated at their homestead.

The paint was peeling on the north side, while mould grew on the south side. Joe and the boys had repaired the spouting so often it ran at different angles all around the house. Many of the windows didn't shut properly, letting in cold winter draughts, and the lean-to bathroom was as dark and dreary, and cold, as ever. But they now had a toilet on the back verandah, a vast improvement from the long-drop in the garden. Elinor constantly nagged the landlord about repairs, but while they took interest in the farm, they had no interest in the house.

But on that day, neither Elinor nor their guests cared a jot about the state of the house. All they cared about was being together. Chairs were dragged outside, extras borrowed from the local hall, and groups of people sat chatting, drinking tea, soft drinks or beer until lunch was called.

She could still smell the aromas – meats slowly baking in the oven, fresh bread, butter softening in the heat. Cakes, pavlovas and fruit tarts were put indoors until needed. Amid the chatter and clink of crockery, salads were tossed, dressings made, cold meats carved and drinks put into an enamel bath of water to keep cool.

With hardly enough space for all the dishes on the table, empty platters were quickly replaced with full ones. The party atmosphere continued all day. The younger ones played games, ran around and generally annoyed their parents; the older generation snoozed in their chairs. Not a single person stood alone until the men went off to do the afternoon milking, signalling time for many to leave. For those who remained, leftovers were picked at until the wine and spirits were brought out in the evening.

That's when Elinor's miracle happened. The radio had been on, they'd listened to the King's Christmas message, and the latest news bulletin, but the volume was turned up when the music started. The young ones danced in the limited space and sang, many of the older ones joining in with the words they knew, and then Elinor heard the piano. Evie loved music and dancing so much that Elinor had bought an old piano, and the girl was having lessons.

Evie was sitting there, a smile lit up her entire face, her eyes full of joy and laughter. She was a natural and could pick out a tune off the radio after a few attempts.

It was a start. A wonderful start to an imagined future.

* * * * *

Months later, that Christmas was still talked about in conversations that started with, 'Remember when …' and Elinor certainly did remember. She wrote about it in her diary to be certain she didn't miss anything.

Many such happy moments filled their life that year. Elinor often lived in fear of something happening, some tragedy affecting their lives, some disaster that would again ruin her hopes and dreams, but as the year progressed, her doubts lessened.

She had become a stalwart at the Women's Institute over the years. When she'd first considered Ella and Millie joining the local branch about five years ago, she'd worried that taking her single daughters to the meetings might be frowned upon, but that wasn't the case. The young women were welcomed and encouraged, and they'd done well. But this year they had excelled themselves.

"Ella has won the national award for sewing, and Millie the baking award," announced Elinor to the family sitting around the table. "That is quite some achievement when you were up against the likes of Mrs Jones and Mrs Stanley, long-standing holders of those prizes. Congratulations to you both."

"And what you about you, Mam? You won the national spinning prize," said Ella. "Thank you for introducing us to WI. We've enjoyed the meetings."

Those meetings had drawn the girls out. They attended the local dances and joined the table tennis club. Elinor noticed that one young man had taken a particular liking to Millie, but he appeared to be quieter and even shyer than she was. For the time being, Elinor would let nature take its course, but maybe she should give it a poke in due time.

While Elinor revelled in the cosiness of family life, her children, and all things domestic, now they had more money in their pockets, Joe worried about the farming industry in general. The fickle summer weather was causing havoc. With major flooding in the north, extensive but less serious flooding around their region followed by a drought, and a major drought in Canterbury, productivity was down. The drop-off in milk yields meant less by-products for the pigs, and the industry was suddenly struggling to fatten the pigs for the bacon market. The usual February and March sales were well down on previous years. Even Joe had suffered in the downturn.

"We're going to have to supplement the feed if the rains don't come soon," he said.

To Elinor's surprise, he'd become quite an expert in

raising pigs, but his greatest love was horses. He'd joined the local racing club after the previous year's outing and followed the breeding and training programmes with interest.

"If we must, but I'm sure it'll rain soon enough. Shall we go to the race meet this weekend?" asked Elinor.

"Of course. There's a few I'm following who are racing. I'd be keen to see how they get on."

Elinor had long since added Joe's dreams to her own. A home on their own farm where he could graze a racehorse or two. They weren't there yet by a long way, but they certainly had more savings and more money in their pockets than at any time in their lives.

She would write about it in her diary.

November 1935

As the year progressed, both Elinor and Joe took a greater interest in the forthcoming election. Resentment at the existing government's harsh policies over the last four years and its failure to address the effects of the depression of the average family grew exponentially.

"I like the sound of this Michael Savage. He's thinking about the ordinary bloke," said Joe, as he read the newspaper.

The Labour Party promised a 'cradle-to-grave' welfare system, that they would build state houses to assist people into their own homes. They had plans to improve both the health and education services and offered a guaranteed price for dairy products.

"That's got to be the best news I've heard," said Joe, his increasing optimism reinforcing his decision. "I'm voting for them."

"So am I," echoed Elinor.

Not only did they, and the others in their household old enough, vote for Michael Joseph Savage and his Labour Party cohorts, so did the majority of the country. Labour surged into power.

"Our future is secure," said Joe, lifting Elinor and swinging her around. "Never again will we see such poverty and deprivation."

She wanted to believe him. She wanted to think her dreams were inching nearer.

How they had partied that night with family and friends, and again at Christmas – one tradition now thoroughly established.

Each day brought better news, and Elinor's hopes knew no bounds.

"I'm having another one," whispered Elinor as she and Joe cuddled up.

Joe chuckled. "Seems to be a natural and regular occurrence, doesn't it, my dear?"

He kissed her deeply, whispering words of love, but she sensed he wasn't as joyful over this one as he had been over the others. If she was honest, neither was she. If her calculations were correct, this one would be born a matter of a week or so before her forty-seventh birthday. Her body was getting too old for such strain. She responded to his kiss and let her worries be taken away by the happiness they shared.

23

Hard Choices

Auckland
22 February 2021

The medical staff at the rest home came running. Anne was still breathing, but they shook their heads. The prognosis wasn't good. She had taken the final turn while her two daughters argued. Jess and Lily clung to each other, seeking forgiveness.

Emma decided to leave them alone. "Don't worry about a thing. I'll get Olivia from school and take her home. You stay here with your mum. She needs you." Emma hugged her friend as she collected her bag. "Lily, is there anything I can do for you? Do you need to tell someone?"

Lily looked up in surprise. "No. Thank you." She hesitated, extracted herself from her sister's embrace and held her hand out. "I owe you an apology. I behaved badly, but I had my reasons." Emma shook the proffered hand as Lily turned to watch Jess fussing over their mother. "I think those reasons are no longer valid and the truth will come out anyway."

"Apology accepted. For now. There's a time and place for everything."

Lily's expression changed. "I can see why you and Jess are friends. Can we talk some time?"

"We can," Emma agreed. She had a fair share of questions to ask. "But I'd better go now." She texted Luke to say she'd pick the girls up from school and she'd explain when she got home.

Forty minutes later, she was pulling up outside Jess's house, still on edge about the strange note jammed into the passenger door. She hadn't noticed it until she let the girls in. The words *I'm warning you* sent shivers down her spine. Who'd put it there, and when?

There was a black SUV parked in the driveway.

"Let's go in together," she said, and walked with Rosie and Olivia to the house.

Olivia put her hand on the knob to discover the door was locked. Banging with her fist, she yelled, "Dad! Let me in."

A surprised Martin opened it and blanched when he saw Emma. "Oh, it's you." He stepped out of the house as the two girls slipped in behind him and checked the driveway where the vehicle was parked. He looked back at Emma, but their eyes didn't quite meet. "Where's Jess?"

"She's at the rest home. Her mum had a turn and appears to have slipped into a coma. She was rather upset, but Lily is with her. She'll call you when she knows more."

"Lily? That troublemaker. I told her …" Martin stopped short. "What's she doing there?"

"She wanted to see her mother." Emma sensed she

277

was stating the obvious, but nothing seemed obvious at the moment.

At a loss, Martin didn't reply. His eyes kept darting back and forth, and Emma's tension mounted.

"Martin, can I do anything? I could take Olivia home with me if you need to go to Jess." She waited for a brief second, but when he didn't answer, asked, "New car?" nodding towards the SUV.

"No. That's not mine. It's … um … it's a … a work colleague. And I don't need your help. I'll send Rosie out."

He left Emma standing on the doorstep while he called Rosie. The front door shut after them without another word.

On the drive home, Emma contemplated all that had happened – Lily's presence, her change of attitude, the black SUV, Martin's behaviour, and her instinct that something was coming to a head.

"Rosie, was there anyone else in the house when you went in?"

"Not that I saw," said Rosie. "Is Auntie Jess going to be okay?"

"Yes, sweetheart, but she's going to be sad for a while longer. And she's going to need our help. You'll be kind to Livvy, won't you?"

Rosie shrugged. "Why's her dad so jumpy?"

Once more, Emma was taken by her daughter's perceptiveness. "I don't know."

Luke was waiting. "Are you all right?"

"Jess's mum took a turn. It's not looking good. But yeah, I'm okay."

By the time she had told him everything, Luke was

furious – and as confused and astonished as she was, and trying to control his desire to confront Martin that minute.

"You're telling me that Lily harassed you twice with texts, and followed you to the library, but you're not certain she was the one who pushed you in the park, but possibly, and she's likely to have been the one to coin your car. You found a note jammed into the car door, saying 'I'm warning you', but you don't believe she was the one playing cat and mouse in the car park because you *think*, and only *think*, the SUV you saw at Martin's is the same car. And now you want to meet with this Lily because she's apologised and you want to forgive her. Have I got that right?"

Put that way, Emma understood why Luke sounded exasperated, but it seemed they were being drawn into the tangle whether they wanted to be or not.

"More or less. Not forgive, so much. I might, in time, but yes, I want to meet her. I want to find out what this is all about. I think she's going to tell me, us – Jess and me – a bunch of family secrets that will put all my research into perspective."

"And why would you trust this woman?"

Instinct, but Emma didn't know if Luke would believe her. "I'm not sure I do, but I need to know. If she wasn't driving that car then who was? And why are they threatening me?"

Jess appeared at the door next morning looking pale and distraught. Lily was with her.

"Oh, Jess. Has your mum gone?"

Jess nodded. "Early this morning. We wanted to talk to you."

"Come in, I'll make us a cup of tea."

Emma steered the conversation to 'what next'?

"I honestly can't answer you," said Jess. "I just know I'm at the end of my tether. Martin drove off somewhere in that stupid SUV he's bought. I've not seen him since."

So that black car is Martin's, thought Emma. Why would he want to frighten her? She hadn't mentioned the bullying tactics to Jess, but somehow it made a difference knowing it wasn't Lily who'd played cat and mouse with her.

"He can take care of himself," said Emma. "You've got more than enough on your plate. Now, what can I do?"

Lily put her teacup down and spoke for the first time. "We're seeing the funeral director later this afternoon. We decided to have a simple, private affair to say our farewells but, in reality, we said them a long time ago. Mum hasn't been herself for some time."

Emma had a sudden desire to write about Anne's life, to let the world know who she really was and what she'd achieved, for her daughters to remember her as the vibrant wife, mother and teacher she had once been. And at that moment, it seemed even more important to write the family history stretching across the five Es their father had talked about; those indomitable women of the past.

Eager with anticipation, Emma said, "Not now, of course, but when you feel up to it, I'd like to write her story, if you'll let me. If you tell me your memories and share some photos that remind you of who she was."

"That's very generous of you," said Lily, "considering what you've had to put with recently. Thank you. That would be a wonderful keepsake. But, please, first I must pay for the damage to your car. I'm sorry for that. It was petty of me, but …" She paused, considering her words. "I meant no harm. I wanted to protect my baby sister, but instead, I made things worse. And now I want to make amends, to her, and to you."

Emma had no idea what Lily was talking about; protect Jess from what? Jess said nothing. She sat nursing her mug of tea, looking out into the garden.

Stifling her desire to challenge Lily head on, Emma decided to be charitable until she knew more. "I'll accept your offer to fix my car. I think that's the least you can do in the circumstances, but beyond that, time will tell. I do believe you owe it to your sister to tell her what is going on. None of it makes sense," said Emma, keen to know the truth. "But just to be certain … it was you who sent me the texts saying 'Mind your own business' and 'Back off'?"

Lily nodded.

"And now I've met you, I know it was you who followed me to the library, but did you also run past me in the park?"

Another nod.

Emma trembled. "Did I trip or did you push me?"

"I didn't push you deliberately. But I did want you to know I was watching you."

"Why?" Emma demanded.

"Hoping I could stop you telling Jess what you'd discovered. I didn't mean for you to fall. You weren't aware of your surroundings because of your music. I could hear it as I got closer, but then I got too close and out of stride. I nearly tripped myself on your heels. I reached out an arm to steady myself. I barely touched you, but it was an accident. I hope you'll believe me?"

Emma considered her comments for a moment but decided her tale was plausible. "I feel better knowing it wasn't deliberate, but you should have stopped. I could've been badly injured. And why did you coin my car? And leave the note? And I have no words for the breach of privacy letter."

Jess turned to her sister. "You did all that? Oh, Lily, how could you?"

Lily kept her face passive, but Emma saw a faint blush of embarrassment. "I won't make excuses. I was wrong on so many counts, and I apologise."

You've got that right, fumed Emma as Lily continued.

"I've got a lot of owning up to do, especially to Jess. I saw you get out of your car and head to the beach. I don't know what came over me. I was angry and upset. It was a stupid thing to do. And I apologise again."

"Why the note then? Why warn me?"

Lily looked at Emma, a puzzled expression on her face. "What note? I didn't leave any note. I ran past your car with my keys between my fingers and kept going. I live nearby."

Emma shuddered. If it wasn't Lily, then who wrote the note? Who else was threatening her? "Did you see a black SUV in the car park by any chance? It blocked me from leaving a couple of times before I got ahead of whoever it was."

"Sorry, no. As I said, I kept going."

"A black SUV? When was this?" asked Jess. "It better not have been Martin. I'll kill him when I see him if it was. I'm sick of it! I'm sick of his coercion and bully-boy tactics." Jess rested her head in her hands, scrunching her fingers into her hair. She lifted her head, her eyes resigned. "But we didn't come here today for that. Lily has something else to tell you."

Endeavouring to remain impassive, Emma said, "Sounds interesting," but felt a surge of anticipation.

"It's a very long story," said Lily, "and I won't tell you all the hows and whys now, but the two of us talked a lot as we sat by Mum's bed, and again when we got back to Jess's after Martin drove off. He wasn't pleased to see me."

"I can imagine," muttered Emma.

Lily settled back in her chair. "I've decided it's time to stop all the lies and pretence."

"Surely, this is something between you and Jess?"

Lily shook her head. "She tells me she wants you to know our story, warts and all, so I've agreed. She also tells me you're a great writer and would do a biography justice. If Jess trusts you, then so will I."

"I'll do my best. As long as there's no more antagonism."

"There won't be." Lily waved away Emma's comment. "Jess says you've done a lot of research already, but there are gaps. I might be able to help fill them."

"That would be wonderful, but how?"

"I have Elinor Somers's diaries."

24

Out of One's Control

March 1936

"Mam, Mam, come quickly. There's been an accident."

Elinor's heart sank and she shook as she put emergency supplies into her basket and changed her shoes.

"Where? What happened?" she demanded as the farm truck bounced its way down the race and through the paddocks.

"That tree that came down in the storm last year," said Ricky. "We were chopping it up and, I dunno how, but Pa slipped. He fell amongst the branches and got tangled. The cross-cut saw got jammed and ripped into his thigh, and his leg was at a funny angle when we tried to pull him out. He's bleeding awful bad."

"Drop me at the tree, then go to the neighbours. Ask to use their phone and call the ambulance while I see what I can do."

Joe looked grey as he lay on the grass surrounded by bits of branches, sawdust and debris. One leg was still trapped by the twisted branches, the other bleeding and bent beneath him. They needed to free him, and fast.

"Joe, my dear," Elinor said, as she knelt beside him and wiped his brow. She lifted his head and dripped water through his lips. "Let me see."

She edged closer to where Ted knelt by his father's knee, putting pressure on his thigh.

"Ted, let me have your belt." She tied it tightly around Joe's thigh, slowing the blood supply. "Bite down, Joe," she said, putting a folded cloth between his teeth.

With Ted's help, she pushed the torn edges of flesh together and bandaged his thigh as tightly as she could. The medical people could worry about cleaning it up later.

"Right, Ted, cut off those smaller branches so we can free his leg. I'll hold it still best I can."

Ted carefully sawed all around Joe's ankle.

"Be quick. There's not much time."

Joe cried out as his foot suddenly came free after the last branch fell away. Elinor took the weight until she and Ted could gently lower his leg to the ground.

"Let's get his boot off before the swelling gets too much. Bite down again, Joe." She cut the laces and opened up the tongue. "Ted, hold his calf while I ease this boot off. Gentle now."

Elinor concentrated on what she was doing, blocking out the sounds of pain Joe was trying to muffle. Fortunately, the boots were old and loose, and it slid off easier than she expected. "Good. No skin broken, no blood. With luck, this is a sprain."

She gently fingered the lower part of his other leg, and checked the bandages around his thigh, satisfied the bleeding was minimal. "The shin bone hasn't pierced the skin. I won't take this boot off, though. You'll need more than I can do. We'll wait for the ambulance."

No sooner had she spoken than Ricky appeared leading the ambulance to where Joe lay. Elinor was glad to leave it to more experienced hands now. She was shaking so much she doubted she could have done much more.

The two ambulance officers assessed the damage and eased the leg into a better position before lifting Joe onto the stretcher.

Elinor returned to the house, feeling empty and anxious, as the ambulance took Joe to the hospital. She wanted to be with him, beside him, but wasn't allowed in until visiting hours.

But with only short stays allowed, the days Joe spent in hospital were torture for Elinor and the nights lonely. She still blanched when she realised how close she had come to losing him, but he'd been fortunate. A sprain to his left ankle, a clean break to the right shin bone and the skin flaps had been sewn back successfully. The saw blade hadn't cut deep and had missed the artery.

Elinor moved furniture around, pushing some back against the walls to make a clear passageway for the wheelchair.

"Stop fussing," said Joe as everyone clamoured around when they brought him home, but Elinor could see he was delighted to be out of hospital. He needed to stay off his ankle for a few more weeks but could then use crutches for another month.

"I'm bored," he stated a matter of days later.

"And what am I supposed to do about that?" asked Elinor. "You have the radio to listen to, books to read. Play a board game with the children. Or I can give you fruit to peel. We can't bottle apples with the skins on."

He grumped and grumbled. He bossed the boys about, telling them what to do on the farm, complained about anything and everything – even the visits to the hospital for check-ups – until none of the children would try to entertain him any longer. She nursed him, washed him, cajoled him, loved him, as the girls picked up the rest of her chores.

Three weeks later, he was finally cleared to use the crutches. They, in turn, caused their share of arguments and frustration until he worked out a way of getting up and down the three front steps and could hobble out to the sheds.

"Away from the house. And all you chattering women," he threw over his shoulder.

Elinor let him go. She was tired of his persistent bad moods. She was six months' pregnant. Her back ached and she was having headaches that forced her to lie down some days, like today. She hated leaving the girls to do the housework, but she had no choice.

"How are you getting on with the apples?" Elinor asked, emerging from her darkened room.

"Depends on how many more are on the trees, Mam," said Ella, "but we've finished this batch."

Elinor thanked the girls as she admired the line of jars alongside the summer peaches and plums on the larder shelves.

Work on the farm continued, and Joe oversaw the

new litter of piglets and monitored the milk yield as the cows began to dry off in readiness for calving. As autumn came to an end, he was finally free of the crutches, the cast and the stitches.

Thankfully, Joe's mood improved once he could get out and about again, but Elinor found the endless grind of chores exhausting. She didn't understand why, especially since the girls had taken most of the load off her shoulders of late.

June 1936

The moment Joe walked in the door that afternoon, she knew something was seriously wrong.

"What's happened?"

"Let's put the kettle on and have a cuppa."

Suspicion mounted in Elinor's mind.

While they waited for the water to boil, Joe told her the news as gently as he could. "We've an opportunity ahead of us, Nellie. One we should look at seriously. We should even talk to the bank."

"Why would we talk to the bank?"

"We've been given notice."

Joe ignored Elinor's gasp.

"The boss says he wants to amalgamate the farms and have one manager oversee them all. And he wants the house."

Elinor's mind went blank. She could hardly comprehend what Joe was saying. She'd always known that one day they might not be able to renew the lease, but they'd lived there for twelve years. The longest she'd lived in any house, ever. Why now?

No, it wasn't her house, but she'd made it a home. The children all lived there still, other family and friends came to visit, they'd had good times – and sad times, when she thought of little Matt.

"When?" Her voice was barely more than a whisper.

"Twelve month this Gypsy Day. He's giving us a whole year to find a new place."

The first of June – commonly known as Gypsy Day, the day when sharemilkers, contract labourers and tenant farmers moved to new placements, new farms, taking their herds with them. Up and down the country, roads became congested, and the air filled with the sounds of horses' hooves clip-clopping, cows mooing, farmers whistling and dogs barking.

'Good luck.' A friendly wave from one family as they headed the opposite way to set up a new home, a new life somewhere else. A toot from another car as they passed.

Good for the industry, they said. Good for those wanting to make something of their lives, a step up the ladder to owning your own farm, they said. Good for the economy, they said. Harrumph, she said.

Within days, Elinor felt a change in her body. The headaches increased and at times she felt her stomach cramp. *Nothing to worry about*, she told herself. *Nothing to tell Joe about yet. It's too early.*

Another day passed, and Elinor began to look for the usual kicks and turns, pressing her hand against her stomach in search of an elbow or fist. At times, her body felt heavy, and she needed to lie down more often. She put it down to her age, but oh, how she loved babies. Their soft, dewy skin, their unique smell after a bath, all soap and talcum powder, swaddled tightly leaving a cherub face showing, the cuddles, watching them sleep, that first smile. Another baby would rejuvenate them all after a year of worry.

"Nell love, are you well?" asked Joe, interrupting her brooding. "You're not your usual self. Should you see the doc?"

"Leave me be, Joe. I'm fine. A little tired is all."

"Yes, Mam, I agree with Pa," said Ella. "I think you're coming down with something. You *should* see him. You need to look after yourself."

The rain fell to match her mood as Ella drove her into town. It was easier to give in than argue. Maybe she was coming down with something. That would be better. It couldn't be .... It couldn't.

"Mrs Somers," said the doctor in a tone that set Elinor's pulse fluttering. He'd examined her, and now she and Ella were sitting on the other side of his desk. "I'm sorry to tell you, but I believe your baby has died." He looked at some notes. Linked his fingers together and faced her. "I can detect no heartbeat, and given your age, amongst other things, this is not unexpected."

She listened as Ella asked questions and the doctor explained, knowing she would have to carry her dead baby for another two weeks or more before she was likely to go into natural labour. She would deliver a baby that would be taken from her forever. She would never feed it, bathe it, never see it smile. Never …

"Noooo, no … no." She broke down and sobbed, letting go of all the tension and anxiety she'd bottled up for so long.

Ella guided her from the doctor's rooms, leading her to the car and home.

She wouldn't even be able to give birth at home, like all the others. The doctor wanted her to go to the hospital, that clinical, soulless place smelling of disinfectant and despair.

Elinor walked straight through the house and retreated to her room. Her beautiful blue bedroom. She couldn't bear to talk to anyone, to see anyone, to explain. Her baby was dead. She had failed. She'd not protected her child the way she vowed to protect all her children. Her dreams vanished and she lost faith.

Joe came to her, took her in his arms, and together they wept for what they had lost.

They named her Julie, after the month she was born and had died and been buried. In the plot next to Matthew.

Every one of their children came to her, said, "I love you, Mam."

Later, Evie danced and played and sang. "For you, Mam."

With so much to hold dear, a large family and so much love, Elinor resolved never to let anyone or anything hurt any of her children ever again if she had any say in the matter.

By October, while the rest of the country, her children included, celebrated and rejoiced in the story of Jean Batten and her brave flight across the oceans from England, Elinor walked through her days numb with pain. Giving birth to her last child – because she knew with an inner certainty it would be her last – had drained all resilience.

Her cries came from her inner core. She'd given birth many times, she'd never miscarried. Her grief would not leave her.

With a matter of months remaining in which to pack up her life and start again, she couldn't bring herself to touch anything.

She should feel joy, optimism, hope for what lay ahead. Joe had called their next venture an opportunity. Why then, did she feel so burdened?

She would talk to her diary.

* * * * *

Elinor could pinpoint the moment her courage returned.

Christmas Day. Surrounded by her ten children – and she included Evie in that number – aged from twenty-seven down to seven; five girls and five boys, and Joe, her dearest Joe, Elinor acknowledged the extent to which she was the centre of their lives. She was the one they turned to, she was the one who shaped their lives, she was the one they pined for when lost in the mist of melancholy.

Not because they couldn't manage without her, but because they didn't want to. Each of them had their roles, their jobs, their position in the household and on the farm. Each of them had carried out those duties.

"You shouldn't have," she cried repeatedly as gift after loving gift was showered on her. "It's too much. I don't deserve all this," she said as she read so many wonderful words in the handmade cards.

"You absolutely deserve everything," said Joe, who knew more than anyone how she'd lain awake mourning.

The outpouring of affection was the glue for her soul. All the months where she had functioned but not engaged, vanished in that moment as she took in the lavish meal spread on the table, the decorations on the tree and the smiles and laughter of those she cared about.

"We love you, Mam," said Ella.

"Mam," said nine-year-old Evie, clinging to Elinor. "Are you coming back soon? I've missed you."

"Yes, my darling, I do believe I am."

In that moment, life returned. Her heart opened like a flower in the sunshine after the spring rains, and she was imbued once again with the joy of family. They sat around the table, pulling crackers, wearing silly hats, laughing at sillier jokes, bursting with jubilation. Evie played the piano while they sang and danced. Extended family and long-time friends visited in the afternoon and applauded Evie as she entertained them.

"I love you, Sprout," Elinor said that night, wrapped in his arms. "Thank you for filling my life with hope."

Somewhere during the traumas of 1936, the quietest and least forthcoming of all the girls, Millie, had grown up. The day after Christmas, when other family and friends arrived, more food was shared and conversation drew people together, Millie had a surprise.

"Mam, Pa, I'd like you to meet Bob."

Politely shaking hands and saying the right things, Bob looked nervous, unsure of his reception, but the way he looked at Millie convinced Elinor that her daughter had chosen well. She softly nudged Joe in the ribs.

"It's nice to meet you at last," said Elinor, knowing she hadn't taken enough notice of the things Millie had said about this lad.

Later that evening when only the immediate family were left, Bob stood up, pushed his chair under the table and gave a cautious cough. "I would like to ask your permission to marry your daughter," he said formally, bringing back memories of another lad at another time asking the same thing. "I believe I can make Millie happy, and I have good prospects for the future."

Bob wasn't a farmer. He was a merchant, working for his father, and expected to take over from him one day. Elinor knew the shop, a busy general store, but obviously Millie knew both it and the shopkeeper's son far better.

They asked the obvious questions and chatted about where they'd live, and how they would pay the bills, while Millie squirmed, but Bob did well for himself. Elinor squeezed Joe's hand under the table, giving her consent. Not that the girl needed it. At twenty-five, she could have decided for herself, but Elinor knew she would never marry without permission.

"Very well, lad," said Joe, standing up and extending his hand. "If our Millie is willing to accept your proposal, we are happy to give our consent."

Joe and Elinor watched as two people very much alike looked at each with love and deep contentment.

A wedding was on the horizon.

25

Unexpected Disclosures

Auckland
25 February 2021

The revelation that Lily had Elinor's diaries took them both by surprise, but since she refused to elaborate until after Anne's funeral, Emma had little choice but to wait. But if they were anything like the notebook she'd found with the dozen or so jottings, she was in for a treat.

Meanwhile, Emma's other issue, which she didn't know how to address, was the black SUV. How could she front up to Jess with the suspicion that Martin had deliberately tried to scare her? Especially now.

Jess had said Martin was back on medication, that he was calmer, that he was sorry for his behaviour, that she understood him and would stand by him. That everything would be back to normal soon. Emma doubted all of it. Martin was a bully. He knew what he wanted and when he got it everyone could relax, but if not, he kicked up a fuss.

Emma had no experience with mental health issues and the various phobias Jess talked about, but she believed Martin was more cunning than that and was using those as an excuse to dominate Jess. Emma was back where she started months ago, believing he was mentally abusing Jess. He was certainly trying to keep her and Jess apart and didn't want Lily around either.

But there was no doubt in Emma's mind now. If Lily said she wasn't the driver, then it must be Martin. What was he playing at? Maybe she should do some spying of her own. But how would she explain that to Luke?

"Are you sure you want me to come?" she asked when Jess invited her to attend the service for Anne.

"Of course I am. You're my best friend, I want you with me. It's not been easy these last few months, but you've stuck by me throughout."

Emma clutched Jess to her. They'd hugged a lot recently. "I haven't done much, but I'm always ready to listen."

"And now you're going to help me discover all the family secrets. Even Lily says she trusts you. So there you are."

Jess might have forgiven her sister, but Emma was wary, the memory of how that woman had harried her still fresh. "I'll do my best."

Emma found the simple service held at the chapel of the funeral home surprisingly moving. The numbers were small since Anne's friends from her previous life had dwindled and none remained to mourn her death.

Jess and Lily had chosen the music, the candles and flowers to welcome the family. The celebrant spoke words the sisters had written, read a poem that had been one of Anne's favourites, and let each person's memories fill the space. Emma noticed how Martin fidgeted and checked his watch, and looked bored the whole time. He didn't want to be there, and Emma wished he wasn't either. He was no support for his wife or child. Fortunately, Jess, Lily and Olivia clung together and didn't miss him.

They grieved for what had already gone from their lives and let their sadness slip away as they said their final farewells. They had mourned their mum over many years. Now she would be at rest with their dad, and through their loss they had found each other again.

Emma hadn't known Anne, but she would learn about her life and passions, write about her and give the sisters as much of their mother back to them as she could. She took in the atmosphere and watched the sisters draw strength from each other. A future beckoned.

As soon as the service was over, Martin whispered something in Jess's ear. She looked surprised, but he walked out without a backward glance. From where Emma stood, she could see him stride through the car park to a black SUV and drive off.

"That was a lovely service," said Emma. "Thank you for inviting me."

The two women looked drained; emotional exhaustion was taking its toll.

Lily looked around as Jess and Olivia spoke to the celebrant and funeral director. "I see 'he' has gone. Thank goodness. He's such a waste of space."

Emma forced herself not to comment. It wasn't her place, but she agreed wholeheartedly.

"Would you come to the interment, please?" Lily asked. "It would help if you could drive us."

"Of course," answered Emma. "Anything I can do to help."

Lily smiled then. A weird, brief grin edged with bitterness. "Can you find out what Martin is up to and get rid of him?"

"That may be beyond me. I'll text Luke and tell him what I'm doing."

"Martin said he had some business to attend to and would be back shortly," explained a dispirited Jess when she joined them. "He shouldn't be long."

"We don't need to wait for him," said Lily. "He can meet us there."

"Okay," Jess said with resignation.

The four of them piled into Emma's car, and she followed the hearse towards the cemetery, tailed by the celebrant.

"We both would have preferred a cremation," said Jess, sitting in the front. "But Mum wanted to be buried beside Dad, so that's what we've done. Our parents weren't churchgoers, but they liked to follow traditions."

"When were you here last to visit Dad?" asked Lily, after the car pulled to a stop and the four of them began to walk across the grass to the open grave.

"To be honest, not since the funeral. I've had so much on my plate."

Lily hooked her arm through Jess's. "I've been a few times, so there are some flowers already here, but we can put Mum's wreath on top."

"You make me feel guilty," replied Jess.

"Well you shouldn't. Not at all."

"I made a donation to the rest home," said Emma quickly, thinking it better than getting involved in any sort of discussion about family quarrels or Martin at this point. "Rather than bring flowers. I hope you don't mind."

"Not in the slightest," replied Lily. "That was very generous and thoughtful of you."

Emma wished Lily wouldn't answer for Jess all the time.

The celebrant began the traditional blessing, halting further conversation. Emma glanced up and saw the SUV pull up further up on the opposite side of the car park from where she was parked. Whoever was inside sat watching until the celebrant made her closing remarks.

Once the sisters, Olivia and Emma had thrown the flower heads the celebrant had supplied and said their silent words, and the thank yous were completed, they began to make their way back to the gate. Martin got out of the car and walked towards them.

"You're too late. You've missed it," said Jess as he got within hearing.

"Doesn't matter," he said. "She didn't mean anything to me. Daft old bat."

Emma swallowed her intake of breath but heard Jess's gasp.

"We'll talk about this later," said Jess. "But we have guests …"

"Who? Those two?" growled Martin. "Don't make me laugh. Bloody troublemakers."

"Please, Martin. Not now. I've invited them back to have refreshments. Will you drive us home, please?"

Martin glared at the three women in turn. "It's not

quite the way I planned it, but you had to know sooner or later."

Unlike the upset, pleading Martin whom Emma had seen in her house a short time ago, this Martin was a gloating, smug parody. She'd guessed he was up to something but even she hadn't expected this outburst.

"What are you talking about?" Jess's voice was shaking.

"I was going to say I've had enough, I'm leaving you, but today, at that bloody service, I decided it's you who is leaving."

"How dare you!" Lily's imperious voice was enough to bring everyone else up sharp, but Martin stared at her with a supercilious stare.

"I dare because I'm sick of being treated like a second-rate citizen by you, and her." He pointed at Emma. "Interfering bitch."

Martin took two paces forward and poked Jess in the chest. "And treated by you as a mental case in need of pampering. Those drugs you want me to take are evil. They're out to get me, all of them. You'll see. Well, I won't let them."

"I don't believe this is happening. Martin, what are you talking about? Why are you behaving like this?"

"We're done. No more talking. I'm not letting them control me any more." He strode towards the vehicle, lifted the boot and hauled out the suitcases and bags that took up the entire space, dumping them on the ground. He slammed the boot shut and walked around to the driver's door. "I'll send whatever else I find of yours to that bitch's place. If I feel like it."

Emma wasn't sure whether he meant her or Lily but either way, she could hardly believe how he had humiliated Jess, and worse, what he was doing to Olivia.

"Stay out of my life. Do you hear me?" His rage was so great he was almost screaming. "And don't try to come round to the house either. You're not welcome. I've changed all the locks." He pulled the door open and climbed in. "You'll be hearing from my lawyer!" he yelled through the window and drove off, wheels spinning, sending gravel chips flying.

Emma watched him leave, relieved that he would be gone from Jess's life for good, but appalled at being a bystander unable to do anything to alleviate her friend's pain.

Lily led Jess to a seat under some trees. Their soft rustling did little to relieve the lingering hostility. No one spoke for some time.

Olivia clung to Emma, her head buried against her side. Utter fury vied with Emma's struggle to stay calm for Jess and Olivia's sake. She didn't think Jess, or Lily for that matter, would be capable of coherent thought. She needed Luke. Not knowing how to explain, she texted, *Please come.*

"Would you like to be with Rosie?" she asked Olivia, smoothing back the hair from her tear-stained face. "You don't have to tell her anything if you don't want to. Just to be with someone while your Mum and I and …" Emma paused briefly, wondering how the child would make sense of all that had happened, and if she called Lily auntie. "… your aunt decide what's best."

Olivia nodded. Emma took her hand and they walked together to where Jess and Lily were sitting.

Emma's heart shattered with the look of despair and defeat on Jess's face. "I'm so sorry this happened. Please come back to our place. Olivia says she wants to be with Rosie, and we can have a couple of stiff drinks while we come up with a plan."

Lily appeared as shocked and angry as Emma but refrained from saying what she clearly wanted to say. "I think that sounds a good idea. Can you get all those bags and us in the car?"

"I've texted Luke. He'll be here soon," she said as Luke turned into the driveway with Rosie.

She walked over to him. "I'll explain more later, but Martin finally lost it, in front of us all. Those are their things. Jess is devastated. Rosie, sweetheart, Olivia is very upset. Can you play or sit with her and watch a movie? Can you do that for me?"

"Okay. Has her dad gone?"

"Yes, he has. Go to her now, while Dad and I load these things in the cars." Emma watched Rosie run to her friend and take her hand.

"I think I'll come back with you, Olivia and Rosie. Lily can drive Jess in my car. It'll give them a chance to talk privately."

"Are they staying?" whispered Luke, lifting bags and fitting some into her car and the rest in his SUV.

"Don't know. Olivia might want to. Jess may go with her sister. It could be a long night. I hope there's plenty of wine. And you're on takeaways." She kissed him on the cheek. "Thank you. I'm sorry I've had to bring this mess home, but I can't leave her."

"I wouldn't expect anything different of you. But what next?"

"Who knows?"

26

A Wedding and Other Possibilities

Glen Oroua, Manawatū
January 1937

The year began with a flurry of fabrics and patterns.

"Can I get married this summer, please? Before we move," asked Millie of her parents. "I've spent half my life here. I'd want to leave from here not some other place I have no connection to."

Elinor could understand her daughter's sentiment and since they needed to vacate the house by the beginning of June, there was no time to lose. Easter falling at the end of March seemed a good time for a wedding.

"Very well," agreed Elinor. "If that's what you want."

"Show me the sort of dress you'd like, and I'll make it," Ella told her sister, never once referring to her lost opportunity or the ideas she'd had for her nuptials nearly a decade earlier.

Amidst Millie's happy moment, Elinor couldn't help thinking about all Ella had missed out on – being a wife, a mother in a true sense, a home of her own. Selfishly, she was glad to still have Ella at home, but she would never deny her the chance of happiness when the time came.

A few days later, the three women shut themselves in Elinor's room.

"Ella, would you be my bridesmaid?" asked Millie, as Ella pinned the pattern base on her, taking Elinor by surprise.

Ella carefully removed all the pins from her mouth and pushed them into the wrist cushion she wore.

Elinor watched as Ella placed both hands on Millie's shoulders and looked into her eyes. "You are offering me a great honour and I thank you, but it's not a good idea."

Millie started to say something but was stayed by Ella.

"Not because I don't want to, or because I'm not grateful, but because I think it would spoil your day. People will look at me and pity me that my younger sister is getting married before me. Many will remember what happened and be sad for me. You don't want that. You want the happiest of memories. Ask Evie. She will light up the day for you, and everyone will remember what a wonderful day it was."

Elinor's heart overflowed with pride. She often wondered if any of the family had guessed that Evie was Ella's child. She doubted it. It had never been raised, not once, but she admired Ella's foresight.

"And match her up with Sam and you'll have a delightful wedding party," added Elinor. "I'll make a ring cushion for him to carry. I read about the idea in the *Woman's Weekly*."

The day arrived and the weather couldn't have been more perfect. Elinor fussed over the men's buttonholes, handmade from flowers in the garden, and straightened ties, making sure they looked their best.

"Ow, leave be, Mam. You're pinching me," said Ricky.

"Do I have to wear this stupid flower?" asked Archie.

Elinor ignored them all. Nothing would spoil Millie's day. "You look wonderful, Millie," she said, as her daughter emerged from the bedroom in the softly tiered dress that flattered her fuller figure.

Millie's veil, held in place by a circlet of fresh flowers, fell to the floor and extended a short distance behind. Beside her stood Evie, looking as if the world was at her feet, wearing a blue floral gown that frilled out around her knees. The girl never appeared anything but happy.

"What about me? " said Samuel, pushing forward to join his sisters, attired in a white shirt and dark-blue waistcoat and matching shorts, holding the cushion in front of him.

"Wait. I'll take a photo," said Elinor.

Joe handed the camera to her. "Happy?" he asked, grinning.

Elinor grinned back. "Go stand beside your daughter. I'll take one of the two of you."

A click and Elinor had another memory to add to her heart-filled store. A father and his daughter. Minutes later, they were in the cars, ribbons fluttering in the breeze, on their way to the church.

Elinor dabbed at her eyes from time to time during the service, thinking it strange she'd been to so few weddings in her life. Her own, nearly thirty years ago, but none of her brothers or sisters yet, a couple of Joe's siblings, and now their daughter. A day full of promises and happiness and the start of a new life, a new family, embracing whatever life threw at them. No one knew what the future might bring, but she prayed that Millie and Bob would have a prosperous life together.

Guests threw rice and confetti over the pair as they emerged smiling from the little country church. The photographer snapped photos of the happy couple and extended family. Briefly, Elinor wondered how Bob, as an only child, would cope being part of such a large, noisy family. But that wasn't her problem to worry about.

Noise inundated the little local hall, plate of foods satisfied empty stomachs and goodwill strengthened hearts and minds. Ella had been right. No one considered whether Ella should have been first or not.

The experience was a novelty for Elinor, one that left her elated, far more than she expected. She was letting one of her own leave the nest to make a new one. She was both losing and gaining, and she felt confused by the emotions flooding through her.

"Congratulations, Millie," she said, hugging each of them in turn. "And to you, Bob. I wish you every happiness and hope you'll know the love Joe and I have had in life."

Fingers crossed, they wouldn't know any of the pain or hardship.

Now the wedding was over, Elinor turned her mind to what next for her and Joe and the rest of the household.

Ever since Joe's announcement the previous year, they had spent every spare moment farm-hunting – with little luck. Either the land was beyond their reach – they'd found nothing they could afford that had a large enough house to go with it – or the better leasehold contracts had already been signed.

"I'm just too old," said Joe despondently one day after another possible farm contract had slipped through his fingers.

"Nonsense! There's years of farm work left in you, and you've got the boys."

Although she was also beginning to doubt if they would get a leasehold farm again. Many owners wanted younger men with young families as sharemilkers and farm labourers. Not a middle-aged man with grown-up sons and daughters. The owners were looking for security.

So was she.

She couldn't imagine them ever settling in a house in town, either – such as those new state houses that the government proposed. It sounded good in principle, but it would mean Joe and the boys finding work elsewhere. She hated the idea. They still had three at school, and it was enough that Dot and Connie had shop work, but the boys having to find other employment and live elsewhere was out of the question. It would split the family to shreds, and she couldn't allow that to happen.

She wrote letters, she scanned the daily newspapers, she asked around the community. She even briefly contemplated asking her brothers. But that would never do. She'd never shame Joe that much.

The month passed and it seemed likely they would

have to rent a house somewhere to give themselves time and then see what was available. But time was running out.

"I'll find something, anything, Nell," said Joe, his natural tendency to accept whatever fate sent his way coming to the fore. "I know nothing is quite working out as we'd planned. I'm sorry, love. I've let you down again."

Elinor was having none of that. "Don't you speak like that, Joe Somers. You've never let me down. We've always had a roof over our heads, food in our tummies and love in our hearts. That's all a body needs."

She shifted her thinking once again. Opportunity wasn't knocking, and her dreams would not yet be fulfilled, but she'd find a way.

"Hello, Millie love," said Elinor, surprised by her daughter's arrival in the middle of a weekday. "What brings you here at this time?"

"I've come straight from the shop. I just had to tell you. I think I've found something." Her excitement transferred itself to Elinor.

"Well, then, I'm glad you're here. I'll put the kettle on and you can tell me all about it. Ella's gone out, and your pa and the boys are down on the farm somewhere. He's not due back for a while yet."

"I can't stay. We had a customer in today. She's a regular, but today she looked very down in the dumps and upset. I got talking to her, and she told me her husband had died recently and they'd held the funeral a few days ago."

"No wonder she's upset," agreed Elinor. "Was he elderly?" She didn't want to imagine the day Joe died.

"I'd say she's in her late sixties, seventies maybe. They've lived on the farm all their married life, but here's the thing. They lost both their sons in the war."

"Poor woman," said Elinor, feeling genuine pity for this unknown widow. "Is there anyone to help her?"

"No. That's the problem. It's been the two of them and some workers running the place ever since. She wants to sell up and live with her widowed sister in Wellington, but she doesn't know how to go about it. She hasn't asked the estate agent yet. I thought you and Pa could talk to her. Maybe make an offer. It can't hurt."

Hope surged through Elinor's body. Was it possible?

"Here's the details," said Millie, handing across a piece of paper. "Please, Mam, give it a try. I think it's quite a few acres. They've been running sheep but there's a milking shed on the place. The house might be a bit old, pre-century even. I've got to go now."

"What about your tea?"

Millie hugged her mother. "Haven't the time, Mam, not today. Go talk to Pa."

Moments later, Elinor took off her apron, changed her shoes and began the walk down the farm. She had an idea where she'd find them. Joe had said something about fencing and firewood.

She heard them before she saw them. She was almost upon them before they heard her calling.

"Nell? What are you doing here? Is everything all right?"

"No. I mean yes, everything *is* all right. Joe, listen, Millie's been."

She explained everything and saw doubt in his eyes. She handed him the piece of paper with the address. "I think we should knock on the door and ask," said Elinor.

"Wouldn't that be rude? So soon after losing her husband?"

"She's on her own. She might welcome the company, and it might bring her – and us – peace of mind. Come on."

With instructions to Ted and Ricky about the work left to do, leaving a message on the table for when the others came back from school and Ella came home, she and Joe changed into their best clothes and climbed in the car. They chatted nervously about the what-ifs and maybes as they drove the ten miles to the farm.

"I can't see the house from here," said Elinor, "but those sheep are nice and healthy."

"They are, and the grass is doing well for this time of year. It's good flat land. I expected this area might be hillier."

"It could be down the back."

"Let's drive around the block and see what's what."

They slowly followed the fence line, seeing when the style changed at a boundary. Joe looked around at the expansive landscape and the line of trees, repeated in blocks and wrapping around corners, indicating the wind direction. "It could blow a bit here. It's nearer the coast."

"Maybe, but that tree line there could be their buffer," said Elinor, ignoring his pessimism and pointing several paddocks up the road. "That could be one boundary, and there's another stand over there."

Joe didn't speak for several minutes as he surveyed the area, taking in every dip and hollow, every tree leaning away from the wind, every animal and whatever buildings were in sight. "I think many of the buildings are hidden by the trees. This area has been well laid out in the past. It has a good feel about it."

"Then we should take the bull by the horns and go see this lady."

They made their way down the track, careful to shut the gate behind them. Loose gravel packed the wheel tracks but grass grew freely down the centre of the long driveway.

"Look, there's the house," said Elinor, seeing a building hidden behind several large bushes and backed by a stand of trees. "In a very sheltered spot." She twisted her head around to check the direction of the sun. "It'll have a nice sunny front porch."

Joe pulled up near the house. As Millie had said, it was pre-war, with a large bay window at one end, a full-length porch, several chimneys and an extension at the back.

"This was painted not that long ago," said Joe, getting out of the car. "It's in good nick."

"That's a hopeful sign," agreed Elinor shutting the passenger door. "That could mean the rest of the farm is top-notch."

"Good afternoon," said a voice from the porch. "Can I help you?"

Elinor and Joe introduced themselves to the woman looking down at them. Her white hair tied back in a bun and her wire-framed glasses added to the impression of a crushed soul. They explained how Millie had told them of her plight.

"Our condolences, Mrs Johnson," said Elinor once they'd been invited inside and had been given a cup of tea in the living room. "Losing your husband must be very hard for you."

Elinor admired the large, well-lit room. The high ceilings gave it an elegance she wasn't used to. But in many ways, it was a simple room, with a fireplace, windows on two sides and spacious.

"It is, as it was unexpected. He'd not shown any signs of being ill, but his heart suddenly gave out." She dabbed her eyes but smiled at them. "But what can't be changed must be endured. Now, what can I do for you?"

"If it's not too much of an imposition, I, that is, we," stumbled Joe, "we were wondering if you're thinking of selling."

The woman looked so sad, Elinor's stomach lurched.

"I might be," said Mrs Johnson, not giving away anything about the farm or her expectations. "It's not the same now he's gone. Archie and I came here when we were first married in the 1890s."

"We have a son called Archie," said Elinor.

"That's nice," replied Mrs Johnson, glancing Elinor's way. Pulling her shoulders back and sitting straighter, her demeanour changed and she became more intent. "Our boys were born here, but we lost them both in the Great War. Nothing great about war, in my opinion, but I can't change what's past. How many children do you have?"

Joe nodded to Elinor, indicating he wanted her to do the talking.

"We have ten children, five boys and five girls. One girl got married at Easter, but the rest are still at home.

We've been married twenty-eight years. The older boys work the farm with their father, the older girls are working in shops in town, except for our eldest, Ella, who helps me in the house. There's a lot to do looking after such a family. Three are still at school, although Archie will be leaving at the end of the year."

"A family," sighed Mrs Johnson. "How delightful. And where have you farmed before?"

Diffidently, Joe outlined their farming life, his knowledge, the boys' abilities. "We've been on leasehold farms … but … we have an idea … of maybe owning our own place. One day. I don't know if we can … but …"

"Young man," interrupted the woman, "stop dithering. If you don't try, you will never succeed. After our boys went, we had to rethink our lives. We were your age and farming was all we knew, but we had to change how we farmed. Sounds to me as if now's the time for you to change. You've a family to think of."

Taken aback by the sudden forcefulness of this seemingly meek old woman, Joe was speechless.

"Why don't you take a walk over the farm while I talk to your wife?"

Suitably dismissed, Joe did as he was told while Elinor and Mrs Johnson made small talk about the house, Elinor's family, Millie's wedding, Mrs Johnson's wish to go to Wellington to live with her sister.

"Now, just for your information. Don't tell your husband until you need to. I don't plan to take any of this stuff with me," – she waved her hand around the room – "apart from some personal items. It'll remind me of my life here with Mr Johnson, and my sister already has a house full of furniture. I don't need any of it. When I sell, and if I sell to you, if your husband can make his mind up, then it stays with the house."

Elinor began to think all her dreams were coming together all at once, but she held herself in check. Such good fortune had never been theirs before. "Surely not," she said, feeling she should protest a little. Mrs Johnson's furniture was far better quality than anything Elinor owned or was ever likely to own. She hadn't seen any of the other rooms, apart from the entrance hall and the living room they sat in, but it wouldn't matter. Either way, Millie's description of an old widow unable to handle the paperwork didn't fit with this resolute woman before her. "It's much too lovely to part with."

"But part with it I will. I've made my mind up. Now you need to decide what you want and get that husband of yours to make up his mind. Where is he?"

Looking at the big grandfather clock, Elinor realised Joe had been gone over an hour. On cue, they heard a tentative knock and a quiet 'hello'.

"Come in, man, for goodness' sake, come in," called Mrs Johnson.

"You have a very nice farm here, Mrs Johnson. Your husband … and you," he added, "deserve to be congratulated."

Elinor heard a quiet chuckle. Mrs Johnson was obviously pleased with the compliment.

"We should take our leave," said Elinor, gathering her gloves and handbag and standing up. "Thank you for your hospitality and letting us see your property."

"Goodbye, Mrs Somers, Mr Somers. I'll think it over and let you know my decision in due course."

On the way home, Joe crushed any hopes before Elinor dared raise them. "Forget it, Nell. We can't afford it. Never mind what. It's too grand for the likes of us. The outbuildings are well kept, even the milking shed they'd used for storage and shelter. The grass yield looks to be at the upper end, and the sheep are in excellent condition. The lambing numbers will be high come September, I should think. The two blokes I talked to said the Johnsons had been good employers, but they were off at the end of the season before new owners took over. She'll sell all right. As a going concern and a top price. Put it right out of your mind. It's not for us."

Elinor said nothing. Mrs Johnson hadn't mentioned price or when she wanted to sell exactly, or if she would sell to them. They hadn't visited the bank or applied for a loan, but if Joe was right, their budget would not be enough. There seemed no way forward.

Elinor put her dreams back in their box and shut the lid, but her mind began to scheme.

27

When Good Follows Bad

Auckland
25 February 2021

No amount of talking, glasses of wine or platitudes could solve Jess's longer-term problems, but Lily was surprisingly logical about the short term. "I've been thinking, not because of today, but because of lots of things lately, and I've changed my mind. We shouldn't sell the house. Not until *you* want to."

Jess looked astonished. "So why have you been so insistent on selling it quickly, with everything gone as soon as possible? I've been at my wits' end trying to meet your demands. I don't understand."

Emma kept silent.

Lily carefully replaced her wine glass on the side table, gathering her thoughts. "Because I truly believed I was protecting you and I wanted what was best for you." She held up her hand to stop Jess interrupting. "I know you'll find that hard to accept. I was mean towards you. I meant for that to happen. I wanted you to think badly of me. That I was uncaring. I wasn't. I visited Mum as often as I could when I was in the country, and I kept in constant touch with Dad and helped him finance Mum's care. Don't blame him. I made him promise not to tell you anything about what I was planning. He believed he was doing the best thing. Setting you free."

Jess appeared increasingly at sea. She stared at her sister. "You think what you did was setting me free!" she scoffed. "You have no idea."

Lily went on as if Jess hadn't spoken. "Until these last few weeks, I was convinced you'd be better off not knowing, but I was wrong. And I was wrong to make that judgement for you. I'm sorry. I promise to be a better sister in future – if you'll let me."

"I don't know what you expect me to say," said Jess. "I still don't have a clue what you're on about."

"Don't say anything yet," replied Lily, taking a fat envelope from her bag. "It's a long and complicated story, but you'll understand more when it's told." She stood and held the package out. "You'll find what you're looking for amongst these papers."

Jess stared at it as though afraid of what it would reveal. She shook her head. "Give them to Emma. We agreed it would be best for her to unravel everything and write the story."

"If you're sure."

Jess nodded and Lily handed Emma the envelope. "Tomorrow I'll bring the diaries around for you to read. They're enlightening, both about life as it was and why so many secrets were kept then, and have been, until now."

Emma accepted the envelope and put it to one side, resisting the urge to open it and satisfy her curiosity.

"Thank you. I'll do as you ask. There's an adage about secrets being revealed one person at a time – sometimes one generation at a time. We need to respect the people who kept them. They had their reasons, even if those reasons don't seem relevant to later generations."

"I'm glad you understand," said Lily, before redirecting her attention to Jess. "Now, back to the house. It's yours – well ours – but you and Olivia should live there."

"I couldn't. What about you?" whispered Jess. "It's not fair."

"Of course you can – and who said anything about fair? Life's not fair. Haven't you noticed? It's time I evened up the balance," said Lily. "And you and Olivia need a home."

Emma winced at Lily's bluntness but concurred.

"My place isn't far away," continued Lily. "When the pandemic hit, I came home and bought a modern, lock-up-and-leave apartment suitable for when I travel. Not that I've done much in the last year. But the house is more to your taste and you know it. You love antiques and period furniture."

Jess nodded, accepting what Lily was saying.

But Lily hadn't finished. "It's a good-sized property but we should modernise it. We can redesign some of the rooms for easier living and outdoor flow, put in new bathrooms and redo the kitchen without losing the original bungalow features."

Emma listened to Lily, slowly putting together something about Lily as a person. She lived alone, early forties, travelled for work, owned her own business, knew about design and property, was financially independent, and far more caring than anyone had given her credit for.

Emma realised that Martin's cryptic criticisms and Jess's tales of how she'd behaved had clouded her judgement of Lily, but she was beginning to like this woman, for her sincerity and forthrightness. Emma was a long way off forgiving her behaviour but at least now understood Lily had a motive. Forgiveness might come more easily once she knew what her motive was.

Lily was right about Jess and the house. She did belong there, amongst the memories and the furniture and belongings she reluctantly agreed to let go because Martin wouldn't want them.

"Ems?"

Emma dragged her thoughts back to Jess. "Sorry, I was away with the fairies. What did you say?"

"I asked if you agreed?"

"It's not my place to tell you what to do, but yes, I think it would work. Remember that day when we were sorting through everything and we opened up your father's desk. You loved the idea that your dad had made it. It brought back your childhood. I think you didn't go ahead and push through getting rid of the furniture or the house because deep down you didn't want to let it go."

Jess smiled for the first time in hours. "You're right. Both of you. I do love the house and the things in it. But I knew Martin would never let me keep any of it, and I thought you wanted it gone, Lil."

Lily coughed to cover her own emotions. "You don't have to battle that offensive brute any more. It's time to think of yourself and Olivia first. You can be who you want to be now. Go back to floristry and decorate the house with beautiful flowers."

Jess's face lit up suddenly. She fixed Emma with her eyes. "That day, when I was cleaning out the house and I told you I heard something …"

"I remember, but you didn't elaborate. You said it was the wind making the house creak."

"It probably was, but something spoke to me. Not real words, I'm not that crazy, but a sense that someone wanted me to stay. To make the place the heart of the family again. Silly, I know. There's no family left. Mum and Dad have gone, there's just Lily, me and Olivia now but still … like it was my legacy."

Silence filled the room as Emma, Lily and Jess contemplated her words.

"That was Evie," said Lily eventually.

"You know about Evie? Who *was* she?" asked Jess, mouth agape.

"A little," acknowledged Lily, "but let Emma discover what she can first, then I'll tell you what I know. Meanwhile …" She looked at the clock, drawing Emma's attention to how long they'd been talking and how hungry she was. The afternoon had disappeared into evening, and it was well past their usual dinner time. "… you and Olivia can stay in a hotel tonight, and tomorrow the two of you can move in."

"I can't afford that!" said Jess dejectedly. "I don't have much money. Martin controlled all our finances. I realise now he controlled everything. I've saved a little from when I was working, but it's not much. I'd love to give the house a go if I can. I have nowhere else. But I won't be able to do any of the fancy renovations you're talking about."

"Jess," said Lily sternly. "Listen to me. When I said

'we', I meant both of us together, or rather, when it comes to costs, it'll be me, because I have money. More than you realise. I'll do the renovations because they will add value to the house should we ever decide to sell. There's no room at my apartment, so I'll pay for whatever you need to be free of that hateful man and establish your new life. I will not leave you to flounder on your own again. Not ever. I promised Dad."

Emma had found more tears filling her eyes in the last few weeks than she'd had since Charli died. It was as if Lily had become the guardian angel sent to rescue Jess. She looked at the two sisters, seeing their eyes pool with love and gratitude. She cleared her throat. "You don't have to go to a hotel. You're both welcome to stay here until you get sorted. Olivia could sleep with Rosie, and we have a spare twin room. As long as you two don't mind sharing. I think we've all had a bit too much to drink to go driving anywhere."

The sisters looked at each other and nodded.

"That's settled then," said Emma. "I don't know about you, but I'm starved. Shall we see what Luke's concocted for dinner?"

Jess looked exhausted, but the tense, fearful expression had gone and her eyes were brighter. "Thanks for everything, Ems. You've been a good friend. And I've got my sister back again. Despite everything, I feel there's hope for the future now. But what a day!"

"What a day, indeed," agreed Lily. "But the law of opposites means that good comes after bad. And today brought good in the end."

Surprised by Lily's philosophical turn, Emma wondered where her thoughts had stemmed from.

"What do you do for a living?"

"Didn't Jess tell you? I'm an interior design consultant. A very good one. Mostly overseas, but I'm about to set up business here."

No wonder Lily had big ideas for Jess, if she was prepared to accept them.

After packing the girls off to school the following morning, Luke helped reload their two cars with all Jess's bags and belongings, and unloaded them at the house.

"Thanks, honey," said Emma. "I don't know when I'll be home."

"Do what you have to." He waved goodbye and drove off. When all of this was over, he would be waiting for her and they would pick up where they left off, the three of them.

Entering the house, she found Lily had thrust back all the curtains and opened the windows. Sunshine and fresh air flooded the rooms.

"I'm glad now I didn't turn off any of the services," said Jess, inspecting the kitchen cupboards, "but someone better get some groceries or we're going to starve."

"Give me an idea of what you want and I can do an online order then pick it up," said Emma. "I'll also shout us lunch later while you two do what you have to to get settled."

"First things first," said Lily. "This furniture needs rearranging. Just because Dad left it exactly as Mum had it is no reason for us to leave it as is. Let's check the bedrooms."

After completing the grocery order, Emma wandered around the living area. Jess and Lily were still deep in conversation and making lists. As before, nostalgia filled Emma as she let her gaze drift on the chiffonier, the lamps, the desk and much more, bringing the past into the present. A sense of peace came over her. Jess was right; someone wanted this house to come alive again.

Some of it was in serious need of an upgrade, but with a wall taken out here and there, and painted in lighter, brighter colours, it would be a wonderful home.

"Didn't I tell you?" said Lily as they returned carrying a throw rug each. "This is the perfect home for you."

Emma regarded the two sisters in animated conversation. The shadows under Jess's eyes told their own tale, apart from the shared grief obvious in both sets of eyes, Jess had a long journey ahead of her. Divorce was never easy, but Emma suspected this one could be messy. But with a roof over her head that Martin would have no claim to, her sister holding her hand along the way and her daughter to care for, she felt certain Jess would find her way. Some things even Martin couldn't take away.

For the rest of the day, the three women pushed and shoved and turned furniture until it was where Lily wanted it. The rooms began to feel different with each change. They threw out rugs and cushions, pulled down unnecessary curtains and lifted the hall runner to reveal kauri floorboards. With each move they made plans. Even Jess began to show more energy and enthusiasm as the day lengthened.

"Look at that floor," she gasped. Light from the stained-glass front door reflected on the rich, native-timber floors almost hidden under the old runner. "I never realised."

"Fabulous aren't they? We should lift all the carpet. With a fresh polish, the floors will look amazing," agreed Lily.

The sound of squeals and laughter charged the air as Rosie and Olivia ran down the hallway, their footsteps ringing on the newly exposed wood.

"Hello, my darling girls," said Jess, hugging both girls.

"Is this where we're going to live?" asked Olivia, her eyes agog.

"It is. Are you happy about that?"

"Oh yes, happy people have lived in this house, Mum."

Jess's eyes sparkled. "Then happy we shall be," she said, her voice croaking. "But how do you know people were happy here?"

Olivia shrugged. "Dunno. Just do. They're here all the time, especially in that front room. Can I have that room? Mum? Can I?"

Emma never knew where her instinct came from, that sixth sense that said something, good or bad, was in the air, yet she never expected someone as young as Olivia to feel it. She'd read about highly perceptive children, but they often had other signs and behavioural issues. Olivia had none of those, but Emma 'felt' the good vibes this house gave out.

"Will you put those photos of Dad's family back up?" asked Lily.

"Which ones were those?" asked Jess, looking confused.

Emma knew immediately. "The ones of a man standing beside a seated woman, a sad man holding a young toddler, and a family group?"

"Yes. How do you know them?" asked Lily.

"They were in the box of photos and letters Jess gave me to help my research, but I have no idea who they are."

"I know."

And in a moment, the family was back where they belonged, in a home that mattered to them, with a story to tell.

28

Never Again

Glen Oroua, Manawatū
May 1937

Elinor was riled, and she didn't care who knew, who heard. She was going to say her piece. She rarely challenged Joe about money, how he ran the farm, or about his inability to see that he … they … were more capable than he believed possible. But he'd gone too far this time.

"Joe, stop thinking you're second class. Maybe once you didn't know as much as my father and he made you feel guilty about that our entire married life, but he's gone. You can't carry that with you any more. You are your own man. You've managed this farm well, and we've done all right. And we'll do better on the next place."

"If I can find a next place."

Joe's despondency was getting on her nerves. How was she going to get him to buck up? "Stop it, Joe. Just stop. Stop putting yourself down. I'm sick of it. I'm sick of being in someone else's debt. I'm sick of kowtowing to the boss. We can look elsewhere. We can move further afield. We can, Joe, we can."

"I'm sorry …"

"Don't you say you're sorry again, either, Joe Somers. You've been sorry all your life. I'm sick of sorry. Do something."

Elinor stomped out of the kitchen, leaving Joe and the rest of them sitting in stunned silence, and retreated to the bedroom. Her precious blue room, with all her treasures, the place where she and Joe were one, where nothing else mattered except the love they shared. But not right now, not today.

She sat on the dressing-table stool, where she wrote all her thoughts, both happy and sad, in her diaries. She couldn't bring herself to write anything yet, she was too angry. Far angrier than she'd ever been. Angrier, even than all those years ago in Pahīatua when the bank had threatened to foreclose and they'd had to give up the first house she'd begun to call home.

In the end, the insurance money for the fire had saved them from bankruptcy. From there, they'd come to this place, survived the worst of the depression and, if not thrived, had grown. Until now.

This time, it was the owners, wanting more for less, wanting bigger returns with less responsibility. They would be out on Gypsy Day whether they had a place to go to or not, such were the rules.

It's not right! It's not right that they can take my home away; take the roof from over the heads of my children.

Fighting back the tears – of anger, of despair, of misery – she tried to make sense of what Joe had told her. She stared at their wedding photo and slammed it face down.

He'd accepted a job as a farm labourer and agreed to rent an old house down by the swamp near the river in the Moutoa area, near Foxton. That he'd done all that without telling her was more than her temper could take. Worse, he'd told the boys they needed to find work and live elsewhere.

Given time, she'd pull herself together and make the move but not before he'd suffered the consequences of his decision. And she had a plan. She would never put her family in jeopardy again. She'd lost one to pneumonia in this cold, draughty place. She'd not live by the swamp. Not if she had any say in the matter.

With less than two weeks to go before moving day, Elinor paid a visit to Mrs Johnson.

"I was hoping you'd come by, dear. Did you get my letter?"

"Letter?" asked Elinor. She'd seen no letter. She wondered what Joe hadn't told her; what he'd kept hidden.

"The one with my offer, of course."

Elinor followed Mrs Johnson up the hall into the kitchen. Her mouth nearly fell open at the sight before her. It was light and bright with a hanging rack stocked with pots and pans above a central table, running water, a window above a large butler's sink, and a coal range in pride of place. It was the loveliest room she'd ever seen.

"Your offer, yes, of course. Yes. That's while I'm here, well partly. Yes." She accepted the proffered cup of tea and sat down.

"Is that a yes, you are accepting my offer, or a yes, you know about the offer, but no, you don't want to take it?"

"Neither, actually. I'm not sure, but I did want to talk to you."

For well over an hour, and several cups of tea, Mrs Johnson and Elinor chatted.

"Thank you, my dear," said Mrs Johnson as Elinor was leaving. "I feel happier now. I was worried about you and your family."

"Thank you for your advice. I would never have thought of such a thing without you."

"Two heads are always better than one, especially when they are female heads." She giggled and Elinor could see the sort of young person she must once have been and wished she'd known the woman longer.

Later that afternoon, Elinor spoke to Ella. "Promise me you'll say nothing of what you see to your father?"

"What are you planning, Mam?"

"I'm putting some of these boxes I've packed up into storage, that's all. I don't want them at the swamp house. I don't intend to be there long. It's a roof over our heads until I find something else. I'm not leaving this to your father any longer. Trusting him to do the best was the worst mistake."

Deciding she'd said enough against Ella's father, she and Ella loaded up the car and Elinor headed off. A while later she was back to repeat the exercise.

"I'll do another couple of loads tomorrow," she said after the second trip. "I don't want your father to catch me."

She and Ella bustled around the kitchen preparing the meal, seeing to the younger children returning from school and finishing off the chores. "Have you done your packing, Ella, dear? Is there anything you want to go into storage? There's so little room at the swamp house."

She wouldn't tell Dot and Connie what she'd done until they discovered what was missing – if they did. The boys wouldn't notice at all.

"I could probably find some things I could put away that I won't need straight away," said Ella. "My summer clothes and some bolts of fabric, for a start. I wouldn't want them to get damp."

"Could you do it soon then, love? I'd like to get this finished so we're only left with the basics and essentials to move on Monday."

On Friday, 28 May, the cold wind howled, whipping the trees left and right, rattling anything not tied down.

"Careful of the doors," shouted Elinor as Ricky came in, narrowly avoiding blowing everything over inside.

"We're off now," he said. "Pa says we should be back by dark, all going well."

Joe and the four boys including Archie, whom she'd allowed to duck out of school, were taking the hay bales and some of the smaller farm equipment over to the swamp house.

"Be careful," she said automatically, her mind racing ahead.

Being a Friday, Dot and Connie planned to go to the movies after work as usual. It would be bedtime before she saw them again. Ella had gone out for the day, saying she'd be back in time to make dinner. Evie had dancing practice after school, and Sam would be with her.

Elinor was on her own. She needed to make the most of it.

As soon as the truck was out of sight, she raced around the house grabbing the last of the things she wanted. She stripped her dressing table of all her treasures, taking a few moments to rub her hand over the photograph of her and Joe on their wedding day and reflect on what life had brought them. Shoving it in a bag along with other last-minute things, she gathered the other bags she'd packed and took them out to the car, delivered them to the storage place and returned. She stoked up the coal range, put a pot of soup on to simmer and carried some other pots and pans out to the washhouse ready to clean later.

The day grew dark and Elinor turned on the light. The single bulb hanging from the high ceiling in the centre of the room barely made any difference. She lit a few of her old lamps. She preferred them in many ways. They were gentler, washing the walls with warmth. She switched on the radio, thinking how much she loved its company. She sat in her fireside chair, listening to the music, hoping it would help calm her nerves. She picked up some knitting, winding her way to the end of the row and back, but couldn't settle. She left it on the chair, the skein poking out of the canvas bag on the floor, and put the kettle on to boil. Pulling a cloth down from the rack above her head, she lifted the lid on the soup, stirred and tasted it. Satisfied, she put the lid back on, the cloth folded neatly over the handle. She rechecked the house, inspecting every item, deciding whether she needed it or not. There wouldn't be time to decide later.

Time passed slowly. She looked outside, considering if she should battle the wind and get more firewood. She pulled her coat on, buttoned it up and dashed outside, returning a short time later with a small armful of wood. It would keep the fire going for now. She spread newspaper on the floor and stacked the wood on top, brushing the loose bits of debris off her front.

Finally, the hands on the clock ticked around. She could pick the children up from school and take Evie to dancing. She opened the door ready to leave. The wind whistled in, lifting the edge of the cloth on the table. A flame flickered under the hurricane glass, and the fire in the coal range flared. She heard a door slam at the back of the house.

One last look around, satisfied that everything was as it should be, she left without a backward glance.

The house was well alight by the time she returned with the two youngest an hour or so later, as dusk was falling. Somewhat to her surprise, Joe and the boys arrived soon after. A neighbour had tried to throw buckets of water at it, but it was hopeless. The area was well outside the fire brigade zone. Nothing would save it.

"Oh, Mam," cried Evie. "The house. And all our things."

Joe helped calm Evie and Sam as they braced against the wind, watching the flames whip into a frenzy, and listened to the roaring crackle and bangs as the house collapsed, bit by bit, before their eyes.

News spread quickly; neighbours raced around to do whatever they could to help. Using coats, sacks, tarpaulins, anything they had in their vehicles or could find, they soaked them in the water troughs and beat back any stray embers.

"Take this," one called.

"Be careful," said another.

The wind fanned every flame, the work hot and dirty, and the noise drowned out many calls of warning.

As soon as they could get near the house, they made sure everything was smothered and confirmed the outhouses were safe. Fear of the fire spreading galvanised them to keep working until they were certain every ember was doused.

"Where are we going to sleep?" asked Evie, clinging to her mother, her spirit dampened for once.

After the initial panic, realising all they had was what they stood up in and what was in the sheds and outhouses, came the decisions about what to do next.

Elinor looked at Joe, who'd appeared beside her wiping his brow of sweat and dirt, leaving a streak of ash smeared across his cheek. "Good question. What's your answer?"

Eleven people to house was no easy task.

"Could the girls go to Millie?" he asked, knowing their cottage was small, with limited space.

"Dot and Connie, possibly. They're still in town at the movies, but Evie and Sam stay with me."

"I'm staying with Mam," said Ella, who had returned with the shopping to stand mute and watch the fire burn itself out.

Elinor briefly hugged Ella. "What about the boys? And you?" she asked Joe.

"Me?" He looked at her in utter shock, but her steely-eyed gaze forced him to glance away sheepishly, accepting his role in their troubles. "We'll have to go to Ma's and my brother's place, I suppose. For the night, anyway." It would work, at a push. Five men took up a lot of space. "Could you and the girls go to your mother?"

Elinor shook her head. "Too far away, and there's no more trains tonight."

More people arrived to help. Someone shouted, and Joe turned to answer. He walked towards the group saying thanks to everyone he passed.

Millie and Bob left minutes after they'd arrived to collect Dot and Connie from the movies and keep them for the night. Then her nearest neighbour and Women's Institute friend, Sally, arrived with flasks of tea and sandwiches, a first-aid kit, blankets and towels. She wrapped a blanket around Elinor's shoulders.

"Come and stay with us tonight. We've got space for you and the little ones."

"And Ella?" asked Elinor.

Sally never missed a beat. "Of course, as long as you don't mind sharing."

It wouldn't be the first time in their lives her family had shared beds. "That would be lovely, thank you."

Those remaining stood in silence. Too shocked to make conversation. Once the helpers had said their farewells, only the family was left.

"What about you, Nell?" asked Joe, looking utterly worn out and defeated.

"For once, Joe Somers, I'm looking after myself and mine. Off you go. I'll see you tomorrow. We've a lot to talk about." She pulled the letter she'd found from Mrs Johnson out of her pocket, and waved it at him. "And you have a lot of explaining to do."

"You've done what?" demanded Joe the following day as he and Elinor sat around Millie's dining table. The family had found plenty of reasons not to be around.

"I've accepted Mrs Johnson's offer," repeated Elinor, although she knew perfectly well he'd heard and understood the first time.

"Without talking to me?"

"Don't try that one with me, Joe Somers." She always used his full name when she was mad, and she was as mad as hell. "You hid this from me, you didn't tell me about it at all. You would have let me live in that swamp house while you worked yourself to death as a labourer. I'm ashamed of you."

"Enough of the arguing!" He thumped the table. "What choice did I have? Tell me. What choice? We had no choice. We still have no choice. We can't afford the place, Nell. We don't have the money, so what's the point in talking about it?"

"I managed to talk about it." Elinor forced herself to calm down.

"Doesn't change a thing. You'll have to go back and tell her we can't take it. We can't afford it, Nell. Don't you understand? I asked the bank and they said no. And now we have nothing except the animals, and nowhere to graze them. Not even a stick of furniture."

"That's where you're wrong, Joe. There was a choice, and I took it. And we have the insurance money."

He looked at her suspiciously. Nothing would change the outcome. They'd lost everything. "I don't agree with you. And the money for the furniture won't be enough. I can't see how …"

Elinor didn't let him finish. "You went too far expecting

me to live in the swamp, and now you're underestimating me again. Mrs Johnson's offer is a good one."

She could see the bluff and bravado drifting away, leaving the uncertain, self-doubting Joe.

"I'm sorry, Nell love. I know I've failed you …"

"Not that again. Stop, Joe. I don't ever want to hear you say I'm sorry again. This is more important than self-blame and accusations. We can do it. I've done the figures. I even had the bank check them."

"You went to the bank? Alone? Without me? Without telling me?"

For the first time in her life, and she hoped the last, she had challenged the head of the house about money and major decisions. He was as incredulous and angry as she expected he'd be, but she couldn't give in now. "So it's my turn to apologise for not consulting you. But it was the only way I could make you see sense. This is right for us, I promise. Look at the figures, what she is offering and you'll see for yourself."

Elinor watched Joe as he scanned the papers she'd passed over, saying nothing, letting him absorb the details. Then she slid a little bank book across.

He stared at the balance and then back at her. "What's this?"

"My savings, from selling eggs and some of my spun wool, and from the housekeeping. Ella's garden and sewing saved us a lot of money. Little bits I stashed away over the years. It's enough for us to start again, Joe. All Mrs Johnson wants is a first-year payment up front, and equal sums over five years. The bank said on that basis they could lend us enough to meet the initial payment and get established."

Elinor watched Joe as he sat there, silent, staring at the papers, a frown creasing his brow. She had taken his pride, something she'd promised never to do. She got up from her chair on the opposite side of the table and knelt in front of him. "Dearest Joe. You are a wonderful father, a loving and caring husband, you've given me a family, and love, and a hearth. Everything I'd always wanted. Now we have a chance to have a home of our own. That opportunity you talked about last year. Please say yes. Please don't let it slip through our fingers. Say yes. And say you'll forgive me for forcing your hand. For not talking to you first."

She waited, expecting his anger, expecting him to fight, to rail against what she'd done. She pulled out her last argument. She reached up, and touched his face. "We'd be doing Mrs Johnson a favour. She's been so unhappy since she lost her husband. It brought back memories of her sons. She doesn't want to live there any more. She's even leaving the furniture. Can you believe that, Joe? She wants us to have it, since she won't need it at her sister's. She want us to have it. She's done all this for us, so she can see a family live in the house that hasn't had one for so long. She set it all up. We can't say no."

Elinor watched expressions of disbelief, defeat, relief and reawakening cross Joe's face before he wrapped his arms around her and stood up, lifting her up with him.

"You are the most amazing woman I have ever known, Elinor Somers. I don't know what my life would have been like without you, and I hope I'll never find out. You've stood by my side through thick and thin. How can I deny you this?" He kissed her deeply.

"Do you mean it?" Elinor might have done the hard work, verbally agreed to Mrs Johnson's terms, but if Joe refused to sign the papers, then everything was lost. "Do you really mean it, Joe? Will you sign the papers?"

"I'll go to the bank … No, *we'll* go to the bank – today. Now. And double-check everything, but if what I'm reading is correct and the bank confirms it, then yes. We'll do it!"

He reached for her again, but she ducked, laughing. "Behave, Joe, now is not the time."

"Thank you, Mr Somers," said Mrs Johnson when they signed the papers the following Monday. "I hope you will be very happy."

As part of the agreement, Joe agreed to manage the sale of the sheep on her behalf, providing Mrs Johnson with extra cash in her hand and clearing the land for Joe's milking herd and the other animals.

She smiled at Elinor. "I can't wait to be with my sister. I'll leave this afternoon. I'm all packed, and you need a place to live right away, so I hear."

She left them, promising to organise a carrier within a few days to collect the remaining possessions she wanted to keep.

"Don't rush, Mrs Johnson. I'm happy to keep them safe until you need them," said Elinor, knowing she still had to tell Joe about the boxes she'd put into storage in Mrs Johnson's garage. All the things they treasured most, none of which had been lost in the fire. She had no idea what she'd have done if Joe had refused to accept her plan.

Later that afternoon, the convoy of farm trucks, the boys' vehicles, their car, Ella's car, followed by Millie and Bob, brimming with food, made their way down the driveway to their new home. Tomorrow they would shift the animals. Joe needed to quit his labouring job before he started and sort out the swamp house. But she'd think about all that later. Tonight was for celebrating.

They walked into the house in awe of the character and style of the well-kept old villa. Each room welcomed them with open arms as if it knew they belonged there, but the note on the table brought a glow to Elinor's eyes.

Welcome to Elinsmore.
Your forever home.

I've renamed it after you. Your dreams have come true.
    A new sign will be erected on the gate tomorrow.
    My mind is now at rest and my heart at peace. There is a family, not mine and Archie's as we'd planned, but a loving family nevertheless, to continue our legacy.
    I wish you happiness.

Thank you.
Betty Johnson.

"Elinsmore!"

29

The Truth At Last

True to her word, Lily had presented the diaries to Emma. She'd sat up half the night, that first night, reading, turning page after page, wanting to know what happened next. Not that any of them were chronological or sequential. Occasionally, they were dated. Which month or which year would require more reading and date matching to be certain, but Emma found that didn't matter. A life story unfolded before her eyes, representing several generations and many individuals.

The papers Lily had given her allowed Emma to finally assign the generations correctly, but none of them fitted as smoothly as she'd hoped. She debated how to present the truth, as Lily called it, in a way Jess would appreciate. Lily, Emma discovered, had known some of the facts, but only since their father's death had she been given the full picture.

Unbeknown to anyone, the mysterious Evie had revealed every secret the family had ever held, to be shared only after the death of Edward Shaw. Her lawyers had been instructed to pass on the family papers and diaries to his eldest daughter.

'I'm glad I was home when I received the package,' Lily had told her. 'I don't know why exactly, but it felt right that I could visit the places and cemeteries and see for myself. It's taken me all this time to decide Jess needed to know, too. My secret wasn't hers to share. The wider family secret was.'

Emma had closed the cover on the final diary, feeling emotional. Since then, she'd had time to reread some parts and recheck her facts. She could understand Lily's dilemma and needed to present those facts carefully. Jess would be hurt by both the truth and the ongoing deception, whichever way she looked at it.

A few days later, when the current round of restrictions had ended, Jess called, full of enthusiasm. "I'd love you to come around and see what we've done to the house. I feel so at home surrounded by the things I grew up with. Lily's here. She's been marvellous."

"I'd love to," said Emma instantly. "And I'd like to talk to you about what I've come up with."

"Can't wait! See you tomorrow."

Jess was so excited she showed Emma through the house before giving her a chance to sit down. A semblance of the old Jess shone through as she grinned at Lily at every turn. She chatted about the soft furnishings – the chair covers, brightly coloured cushions, duvet covers and towels, the odd vase and bowl. Small things, but with an eye on when it would all be completed.

She showed Emma the plans Lily had sketched for the alterations scheduled for the coming months while Lily looked on with a smile of satisfaction. Emma was impressed. She could see the renovations had become a welcome distraction and were helping to relieve the depths of Jess's grief – for her father, for her mother, for her marriage. But she noticed Jess was also using them to put off the moment when Emma would reveal whatever she'd found.

Jess had gone from desperate to know, to being afraid to know.

Finally, the three of them sat in the lounge chatting over a cup of coffee.

Their father's desk, with all its secrets now revealed, sat in pride of place against one wall freshly wallpapered with a large floral design reminiscent of days past but modern at the same time. The three photos now identified as Elinor and Joe Somers, Joe and their son Matthew, and an older Elinor and Joe surrounded by their ten children, were artistically placed on top.

Lily set her cup down. "Let's start, shall we? I'll let you do the talking, Emma. You'll do a far better job of explaining than I would."

The time had come for Emma to reveal what she'd discovered.

Suddenly nervous about the task ahead of her, Emma turned towards Jess. Explaining it succinctly was going to be difficult enough, but she had no idea how Jess would respond to the bombshell to come. Lily had struggled for months to get used to the idea, and much of her unpredictable behaviour stemmed from that knowledge.

"Stop me if you get confused," said Emma, "but only if you must. It would be easier if you let me finish and ask questions after, because some things become clearer the more they develop."

"Okay," replied Jess. "I'm a bit nervous, if I'm honest. But Lily says it's a good story."

Emma made herself more comfortable in the armchair.

"I'll start the story of the five Es, as you've always called them, with the original Eleanor, known as Nora. She was born in 1846 and married James Marshall at age twenty-three. She remained in the Canterbury region her entire life. The men were mostly butchers and slaughtermen and, from what I can gather, some of them lived in close proximity to each other. She died in 1922, aged seventy-six. They had eight children, the eldest of whom was Emily."

Emma shuffled some papers, put aside those she had finished with, and moved on. "Number two in line is Emily. Born in 1870, she married a Robert Harwood at the age of eighteen. Why Emily and Robert left Canterbury is unknown, but they moved from place to place, probably in search of work, and finally settled on a farm in the Pahīatua district, where she lived out her life. She outlived her husband by twenty-three years and died in 1955 at the grand age of eighty-five. They had six children, one of whom died as a baby. The oldest was the second Elinor."

So far, so good, thought Emma, settling more easily into the story.

"I am assuming this Elinor was named after her grandmother, Nora. That was a common naming pattern, but the spelling is different. But, dear friend, *she* is the indomitable Elinor Somers. Number three in the line. The one we have been searching for since you first brought me that funeral notice. She is the author of the diaries, and her life is the core of the biography I will write for you – separate and different from Anne's. Everything and everyone else revolves around this Elinor. I can see why she was considered so steadfast and strong-willed. She must have been a true lionheart. She was born in 1889. She married Joe Somers at age nineteen. They had ten children.

"If we think about that era, we can understand something of her life. She experienced two world wars, the Spanish flu pandemic, and the Great Depression of the late 1920s and into the '30s. They were desperate, frightening times, when money and food were scarce. She would have encountered major floods and devastating earthquakes, including the Napier one in 1931. She lost two children – one as an infant and one a stillborn girl. The family was constantly on the move until the late 1930s. Her eldest was Ella. Number four of the Es."

So far Jess and Lily looked content with her explanation. Emma had knowingly skimmed over a lot of the finer details wanting to create an overall picture before they got bogged down. Ella was more complicated.

"Ella Somers was her mother's right hand, helping her raise the children, grow the vegetables and survive the worst of times. In 1928, three important things happened. Ella's fiancé was killed in a riding accident, her brother Matt, Elinor's fifth son, died aged two years eight months, and a baby girl was born. According to the records, Joe registered the child as Evelyn Jackie Somers and named the parents as himself and Elinor."

"Evelyn?" queried Jess, taking note of the name.

"Yes. However …" Emma paused. She'd reached a point where the details were vital to understand. "The diaries tell a different story. And I have drawn up a chart to help you understand it all better when we're finished." Emma hoped the family tree would make sense to Jess.

"In truth, the baby girl was Ella's. To save her the shame of being an unwed mother after her fiancé died, her mother Elinor pretended the child was hers and incorporated her into the family, counting her as daughter number five. But there's more to come for Ella."

"Truly? That's astonishing," said Jess, sitting forward in her chair, hanging on Emma's every word.

"In 1944, Ella married John Shaw. She was thirty-four. I can't find out much about him before he appears on the scene, but the diaries say he was a mechanic. Their first child was born early in 1945. A girl, named Elizabeth. At the time of their marriage, conscription was in force, and he was a late call-up. Ella returned to live in her parents' home while her husband went to war. Before long she was a widow. He was one of the last thousand or so men taken in the final battles."

"That's sad. Poor woman," murmured Jess.

Emma shifted in her seat and put aside another page. Her nerves were starting to get the better of her. "Meanwhile, Evelyn is now seventeen and a talented dancer and a gifted pianist. She goes to Auckland with her dance school for a contest, which they won, but she doesn't return with the group. According to the dance mistress, or so Elinor wrote, Evelyn was swayed by the charms of one of the international theatre managers."

Emma let Jess digest each piece of information before she added more. "In 1946, Ella gives birth to twins: Edward and Elaine. At least, that's what the birth certificate shows. The father is listed as deceased."

Jess has been following Emma's recitation, nodding to herself. "So Ella was Dad's mother! But he said he was number six in the direct line of Es. Who was number five? And I've never heard about a twin. Have you, Lil?"

"Not until I read the diaries, no. But don't jump ahead, Jess. There's more to come."

"That's where these diaries have become so precious in uncovering your family history," continued Emma. "Ella raised Elizabeth, Edward and Elaine as Shaws, in her mother's home, as part of the wider family. But do your maths. Ella and John married in 1944. Elizabeth was born early 1945. He was called to war and died in the last few months of 1945, and the twins were born in 1946."

Jess gasped. "So if Ella wasn't their birth mother, who was? Was it Evelyn? Was she Dad's mum?"

"She was," confirmed Emma.

Anger flared. "Why didn't we know? Why wasn't she a grandmother to us, like everyone else had?" Jess continued to fire question after question. "Did she get pregnant that time she stayed on in Auckland? Where did she go? Why didn't she keep them …?"

She suddenly ran out of steam. "I don't understand. What was Ella to Evelyn again? Her sister?"

"Ostensibly, yes. According to official records. But

remember, Elinor wrote that Ella was Evelyn's birth mother, even if she grew up believing Elinor was her mother and Ella her sister. She believed that right through until 1978."

"1978? Why then?" asked Jess. "Oh that's when Lily was born."

"Yes. More importantly, it was the year Elinor Somers died and other truths were revealed."

"Such as?" asked Jess, no longer sticking with the request to wait until the end of the story.

"In 1978, Elaine, your father's twin sister, died giving birth to her baby daughter."

"Oh. Poor Dad, to lose his twin and his grandmother in the same year. How terribly sad. What happened to the child?"

This was the moment when the secret that had bound Elinor, Ella and Evelyn together for generations would change everything Jess believed.

Emma hedged. "I'll tell you shortly, but first you have to understand how Elinor's death changed the family dynamics. Elinor Somers died a few weeks short of her ninetieth birthday. She had been the matriarch for decades, holding her children close. At the time of her death, her eldest daughter, Ella – herself approaching seventy – still lived with her.

"Ella became the new matriarch, but without Evelyn, the story would have ended there. And the truth would never have been known. Elinor's last entry before she died freed Ella to acknowledge her daughter, and on Evelyn's fiftieth birthday to give her Elinor's diaries."

"Wow, that's some story," said Jess sorrowfully. "Evie was my grandmother but I never knew her. Do you know why? Did she continue the diaries? Is that what you're saying?"

"Yes. Evie continued to write the family history. Not daily entries, and less about everyday life and minor things. Her entries covered major events and changes. But we need to backtrack a little. Remember, Ella is approaching seventy and for the first time can call Evie her daughter. Ella wrote a letter saying she wanted to keep silent, so as not to shatter Evelyn's lifelong beliefs, but the diaries were too valuable to be ignored and Elinor's wishes must be followed."

"Oh, dear. What a dilemma."

"For goodness' sake, Jess," snapped Lily, "will you shut up and listen."

Chastened, Jess indicated Emma should carry on.

"For Evelyn, who had lost the person she thought was her mother, the revelation comes as a great shock. Her mother became her grandmother. Her sister became her mother. Her siblings turned into aunts and uncles. And she discovered she had a new half-sibling in Elizabeth – Ella's daughter by John Shaw. In that same year, Evelyn's daughter Elaine died. All of which puts a vastly different perspective on family relationships."

"How complicated. How would anyone untangle news like that?"

"Jess …" warned Lily.

Emma looked towards Lily, implying she should say something. She'd already read the diaries. She knew what they revealed, but she appeared content to sit and listen. A small nod came in answer.

"Maybe they didn't tell anyone else," Emma continued. "There's no way of knowing. She doesn't say in her diaries. But whatever their relationship – as mother and daughter, or as sisters – Ella and Evelyn still shared a secret they were forced to reveal when Elaine died."

Emma starts to feel more uncomfortable. Her next words are about to change Jess's life. "Your parents had been married for several years at the time of Elinor's death. Throughout Edward's life, to him Elinor was his grandmother, Ella his mother, and Evie his aunt. Then came Elizabeth, his older sister, and Elaine his twin. A different set of Es to the five he mainly talked about if you include the original Eleanor and Emily. But his twin's death changed everything."

Emma thought of an easier way to fill in the gaps. "Remember that time we visited your mum in the rest home? She said something about Evie changing their lives. Whatever sparked your mum's memory, I now know what she was talking about."

"You mean, Mum's memory was real? What she said was true?" Jess sat on the edge of her seat, clasping her hands in front of her.

"Completely true," agreed Emma. "One day, Evelyn turned up at their home, this house, and told your parents the truth."

"In this house? Of course, they lived here most of their married life. Goodness. Evie was in this house, how amazing, and she told them she was Dad's mother?"

Emma nodded.

"So Dad was right. He was number six in a direct line of Eleanor, Emily, Elinor, Ella and Evelyn or Evie or whatever she called herself. Evie was number five," whispered Jess, finally understanding.

Emma needed to clear her throat before she could answer. "Yes. Plus his 'sister' Elizabeth and twin Elaine."

"They were generation six, too, weren't they?"

"Elaine, yes, like your father, as Evelyn's child. Elizabeth was generation five, Ella's daughter, Evelyn's half-sister."

"How confusing but I'm glad that's sorted. But why all the secrecy once Elinor had died? And why didn't we know about Dad having a twin?" asked Jess.

"Ella was still alive," answered Emma. "I suspect Evelyn wanted to respect her privacy and not upset the family as a whole."

"But what happened to Elaine's baby?"

Emma could feel tension suddenly fill the room. It wasn't her place to answer.

The silence lengthened as Jess looked between her and Lily and back again. "Well?"

"You're looking at her," said Lily eventually.

"What!" Jess turned towards Lily.

She met Jess's eyes with an unflinching gaze. "I am Elaine's daughter. Mum and Dad adopted me."

Confusion, anger and dismay filled Jess's eyes. "Why wasn't I told?"

Lily took up the narrative, much to Emma's relief. She sat back in the chair, put the papers to one side and listened to the rest of the story unfold.

"I didn't know until after Dad died. I did know I was adopted. He told me after Evelyn died in 1999. He was her heir but she also left me an inheritance. I was twenty-one. I thought she was some benign aunt. I had no idea she was his mother, or that he had a twin until the diaries arrived on my doorstep. What he did tell me was that Mum had suffered several miscarriages and they decided to adopt to protect her health."

Jess fidgeted uncomfortably, clearly aggrieved. "That makes sense, I suppose, but it still doesn't explain why I wasn't told."

"I asked him not to," replied Lily.

"Why would you do that?"

"Because we were sisters. I didn't want that to change. I was worried you might think of me differently."

"But I wouldn't have."

"You don't know that, and neither did I back then. We've not been as close as we once were. And that's my fault. I didn't like Martin so avoided him, and I travelled a lot. I left you to cope alone, and I'm sorry."

"All these secrets. And what difference do they all make now?" Jess twisted the handkerchief in her hands. Suddenly, she glared at Lily. "Did you know Evie when she was alive?"

Emma knew how important that was to Jess. She'd been desperate for a grandmother figure but the woman had deliberately kept her distance. If Lily had known her, it would destroy Jess.

Lily shook her head. "No. I didn't. I knew nothing about her until after her death. She felt undeserving and guilty for abandoning her children, and made Dad promise not to tell either of us about her until after he'd gone."

"And all of this is in her diaries?" asked Jess, looking at Emma.

"It is." Emma breathed a sigh of relief. "She didn't hide anything in her diaries, only in real life. For reasons she doesn't explain, Evelyn gave Edward and Elaine to

Ella, who she believed was her sister, and disappeared overseas. Following her lover, possibly. She had a successful career as a dancer and teacher in the States for more than thirty years. She came back because Elinor was sick. After Elinor died, Evie moved in with Ella, who she now knew was her mother. She wrote she felt she owed the women who'd shaped her life – Elinor and Ella – a debt of gratitude for protecting them all.

"Ella was ailing. She had lost her mother and Elaine, the child she'd raised. She was distraught but happy to see your parents raise Lily as their own. She needed someone to look after her. Evelyn fulfilled that role."

"When did Ella die?"

"1983. The year you were born. It was a big funeral by all accounts. All her siblings and their spouses and families, and her pregnant daughter Elizabeth turned up. Your parents. Everyone who could call themselves family."

"Elizabeth? Ella's legitimate daughter? Right?" said Jess. "I've not heard of her before. What happened to her?"

"I'm guessing a bit," said Emma, "but it appears she discovered some or all of the twisted secrets, which sent her over the edge. Evelyn wrote she'd rescued the baby but couldn't save her half-sister from self-destruction. She barely mentions her again. Elizabeth was much younger, only eighteen months older than Edward and Elaine. Those three grew up as siblings believing Ella was their mother. I don't think anything changed your dad's thinking until after Evelyn died."

"Jess." Lily's voice was soft, full of warmth and understanding. "You need to understand our Mum couldn't have children of her own. Dad said …"

Emma could hear the panic in Jess's voice. "What are you saying?"

Lily took a deep breath, her shoulders pulled rigidly back. "We're both adopted," she sighed.

The bombshell was released.

Jess's face lost all colour. "Are you saying we're not related? I'm not Dad's daughter?"

Lily's voice was the kindest Emma had ever heard. "No. My darling Jess, we're still blood. Me through Ella, my great-grandmother, to Evelyn, my grandmother, to Elaine, my mother, and Dad, her twin. You are Elizabeth's child. We don't know exactly what happened to her, but we can try and find out if you want to. Ella was your grandmother. Dad believed he was raising the daughters of his sisters. It made their loss easier to bear, knowing they lived on in us."

Emma filled the shocked stillness. "According to the diaries, once Elinor died, Ella was free to tell her secrets. Five years later, Evelyn felt the same after Ella died. Each protected the other until they'd gone. There was a gap of sixteen years until Evelyn herself died, and the diaries stopped. But Evelyn wanted the secrets known, which is why she told the lawyers to release them when your dad died and there was no need to protect them any longer. She sent the diaries – hers and Elinor's – to Lily because Lily was her granddaughter. She wanted to pass on the mantle."

Lily let her shoulders relax and kept her voice smooth and calm. "The truth is, I panicked. I read all this information which turned our lives upside down. I didn't know what to do, but my instinct said I had to protect you. To keep the secrets and not destroy your world. You were so close to Mum and Dad, Dad especially, that I thought I could keep the truth to myself and you would continue your life blissfully ignorant of the facts. But then you asked Emma to investigate the family tree. You wanted to dig into the past, and I knew she would find bits of the truth, if not all of it. I tried to stop you but finally came to realise you had a right to know." Lily took a deep breath. "The both of us come from a long line of indomitable women. Women who shaped our lives. Women who faced whatever fate threw at them, and survived. And so will we, sister dear. So will we. The secrets and lies and deceptions end with us."

Emma's heart reached out to Jess. She looked utterly shell-shocked from all the blows coming from so many directions. She would take time to absorb it all.

"Why does my name not start with an E then, if I'm Elizabeth's daughter? Yours does."

"To break the curse," said Lily. "Evie believed the women who came after Elinor had been cursed. They suffered too much tragedy – died at a young age, lost their children, or both. She wanted it to stop. Jessica means gift. And you are a very special gift."

Lily stood and pulled her sister to her feet. "I want us to continue as sisters, with no more secrets. Will you ever forgive me?"

Embracing through tears and whispered promises, their reconciliation was complete. Sisters through love, if not by birth.

The house sighed and settled as harmony was restored.

There would be a warm hearth in the home once more.

Epilogue

Six months later

Emma wrote the final page of the biography Jess and Emily had asked her to write, feeling honoured and privileged to know their story. Secrets abounded in all biographies – by nature, people wanted to protect those they loved from embarrassment, shame, and ridicule. Few touched her as much as this one. The tenacity shown by the women, and the loyalty between generations, was uplifting.

She let her fingers flow over the keyboard, bringing the story to a close, remembering, as she did, her own story and how fortunate she was to have known her grandmother, Charli, even for a brief time. Charli would have been of Evelyn's generation, a little later perhaps, but with that same sense of purpose and determination to keep her secrets.

Emma would have liked to have known Evie, the woman who had shaped the lives of so many: her grandmother's, her mother's, her son's, and those of Lily and Jess.

Elinor Somers was a remarkable woman, who, beyond her family and the pages of her diary, would be lost to history as yet another farmer's wife and mother in the era when they were the backbone of the country. In the annals of time, she achieved little of national importance worth recording, but to her family and those who followed, she was the matriarch, the one to remember.

Her legacy was her love of family.

A welcome mat lay at the hearth. Food was put on the table, no matter how hard that was to achieve, love was dished out in large quantities and every person was enveloped within her circle and protected from the harsher realities of life.

Elinsmore fulfilled her dreams in every way for the following forty years. She lived the rest of her life believing anything was possible if you dreamt hard enough; fought hard enough. Hadn't she proved it? They had a home, a hearth, a farm that supported them, where Joe indulged his love of racehorses, and descendants by the score. She asked for nothing else.

She lost the love of her life not long after they celebrated their golden wedding anniversary surrounded by their many children, grandchildren and great-grandchildren. Some of those children, whom she hadn't been able to protect, for all she tried, who'd lost their own loved ones, who needed a retreat, returned to her hearth and lived in her home where she held them close.

Laughter filled the house and echoed down the generations as tales of her deeds and survival were handed down. Nothing defeated her – not illness, not accidents, not heartache, not even a second world war – until finally, her tired body waned.

Her spirit lives on. In other homes, at other hearths, in photographs, in memories. Never to be forgotten.

This book is dedicated to the five Es.

Emma wrote 'The End' with a sigh, believing she had done justice to the memory of the indomitable Elinor Somers. She hoped Jess and Lily would agree.

* * * * * * * *

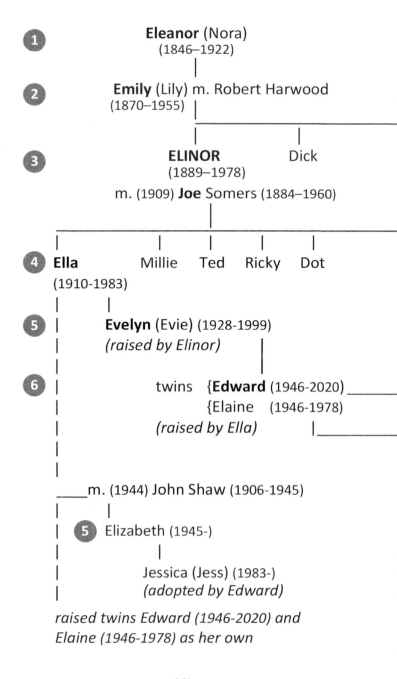

1 **Eleanor** (Nora)
(1846–1922)

2 **Emily** (Lily) m. Robert Harwood
(1870–1955)

3 **ELINOR**   Dick
(1889–1978)
m. (1909) **Joe** Somers (1884–1960)

4 **Ella**   Millie   Ted   Ricky   Dot
(1910-1983)

5 **Evelyn** (Evie) (1928-1999)
(raised by Elinor)

6 twins {**Edward** (1946-2020)
{Elaine (1946-1978)
(raised by Ella)

____m. (1944) John Shaw (1906-1945)

5 Elizabeth (1945-)

Jessica (Jess) (1983-)
(adopted by Edward)

*raised twins Edward (1946-2020) and
Elaine (1946-1978) as her own*

The Five Es

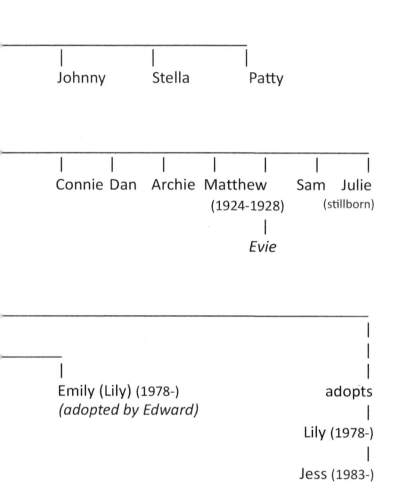

Johnny   Stella   Patty

Connie Dan   Archie Matthew   Sam   Julie
                      (1924-1928)   (stillborn)

                          |
                        Evie

Emily (Lily) (1978-)   adopts
(adopted by Edward)
                                         Lily (1978-)

                                         Jess (1983-)

Thank You

If you enjoyed this book, discover more unforgettable family heritage stories inspired by immigrants seeking a better life in a foreign land.

THE NEW ZEALAND IMMIGRANT COLLECTION
suspenseful family saga fiction about overcoming the odds.

The Cornish Knot
Portrait of a Man

Brigid The Girl from County Clare
Gwenna The Welsh Confectioner
The Costumier's Gift

The Disenchanted Soldier

* * *

THE ART OF SECRETS SERIES
dual-timeline stories about discovering your roots.

1 *The Art of Secrets*
2 *Elinor*
3 *Lucy (2023)*

* * * * * * * * *

Available at
Amazon.com/vickyadin
www.vickyadin.co.nz

Please consider leaving a customer review.
I'd be delighted if you would sign up for my newsletter on my website.

Author's Notes

As a genealogist, I feel honoured to write about the women of past generations. Women who adapted to the harsh realities they faced, and shaped the lives of their families and generations to come with resoluteness.

Life between the two world wars in New Zealand was difficult. Small, family-owned farms were common and the work relentless. The Depression years caused endless hardship few fully recovered from. I remember the way older family members saved string or wrapping paper and carry bags, and newspapers, to be reused time and again. They continued this habit long after they needed to because they remembered when they had nothing. In our throwaway society, we could learn from them about living with penury. We are far more fortunate that they were.

There are also times, like now, when we become part of significant events, just as our ancestors did, which in the future will become major historical moments. As this book is launched, the world is still struggling with a pandemic a hundred-odd years after the last one, and watching a war unfold in Ukraine. In the years to come, other authors will write about these times, fascinated with the enforced rules and regulations, the behaviour of the compliant and rebellious, the greed of the wealthy, and bemoan the tragedy of war forced upon us by authoritarian rulers.

Let us never forget those ordinary people who forged a life for themselves amid the chaos.

About the Author

Vicky Adin is a family historian in love with the past. Like the characters in her stories, she too is an immigrant to New Zealand, arriving a century after her first protagonists, and ready to start a new life.

Born in Wales, she grew up in Cornwall until aged 12. Her family emigrated to New Zealand, a country she would call home. Vicky draws on her affinity for these places, in her writing. Fast forward a few years, and she marries a fourth-generation Kiwi bloke with Irish, Scottish and English ancestors and her passion for genealogy flourishes.

The further she digs into the past, the more she wants to record the lives of the people who were the foundations of her new country. Not just her own ancestors, but all those who braved the oceans and became pioneers in a raw new land. Her research into life as it was for those immigrants in the mid-to-late 1800s and early 1900s gave her enough material to write for many years about the land left behind and the birth of a new nation.

Her first book, *The Disenchanted Soldier,* is the most biographical of all her books, inspired by her husband's great-grandfather. For the rest, while the history of the time is accurate, the characters are fictionalised to fit with the events and happenings as they occurred.

Vicky holds an MA(Hons) in English, is a lover of art, antiques, gardens, good food and red wine. She and her husband travel throughout New Zealand in their caravan and travel the world when they can. She hopes younger generations get as much enjoyment learning about the past through her stories, as she did when writing about it.

The Art of Secrets

An uplifting tale of friendship, grief and lies.

Emma wants to forget;
Charlotte never can.
Together they remember.

First in THE ART OF SECRETS series.

A young journalist and an ageing author have little in common, until their secrets tear them apart.

Emma is an enterprising young journalist with a bright future, but her life and career are falling apart. In a last-ditch attempt to save her position, she accepts the assignment to interview the bestselling author, Charlotte Day.

The ageing Charlotte has a reputation for being cantankerous and is highly secretive about her past, one she considers too painful to relive and too shameful to share. Preferring her roses to people, she grudgingly agrees to meet this girl who gets through her defences, forcing her to confront her past.

As Charlotte and Emma's relationship deepens, they become enmeshed in a tangle of secrets that changes their lives.

The art of great writing! ... Adin keeps a tight rein on her leading characters, their actions and reactions credibly grounded in genuine emotions. The change of tone from Emma to Charlotte, from young to old, works, helps the reader see behind the lies and half-truths they tell each other. Their progress from antagonists to friends is seamless, as the layers of the story peel back like petals, exposing the truth at the flower's heart. Bev Robitai, author of *Sunstrike*

Book 1 of THE ART OF SECRETS series

The Cornish Knot

One woman's emotional quest to discover her family roots

Can one woman's secrets change the life of another a century later?

Prequel to *Portrait of a Man*

A grieving widow, a century old journal, a missing portrait, and an engaging art historian. What will the secrets of the past reveal?

When Megan receives a journal written a century earlier, she sets out on an irresistible path. Following in the footsteps of the diary's author, Megan journeys from her home in New Zealand to Cornwall, France and Italy, uncovering an unsettling past. She meets a fellow countryman in Florence and is soon caught up in the aesthetic world of art where the truth lies hidden beneath the layers of paint.

Charmed by the man her daughter disapproves of, and captivated by a series of unknown paintings, Megan is drawn deeper into the mysteries and conflicts of long ago. As she unravels her family history and reveals its life-changing secrets, can she find love again?

An engaging tale of grief, loss, love and family intrigue ... wonderful story, and a real page-turner, which leads the reader through all the twists and turns of a well-constructed plot. I loved the insightful descriptions of family relationships, the fully realised characters and the various locations in which the action takes place. Seldom have I read such a poignant and faithful account of the effects of bereavement. I can't wait to read more. **** 4-star Amazon review

THE NEW ZEALAND IMMIGRANT COLLECTION

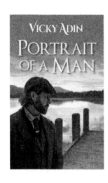

Portrait of a Man

The gripping multigenerational tale of lies, lost chances and misplaced love.

Will the secrets of the past destroy an artist's legacy?

The soul-searching conclusion to *The Cornish Knot*

An Italian artist, a Cornish knot and a Māori koru lead to a shocking exposé. As World War One escalates, can he keep his secrets safe?

In 1863, Matteo Borgoni is a desperate man. If he is to free his beloved wife held captive by her father in Melbourne, his picture framing business must succeed. Haunted by the memory of failure, he has many obstacles to overcome before he can establish himself with the artists of Dunedin, New Zealand and be reunited with his love.

Fifty years on, Luciano, a rakish Italian portrait artist fleeing from a life of lies, turns up at Borgoni Picture Framers seeking refuge. As the ravages of World War One escalate, an unusual friendship and newfound rapport brings unforeseen repercussions. A terrifying pandemic is the last thing they need.

Over a century later, a man recognises a portrait in an Auckland gallery, and demands it back. Amid another global pandemic, a marriage on the brink of failure, and a life-and -death struggle, the portrait exposes generations of family secrets and deceptions with life-changing results.

Portrait of a Man is told over three timelines through the eyes of different generations.

THE NEW ZEALAND IMMIGRANT COLLECTION

Brigid
The Girl from County Clare

The heart-rending tale of Irish immigration in the 1880s

Like making lace – she pieced together a new life from a single thread of hope

Counterpart to *Gwenna The Welsh Confectioner*
Prequel to *The Costumier's Gift*

Eighteen-year-old Brigid faces an unimaginable choice. If she stays in her beloved Ireland, she is another mouth to feed in a land plagued by starvation and poverty. If she leaves, she will never see her family again. But leave she must.

Heartbroken, she travels by ship with her cousin Jamie to a new life in Australia. On the journey, Brigid meets a rough-and-ready Scots girl who becomes her best friend, a man who beguiles her, and a fellow Irishwoman who causes no end of trouble.

Brigid's skill as a lacemaker soon attracts attention, but it is her selfless nature that draws people to her. When the burden of choice is forced upon her once again, Brigid must find an inner strength if she is to fulfil her dream.

A new start in New Zealand offers hope – until the day she encounters the man who seeks her downfall.

The historical aspects of the story are so accurate and described so perfectly that the reader will frequently need to remind herself/ himself that the story is fiction ... This is a thoroughly satisfying read. It is the kind of story that passes the test as a work of history, and is equally satisfying as a novel that will have your attention from first to last. **** 4 stars – Frank O'Shea, *The Irish Echo*, Sydney

THE NEW ZEALAND IMMIGRANT COLLECTION

Gwenna
The Welsh Confectioner

A powerful tale of family life amid Auckland's bustling Karangahape Road at the turn of the 20th century

Against overwhelming odds, can she save her legacy?

Counterpart to *Brigid The Girl from County Clare*
Prequel to *The Costumier's Gift*

Gwenna's life is about to change. Her father is dead, and the family business is on the brink of collapse. Thwarted by society, the plucky sweet maker refuses to accept defeat.

Gwenna promised her father she would fulfil his dreams and save her legacy. But thanks to her overbearing stepbrother, that legacy is at risk. Gwenna must fight for her rights if she is to keep her vow.

She falls in love with the cheeky and charming Johnno, but just when things are beginning to look up, disaster strikes. Throughout the twists and turns of love and tragedy, Gwenna is irrepressible. She refuses to relinquish her goal and lets nothing and no one stand in her way.

But blind to anything that could distract her, Gwenna overlooks the most important person in her life, putting her dreams, her family, and her chance at happiness in jeopardy.

Utter brilliance. Vicky really brings the characters to life and you can really engage with what it must have been like to be a young girl like Gwenna going into business at the turn of the century in a male domi-nated society. Every character contributed to make this a truly wonder-ful story; my only disappointment was when it ended.

***** 5-star Amazon review

THE NEW ZEALAND IMMIGRANT COLLECTION

The Costumier's Gift

An absorbing multigenerational dual-timeline family saga

Why does a stranger hold the key to untangling Katie's family secrets?

Continues the lives of *Brigid The Girl from County Clare* and *Gwenna The Welsh Confectioner*

Jane thrives in the one place where she can hide her pain and keep her skeletons to herself. As principal costumier at Auckland's Opera House in its Edwardian heyday, she is content – until the past comes back to haunt her.

Her beloved foster mother Brigid and her best friend Gwenna are anchors in her solitary yet rewarding life. When the burden of carrying secrets becomes too great, Jane surrenders her role as keeper of the untold.

Generations later Katie seeks refuge from her crumbling life with her Granna, who lives in the past with the people in her cherished photographs. Katie discovers she must identify the people behind the gentle smiles and reveal generations of secrets before she can claim her inheritance.

Through Jared, an intriguing new client, Katie revives her stalled career until she learns he holds the key to uncovering her past. Despite an increasing attraction, she shies away from any deeper involvement ... but without him she will never know the truth.

THE NEW ZEALAND IMMIGRANT COLLECTION

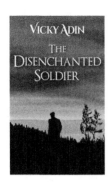

The Disenchanted Soldier

A heart-breaking dual-timeline family saga

From soldier to pacifist

In 1863, young Daniel Adin, a trained British soldier, embarks on an adventure of a lifetime. In pursuit of a new life and land to farm, he travels to New Zealand to fight an unknown enemy – the fearless Māori.

A hundred and thirty years later, Libby is fascinated by the stories of Daniel as he looks down at her from the aged black-and-white photos on the wall. Surrounded by four generations of his large family, she wants to know more, to know what he was really like.

As she researches his past, Daniel's story becomes so much more than she expected.

I loved this book and so will you if you like historical fiction and family sagas set somewhere you likely know little about. This is beautifully and sensitively written. The characters are terrific. The fascinating part to me was how Vicky was able to take us on the family's journey in a thoughtful and non-judgmental way.

***** 5-star Amazon review

THE NEW ZEALAND IMMIGRANT COLLECTION

Acknowledgements

I'm delighted when I can write a contemporary story set against a historical background. We can learn so much from our forebears about resilience, endurance and gratitude. To ensure the history of the period is accurate, I am always thankful for our easily accessible websites such as New Zealand History, and Te Ara: The Encyclopedia of New Zealand, but to find out about the people and how they lived, I turn to the newspaper archives at PapersPast at the National Library of New Zealand, my favourite source of social history.

However, no book comes to fruition without the assistance of many people – editors, designers, readers, library staff, historians, friends, and my family. I am certain that in naming individuals I will miss out some I should have included, so please take it as given – if you have contributed any information, advice, guidance or support, I am deeply grateful.

I would like to especially thank my team of beta readers and critics: Bess Reynolds, who is the perfect reader; my husband who knows New Zealand's history better than me; and fellow authors Jenny Harrison and Erin McKechnie, the toughest of critics. I could not have completed this book without your honesty and insightful suggestions.

My eternal thanks go to my editor, Adrienne Charlton, of AM Publishing New Zealand, for her sharp eye, and her willingness to check and correct every detail to her complete satisfaction. Any errors remaining are mine and mine alone.

My thanks, too, go to Bev Robitai, photographer, for helping me put together vague and disparate ideas for the wonderful cover design, and to Adrienne Charlton for adding her flair.